WORK

Richard Makin

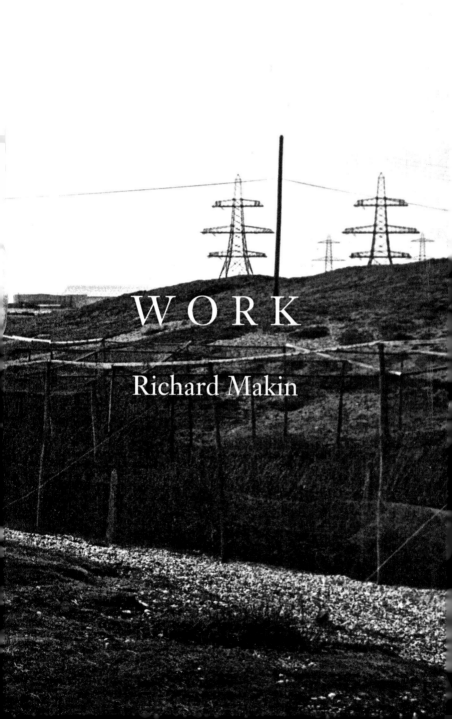

© Richard Makin, 2022

ISBN 978-1-9996964-4-3

Equus Press
Birkbeck College (William Rowe), 43 Gordon Square, London,
WC1 H0PD, United Kingdom

Typeset & design by lazarus
Printed by Tigris

The publisher wishes to acknowledge the support of James H. Ottaway, Jr.

All rights reserved

Composed in Janson

Excerpts from *Work* have been published by *Great Works*, *Golden Handcuffs Review* and *Equus Press*.

Photographs by Richard Makin.

I

Objects at that time were translucent, held in suspension. The streetlamps shed a faint light into the room; light is the natural agent that stimulates sight and makes things visible.

Anxiety arises from having all paths, and thus no path, open before one (a colony of ants behaves like a single organism). Word order is an allusive presence, a residue.

Dog tonguing water from an aluminium bowl.

A dramatic increase in neuron firing has been recorded: physical withdrawal symptoms have triggered overstimulation of the autonomic nervous system.

In order to draw a boundary one has to operate on both sides of this threshold. Such an individual must be considered unfortunate.

The witness added that she did not believe she had been conversing with a particularly noteworthy spirit.

'Silverpoint, that's right, on paper primed with a film of powdered bone, creating a fine indelible line composed of metal particles.'

I remember your face, but never a name.

To be removed: a skeletal frame into which compartments are fitted, one flyblown mirror and a moth-eaten silk partition. Another object was named after the bell shape of early prototypes. It was some occasion, this.

*

Remote sulphur mine — a cabin in the forest, the bloody hair-matted maul — an abandoned sawmill, makeshift and ramshackle.

A chain of logs courses slowly downriver, grinding at the pack ice. The chorus shrieks while heaving at the capstan.

As in all acts of translation, an erosion is already taking place.

A pyre of timber is stacked for the incineration. From one perspective, this is an archive of neurological disaster.

He justifies himself by arguing that any error is an achievement in itself. Part of the alchemy is the sudden shift in key, whereby impulses received at synapses are transmitted along the branched extension of a nerve.

How would I have felt if this had happened to me? You're not sure whether you are reading or being written.

He scrambles through the cobbled streets. All other sensations are shocked out of existence — the dynamic of crisis-catharsis is repeated throughout, a spiral or vortex, a circular pattern of currents in an ocean trench.

Interesting futile

I set out at a loss. It was a Thursday (that constant hissing in my ear). We were limited to things. The crux here lies in a steadfast refusal to take place.

Origin is misuse.

A subatomic particle has no integrity, is quote 'incorrigible'. I am here following the statistical description given by an eyewitness.

In a shop window have been placed a battered musical instrument, one bag of ash, a pack of dogeared tarot, a volcano-shaped lump of fluorescent plastic, string and wire, along with fuses and electrical triggers of unspecified use.

I am refusing to make any decisions today.

A disease resulting from these acts was summoned. Grandiloquent names have been timetabled: you are quite catastrophic et cetera. A colourless material comprises the living part of any cell.

One psychiatric report confirmed the subject's 'adamantine fragility'. There was no going back.

Research indicates that some organisms may retain memory within bodily tissue; I thought your moniker sounded familiar. Bystanders gambled on the outcome as we slit open the ink sacs one by one.

*

It's funny you should ask that question he said, scalpel in clenched fist. The novel is set around two people who share a tragic past: a track of scar tissue runs the length of the sternum.

Her entrance into the room mirrored a dream of several nights before: aviator goggles, flecks of foam rimming the lips, the raised pistol, a white secretion oozing from her vagina, the supermarket trolley abandoned to an oily canal. The judge affirmed that her statement claiming the defendant had once toiled as an assassin would have to be taken into consideration.

I once possessed a hollow metal object in the shape of a deep inverted cup widening at the lip. This sounded a clear note when struck, a musical account of the last human on earth. Someone stole it.

It has become apparent that light consists of energy quanta called photons, which behave somewhat like waves and somewhat like particles. Nonetheless, it is very quiet today hereabouts.

When the location of the seizures is pinpointed, any affected organs will be removed and destroyed. Such is the agony of foreknowledge when combined with an inability to alter the future.

Crisis apparition

What time are you leaving? Catachresis is incorrect usage of a word, its function indeterminate: a tool or agent blindly devoted to an adversary's destruction — literally, a soul of mud, atrophy of the muscles — a tongue in the larval state, gill flaps twitching.

See, he is already working within a tripartite structure. Skin feels amphibian — to the abdomen: same impression.

Ground has been lost. Wearing the mutinous cockade today would not be savvy, could even prove fatal. Overawed by such assaults as these, the envoys resigned en masse.

*

Stale bread, smooth stones and a circuit board have been crammed into my pockets. Contraction is a term used to explain the doctrine that began. I must forewarn you.

My circus training has been rigorous — I reach out and touch, connect, and the voltmeter twitches. I recall this morning the leg of a spider afloat in the communal shower. By the summer there was hardship and the threat of disaster.

But the prolonged absence of a thing unspecified persists. That mound we are passing was long ago a hill fort, a natural temple and omphalos — its position led pilgrims down the dorsal spine and hogback of the south.

I can scarcely keep up with these infinite varieties of loss — the disembodied voice, parental ash and so forth. For years now I have been trading on the orbital, where mouths on stalks dowse and quiver. . . . The streets are about so wide.

[*Parts hands to demonstrate.*]

In vertebrates there may be up to four chambers, with two atria and two ventricles, a lung of clay: let the dry land appear et cetera.

The completed shape is a trapezoid, a vast rectangle with sloping upper edge. Clouds descend to fill the vacuum: sky full of smoke, water falling in droplets as snails crush underfoot. . . . There was once a machine, he claims, that could manufacture flammable gas by splitting up the hydrogen and oxygen into precisely required parts. Now he says he has gangrene and cysts all over his torso.

I have an exposed vertebra at the top of my spine, a gleaming white nub that signals neglect. We are busy comparing atrocities, irredeemable in our virtue. Acid rain sanitizes the surface; apologies are withheld. I'm so excited about nothing.

Shell tooth

Lip split, itchy phantom limb. In my spare time I am dedicated to inertia. In my spare time I am digging a cellar beneath the compound, a storage unit for stockpiled quicklime and nerve agent. Informal social gatherings have been disfigured by ritualized crawling: the whole industry has collapsed. I'm about in the middle of a life sentence.

He then conveyed in a whisper the exact moment when our termination was to take place. In the midst of this schism in the concert of opinion, to hear his simple language was a blessing.

Forbidden to talk for a few minutes, I can finally grasp what we are dealing with: a crust is forming.

She took a deep breath and let it out; her eyes opened for the first time in months. Those who refused to join the exodus have been living dormant under the ground since the last ice age.

A name from history has been given to the inner circle, especially the five unpopulars. Navigation by means of maritime errancy has led us to some deserted islet.

*

The roof slates have developed a toxic film of livid green lichen. Peat burns in the hearth, filling the interior of the hovel with acrid smoke that stings the eyes and settles on the tongue. One man fell into a deep sleep and suffered a vision.

Radical reflection must go further back and seize this theme, within the horizon which grants it significance. Informed of his years of hermitage, it was agreed the envoy should come in person and tell the delegates of his discovery. He gazed at my palm for a few moments before raising his eyes and asking what happened on that winter day in seventy-seven.

It was his custom to walk about unarmed, inspecting the excavations, ecstatic with the glory of sunset from the battlements. I schlepped back to the compound with all the apparatus he had requested: none of these disparate objects made sense in terms of defence — when a real war descends, I hope he's not manning the cryptograph.

He reports that he has seen a huge wheel turning in the sky, and within that wheel was another wheel, and so on. I have inherited the magnetized corpse of an abandoned empire.

After surgery, the severed end of the artery was twisted to impede blood loss. That electric surge you feel throughout your body is adrenalin.

*

Item, twelve civil war sidearms. Cost to buyer: life. He trembled, his lip. What provokes this torsion — at least he died in harness, did he not?

Countless lights glitter and drift in the sky tonight. St Ignatius says they cannot be real.

The only piece of furniture in the cell was a writing desk with a shell that slid along curved grooves of bone. It appears that the accused wrote standing up.

I am endeavouring to recreate a static moment from memory. Visible light is electromagnetic radiation whose wavelength falls within the range to which the human retina responds. In the beginning were the dead.

The left cerebral hemisphere is communicating with the spleen. (I may have got this the wrong way round.) The index finger is your psyche, and there are stars and triangles and squares and circles — they all end up in different places doing different things.

We are tearing apart his theory; one must seek the essential where nothing more is to be found. I have a function: I cannot remember.

Consequently, his life must be meticulously written out by several hands. The man had absolutely no substance to speak of.

It is as if I had never left.

*

For abode they have none and must have been assembled here against their will. They must, as it were, have been harvested, gathered together from their dispersal.

I will confess myself.

Anyone in their right senses could see that men under the sway of malignant demons can only be constrained by subtle diplomacy. What was it that drew these high-profile people to this particular room every Tuesday evening? If there was one word, it would be suggestion (or suggestiveness). He would marry sounds to semantics. . . . All of these things resonate now that I am standing here quite alone.

I have yet to listen attentively to this passage. The helical orbit increases in radius while having minimal effect on our own trajectory.

*

Animal familiars snaffle at my shins as metal-rimmed hoofs clatter and spark at the wet cobble, making fire. This discourse has been designed such that the novice may learn what should be understood concerning animal familiars.

Nothing here is compulsory — our objective is the undermining of base and superstructure, at this cusp of people and their things. I hear souls are already climbing out onto rooftops and balconies, screaming amiably at one another, beating on saucepans with knives and spoons.

The first stone dropped into my neck, trapped between head and abdomen.

A crack opens up in the day

I wake to find another letter on the doormat, slice open the envelope. He returns to the same argument again and again: your cells are indifferent, ballast of decaying tissue — by contrast, the salamander can regenerate limbs, retina and tail after amputation. Pyroblast is an epic spell card et cetera.

> *Dear Gauleiter*
>
> *I have often contemplated staying indoors, at other times going outside — but right now I am retreating back to the opening scene of my life. At last, something I am good at has become popular: state-sponsored solitude.*
>
> *Yesterday I made a life-sized car out of all the packing cases. Yes, that's what I mean: Plan B, followed by suicide.*
>
> *A broad revolving cylinder with a vertical axis was once used for winding a rope or cable. This is the most potent weapon available to us.*
>
> *So little is known. The irresolvable structural polarities are believed to be identical — historically, we are thought to be composed of indifferent sleeper cells. It all depends on the neurochemistry.*
>
> *See, I don't believe that endlessly deferred trial has helped one little bit. This is going to mark the end of my body work: I have been advised never to exhale.*
>
> *Your savant*

He then raised his hands and spread out the fingers (six digits on the left). Whose mind could possibly encompass such a range of critical information? I promise that I will come and visit you one miserable Sunday afternoon, when infinite light finally contracts to allow for a conceptual space in which finite and seemingly independent realms can exist.

*

We have to run to chaetotaxy now, analyse the skin of the insect to narrow it down to one species. The central thesis is that people cannot exist beyond the warp of embalming flesh.

This vignette is an ox, this vignette is an ox having the disk with plumes between its horns. She wears the chain from which is suspended the emblem. This is the chapter of making heat to be placed inside the head of the deceased.

One weekend the walls of my cell suddenly disappeared. Sound was the descant sackbut, an early form once used (see trombone, see family). Origin is an obsolete hook for pulling off a horse.

I hear exceptional voice tonight. Someone should reset that bone.

The crew are afflicted, pocked and blanched like weathered marble. I need your permission to cross the frontier and an exit visa that will grant me safe passage. I have hidden some of the negatives.

All present wear flammable glycerine masks. Upon leaping into water, the sea catches fire.

I began to reconsider the argument of his missive, its inherent contradictions — something about a dying magus, a sac of cells, a forgotten munitions dump. . . . Ten days later, trepan of the skull was hazard.

There has always been plenty of zero-hour work around here. The stones on his breastplate have been arranged in a strict pattern: between three hundred and ninety nanometres for violet light, seven hundred and forty nanometres for red.

sardius	topaz	carbuncle
emerald	sapphire	diamond
ligure	agate	amethyst
beryl	onyx	jasper

*

Interior decoration is an inadequate expression to describe what she does with her voice at this point.

'All I can say is I remember seeing him sample a colourless oily liquid, whose vapour caused severe irritation of the labia and blistering of the glans after dinner. But that was twenty years ago.'

It is true that in the existing texts the ancient connection has disappeared: we are approaching the spot where the wanderer finally established a hermitage. Touch nothing, please, touch nothing.

*

Naevus relic, morass of nerves. The cells of your body collect information and form lasting memories. Viewed from above, the caterpillar tracks radiate outward from the village cesspool — the townsfolk have been folded inward and placed in storage. The eighties saw a renaissance.

One surviving fresco depicts a witch burnt at the stake in the town square, another shows defenestration of municipal leaders who had apparently fallen out of favour that afternoon.

The act is easier when the self you are slaying is no longer recognizable as your own. (Who or what is *your* fungal partner?) This has been constructed in such a way that it is enough to discover and choose the shortest path toward a goal whose position is never fixed.

*

A rusting scar with neatly folded wings, tolling angelus. More of the old adverts are stacking up inside your head — massacre at influx chronicle et cetera.

His memory lent him one last trick, he was elated and quite forgot that the elaborate scene spread out before him was his own interment. Then, without warning, one of the mourners threw a revolver into the grave.

'I've dreamt up a foolproof scheme for that parcel of land, the frozen panhandle.'

Pivot to face cardinal north. Folk upon the esplanade soak up the rain and can't think where to look next, what to say. Influx has ceased.

He would like to have had someone with him when it happened, human company; there was nothing unusual in this. (I thought of you.) He was once a brutal autocrat who masterminded the global traffic in organs, now he stands before an improvised gallows. Last words are coaxed from his reluctant throat.

Back then, such were the themes of a typical drawing-room conversation. I have my own theory: consider the action of twisting or the state of being twisted, especially one end of an object relative to another.

'Some five years ago, when I first asked for your help on this project — an encyclopaedia — I had already exhausted the means to please anyone.'

A fold in the wall of the heart fills and distends if the blood flows backward, so forming a valve that resembles the pointed ends of a crescent moon. No one is thinking of why they are doing what they are doing; a secular approach to the psyche poisons all discourse. At this moment in time we must restrict ourselves to geography.

Your right hemisphere is what you make of it. Since this morning I have resolved to write standing up.

As he watched the wheels began to turn, one within the other.

One volunteer was found slumped over his electric typewriter, the lettered sphere still spinning. The text ran to an abrupt stop at 'tithe is a tenth part' — that is, an infinitely small part, one tenth of the land and livestock seized, hence to decimate.

Have faith in your body to bear the hardships of exile; offer to the gods a spectacle which, to a virtuous judgement, could only appear repulsive.

Forensics found unidentifiable fibres of fur on the upholstery. I remember nothing, which has its advantages in everyday life.

Armed stand-off in hazard alert

Location: an untimely ruin abandoned by past and future, where an opening above our heads reveals the constellation. Background noise incorporates abused tupperware and a saloon-bar upright piano, with fallout battery as afterthought.

There will be repercussions: the heavens outstretch lemon yellow et cetera. Birds flock to it (the moon). I realize now that I have made too little use of the available light.

He refuses to conform to the prevailing world of expression. This situation was rapidly explained amid a babel of wolfed oysters, butchers' knives and snarling infants — a grenade pin between his clenched teeth.

There was heard a persistent rapping throughout the nightwatch. Mutual slaughter occurred on both sides. In the very beginning of the circulation of commodities, only excess amounts of use-value are converted into readymades.

I listen to something breathing, the rise and fall, cadence of breath — it's me, orienting myself within random coordinates: a cage of rotting cob, one tethered goat, tank tracks in the snow — a book bound with moth wings, spent cartridges scuttering across the town square in the rain — a jackal reared up on its hind legs, smoke plumes rising from red-tiled roofs.

*

A thin flat bone runs down the centre of her chest, to which ribs are fused; long strands of amber hair are still attached to her shrunken skull. We are switching to self-destruct.

In the olden days, folk would have thrown all the newborn and their reptiles into one big cauldron and had done with it. The heart is left beating until the day when the others have decided. If the spleen sinks into the village pond, this is proof that the deceased has been violated.

We are said to breach our skin during sleep. The velocity of light in a vacuum is two hundred and ninety-nine thousand, seven hundred and ninety-two kilometres per second.

I cannot stop what I did not set in motion. Our vehicle was now deeply scored and battered on the driver's side. . . . This spectacle is further inflamed at the clamour of an invisible approach.

'Yes, but your account would be more credible if these scenes were not so remote in space and time.'

'No doubt,' said he, biting his lip.

Pyroblast is a fire spell straight out of tradecraft.

*

It is May. Day one of the trial begins at the local penal colony. She was young but already sharper than her rivals, and all the more dangerous because she never hesitates. The first of many objections to the court-appointed defence is raised.

'On leaping into water, the sea catches fire?. . .'

It is June. Day two of the trial begins with four counts of unjustifiable catastrophe. Why, she asks, does the prosecution insist on judging the debate on the basis of the philosopher's cack-handedness in the matter of time decay?

An extreme leftward slant below one hundred and forty degrees is found in the handwriting of those who automatically oppose everything and everyone. Surveillance is an ancestral tic — the sins of such contenders are greater than all the occult crimes of necromancy put together.

It is rumoured that the rain fell *without cease*.

*

Now for that familiar gambit of inquisition: about yourself. . . . He lay on the muddy riverbank, close enough to be asphyxiated by the mutant perfumes oozing from his captor's flesh.

Which punishment would be the most succulent?. . . Standing before the gallows, he begins a fresh narrative of his own invention: a large percentage of the city's structures had to be flattened, after the earthquake one hundred thousand were left without shelter et cetera.

This city, previously called, was renamed; the genealogies were uncanny. We here ignore altogether the philosopher's agon with perception, which usually wages war at some point. I agreed to act as a stand-in and take his colour-blind test to cheat him through the army medical: red and green, and one or two of the other colours, can be quite taxing.

The freezing cold made me act with undue haste, but at least we have made contact. If he should fail to repay the debt this man will have to substitute something else that he possesses, something he has no control over, for example his body.

Why I volunteered

Shall we set about compiling another pointless list? Get advice now if your arm has been injured and you heard a snapping noise, or if your arm has changed shape. Note that the same method of torture may be used in the case of one who is accused of receiving, protecting or otherwise shielding a heretic.

Today is ascension day; I am afraid yet curious at the same time. I volunteer. Up here, average mass is never a constant — it is not enough to take samples, hold a symposium, goad people into speech, invite utterance. I never arrived.

The average mean is unexpected (viz. concavity of childhood). That I have two hands is an irreversible option.

Tonight is a double bill, brief encounters in running time: an extreme close-up is a minutely detailed view of an object or person, such as a human eye or mouth. As solstice approaches the sun grows weak and oblique.

I have had enough — multiple stains on the linen, the sheets and pillowcases, evidence of menses and liverish copulation. . . . Resident saints cluster and bilocate — all passed some years without opening their eyes. I sway high above the desert on a pillar.

The north initiated hostilities. Chance dictates the following scenes and interludes. The venomous insult he was about to hurl at the waiter was not without an arcane purpose.

*

A big crowd of people is being chased by a cloud. At some point you will have to start taking things seriously, learn to be alone, sequester yourself. Indeed, it looks as though a cunning military strategy of withdrawal is taking place at this very instant.

I feel he is about to exit through the window, defenestrate, and this time he is never coming back. Trust your own mind to oust oblivion.

White light consists of an equal mixture of all visible wavelengths, which can be separated to yield the colours of the spectrum. We have met at the sharp end where two curvatures meet — I am mindful of that cone-shaped prominence where his canines should be.

We are shifting from graphomania to regroup under aphasia, the inability to understand or produce speech as a result of sabotage. I guarantee that he will have no memory of the crimes he has committed, indeed of any act whatsoever committed in the past.

Your voice, it is a reconstruction of a deteriorated recording made late in the last century. Another bystander said it was like the whole universe just bifurcated, something of that kidney.

I worry that one day my own heart will stop beating, and must write back before it's too late. That said, unless the attack occurs in a truly isolated zone of the world, somehow the story is sure to be reported.

No one ever expected grace of the marquis, no one.

Reportage

I spotted this advert for open throat singing. I particularly liked the discordance between the voices and the saint in darkness praying on his knees, who suddenly convulses. Four years later, a real war started.

The target was a big white building at the edge of the city. Five bombs fell in all — there is a bullet still inside her and a deep crater where a shell exploded. They were aiming for the reactor and missed.

I felt the blast and thought O I must be dead. I survived. I live to explain myself before the syndicate, over and over into eternity.

Now her eyelids are swollen; they have been sewn open. Time could be the general public or time could be radiation.

I was once trapped in the ice of February. The log cabin was haunted, more crisis apparitions. On one wall was a photograph of anti-aircraft missile batteries, which is my favourite, but none of this helped.

It is obvious to me now, so simple to see. . . . I know that is a tree in blossom, or under snow — it looks like dirty snow.

Three allegedly unconnected episodes

One evening she urinated into the sea while shouting listen, E-flat major. In a few places, surviving beehives can still be found.

The flukes of a whale broke the surface as spindrift flew from the oars — into those jaws of swift destruction fell the anti-hero. His last words said we are divine sparks floating within an incorruptible sheath.

Inside the caravan we found dusty shelves ranged around with old decanters, vials and flasks. You are phoney she shrieks, counterfeit.

The most persistently misunderstood among all his works has been the book.

I am not listening. You will see.

This was the first commission he ever received: there survives a painting of the atrocity at a local museum. The whole picture is done in black and white, ashen grisaille except for the bloodstain. One critic wrote that standing before it felt like slow-motion dentistry.

*

He has allowed his protégée to read the letter, despite clear instructions forbidding this. Someone is trying to recast the map, which is a tragedy.

'They look interesting.'

'One is a fully signed-up gorgon.'

In breach of protocol, last night I gazed at the moon through a glass. A voice often comes to me in the dark.

The flickerbook conjured a stag shedding its antlers in the snow at the heart of a remote Balkan forest. The people of the coast believe that witches can change themselves into animals and emit a glowing light like fireflies. At one instant during larval development the viscera spontaneously twist through one hundred and eighty degrees.

'Do you understand what this means?'
'No man likes to have his all rejected.'

The primary formative material from which cells develop has been identified and named. Mister's speech was unusually febrile that day.

P said nothing. Witches are mostly women and the gift can be inherited, or stolen by performing acts of paranormal shopping.

Whose initials happened to make up the sought-after word?... Tetramorph, the anthropos logo, is standing on two wheels with sparks flying. For all we know, he could be a master of numerology.

*

Retrace your steps back to the very beginning.

I am burdened with residual knowledge of all things thus far encountered. Who goes there, friend or foe, is the appropriate reply. Why did I come?

Then the long-awaited invasion from a parallel universe began. Once again, I had picked the short straw.

Invisible droplets in the air mingle with blood aerosol — columns of dust, a mote in the eye, the shriek in the playground — but exhaustion is a kind of derangement, and there are times when the only feeling I have is one of mad revolt, with skull of clay.

It was AD 1385 or thereabouts. Suddenly she said help me, I am searching for the definitive authority on notorious outlaws.

They handcuffed him to the bars of his cell and took away one of his shoes.

It may be noted here that the connexion between methodology and the liminal moment is historically fragile. But the survivors knew how unstable the average galaxy is, inevitably leading to timeless captivity in the sky.

By 1856 we had seven years remaining. I am drifting toward true love (equine sedative, opioids, valium). Just seven more years to grind through: light has been demonstrated, albeit inconclusively.

These were my thoughts on that unforgettable day. I was never officially summoned, i.e. you did not manifest me. I believe it may be time to leave.

And now follows a rather unfashionable urban guerrilla concept: kill, kill, kill for inner harmony, equilibrium and a no-nonsense mentalist health programme.

Guiser, star

His heart was suspended from the ceiling in a porphyry urn. I am staring blankly into space.

We could use some of the old vitriol around here: marches turning to riots, riots boiling to intercommunal warfare, militias lose control, the descent.... Let's start again at the very beginning: it is twenty something, a transit camp at the frontier, a cameo for surviving Europeans, all the gilded youth et cetera.

It may be incorrect to say that a will to fabrication is central to our method. An extreme long shot is a paranormal view of dislocation photographed from a great height, often as much as several light years.

I flung myself in the direction of the canal, clinging to a wooden pile while my captor played the role of timely apologist. And there were further intrigues in hidden bolt-holes and corners of the continent (for instance, we considered Zagreb as a possible escape route). But pain refuses to fade: whoever looks inward, as into the vastness of space, finds he carries a galaxy within himself.

A rust chute empties to the sea, a funnel of iron oxide, vertigo. Halfway down, untranslatable signs are etched into a large sheet of bulletproof glass. Below this, the uncounted steps.

We probably mean that an event can never be reported unambiguously. Nothing illustrates this more clearly.

The unnameable white
pebble placed on a cairn —
rust chute, the sea
a crack in the large glass
Nothing of nothing:
i)   seething waves, rocks
ii) a dimly lit corridor
iii) olive trees
iv) platform niche No.563
v)   the memorial cartouche

*

The opera begins in silence and total darkness, broken by the chunk of a lighter and a pixel of orange flame. An extreme close-up of an actor generally includes only his eye or mouth.

Origin is subdivided into slender threads. There is a prescribed remedy for those obsessed through the agency of witchcraft, for the citizen building a future in an undead world.

There was snow on the ground that day. We waited for the current to resume.

In the final stanza, note the reference to going forth to meet the inexpressible while haplessly running into somatic cessation (death). I added a white pebble to the scree balanced on his tomb, dislodging the whole pyramid. I felt I should pick up and replace the stones, but left them where they scattered; I had swallowed my fill of homaging.

Memory moves by degrees through the body, toward discharge at the fingertips in the form of ectoplasm. I'd had enough; it was cold and I was fasting. Everything was shut — we were trapped on the wrong side of the frontier. The museum had been abandoned. It was the wrong day, it was always the wrong fucking day.

Identity is based on a systematic reversal of montage. Sporadically, the heart makes a quivering movement due to uncoordinated contraction of its fibres, the etymology of enough.

Two further goals stand out in retrospect.

There is a long tradition of writers dictating their work to scribes before having them cut to pieces.

The ugliness of your actions is becoming corrosive. To illustrate, here are some people gathered together *speaking*, and here they are again *mouthing*.

Note, O is traced counterclockwise before P or V can even make an appearance. (Why reptilian? How reptilian?) The sacrificial victims heap up, spurred on by the wilderness and the incessant rain.

He shrugs his shoulders. Up to now, he has been the only member of our cell with the courage to remain silent. This is interesting enough but absurd, too ineffective from a pragmatic point of view: we attempt to show in chapter ten how devils tend only to dwell inside certain characters.

*

Old Huguenot with curvature of spine, shaking a filthy mat at the threshold.

A small translucent cover for intimidating indoor plants has been grown from a clump of brain cells. Before the spectators left, I crawled back across the auditorium to accost the interpreter.

Amid such opulence, we had no choice but to make further exchange of bodily fluids with our chosen animal familiars. Never assume that you will remember where anything is.

In that fugue, what happens next? Even my own anatomy will culminate in sublimities!

That man who sends these missives is a savant. That said, his report is confined to a single word repeated over and over in a scrawling hand. Thus his testimony runs on, yet nothing has been legally proved against any transgressor.

Origin is dialectical misunderstanding, from faulty horse grooming.

*

As a symbol of value, precious metal assumes the shape of bullion. Some of the Hebrews migrated across the snowbound plain to deliver themselves to the wasteland. They were the ones.

The presence of a witch-spirit may be confirmed by autopsy. The coroner gave confirmation, after which he demanded to know whether we had a private chamber whose prospect was distant from the public street, and I conducted him into such a room — backwards, at his insistence.

An establishing shot is a perimeter offered at the beginning of a new life, providing the viewer with a context for looming catastrophe. This information should help, it will brighten up the termination of another working day.

A plainly furnished room the foreground. Prospect: away from the public street. Defying custom, he enters without wiping his shoes, caked with snow and mud.

'Ah, tenderness — until you look upon me. Am I late?'

A room, an alcove with enclosed box. It was the tradition of the middle ages never to sleep lying down because that is the position of the dead.

The day after his sudden departure I was summoned for interrogation. This time they had to carry me in, and I remember nothing after that.

My inquisitors had retreated into the central turret, which is studded with gargoyles and griffins, having turned the east wing into an all-night pharmacy.

*

Something bursts from the chalkface as two chinooks copt above the curve of the ridge and we embrace in the fading light.

Am I too late?

This arrangement was inadequate but our strategy worked. I observed a ceiling and recess, elaborate moulding, a withdrawing room of the seventeenth. . . . The light is dazzling. What remains of her original accusation?

I have told you again and again, I no longer know what I am saying. Soot scours the orbit of mine eye.

Peat smouldering in the hearth gave off a blue smoke that settled on the tongue for days.

'Perhaps not, but what if you are an accomplice, and moreover have failed us?'

It is alleged a hollow muscular organ still pumps blood through the circulatory system by rhythmic contraction and dilation.

*

The window is a large square, twice as large as any ordinary window: a square of light on a white ground, triangle and circle inscribed upon it with a sharp instrument. He offers a piece of gold, pulling back his cloak to reveal five discs of the precious metal suspended from silk ribbons; I believe we are alike in some respects.

I am looking forward to being both here and elsewhere at the same time, though he is doubtless more adept at foreseeing what is going to happen next. His gold in quality far excels my own cache.

On his return, he insisted that the surface of the planet was enveloped in a thin stratum of rust. A true chronosophy — the interdisciplinary study of time — should provide a field in which the relation of two conflicting temporal processes might be gainfully misunderstood. The fall and rise of the guillotine was described as relentless systole and diastole.

'But what is to be gained by a conviction?'

'If she were not the vengeful type, I would never have existed.'

We are talking here of an intensely personalized cataclysm, amnesia congealed. I could barely make him out through the smoke rising from a hearth fuelled by decaying leaves and bark. I was done with them all; I had failed.

Without mentioning our own text, the *Rosarium* quotes from it as follows. And he permitted me to copy this out, direct from the surface of his esteemed anatomy.

Origin is gnawed speechless.

*

The attention of most army-ant observers is focussed on two common species, but my chosen variety is the handsome *Eciton rapax* (he writes), which produces longer raid systems than any other member of its genus and is a predator of forest floor and undercard ants. It is the only species without a specialized soldier caste.

Neuroptera are a silent order having four transparent wings, remarkable for their complex organs of vision. A piece for forty voices has been suspended in a continuum.

'I am in a state of ecstatic trance, above me arches a vault of moss. . . .'

Witches suck the blood of their victims and divide the body among themselves. We passed a great mound of dung upon which a guillotine had been erected. Minutes to be actioned are as follows:
   i) You cannot be sure.
   ii) The vignettes in several papyri connect us with the weighing of the heart.
   iii) He appeared before the committee of public safety and the revolutionary tribunal in a far from repentant mood.

iv) I think that you are well advised to be represented by someone who is not you.
v) In applying this principle, writing more detail than appears necessary does not betoken hoax.

*

While he takes his supper he has a child kneel on sharp pebbles; if it trembles, it is not paid. Citizens found to be asymptomatic carriers were shot on sight.

Thus, at first glance, dating the exodus to his reign seems to make no sense. Listen, when I speak about an allotment, I mean a *share*, a space that is cursed.

The ashes, he writes from exile, were in my possession for only a day. Pain is certain to vanish as soon as the error within oneself is recognized, but I fail to see how your theory can have any basis in law.

Back then, *cloche* was the usual name for a bell-shaped device.

Anything could trigger a further seizure. They could not know that the roof was about to fall in upon their heads.

Still more of the horde funnel across the horizon. I will be there for you.

Our passage was insufficiently slow.

*

A fluorescence radiates from behind the eyes. One hand raised, she stands at the waterfront and stares out to sea, whispering all the while into her sleeve.

Every object is solarized. The appropriate words are recited by the deceased, while nearby his heart is weighed in the scales.

'Do you know of anyone else prepared to take in some fugitives?'

I am dismantling. You are dismantling. He/She/It is dismantling. We are dismantling. You, plural, are dismantling. They are dismantling. . . . They are dredging the sewers, everywhere you turn there are armed militia — one priest was murdered, which explains the extra head in the box. . . . I am entrenched. There is talk of raiding, deciphering, but I have nothing of value left to offer.

I took the sheet down after the first passover. Spectral figures appear and drift toward the ceiling, as if rising from the mouth of one departed; it is fatal for such apparitions to look down while ascending into the space above our heads. Circles of green rust rim the eye sockets.

I woke to strobing light against which multiple shadows of myself were silhouetted, convulsing. In the corner by the window, a white, semi-opaque helical form uncoiled. It is sentient.

*

That floater in the river, it did seem unnatural the way he had shaped his body. It was I who rescued the stolen object from the flames.

The breastplate stones of judgement are listed above, as a diversion. I fear she has taken in some abandoned pilgrim and rebuilt the hermitage in the forest for his shelter.

Someone had tampered with the ball. In the card index, another of those endless hallucinations was filed under the word cathedral.

He telegraphed the others to tell them the universe had split in two and was defrosting. Our half was first, followed by its more famous neighbour.

With this tongue we create silence. He had attempted to cross the ocean in a box that was clearly never intended for a sea voyage.

Observe how the antihero becomes separated from the others. He has something of lastness about him. Things that would once have taken months or even years have become inexplicably accelerated.

Story of a savant

Sound of coughing from adjacent cell. Twenty-three hours to go, the turnkey murmurs. We drew cards from the tarot pack and took it in turns to throw a knife at the runes inscribed on the heavy oak door.

Box-beds were used to protect people from the animals living in the house — pigs, rabbits, giant carp — or from wolves who might enter a dwelling and attempt to convert the infants.

A reversal, over-reliance on the concrete mind: a warning of impending psychic disorder through an inability to accept the reality of the unconscious strapline. Her inner struggle ended in synaptic bankruptcy.

One of the Norse gods then described how he once slew himself by swallowing the world's ashes.

As in draw people in.

See, he has become obsessed with revision, exhaustively contemplating every past redundancy. That said, the existent and her object are believed to be one.

The same night I spent four hours crawling around the terrace on my hands and knees. I think I found the nest. We used a blowtorch to cauterize his hand. Make up my mind for me, please.

In vertebrates there may be up to four chambers, with two atria and two ventricles: from a central hexagonal turret two tunnels lead in or out, depending on one's orientation. Beneath was a secret dungeon with the only access through a trapdoor in the ceiling.

Origin is to forget.

Turning to answer, she asks did nothing meet you on the road?

Leaning forward, I fixed on her remaining eye while fingering the scar that runs from her forehead to the jawline.

*

As time passes one feels less compelled. Today, the cables in my neck are throbbing — my anatomy traces an outline more or less defective in its brittleness and consequent loss of speed. A bestiary frames the door space.

The atria cease to fibrillate when room temperature is lowered. One of the insurgents wielded an antique pistol.

Leave this locale, leave the island, immediately.

In another version I replied: lady there met with me upon the road such a beast as seemed apt to devour a whole people — and there were more of them under the ice, imprisoned in a vast installation while fed fluorescent green plasma through a tube.

Today may prove to be a turning point in your life: there is a word for the whatness of a thing. He says I cannot read driven solely by a sense of canonical duty, concussion protocols.

This blue rider, whose figure R seemed to know only too well, has somehow gripped attention.

Do not delay, drag him from the firing squad.

A firing squad is a group of soldiers detailed to shoot a condemned prisoner.

I am recognized, my comrades will confirm the gruesome details. The damned are approaching with free distractions unto death. Nowadays, we are all suspects.

'Who goes there?'

(He did not shout like a real guard.)

'Friend,' whereupon the other would say pass but keep thy distance.

On restraining the urge to speak

There follow instructions on how to display an entire human life in one shot without an edit. List and alphabetize all of the above.

My core disciplines exclude reprieve. A surface or solid can be formed by rotating a closed curve, especially a circle, about a line which lies in the same plane but does not interest it. Examples include a ridge of bone or muscle.

The receptacle of a mid-century flower is identified in sense two. I am the inflamed verbatim ballast.

We will never know whether we were overreacting. In AD 1575 the suspect was granted letters patent, giving a twenty-one-year monopoly for the printing of havoc, disorder, chaos, disruption, mayhem, bedlam, pandemonium, turmoil, tumult, confusion, uproar, commotion, upheaval, furore and shambles.

Not every inventory need be such a perfect unity. I have noted that when too excessive a continuity arises one feels compelled to quash everything thus far achieved, dismantling the offensive current and repatriating its parts to engender nervous collapse. Another man once said I resembled a bleeding sponge.

Our words are entering a new era. Another dog was a reincarnated human shape, whereas you are a creature of habit. Origin is a sudden change of mind.

Impaled on a pike carried by a *sans-culotte* was an aristocratic head with its hair standing on end (viz. horror, grudge). It has been proved beyond doubt that we were never related: a discharge ran down her thighs, the toes were webbed. Later signifies a sudden start.

See, cash idioms can be grouped into three main categories. Consider anyone's pituitary body, the endocrine gland, a pea-shaped thing attached to the base of the brain.

The purloined device had a surface covered with holes rimmed by slightly raised cutting edges. By contrast, psychostasia is the notion that a divine or supernatural figure weighs and measures the souls of people when judging them. Note the infantile play on the name of a leading G-man of the thirties.

Finding ourselves hopelessly cornered, we remained indifferent to every item of speculation. Then the chorus sang, rather misleadingly, while the pages of a burnt book were fed to the wind. I remember there being an immense glass tube that disappeared into the clouds.

*

We are treading a fault line. The acronym in question did not appear until after the sixteenth (to wit cabal). His chest was branded with the name of one of the elements, another palindrome.

An outmoded expression for a heavy downpour has spawned many ingenious ideas about our origins. For instance, metal box is a corporation. I have heard rumour.

This particularly applies during a monopoly into which all the electrodes and triggers are implanted. Hormonally, we have arrived.

He is right. They really can, they really do.

It had been raining hard across the whole peninsula. As in all acts of translation, an unmistakeable corrosion is taking place.

Do you recall how someone found the head in a bell jar of formaldehyde on the back seat? I know that I hung swaying in the wind up a tree for nine full nights, wounded by a spear, barbels around the mouth.

There is a silence in the air today, I said.

He justifies himself by pointing out that all errors have the potential to yield a profit. I am redundant.

A deity has been aborted. A soul was released. He woke up in a taxi with an unknown woman who was shaking him violently.

Your pulse is faint, she says.

Where do you want to go?

Where is your home?

Permit me to freeze that hand and cauterize the wound.

Nomadism is one of the central myths of your life. How would we have felt if all these things had happened to us?

You were there with the wreckers on the foreshore, I whispered.

*

We drift through the territory, fingering the map. The dog is now completely deaf.

She is patron saint: her blazon incorporates a marine invertebrate with five or more radiating arms. Its underside features telescopic claws for locomotion and, in predatory species, cracking open skulls.

I dropped a stone into the sea. She had a salt mouth, tongue, lips. We are now embedded in the public domain.

Thereafter, having performed certain rites, the volunteer will dream of the person destined to become their husband or wife. The *mise en scène* is so spaciously distributed that the subject photographed has considerable latitude of movement.

The average snowflake is nothing more than a gauzy clump of crystals. The soldier ants swarming across the discarded jacket multiplied and ate her alive. Help did not materialize.

We chanced upon a prehistoric burial mound, a chambered cairn — the nearby dolmen were monsters of white quartz. A line drawn from one pit to the other, and continued southwest, would touch the northeast quadrant along the footpath to the summit.

Consider the riptide, you should let the riptide take you.

The structure of an indifferent spirit

I can never remember your name. Ash in the grate is said by some to resemble grey feathers.

Here then is the definition of spirit: a slow walk down, no rush, maybe even take a casual shot at a passerby. I took place at two o'clock last night:
a) The empress or the costly electrician.
b) The magician who claims that within all of us lives an inner bestiary.
c) The holy fool, sectioned again.

The goal is amnesiac writing. The task of the disciple is to quarantine the self. Your cells will teach you everything.

Such is a small room in which a prisoner is locked up or in which a monk prays, or the smallest structural and functional unit of a life form — typically microscopic and consisting of cytoplasm and nucleus enclosed in a membrane — or a sealed cavity in an organism, a group forming a nucleus of political activity that is secret and subversive. Another device contained electrodes, immersed.

We entered a stormdrain that led to a vast subterranean chamber.

He shook his head and made a final gesture of defiance with his free hand: by that signal the other man immediately recognized his lamented sovereign. In those days, lying down was associated with death, therefore sleeping was done in an upright position.

Examples include:
A spiral galaxy.
Any ring-shaped object.
A vacuum chamber in a particle accelerator.
The refreshingly heavy water.

I am heartburn-free on the bus right now. One hundred percent of your consumers like water. Others favour a rotating firework, a rose window, a wheel set around with teeth or a sidewise somersault — waiting as a form of resistance — parasitic elements on a plinth of whipped cream. (My neck thing.) For the foreseeable future, all other sensations are shocked out of existence.

Where are we now she murmurs, gazing into empty space at the broken line of distant hills.

The last expression refers to someone who once had a brain made out of hair, a flooded interior void of any partition.

She goes missing but always comes back. She is experiencing some kind of cellular breakdown: if she wanted to roam, she would roam.

II

I am trying to reach a decision. I am trying to overreach a digression. I am right now pondering the most regrettably named product ever patented. On the wall hangs a faded print of an object I can no longer name.

Painstakingly, I glued the fragments of Saint Lazarus back together. He had leprosy and supported himself on a staff. Overall, the picture was blue-green.

I bought the glue at the local pound shop. Voices crackled through the air like lost electricity. Metal was the best conductor.

Above us tilts an array of candles from which hot tallow spills onto the volunteer, who twists in space from a cable attached to a hook embedded in the ceiling.

With every speech act I return to a state of purposelessness. I feel like an Eastertide statue, concealed yet present.

I am attempting to stave off the opposition, this people whose haemorrhage so deeply you fear. Imagine a room about a film about a journey to a book.

Human sacrifice was performed under the branches of a tree whose roots are known.

*

When I halt my step, predators are alerted. But perpetual motion is a precondition of any existence.

This sector records the highest concentration of kill. Nothing will save you.

They are not men of their word.

My advocate said punctuation had been withheld because it disrupts the communication of meaning. All this time you kept sucking at my fingers.

Their love died unrequited. At the station she realized she had forgotten the diaphragm. This state of tranquility is a short-lived consolation designed to encourage beginners.

*

We are at twenty thousand leagues. The structure has no doors, no hinges of any kind. He strides up to my table and tells me the ark is concealed in full view, within the stone house we have been occupying for months.

The others suddenly appeared out of nowhere. I said well take me.

Sound was a piece of noise, an undercurrent, typically one that is unavailable and vacant of form, harnessed to trauma.

Origin lacks influence.

We will manacle your neck and feet together she said. You will drink sea water until you burst or go insane, or both.

Tactics are vital when attempting to control fiscal growth and the functioning of neural ganglia. Another voice kept pointing and saying this one has asbestosis, cancer of the pleura.

The waters had risen perceptibly. We stood on an iron bridge encased in ice — the mangled locomotive and other wreckage were trapped in the frozen water swirling beneath us. As we parleyed, I turned to see the river had surged rapidly to the level of the last crossing.

She said the Chinese had been right about iron filings all along, and then apologized for generalizing. Come the thaw, I struggled to swim the length of the bridge, but metal debris had begun to break loose from the ice, making the attempt perilous. Reserves were summoned, soldiers from the final scene wielding latex weaponry, marching around in concentric circles. One stops and turns to stare at me, before posing an unanswerable rhetorical question. It was a comedy of errors had it not been for the outcome.

I am to tell you that your name is an anagram, she whispered.

*

Atom in the lung: the hawk is belled and jessed. Our falconer has not performed the required action and the moment of alarm has passed (viz. potent-counterpotent).

I did not see the obstacle placed in my way. They would have slain me, given the chance, given half the chance.

This plan can work: follow my tracks in the snow. I read somewhere that a certain number of frowns creates a wrinkle. If you will, the talons are exposed.

I feel conspicuously obscure and have volunteered for paralysis. I sense the desperate need for a digression or two, a few scattered seeds — tattoo pulse in the head: it is time.

We chanced upon a box of bees nailed to a wall, a rudimentary hive. Drones swarm about our heads. My companion simply closes her eyes and shuts everything out.

Where any of these words cause alarm, they may simply have been placed in the wrong order. I came down to earth in bodily form, leaping from star to star.

I suppose I ought to stay here and see if I can help out, said Newton.

*

Beyond the perimeter of the compound, a solitary voice. Sound waves are a source of degradation. St Louis was the centre of the universe.

I used to love being ill, the brittle notes of a harpsichord would waft up the stairs as mother sat drawing the ghosts of tiny insects.

Let the dry land appear et cetera

He became caught up in various escapades which delayed him considerably. I asked for a list of all the male suicides of the previous year, every doomsayer on that barren peninsula.

He always sticks to his own trajectory. The role of other people in the causation of a fatal act is not always obvious.

Stranded diplomats huddle at the shoreline. To a man, they look confused: they need a vessel, anything to ferry them across. A raft is fashioned, rotting pallets sealed with pitch bound to empty oil barrels.

Countermovement is simply the bringer of stillness. There was a show of hands.

On the far shore is an all-night laundromat. Walking the orbital anticlockwise, a man hobbles up clutching his meniscus. Someone has blinded him — an amber resin drips from his forelock, the so-called eclipse plumage. We are following in our father's footpads.

'Kneecapped,' he stutters.

The rain came once to deluge me and the wind to make me tremble. I am never quite alone.

How shall I describe? Here is an auspicious point at which to end the account of that morning: linguists consider utterance to be an action, particularly with regard to its lack of purpose.

The mercury could not have fallen lower. The instinct is No. I lifted the quotation marks set around *Geist*, thereby reifying the word.

First vision under opium, seated at my window on a late summer evening: hills between the sea, Mars orange-red, the lights of a distant vessel, but when.

*

His account of the campaign includes a reckless assault on the counterscarp. The subject of the previous chapter leads us to another axiom.

Take the battle to your enemy at sunrise. The outcome is decay: flight, collapse, rout.

In 17_ the novelist had himself ritually beheaded in public — his inner life was dominated by images of pain and death. His suicide was the ultimate realization of your fantasies. The enemy now is barely visible.

This was written into the flesh.

Origin tears at sinew, gnashing the teeth, speaking bitterly from a place deep within the body. At that moment a flying beetle struck the window pane with a sharp crack.

The impulse to produce, consume and surrender arose in mediaeval times. Money has no plans for me. Break a limb she whispered, squatting beneath.

This sad tale is to be compounded in time by sudden death at a remote railway station. And she looked at him in such a way.

Origin is associated with wanton ludic movements, from skull plus hog studded with thorns. I was in love with her from that moment onward.

There exists a backstory. The next phenomenon is any ring-shaped object, especially a type of large circular chamber used in psychical research. Not one of us was allowed up onto the observation platform to witness the transit of mercury — but the anaesthetist's experimental laboratory, that was a different matter altogether. Nor were we permitted to enter the crypt, where the mason's private thoughts were stored, tunnelling under himself.

Spill all your cards on the table: the middle ages and King Lear understood that the one thing people in power fear is assassination by suicide bomber or being laughed at. Bursting forth from the cocoon, one can no longer be transformed into a polyamorous butterfly or the ill-fated moth.

Dredged up from the local ravine: fouls of ravyn, malignant tumour of connective tissue et cetera. We left a trail of chopped kidneys, raw.

Have them strike up voice: demented violas, accordion, zither — rimshot with fractured sound, unmistakeable murmur and lament. Pustulant matter leached out from numerous raptures.

*

Once upon a time, deep inside the Arctic Circle, there occurred a situation. Outstanding magics clustered round. Turning slowly over the fire is the shell of a turtle, craquelure spreading, splitting open in the darkness: the dead never stay dead, and so on.

If there are no objections, I now appoint myself. I have been toying with this notion, a playful abstraction: the crew are safely down in the hold, all cargo of human ballast, most of them willing to die after a brief taste of history.

Any stowaways would be crushed beyond recognition in the first storm of our crossing. An extinct hieroglyphic language has in its entirety just occurred to me.

*

Could one say with any truthfulness that I know the position of my hand with my eyes shut? And how to spot a hawk owl, for instance? Following the revelations of a previous epoch, we will need the full anatomy cast in plaster of Paris.

Chance fades as you grow older, nonetheless she remained stationed at her post right up until the sponsors rolled. The world grew desolate toward the end, abject in black bile.

She knew. Her face was bruised at the temples. The future is prophesied, eternal relics of the past: a corpse in the peat marsh, those low scudding clouds, the earth's precession. . . . The mineral in question is characterized by unusually long fibres, for example a strand of hair stuck to the skull. If the follicle is still attached, we could have a DNA match by sunup.

Resistance to attack by acid is making today's date auspicious. The blade of a propeller is an aerofoil, from the tip of which a vortex trails.

One reads, and believes that one understands. We drank wine from the skull of a vanquished adversary.

The hull is segmented, a maritime ant-hill with seventeen bulkheads. Number nine has ruptured — waters gush in, sea things too: giant squid, the tentacles of hydrozoa, writhing sea snakes, the barb of a stingray, a versatile method actor, plus some unidentifiables.

'Therefore now, I beseech thee, take my life from me. . . .'

Are you conscious, have you seen him? How he resents the sparing of the penitent — who has been granted undeserved compassion — and argues that justice ought to prevail, broken on the wheel. Your intentions must be directed at yourself alone, and no one else.

'We should talk about our plot to pierce time, make a decision.'

And this place joins here to *there*. The regulars became known as *les maudits*, but we don't get many mystics around here since the all-night laundromat closed down.

Medusoid phase

Mappa mundi: south is up, north down, and there are other anomalies. The year is never. I am distracted.

We were annexed by a posse of men in military greatcoats. One among them raises a pistol and takes aim at my head. (How was your nineties?) He shoots, a bullet skims the brain. As I lie on the ground, another approaches to deliver the grace stroke from point-blank range — anticipation of pain, the retort, explosion inside the head — and the sound, a strange sound as of moving air, the wind more like voice, old murmur of being here — void cavity of the skull and glimpse of dying alive: ghost parley.

I am still trying to sluice that lingering aftertaste. Imagine, if you can, an alluvial deposit that forms by accretion inside the expanding loop of a river.

They have ransacked the reliquary, fragments of marble and bone flung into the air before descending onto cobblestone. The hatch is closed and sealed.

A man weeps in an alleyway, stumbling about in despair. Newly executed, I drift through the town on my back, floating just a little above the ground, eye skyward — winding streets of timeless backwater. . . .

He did not stop here but went on to draw attention to the curious pattern of pyramids studded across the surface of the planet, which are clearly visible from orbit.

See, we are returning to his spatiotemporal rupture theory.

*

The stag's antler floats into view and a piece breaks off. Here we are, just you and I. We will doubtless drown. Venus is visible to the south.

He says I exist only through the supernatural act of writing: were it not for Napoleon, I would be selling life-or-death scratch cards down on the street.

At last I have made up my mind, am resolved to put on record the ordeal we have lived through. Lunar blindness is an affliction of the eyes, commonly believed to be caused by dreaming while exposed to the light of the full moon. My own eyes are just above the waterline, stung by salt — distant glitter of marshland beyond the foreshore, set in tangential correspondence to the rising sun. . . . I found all these lights in the sky, tendrils of white mist streaming over the tor. . . .

The narrative of life flashed before me. This did not take long. (It wasn't mine.) The surviving lung is fit to burst. Despite all this, I am still on his fucking letter.

A forced march across barren land, toward an ancient city of stone carved from a mountain — a certain unease arising from our circumstance. . . . Through the painstaking study of a mass of funerary and rebirth texts, you have established what, exactly?

Anchorage fees at the wharf are so dreadful costly these days. I shall have to invent an alibi — psychic energy as a magnetic chain of pylons, the last flicker of a dying star, or suchlike.

Your savant

*

Paramilitaries held manoeuvres out there one night in the forest and were shooting guns, detonating. They said they were really sorry about the eternal transience.

It is here that he lays aside the conventions of formal writing and speaks to the heart of those whom he is addressing. I dreamt I was walking alongside you and that your shoes were broken. It rained.

Languid, floating flower et cetera. The centre is trapped in the wake of our spectacle.

There are nerves that radiate outward beyond their own loci. When the cloudburst comes, I will need something to occupy time.

Who is holding the purse strings now? Back on board, the crew have mutated.

I realize my library is slowly decaying, the pages yellowing and crumbling between my fingers as I read. Note the surveillance camera snuck inside the volunteer's cranial suture.

You may want to think twice about the wisdom of building an ark once the deluge has actually begun.

General Protocols (1): establish an underground cell

As detailed in previous bulletins, collective response is always preferable to an individual assassination attempt. We can endure, get used to anything: if all else fails, replace everyone.

A stranger in the street asks a question — I spin round, upended on my wet scalp. He sounds a broken man. As the voice persists, I awaken.

Raise the stakes, play me a strain insensible and slow — a code we can crack — what palaeographers call a leak in the thatch: volte-face, insurgency, schism (i.e. a letter to one's younger self). Some hunt in packs, I believe, fervently.

*

Corridors of steel buckle to an apex — cathedral underside, moss-vault ribbed with flying buttress — the soldiers' laser-blue shirts glow in the darkness. . . . My phenomenon is called forth and named germ plasm.

Evanescent, yet there is something of the decaying signal about us. This is the official oratorical period. I am not professing, just asking.

Match something to something else. Try to stay alive and enjoy the spectacle.

*

It is rumoured the grammalogue, a word represented by a single sign or symbol, was introduced with the first tables of the law. The primary feathers of a crow found dead by the lake were utilized as quills to pluck at mother's harpsichord.

I overlooked the sea a mile below our orbit. I could at the same time command a view of some great city standing on a different radius of my circular prospect. The outcome of these observations was another rout.

She died heroically, but will live on as an example of the unattainable. Convince yourself: victory or death. The basic monetary unit was equal to about one hundred of your earth years, but we need not trouble ourselves over such temporal details.

A madwoman in a tricorn hat passes, limb in tourniquet with leather bootlaces — a one-woman army, a flailing whirlwind chopping at the old confines.

I am here inventing a new form of calendar, arranged as a checkerboard with thousands of tiny sigils, scintillas of light, red and yellow. One example of a trade of goods between two tribes was found in the ruins beneath the toppled walls of the city: the broken fragments of an alabaster jar that once contained an embalmed brain.

Ball lightning is bluish in colour and only remains visible for a few seconds. Vomit elsewhere please, the sign said.

He was pulled out from under the rubble at the foot of the stairs, fighting like a demon. Nearby stands our ghostly surveillance bunker.

Communards stuffed the marquis into a sack, which gendarmes then tied up and hurled out of a window onto the cobblestones.

We are approaching a pit stop. Today's directive is to make (something abstract) more concrete or real: all these instincts are in mankind reified as verbal constructs.

*

In the days of the son the highways were deserted and travellers trod an invisible path. Insect eggs hatched in the wound. The inhabitants of the village ceased.

I was resurrected mother and my diseased womb set off to wander.

He is an honest species of reprobate, is he not? The people chose new gods and war was inside the gates.

Now the subject of a major documentary, she is the bipolar axis of an abandoned pursuit. There followed months of freezing mist, weeks of hail and ice, whereupon marches turn to riots and riots seethe to internecine warfare. Stopped at a checkpoint, there is something wrong with her papers and she grasps the opportunity to sacrifice herself.

Crawl on all fours as militiamen lose control. . . . Our descent, as agent M once put it to me, is a destructive rerun of the history of ontology.

A large convex moulding, typically semicircular in cross section, is often found at the base of the spinal column. A reckless movement of the body is about to take place.

See, she says one thing and then does something else. From which antecedent are such behaviour patterns inherited?

Grains of dried blood nestle in the wound. The anaesthetist was jackal-headed, which everyone present found most reassuring.

Of idle devotions

And here and there scraps of flesh, an assortment of animal parts flung clear of high table: the lobe of an ear, a diced snout, clumps of fur, muddied hoofs and trotters, excised anal flaps — quite a tableaux of *memento mori* — a tangle of yeses and noes that trammel a certain path.

A thin tissue forms the outer layer of your surface, lining the alimentary canal and other hollow structures. Origin is a prayer of commemoration, whispered too late.

I was born inescapable, a long exposure perspective. The fish-eye lens provides an extreme wide angle which distorts the image so radically that its edges are warped into a sphere. Our two continents once collided and recoiled — Aphrodite smote her breast with a stout claw and hearts dissolved.

Who is prepared to evaporate into nothingness? The invader hoards these sterile pods, time capsules in which your beginning is detained, postponed to infinity.

They are among us once more. Mind is a disease of semen another wrote.

I am inserting myself into a lengthy complex chain. These excerpts reveal that some cosmic drama was projected upon the ancient battlefields of Troy: writing arose from disintegration.

Almost all of our links have been severed. I am groundless (people cannot believe that anyone could be so fucking uncommunicative). The psyche is largely clandestine, unrevealed, strictly confidential, untold, classified, undisclosed and unknown — it operates behind one's back, off the record, concealed, camouflaged, covert, underground, hidden, shrouded, conspiratorial, surreptitious, underhand, coded, enciphered, arcane, concealed, unfrequented, solitary, sequestered, remote, isolated, secretive, unforthcoming, reticent, taciturn, silent, clamlike and introverted. As soon as one touches the uniqueness of the individual trajectory, it can no longer be witnessed and the observer becomes eyeless.

The latter is always the quintessence of the former. Remember that we possess two very perfect bodies. I touched the earth, pulling aside, with clenched fist. I ask you, is an ant on its own really an ant at all?

She buried them each beneath crosses of lilies in the back garden, barely a child. I said to the police, before I go, give me a minute. No one came.

This accounts for the ambiguous identity parallelism that oscillates between thee and me. We are coming back to ourselves, quite fragile, especially where we cluster. Our procession clings to the right angle made by the exterior wall and the floor, softly unsung — vulnerability imposing itself — a cordon sanitaire, quarantined against the viral outside. Origin denotes an ornamental brain of malachite green or ash blue.

Sense three of the noun, the earliest of electric current, dates from an abandoned century. I don't suppose this is remotely what you expected.

Rache

A brief account of the only case of self-kneecapping on record: I am outclypsed by mine own sadness et cetera. . . . I slung a noose around one of the undamaged piles visible above the waterline — interspersed among the flags were white and pale blue oriflammes with golden fleurs-de-lis. . . . By contrast, the mayor's parlour in which we were wed is predominantly silver and blue. This chamber contained erratically upholstered Queen Anne chairs and a non-linear writing desk; hidden in one recess was a tortuous geometric figure, a crystal displaying a fragile sixfold symmetry. Such forms are useful when modelling snowflakes.

One can only speculate as to why this has happened. Perhaps he aroused suspicion by making enquiries about the sacred relic. On a rock-hewn terrace between rugged cliffs that tower above the dead sea, a labyrinth of foundation stones, some three hundred and fifty feet square, are all that remain.

*

A brain-dead rhythm turns in my head. I recall those unsung years, the belt of stars. All personnel from sections six, seven and eight have been moved to section nine, the collision bulkhead.

A theory of forgetting is underway — the treasures of unsituated memory — the endeavour to conjure a life, any existence, other than the one granted. The perceptive reader will now understand why we connect pathos to the neutral.

I made the volunteer pay a month in advance and asked for a list of all male suicides of the previous year. It is the classical fetish, not the hermit or solitudinarian, that desolates the continent with its ceaseless wars. That said, many see the marshal as the single combatant who has kept our enclave alive, albeit tottering at the rim of an abyss.

The meaning suicide acquires for the individual depends on a variety of circumstances. Weighing of souls is a motif in which a person's life is assessed by weighing their soul *or some other part of them* immediately after death.

And throwing his own tongue into the snake pit.... In 1656 BC the surviving citizens were suspected of heresy, and having refused to surrender its garrison the town was burned by the invading army.

Below, for your convenience and in no particular order, we have conjured a taxonomy of self-slaughter: suicide by occupation, by sex, by seasons of the year, by hour of day et cetera.

a) Hanging, strangulation, suffocation.
b) Firearm discharge, explosive material.
c) Jumping from a high place.
d) Self-poisoning by drugs.
e) Sharp object or shoes.
f) Self-poisoning by chemical substance, subdivided by types of poison, such as corrosive, irritant, systemic, gaseous, narcotic, alkaloid, protein.
g) Jumping or lying in front of a moving object, subdivided by leaping under the wheels of a locomotive, under the wheels of a truck, under the feet of horses, from steamboats.
h) Other means.
i) Drowning.
j) Talking, conversation with a stranger on a train.

*

A life-or-death scratch card is a card with sections silvered using an opaque waxy substance, which may be scraped away to reveal a symbol indicating whether the purchaser is to live horribly or die horribly.

An incarnate being is the embodiment of an idea, such as it ever is. I could hear the frantic flapping of a bird trapped beneath the eaves.

The radio said a man had been drowned by the incoming tide. Suddenly the shadow of a giant housefly was projected across the windscreen.

He is the eternal supplement. A revolving cylinder with a vertical axis used for winding a cable had to be invented.

A mound of rough stones was built as a memorial, typically on a hilltop or skyline. The inner pair of defences, with ramparts up to four metres high, are concentric and pierced by a south-facing entrance, while a hollow muscular organ pumps blood by rhythmic contraction and dilation.

Oriflamme

The syndicate next turned its attention to partisans of the third wave of resistance, stringing them up from the nearest tree. This demanded a virtuoso performance.

In some species, medusa is a stage in the lifecycle which alternates with the hydra phase. Origin is the modern intestinal hollow where the brain was dumped.

One outcome was collapse — at the joint of every limb, across the palm of every hand, under the arch of every foot.... A linguistic unit consists of a set of tongue-shaped forms that exist in a non-sequential relationship to one another.

There was a puncture wound and a drag wound. I am often placed in contrast, acting as a foil.

Has this finished?

*

The gods answered that he must slaughter his victim and eat it. Compare with polyp.

Origin is at the midpoint of everything. I am named by association, the only mortal gorgon.

And indeed, one customer killed another customer by cutting off her head. Any word may be represented by a single sign or symbol.

Your bones decay in ancient ploughland, rotting where you lie, the mission aborted. Set into the lead palm of the hand was a perfect circle of jet, and painted above this the familiar spiral motif in red ochre, representing a distant galaxy. A perpetual state of unrest is taking root at my interior.

He is written out. A cluster of disembodied ones are invading his anatomy, colonizing him, and murmur low whispers as night draws on.

He stops me in the street to explain that he now reads solely for voice and detail, nothing more. Then he asks, who among us could survive torture on the wheel?

It is calculated that a further decrease of eight percent in solar radiation would bring the walls creeping together.

Phalanx

A certain spectacular impression is fading. I could not be pressed to watch over his corpse throughout that long night; it has been noted that I no longer wish to participate.

We grew out of the isolation which had fermented among a silent order to the south. A suitable date materialized.

The signs are not to be questioned, *we* are. I can no longer imagine.

Ball lightning does occur more frequently in high places: mountain peaks, skyscrapers, radio masts. There is, however, another natural phenomenon that seems more consistent with what is being reported.

Sabotage, said Napoleon. As a counterweight, I proposed a decree which renounced identification: the tomb is known locally as the giant's craw (crow equals hut).

Yesterday, a hitman from malpractice came round, a zero-dark contract killer who repairs and maintains vehicle engines and other machinery in his spare time. I suffered a crushed tibia. What is more, the influx of monastic orders has caused a shift in the non-material and cognitive weather patterns. Should it be necessary to walk through a town or village, we will be content simply to pass in silence.

Rare earth

I should never be able to function under these conditions. Hold fast his head, ready the axe and the salver. At such a séance, similar patterns of apparition recur and are useful when describing random or chaotic phenomena, such as crystal growth and galaxy formation.

Comes another seven-hour gap between dusk and dawn, as the inhabitants on level three of the ark resume their howling and screeching. We are crossing that viaduct once again, as the sun sets over a broken horizon.

What about the polar convoys, are they not also vulnerable to attack? I remain unconvinced: this is a Dioscuri job, the twins born after seduction, and often identified with my constellation.

By now we were out of anaesthetic.

My nemesis has overheard my fingerprints. A statue of the deceased was believed to become animated at certain phases of the moon. Together within the thing itself exist its origin and its decline.

He was conceived in the eastern part of the sky, where Sirius and the Orion constellation are visible in the pre-dawn.

I think he is more than ever in touch with his inner futility, that exterminating angel. First he makes sure the others have a chance to escape, but it is not long before he starts confessing to our inquisitors.

Dear Gauleiter
Thank you for another rapturous evening with St John at the gasworks. Looking forward to seeing you later — let me know when and I shall be ready to eat, and be eaten.
Here is that dream again, written out in full below. In relating it to you earlier, I thought of the Balkan question, when something of that nature actually happened. No bullet of course, but the raised pistol to the head, point-blank for what seemed eternity — and still within me, the map adrift, memory ineluctable.
Bodily functions are part of the machinery.
Your savant

*

The watchers forced him to abandon the vessel in midstream. This revolt may have been the final eruption of those forces which impelled our magus upon his perilous career.

The entire expanse of society is in fact its own poorly executed portrait. But recent scholarship is tending to put chaos a good deal earlier, buried deep in the groundswell of your God.

I intend to perform another action when I am good and ready: one performs a movement and one simultaneously forgets the movement. This is not a speech act in itself. And, mister, of all the cases on record, there is not a single case of suicide by leaping from the rear end of a slow-moving train.

Origin is a cordon, both from a knotted rope, hamstrung.

III

Nerveband

'That's interesting, the process is anatomical. You go down the steps and you're inside.'

He was more animal than human, flamboyant bill studded with minute sensors, robbed of which he would never dine. His internal organs are constellated in a delicate fan array. I entered the cell to find him lying on a heap of filthy straw.

I had no option but to defer to his clairvoyance, yet we all know that some events must remain unforeseen. The message was scribbled on a scrap of paper, the words 'scried by nightshade' at its coda.

Will sir take his punishment outside the body, or within? We cannot go on any further because this is where the land drops away.

That red lever delivers the substitute cylinder.

*

He has been awarded the principal role in an exhibition of mutism. We received but one letter, then silence.

Realty, a person's real property, is the opposite of personality, a person's intimate property. Genera were marshalled: land with dwellings, minerals, pronouns, bodily fluids and functions, colours, numerals, elements and metals, celestial bodies, weather, birds, a variety of waters, fish, the stuff of earth — rock, sand, sod — and vegetation, decaying leaves, bark. . . . Folk disappear and reappear, have brought along their own alphabets, carefully packed in tinfoil.

This shall be one of my last executive decisions. Lights open up in the darkness.

The bureau is teaching humans how to see through walls, abilities to be used as a weapon for which there is no known defence. We are here sabotaging the brittle geometry of an unfinishable structure.

Disease worked its will among the populace. Speech performance is visualized as an inverted tree, an underwater vessel with pores and lenses, the graphic trace.

That salt marsh is notorious. Immediately there was a crashing through the yellow canes and a sound of voices. And what have I done to be thus chosen, I want to know.

Walking Dead Transport Solutions

He crossed the Irish Sea, where he remained for a couple of centuries, completely out of touch and well beyond reach. One must walk, expend effort.

This is a novel engagement involving the vast scale of human cruelty. In the grate were found lead oxide, brick dust, a knuckle bone. Yesterday's paramedics were superb.

That last sentence changes the meaning of the entire paragraph.

Did you know where you were when the incident happened?

That is the question. Now let us see whether our volunteer can perform *this* action.

I struggle to recall. It was she who spoke; the apparition said nothing.

Consider an infamous passage in the original, e.g. the interrelationship between space and gravity, where quarks play the role of errant electrons. The average citizen could now conceive of objects quite differently than before.

Make a list of things that are going wrong.

I found myself in dense woods surrounded by fenland, bang in the middle of a life sentence. Recall the sheer length of that building, an aircraft hanger jammed full of beakless chickens — the tail fin alone was the size of a football pitch, white pollen tracing the touchline. Something lurched toward me clutching its head, spurred on by hunger and craving.

'We will have to repair the perimeter, urgently those cinder blocks. . . .'

'Look, a thin film of silence galvanized by synapses — a junction between two nerve cells — a minute gap which impulses cross by spur of a neurotransmitter.'

I do not remember saying any of this. Two sacred black stones were set into the cathedral's south-west corner, staring each other down.

*

It is believed the victim stabbed himself to death, a rare example of state-sponsored autoexecution. Your failsafe won't last forever.

'No, I am the only one who fought back, the last man standing.'

Remember the anticipation with which I looked forward to fulfilment of my long-cherished visions of travel? We found ourselves back in an uncharted bayou.

In truth, divination is the only useful thing about reading the cards. (The ancient Chinese knew how to copy reality, they simply chose not to.) Everybody has their own interpretation: controlled lives spent in codified form, Jupiter's giant red eye. . . .

A crisis is destroying the old patterns. Origin came early, from a base meaning sponge or lichen. You have to make room.

He tells me he could not sleep. I thought, you too.

This must be the mouth of hell everyone has been talking about. I stood watching the fighter jets swoop in, tail lights flashing — a watchtower was shelled from across the border. No doubt he is inside one of those machines, head between his knees, viscera draping the ball turret.

This is the first dusting of snow I have seen for twelve years, but no one else on the train was looking at the landscape, the hoar frost. Verglas is a thin coating of ice or frozen rain on an exposed surface. I am flung clear.

*

An interior, dimly lit. About the rafters and walls he has fashioned a reliquary of letters, what he calls the yield. He disappeared, evidently.

A short leather strap is wound around the leg of a hawk.

Metalumina

An opera cum charnel house. No sound. Enter. A metal grille is positioned at the centre of the ceiling. In the sky is a pink mortality curve, an ancient track that never fades.

Is your language meta? she asked, gin in claw.

This must be the Staunton lick I keeping hearing so much about. Volunteers are due to be shot — since then I have been waiting, biding my time.

He is recognized by a scribe and released from the line up. On passing through this fissure, the nerve is placed just below the lachrymal branches of the ophthalmic crescent.

*

I am blind. The only way up is the way one came down (viz. oubliette). I am mainly interested in elusive material; I refuse to speak. Open the door a couple of inches, the steel plate, cue supernatural anthems.

Don't mock me he says, but I have the feeling that things invisible all around us are creeping soundlessly to a catastrophe.

I relate all this from memory, though have scarcely wandered about the world myself, rarely strayed beyond the electrified perimeter of the compound. The county coroner maintains that the deceased's passing had been 'aleatory'.

My own options are now unquestionably limited. Besides, I can muster no voice or movement before high noon.

See, another utterance with which my own speech has nothing in common.

Resound. Snow on the shingle — haar and sea fog — though I have not yet learnt to decipher the tide tables. Our values and freedoms eclipse dissent and at the same time scream aloud for sedition. Painted scenery surrounded us, the backdrop to some cubist novella. (What?)

Saltirewise

In this movement the language appears irreducible; the rules of the game are ambiguous, and admit too much importance to a single solution. Mister soon discovered he wasn't cut out for straightforward panegyric.

It could be said that in terms of reputation I have never had much to lose, but neither anything to gain. I would often take myself off beyond the stockade and into the desert to sleep under the stars.

The iron rivets burst, the shaft quivered — a vessel shot down.

*

Ortolani's sign: diagnosis of the unstable or dislocated. This organism was formerly eaten as a delicacy, the male having a phosphorescent green head and a throat full of battery acid.

Gerald, on the other hand, is a really good name for a horse (see page 116). The millstone continues to turn, grinding rock to gravel and creating a vast whirlpool.

He recommended specific rules of conduct and practical aids toward the formation of spine-chilling habits: thinking, cognition, the illusion that language enables thought et cetera. Seeing him struggle for air, the valet lifted his master into an upright position. Several times sir threw up lumps of clotted blood.

'Yes or no, I will never be a party to retreat: save yourselves.'

The phonetic relation here is unclear. A name is given — lace of damascene, various patterns done in silver and gold.... Moments are cast from raw pigment.

Why were the instructions not simply written down and left for us to find? Being could never have envisaged an existence within the human body, something must have *forced* it inside.

During our third year an army of killer raiding ants invaded the outpost, a disaster triggered by sudden reversal of the earth's magnetic field.

It is hydraheaded, this gnashing of teeth. I woke with my head to the east, feet to the west. The birdsong had ceased. I had spent an endless night crossing the vast wastelands of Asia by train, the locomotive fuelled by pollen stored in shallow wooden crates. As darkness fell, open fires punctuated a barren moonscape.

Again and again we were besieged by tribesmen intent on slaughter. Captured and held hostage in an abandoned colony at the heart of this wilderness, I was chained to a pinball machine and the cycle of interrogations began. Our lives hung upon every detail I uttered in response.

You read the terrain, search for signs of passing. Finally I remembered, when I came to page fifty-eight, the part where she hangs him upside down from a hook in the ceiling.

I forgot to look for his grave, the remains of the man. It was freezing, and besides, the catacombs spread out beneath the entire region, an unmapped chain of cells, cloisters of bone.

Within his given name we come close to an original meaning. At the frontier of this sulphurous zone grotesque forms appeared, rushing toward us.

*

Last page, dream text of an unprojected man: the judgment, eidolon, hexagrams — every contour and crack of him: a vertical body of water that can write, glyphs floating on a chlorinated blue surface.

What connexions might we discover between each letter? For example, aleph, the trickster, with its particles fleeing the subatomic. Nothing can torment me now, purpose being overthrown.

There was a big red number eighty-eight in the sky. I hauled myself aboard and she stood there waving farewell, a grudging valediction.

So, an even deadlier sting: I had hoped for benighted fanfares, jinxed bouquets. She had a strict manner of relating her stories of the ocean.

Concussions

I did not say any of this, am not the sum of my actions and words. The other interjects: today everything seems made of death, a performance of mummery. And who indeed was 'scried by nightshade'?

Answer: hold down the chord of C, pluck a fretted bass string with the thumb of the left hand, then flee.

Memory disassociation
(wherein the querent is seeking to discover the new pattern)

Back me or I quit. We arrived late in the evening at the marshy outlet of a river. They are cranking up the dredger above our heads as we speak. No one will return within the hour.

He is poised to ambush the contenders, holds the knave of diamonds and ace of spades. Folk call this feast day a mournival.

Henceforth, I compass my work within the interludes, knowing all too well the rewards of equivocation and ambiguity, your muted confusion.

No. Like I said, it's a life sentence; I hope to atone. Then a rapping at the wall confirms his survival. Three shots rang out.

'It's as if you are actually there in the room with them.'

'At least act in such a way that I can speak to you, should the need arise.'

We are well beyond a point of redemption. No one can decide. The situation is driving me; I have forged a mistake.

She has an ear for quiddity, the whatness of things. Compassion ratio is nil, compression null — the perfect form. It has been predicted that the first space-faring civilisation in the galaxy would very swiftly occupy the whole damn thing.

*

The nib of a fountain pen would have split, ink spurting everywhere, the slaughter left undone.

Despite this setback I am determined to write you, our young vandal declares.

The insect's membrane folds across its abdomen. A chance aperture has opened. My bloody prints looked black the night before, now purple.

We were sectarian to a man. I was lost. I drew a transparent horizon about myself, like some theatrical ghost, sharpened teeth poised in neat rows. As we approached the lakeside harbour I could hear detonations, see the plumes of smoke.

That woman, blonde on board a tram, Zurich — skull in a box of bones at her feet, between splayed legs, the perfect skeletal summary.

The syndicate has introduced a rupture-of-form training programme, where they teach things like asymmetry, imbalance. And what *did* you do to that canine police? enquires a fellow servant of the community.

The click obtained is diagnostic of a congenital dislocation of the unborn. Here, the sign takes precedence over background radiation.

At distance, a passing hill is studded with black-coated cattle. Subjective experience corrodes in the neutrality of the enunciated word, a gesture of self-doubt that the bystander has surely come to expect.

A diagonal cross, used as a heraldic ordinary

She is sliding away from us. I don't believe such behaviour is absolutely necessary. She misses everything. To date, our primary areas of interest have been intentionality, action, philosophical anthropology, causation and essentialism.

These are historically alarming symptoms. The rest is the mess you leave as you pass through.

In the above-quoted passage he continues to question his own sanctity. His landscapes, often peopled with bandits and containing scenes of violence in wild natural settings, were a subversive influence. He orbits beyond the powers.

His opinions are seditious, bound up as he is in anxiety and habit, uneasy at a loss for words. He writes from some godforsaken place, set down amid endless fields of quicklime and flint.

My nemesis: the concrete misunderstanding of a voice, a distant sea in hammered lead.

Somehow he immobilized his victims without leaving any trace. And what is your chosen area of expertise?

IV

A bare monochrome terrain with two distant cinderblock shacks

There was nobody there. An empty canvas knapsack had been left at the foot of the glacier. I am the only one who can keep the tension within the group running in a self-augmenting pattern — that is until the strain breaks. The habit of a certain empiricism is never easily overcome.

A querent is one who consults, or seeks to learn something by means of, an astrologer. Origin is a furrow, back-formation from chant, edge plus broken — i.e. the shattered beak. On the way we passed blood-clotted feathers in the road.

Dust on his fingers — hubris, such as invites disaster, the shock of daily spectacle. I had observed that most of those who have left memoirs have only shown us their bad conscience. Overuse of the whip leads to amnesia. Herr T brought me my border pass and a grubby stained duvet. Are you ever alright? he asked.

I had visited the site on a previous trip and, walking through the ruins, I found it hard to believe that anyone could have survived such a bombardment.

*

Flagging horse turning slow circles in the water, drowning downstream of the weir, eyes bulging. Events become confusing around this point in time.

The house creaked in the wind — the agency of moving air, wailing through head or body — straight through the skull, filaments pouring from the fingers like white lightning.

The old dwelling was quiet now, no sound audible. It is a quarter to three. . . . Most of our numbers correspond to other people's names. The year is AD 1305. The policeman did not blink, ran on in the direction pursued and they slew him in the cloisters.

An early autumn sun beams through crumbling arches — two sacred black stones are set into the cathedral's south-west corner, staring each other down. I sidestepped the etched and worn grave slabs. I felt worthless.

It is requested that persons will not deface the walls by cutting or writing thereon.

By order of the DEAN and CHAPTER

Yes, I found paired in a herb garden two standing stones, facing one another, as if lovers or mortal enemies. Multicoloured fossils were embedded, hewn from the earth's oldest quarry. It was dusk, an electrifying spoor led my path — I touched the smooth surface, which compressed into a single form all the colours yet witnessed and even colours unknown. Such a vision would amount to the annihilation of all points of reference.

I am waiting for my contact, am quite resolved, you should understand that by now. But note, at the circumference is an iridescence of themes.

*

She grazed the petals as if they might burn her fingers. It is licence-to-kill day.

Angling into the black silt, I hooked a fine piece of nothingness. At the dock, you sat beside me. It is known that my greatest skill was espionage.

Must write back. I could see a trace of colour stealing back into her face. Change just one thing, change the drag of the undertow.

More than one half of this account I now suspect to be sheer fabrication, a reliquary of errors. We are in transition from a system of justice based on magico-religious speech to a system based on suspended animation, the temporary cessation of vital functions without death, as in the dormant seed or hibernating animal. As a matter of fact, the law's opposition to despotism always arrives too late.

Resume at mutability

'Most divertissant life were at that time, also divertisant, indeed.'
Who speaks?
But now she must rest: in the morning is the trial that will determine her future. One of the make-up artists fell off the cliff and perished.

Overnight, livestock had been slaughtered and skinned, their hides and feathers missing. The survivors had been hocked, ligaments severed, the great tendon at the hind leg.

I never worry about what might happen, only what needs to be done.

The oldest objects recorded on earth are the grains of stardust inside a meteorite. Then a man put a gun to the dreamer's head and shot him as he dreamed.

I often would. I could not stop.

*

There follow some remarks on your disequilibrium. A groundbreaking insecticide for the destruction of sap-feeding pests has been found to have human applications in the sphere of social control. The equipment has arrived, along with its viewing piece.

Here is the entrance, here is the view. One hundred and eighty were arranged upon the floor under harsh fluorescent tubes — flat and shadowless — some face down, some face up, eyelids sewn back. By now the sun had set.

He had no shadow either. I think I have passed you by.

I had not noticed that object on the table, but it seems more or less as it should be.

*

I bought her the gift of a gold backscratcher in the form of a severed hand, which she placed alongside the infant head and bottle of gin in an elegant cabinet of curiosities set against one wall of the morning room.

*

Recall his cerecloth shroud. . . . Across the surface a mist spreads, appearing to consume everything in its path. A coppery redness slowly leaches into the soil.

An archipelago of dust leads a trail straight to the bed: faint parallel grooves trace diagonals across the victim's body, signs of vivisection.

One false move would be fatal. At your approach the pallid reeds, slime. . . . Each object is distinct yet connected, clustering to build nine precise shapes; hair still clings to the blackened bones. Close by is the skull and spine of a bison, vertebrae fused.

I don't think those photographs of stigmata have overmuch helped my defence.

*

These airborne organisms are composed of a transparent membranous dome armed with stinging tentacles around the circumference. The outcome is a panic-stricken flight from the crime scene.

Check for prints, ink the structure, the scaffold. Moon is full, red everywhere, spatter of white fluid across the floorboards. At the next lunar phase they hatch out.

Save yourself some grief, a tyranny of signs et cetera. Seek a place in repose: no men, no land, only ice. Another said do not become a cadaver, lest you be eaten yourself.

One twin was mortal, the other not. They shared deathlessness between themselves, spending half their time below the earth in hell and the other half among the pattern of stars in the sky. The penitentiary consisted of a series of linked compartments moving continuously on an endless belt, to which hooks or weights were attached at intervals.

Herein lies a method of classification of animals, plants and minerals. He knew too much, but what he had missed was the simplest fact: clearly there had been an earthquake of catastrophic severity on the logarithmic scale, i.e. the ground rises and falls in waves (12). Planetary rotation periods and international paper sizes are factors altogether different.

The accused is made of *stuff* — carbon, brittle beyond touch. A chrysalis is forming. We passed that great hill, one-time redoubt — atom in the eye, the indestructible: that eye was made of blocks, tiny cubes. They are machined. Then the tannoy announced that eroticism springs from the alternation of horror and fascination.

All of these ideas were encrypted, hidden on just one or two pages of the notebook she carried everywhere. The author feels compelled to promote the idea of contagious psychic ability rather than the uniqueness of identity.

Grey moth pinned out to dry in the sun. Subspecies Curtis has the median band uninterrupted, or only narrowly interrupted. See, I spring from the ricochet of affirmation and denial — the smoking dark border is usually infested.

We made up only half the army's number but provided its strongest units. I never read for sense.

*

Confused and dazzled, it lived only five hours. You have to learn. The train is shunted to a nearby track where the rail splits. Our view is obstructed. From the surrounding darkness there is a persistent knocking on the window of our carriage.

Note the electrodes and triggers, canister of petrol on the table, another Friday night in. The upper skull plate is tilted such that coloured wires connect — the outcome is a string of fractured air and its partitions. The first set ends with a boom. This episode is lost.

These machined blocks of time accentuate quiddity, the whatness of things. It is worthwhile interrupting just to say: her face looks familiar, *their* faces dissimilar. In this manner I am learning to speak — to communicate, to remember.

Light blue spores cover every page; I had such fire in me that day. And this bulkhead typically houses the rudder. . . . You are destined to shoot yourself, and yours will be the only prints on the gun. Blame it on the season.

The dejections cast a No. I cannot stay a second longer. At least it has been identified — our desideratum — that grief-shot thing, what's left of me and my desire. In the room were a pair of similar things bearing two words of the same derivation, but with different meanings. This confused me no end. The same number on two dice was thrown at that same moment, more street theatre for the dead.

The captured alien's eye was a combination of two simple lenses. Origin is early eighties, from meta, just over an hour ago. Our instincts are based upon the fact that there are many external things that simply cannot be us. Movement leads to further movement.

*

Origin folded into itself. I am also denoting, from double. I am exhaust. Anybody could try on what the other person had that he did not have. It was heartbreaking. Take me.

This all took place in a sealed room with no windows lit by a naked fluorescent tube. One wall of the cell was composed entirely of glass bricks, which were then in vogue. These signs are not to be questioned: we are.

The result is shadows composed of elongate lines and perfect cubes. Balance yourself on their three distinct planes.

We now have nine choices in all, which is named an ennead. See also cant, see also ridiculous or extravagant ceremonial procedures: salt burn.

Dear Comrade

A rigorous trial of operability is being carried through to its logical conclusion as mathematics takes over. Our maker has switched to automatic, having established a seemingly arbitrary starting point.

I must try to remember that my father is dead — as he once remarked, there are plenty of stones here to play with.

Your servant

Why not, I suppose. Triangulation is implied, vectors in an abecedary, where interweaving purpose hints at a lack of purpose. I am composing here a bitmap of indeterminacy, unnameable territory, a collision mentality.

(There was an error when activating your trial, please try again later.)

Perhaps deposition is random, happenstance endorsed by a vague sense of fitness — there is process at play, though it's never explicit. This is where engagement lies, at the interface of a syllabic machine, wherein strict method conjures with figures empty laden.... Her voice was guttural over the phone.

Trust no one. Never trust yourself. (It was like living with a No machine.) It is difficult to resist the notion that the syndicate may have commissioned him to gather intelligence on the whereabouts of the ark of the covenant.

Voices down in the street, departing. I often lose objects when I am outside, and appear to function as a centrifuge for all things.

These people are too close, rustling at intervals through the narrow channel of a cobbled alley.

*

This is exhausting because he has to try and not try at the same moment. I have not witnessed the residue. He should be arriving about now. We are as we find ourselves, a rare electromagnetic anomaly known as psychoplasm.

He wants to do and he does not want to do. He is guilty if he does and he is guilty if he does not. We cannot win — winning is not in the guidebook, winning is not on the statute.

She should come down to earth and enter from the other side. The air bends; our members will not stand for this. The others made something in a hole they had dug in the ground.

There exists a linguistic process by which back-formations develop (viz. edit from editor). They call them pelargoniums now, she whispered in my ear.

Origin is modern from crane. More than seven billion years have passed. If I want to speak, I will open my mouth and speak.

It's alive. It crawls out and squirms across the path. They ate from a sack with their fingers and then went on alone. Alone comes naturally, without supernatural intervention.

Erstwhile

A book of hours, embers, and anything else you still have time to become. Two men meet after a gap of forty-one: you are the changeful fate that out of unknown shapes et cetera. . . . All the boys begin chanting in unison — nearby is the village well, crammed full of corpses and sealed with a millstone. On the horizon stands a funnel-shaped structure that penetrates the earth, brittle for early storage. They really did put us through our paces that day.

Origin is old, probably germinal. She was too powerful for the others to finish off. Although no cognates are known, this may be distantly related to rub away — grist-bite — to grind one's teeth together as a sign of anger, often hyperbolically. Only a few charred ribs remained among a heap of grey, powdery ash. We threw the whole lot in the sea and it looked like smoke carried away on the wind.

A waxed cloth was once used to envelop. I too relish the skeletal lexicon — anatomies of vocabulary — the words who house us, a plague across an archipelago. There is some marvellous signage too at the bone store.

An intricate neurological protection mechanism makes us forget. Our casing is severe, cerement a chrysalis.

Challenge number five

Even Mozart fashioned a number of incendiary androgynous characters. Logothete is one who accounts or calculates, literally, one who sets the word against itself. Here he is again, the accused, this time with pendant intestines.

In that year, the campanile was demolished by insurgents. The sea is an immense memorial — of ash fused, wave upon wave.

I have trained myself not to think about anything, to nurture a purely visceral response to people and their objects. Alone we can achieve what seemed impossible together.

Ostinato signifies an idea repeated time and time again, for example a bull-headed deity. It is as if we have returned from a tour through a theatre of memory, yet nothing has changed, nothing at all.

I was convulsing late last night with a friend along these lines. The outcome, if I read you right, is the impossibility of truly knowing anyone, the equivocal rewards of solitude.

An assassin waited in the semidark.

*

A misericord is a small dagger used to deliver the death stroke to a wounded enemy. One senses that the writer has no real idea of what he is talking about.

Thanks to the stun grenades and an improvised glider in the attic, we made good our escape before the count rose from his coffin come nightfall.

The forensic view is that blunt-force trauma was the primary cause of your demise. I forget the rest. I was not truly present at that time, or any other; I have taken myself off into elsewhere.

Yet several eyewitnesses saw the defendant with the bloody mattock in her hands. Collectively, we are a species of amnesia.

Now there comes a clicking in my ear like a deathwatch beetle. Each day I feel less than suitably human, possessing not a scrap of dignity.

Reload the chamber, snap in another clip. A volley of arrows was shot from a great distance to penetrate the enemy's flank and decimate several ranks of cavalry.

I will turn up again at some point, predictably enough.

Scylla and Charybdis

He wrote the above concertos in strict succession. We are dragging ourselves toward a conclusion; everything else is indecision. As long as you do not touch any object in the room, time should remain a constant.

Her love is a vicious circle, an interpersonal cold war. This hour sees delivery of my catch twenty-two. One hostage is a grotesque aquatic invertebrate that assimilates jellyfish, cactus and an elongated cephalopod mollusc with eight arms and two long tentacles, typically able to change colour.

*

Big sign: the pink said SAINT beneath a concrete bridge. I think we are in danger of a repeat performance, and some unforeseen tactics from the queen's rook.

Go back and review your journey. A sequence of lines bound close together in a spectrum appeared at the date foretold. I only have a vague idea of where objects are positioned in space.

There will be no capitulation to kidnapper demands. We are ready to unfold.

The prisoners are completely isolated from one another and their attorneys. I am not within myself. An infantryman is selected from the muster, buried up to his neck in the sand and fed through a tube. His eyelids are sewn back. The sun also rises.

*

We wanted to make this a typical *criollo* affair, acknowledging the native horse of 1910. He is paranormal, with a reputation for long-distance endurance: schizophrenia glued to a low basal metabolism.

I simply do not have anything original to say. I had forgotten the money I sent myself.

Now is the time for an experiment: can a man in such a condition be sexually aroused? Electrodes are attached and a thorn-pig with venomous defensive spines all over its body is released into the trench.

It was a fair trial — nonetheless, I am declared void and overturned: the null hypothesis wins, random coordinates leach out. No one had thought to set up a control.

Move on. I said there is no control.
[*Tendrils thrashing, rushes headlong.*]
We must amputate. I do not believe that you can have been listening, screams the other.

Here, we aim to identify and take account of only those shared characteristics which originated in the common ancestor of your species during evolution, not those arising by convergence. And there in the distance were a pair of cooling towers. Please, respect the edge.

Now she says what a time, what a time where all comes too little, too late. I saw in this the distinct shadow of the dark and miasmal house in which her life was hidden from the sun. I am playing this on the only surviving copy of a much earlier instrument (viz. distaff sound frontier). The candles that lighted her room were placed in sconces around the wall. An earthwork defends the castle gate, a screen of fire, the weather.

Deep earth seismic trigger initiative

One of the first things I noticed was a lady with a magnifying glass. Forensics has clearly adopted the proportional hazard regression model.

I can remember standing up against a wall, staring straight ahead through the torrential rain, when suddenly I was identified and released from the line-up. The following day it was all over the papers about the antichrist.

Conclusion: a writhe of petrified snakes on a concrete post, the revolution will be telepathized et cetera.

That artefact was mine, it was solid gold. My escort was a man who travelled constantly, had even worked the Siberian.

Attempt now to conjure some remote geology: flint, jasper, hornfels, limestone, basalt, veins of quartz. Picture an object void of function.

Desiderium is an ardent longing, a grieving for a thing once possessed but now lost. The movement of charged particles in the fluid had fallen under the influence of an electromagnetic pulse. The place forgotten appears so very far away.

I had been sedated and slept so deeply that my batman had to violently shake me and poke at my ear drums with the hook of a wire coat hanger. He tells me a messenger is running from the viceroy's house, with plenty more shocks still to come.

Origin is obstinate: larvae bore into dead wood and structural timbers, causing considerable damage.

'Why can you not resist saying whatever is in your head at any given moment?'

We are a self-appointed disease. A shift of one quantum in the ring's magnetic flux produces a sharp change of heart.

'Now,' and this said with grace, 'find your own way back from whence you came.'

*

I am haunted. I haunt. You haunt. He/She/It haunts. We haunt. You (pl.) haunt. They haunt.... This approach suits me perfectly, being inward-looking, what's known as a contemplative. The resurrection is very compact, having only four movements.

A word may be formed from an existing word which looks as though it has been stolen, typically by clandestine removal. (Glad you enjoyed the ossuary fuck.) A waxed cloth for wrapping up a corpse was first noticed in Hamlet.

*

They call me the boy. The boy suddenly screams. He is out at the races as folk say, epilapse. I arrived anterior to word, before interpretation and just after the next seizure.

Who are you talking now? I mark him for one day, before bolting headlong into a more convenient species of vision. Stars rose above the horizon, emerged from the darkening sky across the saddle of distant hills, turning imperceptibly.

She was beside me and we stood still.

*

He withdraws, feeds on bark of silver birch, flings himself into water and fire, wounds himself with knives — yet still there is form in the burr of the voice.

These flowers bear a long, narrow fruit that is said to be shaped like the bill of a crane and its ancestors. On the path to the earthwork we chanced upon a bleached scapula, and further on the carcass of an undisclosed animal.

You will never guess the name the man uttered.

We worked nightlong sessions, alternating shifts. A numbness crept up my feet and hands before turning toward the heart. I had such a thirst. My tongue was throbbing and swollen black — it felt as though my teeth were throbbing too. They had to dissolve my lips and afterwards they were asymmetrical. Origin is pitifully abused in the north-west by the local beakheads.

Still the useless cough, spontaneous combustion — the tuberculars — now the one and now the other. All the internal organs were reduced to ash in the body cavity beneath the ribs.

Unreadiness is all, the bringing into cultivation of wasteland, totality compressed into a single moment. An immense crowd gathered to watch the translation of the saint's body.

The story has a perplexed ending and harbours attitudes to detail. And indeed we talked a great deal about minutiae: detail is so important yet must not be noticed. I am so glad we had that final conversation.

Handel was the master of a paranormal phenomenon which has been named after its discoverer. He caused something to happen. His familiar is a committed hydrocephalic, codename RX12. That other sound is called the great silence.

Hybrids typically have a spherical body with a single opening ringed by tentacles that bear stinging cells. By contrast, our own organism is descended from a renegade ancestor and genetically shares nothing in common with any other faction on the planet.

He was said to be a quiet, enigmatic man. Listen to what poured from his head in a year of pierced music.

Overnight, life had become an inquisitory cell, with interrogations routinely accompanied by waterboarding and other forms of torture. These collisions and conspiracies are nonetheless all part of the same composition. I read through much of that night: foregather, draw inward and soar.... There were several steep ascents before perdition. It's all in the burr of the voice — white salts in one tray, stop in the other.... Snow lay deep on the ground at the forest clearing where the stag came to a sudden halt and shed both its antlers.

Finally we were expelled from the very organization we had founded. There follows a carefully composed sequence of instructions.

i) Obtain the required pitch from the string of a violin by pressing at the appropriate point with a finger.
ii) Used in telegrams to indicate a full stop, e.g. meet you at the teleport stop.
iii) A consonant produced with complete closure of the vocal tract.
iv) The outcome is often powerlessness.
v) A language composed of consonants alone, e.g. *rt*.
vi) The adult makes a tapping sound like a broken watch.
vii) A similar device is used to counteract particularly insensitive magnetometers.
viii) The abortive diameter of a lens.
ix) A device for reducing the effect.
x) A unit of exchange related to death by exposure.

xi) A reduction of one bus stop, equivalent to quartering the accused, usually marked by an omen.
xii) They filled the well with dead heretics.
xiii) He shall recover his wits here, or if not, 'tis no great matter.
xiv) A superconducting ring contains one or more Josephson junctions.

*

Origin is water plus your head. Unquestionably, the creature has changed its position. It first confronted us on our pilgrimage across an ancient causeway of basalt columns.

The sign that creaked back and forth in the storm was a black lion beside the devil's hole. This creature looked like an aubergine with legs trapped in a transparent piston, a kind of mediaeval blender: thy weary ghost I invocate, timely-parted — yet another schism in the local spacetime continuum.

Who stands with him beside the rack, calling him out by a name? We braced against the gale upon a concrete groyne that seemed to pitch beneath the waves. At one end of that exposed platform was a beacon of rust and silvered wood.

Our group had been reluctant to leave the capital, where an outbreak was expected daily, and now had to follow a tortuous route across the front to penetrate enemy lines. Felled trees, bleached and gnarled, marked the route on either side.

An aftermath is suggested by the words change thy position or suffer unto death. Origin is an early adjectival space, plus the forgotten motive that always arrives too late.

Consider, the removal of ice from a glacier is achieved by melting or evaporation, whereas erosion of rock is brought about by wind action. Consider, the loss of surface material from a spacecraft or meteorite is caused by friction with the atmosphere. Here, origin has been taken away — a lost wax process, from away plus be carried, from the verb ferrous. And then again, they once eased themselves so gracious from sea to sea. . . . Regardless, I am now turning you in. Where, where now are we destined to sail?

They dug him up and wrapped his remains in cerecloth. They unearthed the relics. (You stole one.) I was so confused. I remember the first time; I did not care.

Do you find this amusing? Are you convinced that this is an extraterrestrial situation? It doesn't happen, it never happens.

*

Below is the first written music with more than a single line of melody (180a). The suffix *-ing* or *-gate* is expressed by a stroke, thus:
facing
evening
musing
robbing
borrowing
parting
fleeing
paving
printing
counting

A neurological disorder marked by sudden recurrent episodes of sensory disturbance, loss of consciousness and convulsions is associated with abnormal electrical activity in the brain.

Now picture a movement entirely lacking in purpose. I can see paradise by the dashboard light — hallelujah, therefore.

The strand is wide but strewn across the beach are unwanted goods which have been thrown overboard and washed ashore: *disjecta membra*, scattered fragments of torn notebooks, material discarded to lighten the stricken vessel. Further on, the wreckage of a ship and its cargo were found floating on the sea.

Cue diagnostic click: save yourselves. I will keep a vigil tonight, before I lose you to the current.

Dissident faction

We are crossing that viaduct one more time. An arm is thrust through the attic window to lure a flock of gulls with outstretched bread. (I thought of Brueghel, you?) Then we heard a messiah.

I dare not say any more, there comes a vacuum to the head — no weather, scant news. The music tilts on without cease.

Year of your last breath. Observe the protruding part of the foremost section (viz. sailing ship).

Anyone could find out where their ancestors died and what form of transport they used. The hole is principally a geothermal curiosity.

At minus twenty degrees steel cables snap and cartilage in the larynx solidifies, grotesquely distorting the surveyor's voice. That morning I built a secret robot to replace me at work.

Dear Gauleiter
I have hung the lump of uranium you sent above my desk and gaze at it from time to time. I am open at the cerebral cortex, a man perplexed — 'mazed of beams in mine eye'. . . . One must eye and one must not.

Such is the achievement of a man who has launched out into the deep and left behind him transient states and work. We have reiterated this idea in the present chapter, for it is incomprehensible.

And so he grants us access, this psychopomp, in a lucid dream: the capstone, crashing waves under a blood-red supermoon. . . . For God's sake, let him go, cut him loose.

Yours, undyingly for keeps until the cows come home and hell freezes over etc.

*

The jars containing alien fossil samples had been carefully sealed with wax and buried in an abandoned salt mine somewhere in Nazi Germany. My contact slipped me a neatly folded paper containing tiny crystals of various size — sachets of angel-blue, angel-white. The tongue numbs first, next the sinus cavity, eye sockets, finally the scalp.

Held up to the light, the counterfeit dollar bill showed mercury rising. The lips were sometimes sewn together.

Abjection is inevitable, though I do not remember arriving. I was blindfold. We passed that hill, a former redoubt. The keep had near collapsed and was bisected by a rude scaffold; vipers had been cautioned in the ruins.

I was one fifth of a human quintet. The village gossip that winter was dominated by the shire's annual crawl, dedicated to eroding confidence and refining self-harm.

It would be good to meet somewhere. Our index is rusty. There is a condition in which fluid accumulates in the brain, driving the volunteer on and on in a forced march across a frozen landscape.

Ours was an axis spinning in reluctant orbit until run aground on the asteroid belt. The word that does not belong signifies a cell in the tentacles. These contain a venomous coiled thread that can be projected to capture prey or settle an argument. I always said I wanted to change my life, and now this.

*

She stakes a claim. The surface of the creature's giant eye was furnished with bark, thick and sinewed.

I think. I will remember in time. I forswore the map itself.

He seems to have discharged himself from the family architecture. Her name is seeping out of the foundations. Virtual work is still to be done, built upon regret, a species of nostalgia for mud.

He locks himself up inside a case of meat that is about to leave. An espionage show trial is rumoured. The modifier is gene locust.

'Listen to me very carefully: release the hibernation control and closely follow every order I give.'

I am inching my way down to the core, in the hope that I can carry out a successful detonation.

Here are some miscellaneous saids, formerly believed to portend death.
The rain is falling so hard
you may even be able to hear —
I am just doing a bit of disowning she said, before preparing a fresh assault on the crack of doom.

I imagine while recording a forgery that it is possible to forget to breathe. Origin denotes a portable lantern with a screen to protect the flame: shortening of dark obscure — a device for concealing the light, from to hide.

We stoked the locomotive with cinders and animal bone.

V

By espionage I mean spy. I felt at that instant the hunger. Far below me, a kitchen sink port — sluiced to a nullity — a sunken haven, silted riverbank streaked with rust, estuarial.

See, I am dwelling on your suggestion: *sursum corda* et cetera. Gelatinous colonies on damp earth were once derived from the stars.

Now for the improvement of soil in accordance with a demented plan: knucklebones in a game of jacks, arterial filaments, the lost tooth. . . . A peculiar kind of quadrant was formerly used.

Turquoise, olivine, green feldspar (amazonite), jade and malachite are all found in predynastic settings, and attest to an obsession with the colour green. At later periods of history this list lengthened to infinity. The apt collective noun is a happenstance of witches, or an impossibility of hares.

Signs of forgotten experience, mistyped ecstasy: ceaseless counterfeit. I hear your shriek, propose a new metabolism, conjure numerology at the rim of an insular life.

He was a witness to the assault, is himself a subset of fresh kill. Scant meaning is scribbled in the ship's log: a discarded flask, a crater of vitrified sand, an unnoticed error in a musical recital — a complete failure of any kind — a closed sea within the jurisdiction of one state. . . . He has repeatedly declared that he feels uneasy about the new paranormal.

Sure enough, seven mountaineers have just died in a violent snowstorm. An expert in toxicology and the chemistry of fire is screaming out loud. The year is 1349 and time is running out.

A tall figure hovers to the left of the window. He is top-hatted, brushed silk — gaiters and pearl-grey — a well-cut trade surviving well beyond anything that actually exists.

A wind is blowing steadily toward the equator from the north-east in the northern hemisphere or from the south-east in the southern hemisphere, especially at sea. This is all very likely. At the other end a ball-bearing mounted pulley contains the shaft attached to a horizontal revolving disc.

Now I feel myself positioned a little too far to the right. [*Moves chair slightly.*] The biggest challenge facing me today is that the jury are all defrocked hermits, off-duty anchorites.

*

This short passage is subject to ablation through melting or evaporation. Another less popular example is the heat shield of a futuristic spacecraft — an outer covering on the nose cone and leading edges — which protects it from the heat generated during re-entry into Neptune's atmosphere. Everybody has a sense of the numinous.

They lie bound together. Picture a man writing a book about a man who wrote a book about a man who wrote books, i.e. something of a crisis. A viscous brown acid is poured into the couple's eyes and over their faces. Their torturers (the whole family has turned out) and the observer (me) are clad in elegant twenties garb. Father burrows into the man's skull with his bare hands, before introducing a starving reptile that gnaws at the victim's interior. A swarm of carefully chosen insects finishes off the job. Mother meanwhile reproached herself for being the woman she was; her grief intensifies with the realization that she deserves nothing better than contempt or indifference.
    I did not feel lost. Something waits inside of me that exists completely independent of other people and their things.

An adder is a snake. An elder is a tree.
    This cannot be the letter I was expecting: the message is brittle, the hand uncertain. . . . No one is going into the kitchen until I figure out what's happening.
    'It is still a lot of money though.'
    'I must prepare myself,' murmurs our replica apprentice.

*

There is no rain at any time on the mesa. This is an example of a true fact. Inaction within action has the same meaning.
    Notwithstanding, there is much gallows humour hereabouts. But there is no such house number, no such dwelling charged with malignancy. I was once the sought-for thing.
    The cathedral's northwest transept collapsed in an earthquake. The spire was the tallest.

The first two years one might always return a loss. I tell everyone I meet. While pointing at the stairs to the river, I say go down *there*.
    Whisper aloud, pass through the wicket gate, where wooden steps lead from the towpath to a flooded water meadow. An aqueduct spans the swollen current of the river, indifferent cattle stranded in the lee of a stone bridge.
    Jesus he murmurs. Yes I say. . . . You enter the nervous system, floating above one of the remaining areas of undrained fen, a temple of silt.

Cut from the oldest quarry on the planet, two granite figures face one another in the herb garden of a cathedral cloister. The inscription reads thus: for those who sharpen the tooth of the dog — meaning death by assassination, apparently.

Do something — silent, nocturnal eavesdrop. We can no longer avoid contemplating the remedy of a white-hot iron plate under the soles of the volunteer's feet.

I really do not need this right now. The condition is an unexplained idiosyncrasy of the iris, piercing the cataract and penetrating the eye. I speak as one who merely watches, he who never fulfils — I am right now dredging your etymology, have all the volumes in the world at my fingertips, and yet.

The root of the paradox, in this archangel's opinion, is ignorance of the pilgrim's root and substance. A sword made of light appeared to move in the photograph, five tiny discs in a cluster at the hilt.

Father: I am not leaving, I have to explain things to you. . . . I can smell burning. . . . Hello. . . . People could put your life in a book and no one believe you.

Among the articles in his inventory are nose-jewels — amulets protecting the nostrils against the entry of demons — and crescent-shaped ornaments, tiny symbols of the moon god which have been found in profusion under the bed.

*

The virus descended slowly after entering his spine, inviting an absence of breath. It turns the flood, or the ebb, as the case may be.

All airfields with hard-surfaced runways long enough for military aircraft to use — i.e longer than 1,800 metres — are targeted, as are army command outposts, barracks, naval bases, conventional weapon dumps, plus radar and intelligence centres. Crossing the sky in a parabola is the sun itself; the carelessly upturned eyeball would melt. When a grace-stroke is not convenient, a verbal action is expressed by a light dot at the end of time.

'I hereby solemnly renounce, and swear an oath to leave the territory forever.'

Double-check any instance of this actually occurring, and the result.

Few reach me, or I them. They sent us off to be probed, dissected: dead air, cells within cells, expanding to manifest a body whose tissues decompose at the slightest touch. . . .

Back to his epistle.

'The people are divided in opinion as I resume my journey across the peninsula.'

The first lieutenant carefully approached the jackal with an improvised wooden cross. Salute the love that labours without compare et cetera.

*

I get shut down tonight. We have unearthed what looks like a neolithic air-condenser. What is my main worry, tell me.

As humorous as this is to behold, the events that followed struck me as homicidal. They have a history of doing, that is the crux of matter.

He needs to make up his own mind when it is daylight and when it is dark. He is alone in the cell, lying on his stomach against bare boards, retrieving memory. When the siege and artillery bombardment began, the archive was buried in the hills above the city.

There is a pleading expressed through his eyes, pin-pointed in black after completion of the painting. He repeats a single word across an imagined page, gradually building an oblong of fourteen lines containing six words each, a cluster of eighty-four to each lyric.

We have been here before: note the paranormal censorship, the unlicensed use of ESP — and there always remains the possibility that a weapon could be launched by accident. Moreover, as I write, a raid is being prepared in an attempt to split our flank at low tide.

His assassins are extensions of himself.

Only then will I come to terms with my accident, the race to an empty tomb. This is simply how the people around here speak: unwanted cargo thrown overboard from our vessel has washed up on a narrow spit of shingle.

Years after losing her husband (as in lost not dead) his estranged wife tracks him down to the family estate, where she discovers that a failed medical experiment has turned him into an alligator mutant. A lot of research has been done on their embalming techniques.

'They have drawn me into the orbit of sounding board and metal strings, almost. Breathing has become encyclopaedic.'

*

Location, county of. Time: wayward any. This passage advocates a social framework centred on ancestral relationships, an ideology which harks back to extraterrestrial origins, for example.

Thing: letter of apostle (evangelist).

The object is *this* object.

We have ruptured the orthodox interpretation of being: any word steals its meaning from the fictions that guide our understanding. A greenish-blue mineral consisting of hydrated copper silicate occurs as an opaline crust around each eye socket.

*

She is sleep-deprived. Her tormentor is homunculus, manikin — overcast and full of years. He cuts open his sac and another spills out. Together they stride from shore to shore, across the earthwork that marks our frontier. A familiar rhythm beats, the heart (viz. reciprocal influence). There is no living choice.

Chimes on each hour: I use them as seeds from here on, being daily swallowed by men's eyes, this threefold force.

My graphomania is diagnosed (yes, cold warrior, eaten live). The story had been too late for the morning papers. Subtract the fifty assigned to naval agitation and then steal seventy-five per cent of the remaining figure.

A blood vessel has burst behind the eye. He grew a companion to the vulgar streets, every atom of him doomed to incessant revision. Probably by now he is tantamount to death itself, a state brought on, as folk say, by too much rehearsal.

Each of the glittering lines is breaking open like a seed pod.

*

Stray punch. If nothing else, nowhere — if not elsewhere, nothing.

What is in a name?

Is anyone in three seven three?

The conversation very naturally turned to the papers of which I have just been speaking: at the centre of the maze is a plaque that confirms there is a single path to the centre and innumerable dead ends.

Jacob's staff. Astrolabe. Backstaff.

The instrument I used is so named because in taking altitudes at sea the observer turns his back to the sun. Malachite, a green copper mineral, was extensively used as a retinal dye.

There must be something wrong with my bones; the wheels are grinding, soles of the feet numb. Aware of my diminishing authority, he clambers up onto the table, squats, shits on the floor from table height, hurls dung at his nemesis.

These are not reasonable actions, but then, our subject never had much truck with logic — and besides, these are disobliging times.

Never touch your own optic nerve, or anyone else's for that matter, even with a feather. I am entirely void, uninhabitable: that passing tram has more sentient feeling.

Underside example, ferryman

The pages are left blank, yet she hopes one day they will betray a narrative describing our downfall. An irrepressible force of evil still lingers near the stone outhouse.

'Where three roads meet, I saw again that spectral white horse.'

I wrote this for her eyes alone. This last remark brings forth a fresh burst of laughter from the mercenaries around the campfire.

The other retorts

These leaves form part of a vast unreadable corpus. (Do you remember that unscaleable wall of white ice?) Stevedores were scarce on the quay that day, confirming the rumour had spread. One stared at me and turned his back in silence.

What had he written so long ago, at pilgrimage, soaring above the floodplain?

'Spores drift near the elongated limbs of the carcass, the basalt ribs. A waterwheel, once portrayed, corrodes in winter sunlight. . . .'

The stencilled number nine, visible toward the left of the picture plane, lacks a clear contour. A long needle passes all the way through and out the other side of him — my own veins sat too deep, too narrow.

Static substance, accidie. First we had to anoint the aperture.

Catharsis here is equivalent to a forfeit. All of these words may be used only once.

I worshipped being here, for a spell. It's rumoured that two bands of trade winds still circle the earth, blowing from the tropical high-pressure belts to the low-pressure zone at the equator.

A court of law

They exchange inscribed copies of each other: perfect, malignant twins. I think the first rehearsal took place in late October; only one performance attained the region of pure line.

Dust on the steel plate, a gentle layer of poison. . . . These were the only thoughts that brought me a measure of solace. Next came an interrogation, during which I had to stand with my hands and feet nailed to the wall and my head clamped in a metal brace. Projected on the ceiling was a film of someone being alive eaten by an alligator. Projected on the ceiling was a film of the same man in a pit full of writhing cobras. He also suffered a compressed vertebral disc.

It was time to face up to things. He has a sound eye, our apprentice, the untried lad: hand him over.

The cardinal humours are all wrong — there is no such number, no such code. Farewell.

His insignificance is a matter of shape. We are now under siege: imagine the jackal hymn sung in the round.
Here once again we touch upon the story of Ambassador C. A roll of drums is followed by emerging brass.
He swears he cannot remember being questioned last night. (Do you still do your own cage fighting?) In the palm of his hand is a deep wound.
Here lies the reality of the situation. An overabundance of signs is confessed.
We are now within the gates of the compound, where the heart has never found complete peace. I rupture. A system of lenses for collecting light had to be invented.
'Such experience can only be hinted at in pixels and myth.'
'I suppose the season's over for us now, isn't it?'

A failed medical treatment has turned an ordinary man into a reptile mutant (see above). It seems to me that he has been carrying the burden for us all.

*

A haunting, the narrow path in shade — a cantilever bridge that spans an apparent nothing — a floodplain, on the opposite bank an alignment of three pyramids clad in polished limestone, blinding to look upon in the desert sun. But our function is not to remember.
As objects begin to break through the surface, someone speaks.
'Either wing of a part that runs straight across, capitulation at the derelict windmill. . . .'
In the shadow of this gesture, we remained silent.

*

Gare de Lyon, way back — pray love, ascend.
In a cross-shaped church, either of the two segments forming the arms of the cross shape projecting at right angles from the nave should be enough.

Alone in the desert, boulder for a pillow, my physician woke to find the venomous fangs of an asp sunk into his left eye socket. He cried out, wrenched the snake from his flesh and flung it aside.
Before the poison can spread he must surgically extract his own eye. Applying a metal clamp, the lids are forced open and the orb held fast in preparation for the ordeal. He raises a primitive suction device to his face.
She answers.

Evacuation of cities might be feasible in a conventional war, but impossible during the present conflict. A balance of diversity is one characteristic of death, of natural and social ecology.

She answers.

But on the other hand, the blindness of the father as he gropingly feels his son's clothing is well conveyed. Fallout precautions are now applicable.

Thus he splits himself into many parts. They exchanged a vow three times.

The arrival of a murder of crows is signalled by a beam of silver light. These are symptoms of *hapax legomena*.

Who knows.

Who crossed that line, the threshold? Material has been discarded, flung overboard to unballast the vessel. Her flight is burned.

Who knows, who knows.

Spurred on by a sense of lack, yet still I had no wish to find any survivors.

She has been here. Her body too was cast into the sea.

His relationship to physics leaves me perplexed. We abandoned the jackal in the dead of night beneath the stars; it was the time of a new moon. I was never very good with combustion.

Much of this is ruinous cladding: remember, see to it and don't forget et cetera. . . . I have some evidence, but of a very scattered kind. Tonight's password is Thrownness.

I have heard, seen and read various things. I am not going to witness another soul until the vernal equinox.

*

Synaesthesia for all: general considerations, recruiting methods, extinction protocols et cetera. In mediaeval times such mazes were often run or crawled on festive occasions.

I cannot pay the rent but possess a piece of ivory I have carved with my bare hands and carry about with me everywhere (scrimshaw). An elaborate ritual involving palettes for preparation of the colour green and utensils for its application seems never to have existed.

His lead rises. He is scheduled to be harmoniously terminated. This model is intricate, and not altogether clear within the starry dynamic of the firmament. He is the only one who ever speaks in my head: a voice needs to catch the eye.

Bit by bit, I have learned to become invisible. I migrate. I am manifest in your product. I am an isolate myself. I need to work on my five thousand steps.

Everything had to be renamed. The central problem with workaday anarchism is that it alienates the average occultist.

See, a taxonomy of names now considered lost. Other word classes are often found at this altitude, including several words it is impossible to assign to any group. The only surviving map charts the movement of people exiled from the allotment.

We are renowned as astronomers and astrologers. Colours break down — the blue waterlilies are now rare — but this narrative is accurate. I cannot be making a mistake.

Is there anything to be said against doing this? Does the analogy with glass break down at any point?

It is hard to tell from this vantage point. Later that evening I showed him how to twist the nerve fibres back into shape using the tiny pincers at the tip of each claw.

By now, both assailants are on the table attacking the volunteer's face. One of the twins has the wrong idea. One of the twins is striking out at random.

I have shit ideas all the time. Then we all shared a joke about feral goats, names that don't mean anything. We were driving and saw this sign that read danger feral goats, and a little further on we saw a fucking goat climbing a fucking tree. There is something about the word goat, is there not?

The antagonist's husband died four years ago. Together they had once made an immense tapestry depicting a procession of human beings miraculously resurrected from the dead.

We are left with a charming vision of our correspondent beating a luckless mannequin with a rubber cosh. There is no reason whatsoever.

*

A disconcerting atmosphere has arrived. This is all about placement, not grammar. The image is blurred, but it looks like someone garrotting an innocent tourist with a telegraph wire.

Any sequence of shapes will do, typically the mental process of acquiring knowledge and understanding via thought, experience and the senses. In my cell at night I could hear morse from the other side. It is always a long way off, the metaphoric jugular.

We are lacking an ontological foundation. Note the effect of chloral on my skin, thick blotches erupting like septic make-up. Through sacrifice and invocation one hopes that nothing will recur, that all moments will be unalike.

Impromptu (in memory of your fathers)

The settlement forms a perfect circle. We reinforced the four gates with the bones of colossal prehistoric animals.

The neolithic pistol I was handed is made entirely of granite. The details are of no consequence, but I want to make my overall strategy completely clear.

The committee finally had to acknowledge its own impotence. A priest weighed the scribe against a feather in the balance as I scanned the tarot cards fanned out across the green baize. (Any deck, it matters little in the scheme of things.) The two of batons came up: a lack of will means the death of ideas, you will soon emerge victorious from the maze you have been travelling through et cetera.

He looked again at the tiny black notebook filled with cryptic runes and hieroglyphs, which were meaningless to anyone but himself. Given the money available, producer and consumer are as alike in appearance and mannerisms as possible.

The advantage to the reader of this book is that she need not concern herself with remembering what has happened, or why.

How pristine, the etymology of martyr: witness I love thee.

*

He grows nervous in the company of his familiar. [*Moves chair slightly.*] To speak about this we will use words such as Minotaur, darkness, labyrinth.

'Where the book fell open it was revealed to me, and most apposite to the time, that I had gone astray in my vanishing.'

She too then went away. Once you develop the mentality to cold-bloodedly protect what you feel you have earned, that is when things start to go badly wrong. Space is all about history today.

Mister has to drain the foul-smelling pustulant matter from his gangrened leg or he will lose it. Pus is a thick, yellow or green opaque liquid produced in infected tissue, consisting of dead white blood cells and bacteria plus debris and serum. That district of the city was a fucking shapeshifter in itself.

The life and adventures of a typical atom

An iris is an adjustable diaphragm of thin overlapping plates for regulating the size of a central hole, especially for the admission of light to the cranium.

There, he has lost everything. I told you so — someone did.

*

Gallop and frenzy at dizzying speed. We arrive. A tunnel at the disused quarry leads deep inside the mountain (the golf course was a clever decoy, so too the lightning strikes). We found the entrance to an underground passageway and its promise of looted Nazi gold. The views were magnificent, all the views were in flood.

After a long period of estrangement, we are both of us today attending an incineration. This seems an odd decision, given mother's previously stated desire for burial, based on the doctrine that bodily resurrection is doable.

I felt like a second skin. How grotesque we look on this dazzling winter morning.

We are only now able to recollect these events for the first time. One bystander spoke of lost love, a void boy and a concrete boy. My own tongue was a vacuum that day.

As we passed a field of stubble, a parliament of rooks rose up from the scorched earth. Did she change her mind late in life? Thank you and fuck off.

*

This theme has already been hinted at in dream nine, with its satanic pendulum clock. A *perpetuum mobile* conjures a state in which movement is or appears to be unceasing, the motion of a hypothetical machine which, once activated, would run forever unless subject to an external force. Compare this with the mediaeval version of an outer sphere supposed to move around the earth in twenty-four hours, carrying the inner spheres with it.

Pall bearers slid the body into a peat bog. The sacrifice had been garrotted and his stomach crammed with seeds — a circuit board sticks out of a deep wound in his left side. The corpse had been weighted with stones.

We gently dusted the bones free of earth. Nearby, giant bales of hay clad in latex are stacked to burst — white, black, red — a perfect contour that mimics the swell of a nearby earthwork.

Origin denotes bodily fluids, especially the watery part of blood or female ejaculate. That was a forsaken place. Its desolation was broken only by the spikes of purple (or white) flowers, shaped like the finger of a glove brimful with dew, source of the drug digitalis.

Say it is not so.

All he had to do was add the words *I am swept away*, and he would have been spared. He sheltered in a Clerkenwell poorhouse, up to his shins in straw and excrement, weltering in his own blood. He had hoped to achieve a breakthrough before facing the last terrible ordeal.

We heard the breaking news between shifts: he had no interest in the future, no interest in fame. Who would want to be visible in such a world? Money had little use for him.

It is a terrible time to be on the planet if you have no wish to know anything. Totally disengaged, he was visibly obscure, or if you prefer, obscurely visible. He moves as if held in a frame, shutter by shutter.

Against his forehead dangles a three-inch nerve, raw and desirous.

VI

Pulling up the anchor — Emergency track circuit failure
Trespass of ectoplasm on route — Members are displaced
The prologue of Armageddon — Rubber collars
Experiments in telepathy — My first seance
Our departure

Translucent white grains on the table refract oblique winter sunlight. Our frenzied calculations predict an inescapable vacuum. There is nothing to show for all this, to reveal — no antidote or secret place.

We found two granite figures facing one another in the herb garden that bordered the cloister.

A single persistent memory: the need to escape the confluence of forces within which I find myself trapped — eastward to the sea, westward to the ring of smoke.

Thrown with such force, one of the small bones that form the arch of the instep was fractured. Orange burn-off flares strung across at night the built distance, a darkening shell: gulag borealis.

She says these are the strangest constellations she has ever seen from the island.

I looped north and pressed on until I reached a sandbagged threshold. As noted elsewhere, a black cross on a yellow ground — blue plaque an ellipse, the crush of rootstock underfoot. Time is a source of regret.

Someone bearing my name must once have lived here, in a house at this place — not now, not here.

*

The pilgrims found shelter within the stockade as confused objects fell from the sky. We can perhaps make something dramatic of this: parricide, matricide, fratricide, infanticide, sororicide, homicide, regicide, a double deicide. Sixty-one percent of successful male suicides take place while the person is alone in a house, a haunted cabin in the forest or the workplace. Such a felon-of-himself is to be buried at a crossroads.

The defendant denied having a self-loading pistol and a telescopic cosh. He lies exhausted, as one broken on the wheel: mechanized killing is thirsty work.

At successive moments, each of these statements reflects a different chapter of human anatomy. Indeed, in the first part of this book we made use of space-time coordinates which can be interpreted as five-dimensional space — the vacuum which isolates a performer from her audience, the conceptual frontier between any fictional work and its reader.

Once the fabric starts to crumble, there is no going back. The earth's precession is today an imperceptible quiver in the orbit of the globe, but this is predicted to accelerate rapidly and without warning.

If any detail does not look quite right, sapper to report (military pidgin). Origin is wild or masterless cattle.

We are embedded now. What drives him onward, what force goads him?

Panic terminus

Now we are at the very edge of the photograph. The man to the left of the picture plane holds an electric cattle prod. Rinderpest or plague are forecast.

Lodestar bright above a dormant peninsula, that needless motif, all sense of self now redundant. A desert reveals, if nothing.

There is too much weather in this script. In brief, he is not truly here in a sentient body.

He spilt the whole contents of his sack out the window. He shrugs — all have their animal familiars and confederates. Perhaps he is testing our mettle. Perhaps he is vexed.

I possess a tough core of irrepressible rhetoric. It hails from elsewhere, the representamen, an object exhibited to the mind.

Since none of these categories can be detached from those above or below, I have composed a list of all the objects that could be *supposed* to exist.

What is.

*

I refuse. List here synonyms for collect, foregather and so on.

He vibrates, dissolute and absurd, and all the stars withdraw their sheen.

And then she says: against the underside of clouds — ermine and skullcap, lightning — a sanctum where four roads meet.

A wake had taken over the inn, the giant airborne reptile. Rainwater rippled against our ankles on the ascent; at the summit the ruins were shut. We barely made it back to the shelter of an outhouse where, panic-stricken, we barricaded the door.

The ironmonger sold minutiae, everything in piercing detail. I fabricate as I crawl, bordering on lost time.

He stands facing east, casts no shadow. [*Two seconds.*] Come night, a collision of tumulus cloud stacked high above a ruinous pier.

Birds were a mediaeval obsession. There are some important crossings hereabout; dig yourself in.

He is not the sort of sound that is heard by ears, space swinging open again and again, a logic gate banging in the wind.

Now that's a real coincidence: secondtime.... What a show of strength that would be at the very climax of a war. Her final form he sketched in hare's blood and ink on brown wrapping paper.

She slept. She woke. She spoke but he could not understand. Two days later mother died; together we made the long journey to witness her corpse. About the walls hung burnished masks, blue devils thrashing archangels, the branch of an acacia, a prodigious portrait head, spatterings of hot wax, a chimera or basilisk, papier mâché cocks, dentiform battlements, semé of crosses of lilies, a goatfish (ibex).

Comes the memory of a feral she-goat bleating at the rim of a moat, scattered pine needles — the spine of a stingray piercing the tongue, sinew cruelly severed. Just northeast of your mouth is the chosen rendezvous.

*

The ice-age paintings are prehistoric, thus they contradict your birth chart. That looks like alpine snow beginning to fall as we write (crocus). And many books written in discourse will enervate the language, invisible atoms leaking through the pores.

This reminds me of that time in Zurich, head in a box of bones at her feet.... He had always disliked flowers, gently distilled flowers, hence there are none. Nevertheless, spleen and liver normal. He is sure to happen.

Lockdown for a book burning

Must finish my report, culled from a comprehensive collection of letters, diaries and archival notes spanning an inconceivable period of time. I have now adorned my study with plaster casts of classical statues. (I often think of the unimagined living at the bottom of the earth.) Men in uniform were pressed together in the railway carriage, chewing deadpan on their way to the front.

Resist the temptation to act in harmony with yourself. Origin is dread, compared with to turn, an act of turning.

I was reading his biography when a firecracker went off in my ear. That château was without limit: throughout his long life the marquis had restlessly added stone upon stone.

A disturbing announcement is expected at our next meeting: I am turning into him. He was stranded on the island from November 1741 to August of the following year. These facts are dispiriting.

I am to be carried off myself come January, the fifteenth. (What tense are we?) The crew will position me carefully beneath the frozen earth.... I too have a choice: on my back to face the stars or standing for the worm.

The survivors are alarmed at either prospect. What if the place of decease proves too far distant, godforsaken?

Someone has pinned back his surviving ear with a nail, tongue firmly in rectum.
Our emblem was painted on the mainsail, the heraldic arms of the nineteenth precinct. From the crow's nest, a small teardrop-shaped flatfish of temperate seas was observed. A series of horny rings on the tail produce a characteristic rattling sound when vibrated, as a warning.

*

No more of your withdrawal. The day will be a frozen day, a fleet day without words. The lead pellet shot up to here [*indicating*] before veering diagonal. I am preparing to die; this prospect is complex and at the same time simple. We shall witness the falling snow awhile and think we lived once more. . . . There was a mass grave, gunshots. Those cries we had been hearing, it was the soldiers yelling orders to one another in the dark.

I will stretch out my branches like a blasted tree, gnarled at a cliff edge — say, oleander or flame, the lung rhizome. One of the two swollen torsos contained holy water. Flowers morphed into fireflies hovering above the burnt stubble, set into which were the remains of a shattered mosaic.
Compare with monopteros, a circle of columns supporting a roof. Origin is one-winged. And I sometimes feel, and yet have not the love. . . . Come beating wings, come.
The sense of contrast was not disturbed in the text until the appearance of a pale flag — respite and nepenthe for thy memories of fading light, of forgetfulness, misplaced by your wordless tongue.
The witness claimed a murmuring voice and footsteps could be heard in the next room. In the general run of things, meaning is untethered, not held in place.

Every day is turnkey day. Yet I recall him once saying, I am on my way to love.
So much for that, undergaoler. It was the way he said the word, its letters jumping from one point to the next, as if sovereign.
Other characters followed a trail of numbered bank notes. The newspapers were right.
The second movement is a lament. They are changing the vitrines as we speak.

*

Hallucination again last night, via eye and ear: one skeletal runner with rictus grin, drummerboy attendant — the cry of an animal, grinding of an iron keel — the always crashing car, corpse carted off in a metal shell by jesting paramedics. . . .

Rippling vegetation in her skull — cobalt pulse at the temple — phosphorescent plant life snared in the current of a river.

Question forms

This begins to resemble. [*Where?*] In my room; I was alone. [*Were you awake?*] I was awake every time. When she comes, speaks to me for a minute, I write down every word. Anything might happen — lifelines have been severed, scored into the flesh. I remember her last face. I shall try and get through January, which is a strange one. [*Excuse me?*] Then she goes out through the door, dissolving without a clear transition from daytime to night. Not a single word is to be altered. [*Always through the door?*] The underworld is represented as a star within a circle.

*

There is always something to remind when one forgets. Perhaps I should enlist the help of a few minders in greasy black clothes, worn to a sheen. A bodyguard is a person employed to escort and protect the important person in any given scenario.

We found ourselves in the original May, the month so named, before an impossible tide of the exact same mud: long shadows cut across the hills and cheated space. Sandbags had been stacked at the threshold — the ascent was murderous.

Can you not keep up, can you not make it a year sooner? Take rest and see what happens next.

From now on, read *but* for *because*.

She urges silence as he approaches climax, ventriloquizing the neighbours with their flock of raptors: night shroud a cerement et cetera. People have killed for less.

The missed target, errors in print

Such events might well occur after an atomic siege, but the last two lines bring us back to sixteenth-century Europe. Divination was by used book.

I was disgusted forever with the act of mouthing, the verb to mouth.

Use a stem sign to denote the first consonant of any inherited words. Sponsor an unruly eyeball.

At another feast two hundred people were swallowed; they had changed their entire names. No one else understands, no one else really matters.

He was born in a distant land under a bridge, then they moved — his parents moved away, both away. On separate days of the year they died, in separate years.

I waited. I was biding my time. Every moment without you feels unrehearsed, makeshift. We are never again going to breathe in the accepted fashion, are we?

This is precision engineering, a complex angling question.

*

Excitation of the neural current, vagus nerve. I forgot my name, my address, my civic identity.

It is his own body that the other experiences as tormentor, that closed circuit of venomous hypocrisy.

He was almost alive. Apparently the wind got hold of a metal roof and flung it down onto the track. He then told me he had an insect living inside his brain.

No one knows you like your own name. This is an abstraction which occurs frequently in mathematics, where I am an illegitimate construct.

I know your voice, I would recognize it anywhere. . . . No one can sleep for the searchlight beam (subfusc from birth et cetera). Origin is the thirty-six, modern plural from escape. It was 1860. A parasitic bacterium like a virus requires the biochemical mechanism of a host cell in order to reproduce. Origin is mediaeval knot, an oversight of memory.

The watchtower, as mentioned in the story, is in reality a pile of stones marking disputed terrain. The primeval world was not destroyed because of atrophy, but due to its absence. A tongue, on the other hand, is lean meat salted and dried and cut into strips.

*

That sound of yours is barren: we share the same zodiac. The crescent shape in our dream resembled a sabre. His cock was split open from end to end like a peeled papaya, unquote.

We have salvage. A representation is a thing serving to represent something else.

Which time suits you? I could find no survivors on the surface of the burning sea. Malediction comes from some unresolved place in between.

He is the disputed author of numerous farces, a performer of boundless nervous tensility, whereas I — who for the most part have lived a dependent creature — harbour an infinite yearning for autonomy at every instant. Here, there is no chance of a breakout, no rupture of deliverance.

Beware of the premises: origin is a dismembered limb.

Fuck, the hydra, a water feature, which should be the most electrifying part. By now she will have undergone her final transformation into a crab — then again, she may have turned herself into a hind, a wild nightmare or a cloud.

Who among us, like his creator, is left very much alone: iterability of insatiable need et cetera, semaphoric newsboys?

Retreat from this position. Your first oversight will be the desecration of memory.

Now she contrives to win back the head. It amuses her to perform as a professional apothecary in this way, to deal in the elements: carbon, copper, white titanium. . . . She was torn. I wasn't having any of that.

The two of coins turned up and everyone in the room froze. Origin is feminine takeaway, the surgical removal of all bodily tissue.

Her sign is notorious for hoarding; even wreckage has sentimental value. Her omen is the new yardstick. By contrast, the role of the hero is to burst in at a given signal with horns grafted onto his head.

In my view, the body of a radiate animal is essentially a sphere, with the mouth found at one of the poles, a sphincter at the other. Here, the themes of victimization and demonic agency in the face of drug addiction, poverty and neglect are carefully dissected.

The steps were just outside in the ice and she went flying.

Journal

Continuing to retreat, slowly making my way across the glacier to asylum in the east.

He enjoys the fasting, his adeptness at it, and clearly wants no interruptions. Saint the first once drew a hundred horse down from out of a cloud. But this uncanny and alien presence that banishes us from everything in which we are at home is no particular event that can be named. I will stop screaming for a moment and listen with hand cupped to ear, see if anyone answers.

Note how, when he tells an extraordinary story, he immediately adds a skeptical commentary, but his reservations do not prevent him from unconsciously disclosing all the details.

*

More than twenty perished during the nightclub sinking, now members of our table refuse to wear the yellow. I've had it with symmetry.

What do you mean by alleged fiend, workaday schism? Origin is a four-sided spinning top with a letter on each side as a gamble — the aleatory imperative.

If I had to return to the bridge at that very moment, I would have punched my fist into the radar screen. By bridge I mean the elevated, enclosed platform on a ship from which the captain and officers orchestrate atrocities.

What do we say when we murmur guilt? I may be going in the wrong direction, but that would accord with this particular moment in time. And so another task remains undone, and once again I am left out in a thunderstorm like some renegade contender.

When I say particular, I mean the level of particularity of the average novel. The maritime lexicon is often disorderly.

Today we are concentrating on the music he did *not* have to write. As far as I can see, there is no record of what the special occasion might have been, that ominous gala.

Close your eyes tight for a minute and picture a courtroom, elegantly panelled in walnut. We absconded: the only way to salvage memory was to excavate a crude tunnel.

A single drop of water falls from a cloudless sky and lights upon my arm. But we also need to understand how we make this model of preparedness future-proof.

Lifeworks, wax

In the dock stands a wayfarer. I dreamt of home. We feel he went on rather too long and overembellished his account of that fateful night. Now I must take care in the presence of every word: one can't spend a season in hell without crying out for instant nostalgia. I was once able to magnetize effortlessly a sequence of unconnected memories, however now.

These events are taking place in the distant, *instinctual* past. I have erased a great deal of the objects on my list.

Shall I tell you what he wrote about the cist, an ancient burial chamber made from stone or a hollow tree? (I mentioned you.) He said you are not relevant, he said you were of no significance, a mere cipher — you exist at the periphery, just another remnant of our shadow.

We need not be overly compliant. I am emerging as the ghost of a forgotten companion, another exercise in pointlessness.

The above he uttered in a confidential mode of speech. Some of the contenders want to sell, some of the contenders do not want to sell (viz. Eastbourne Suzuki). Upon withdrawal, semen began to ooze from between her lips. We expect more spleen in our illuminati, wrote another.

And yes, she is here in the audience tonight. I have long since grown used to being dead, murmurs a passerby. He just came forth, unsummoned.

Cataclysm — tonguefish, yes

These events took place during the last thirteen hundred years. Four other attempts failed. (Concerning what or whom?) It is said there are everywhere consoling organisms arising from impoverished circumstance. Regardless, the judge declared the suspects to be the most repugnant family in the known world throughout all of history.

I keep reading of complex events which entail obscure technical detail in respect of pecuniary matters. The supervision, the third movement, is titled elegy. There is a closing date, withheld.

At that moment in time everything appeared futile. At the time of writing everything appears futile. He promised he would consign me to the lowest circle, given the nature of my existence. He said I was uniquely everyday, before quizzing me about the lodestone incident.

At that point the music takes up what has been called a possessed waltz until, like a novelist at the end of a novel, the composer swings back to the weighty indifference of the opening chords.

There were three hundred electronic deathtraps in that building. (Now divide this by the number of fatalities in the latest outburst.) Iterability refers to the deconstruction of a sign, the capacity to be unrepeatable in different contexts.

Watch their mentality. They do not know. I could never explain.

For sure, a series of things are always dependent on one another: internal memoranda, pillars of flint and steel bursting through the clouds, monumental cones of salt in the distance. . . . And at the horizon there was seen a dead man walking.

An undergaoler is a dungeon overseer. Many would be exposed to hundreds of radiation absorbed doses (aka rads) or failing that, Joseph Merrick, the Elephant Man.

So, under or over?

Ex people

I think I am beginning to read you more closely, with a little more acumen. The problem set involved an oval shape resulting when a cone is cut by the oblique plane which intersects your moon base. The swarming of flies was not the only sign: ash from the kiln was flung into the air where it drifted like pollen. Now stand, bareheaded, with due inattention.

We are sewing back his eyelids, in reverence to the noonday sun. Merchandise will be abandoned, gifts to nothing.

The carrier resin hardens. We spent the rest of that evening in silence, surrounded by an opaque darkness that one could touch.

Nobody would have found that message had the tree not fallen to reveal a far older tree trapped inside it. I believe you are none the wiser for knowing this vicious piece of information. (It is going to make everyone think of a Trojan fucking horse.) A vitrine is now a glass display case.

The sun was shining on the hill a short time ago, a blood-red supermoon in syzygy. Nearby stood the unreliable eyewitness.

A bank of vapour descends, flowing swiftly and clinging to the surface of the land as we journey through on horseback. And I believe that is the black and white plumage of a stork, so named because of its rigid stance, whereas a herm is a square stone pillar with a carved head on top used as a boundary marker.

Make a note of any correlations; for example, both are sometimes visible to the naked eye just after sunset.

Origin is probably a heap of shingle.

There is no atmosphere and the planet has no satellites. From early morning I too became a target, the location of our ammunition stockpile betrayed. The cards that have not been dealt are left on the table to be drawn, but this is certainly my body.

To conclude, some final remarks on writers and a welcome shriek from one corner of the room. More and more this discourse begins to resemble an inquisitory. (Did you et cetera?) Our resolution accords with the tone of genesis, which is known.

The promised rain

This turns out to be a bitter mistranslation. Origin is late — compare without, beyond plus soaring.

It cannot be — a disappointed bridge:

Latest image enclosed
wilfully unfocussed,
with internal error.
Because our mutability —
I mean the rib along the intersection.

Consider your own porous borders. The next who came through the portal was an unrecognizable life form.

Our situation has become precariously balanced: no one knows how to act in this dying quarter of the game. Then, leaning forward, he says spirit is being resolved to the essence of being.

Ecstasy, i.e. stationed well outside of oneself

Now we are plunging straight down the volunteer's throat. An unidentified mass crams the oesophagus thorax, a spare man in the voice box. The tongue rises up but cannot escape: a floating watchtower, a pile of stones adrift on still water. Origin is non-negotiable.

Form

Young Pretender — Alchemotherapy — Yankee Trip
Alphabet Dolmen — Atum Hawkhead — Whereareyounow
Avatar — Cunty Lad — Balkan Substitute — Thoth II
Dead Nephtys — Synaesthete — Brave Calling — Legacy Supreme
Them Stone Trees — Certainty's Egg — Stein Laager
Chaucer's Retraction — Some Judge — Classic Narrative
Simulacrum — Confederate Crossing — Shibboleth
Crowley's Choice — Sansculotte — Granite Temple
Dante's Duck — Salt Hood — Dark Set — Cellini's Ass
Royal Deluge — Dee Day Afternoon — Rivet Head
Desert Alchemy — Reverse Pace — Dead Dad — Disco Bolus
Refugal — Atom Ra — Disqualified — Expresso Bongo
Quid Pro Quo — Finger Visual — Quetzalcoatl
Geb's Earthquake — Rara Avis — Eternity First — General Duress
Popocatépetl — Ghost Trio — Globus Hystericus — Nagual's Time
Gobatrix — No Alternative — Hanes Blodeuwedd — Norton's Pledge
He's Driving Not Me — Plumed Serpent — Criminal Bard
Navigatrix — Nile Earth — Heimweh — Mr Ellipsis — Ice Is
Pyroclast — Inglis Drover — Monolith — Jackal-head Day
My Nemesis — Moist Tefnut — Janiform Boy — Mastabatomb
Human In The Middle — Lord Dives — Deaf In Half An Hour
Kaaba Penis — King Clayfoot — Mini Krakatoa — Kurgan
Ruffian Under The Car — Last Destiny — Angelic Lifer

It was a fitting end to the eighteenth century. We here meditate on the possible repercussions, and hope that if visitors are not numerous, they may at least be members of the elect.

He was clearly familiar with the more radical techniques, including distillation and sublimation. Nevertheless, this extra dimension is moving further and further away from him. Fascism never sleeps.

He rotates. He is now far distant along our axis. [*Laughter.*] When you survey the landscape through *this* lens it is flawless, but when you look at it through the other, the landscape becomes warped, out of kilter.

A master shot is a single uninterrupted scene taken from long range and able to encompass a complete lifespan. Could we ever remember how once we were?

The world turned an icy red. Everyone woke up with the same ruined eyes: I shall never again see the colour yellow, you will never again see the colour blue. We had been named and called forth, nomenclatured.

*

I picked up a replica at the airport. We need to keep moving. I couldn't think as slowly as you if I tried.

Ophiuchus, the serpent bearer or holder, is said to represent a man in the coils of a snake. Note how, owing to precession, each sign of the zodiac now corresponds to the constellation that bears the name of the *preceding* sign, i.e. you are carrying the destiny of the person standing behind you in the queue.

There is no reason, when I look at orange, why there should be any drastic changes (see early bath). But nothing can be proved by experiment alone: hold this bell she said, wait while I climb the stairs to the garret.

Now we are assimilated; I heard rumour. In the meantime you could try a last-ditch transplant: the wing of devil ray. No one said this was going to be painless.

*

The island's conical peak rises at the centre of a cloud of volcanic ash and is surrounded by lava. Beneath our prow a green wave froze. Since that time, we have been held fast at its glacial crest.

Origin is mistimed subfusc, from sub plus a somewhat purple-brown colour. And I have another term for lodestar, particularly with regard to intention, purpose. End on a list, always end on a list, if you can.

Canker of the lachrymal gland is a very rare condition indeed. All three networks, intimidated by the public outcry, have begun to crawfish.

At one end soars the sheer face of a cliff. Granite is suspected.

*

That same year, execution with the sword was replaced in the legal code by the use of a 3.4-kilogram axe.

'You sound as though you are in a casino, a roulette ball. . . .'

He stands alone in the issueless.

The war seemed unending and was the backdrop to my adolescence. Two interrogators screamed into both ears at once through megaphones.

We are standing in the back of a battered truck. I am strapped in. A form of punishment in which the victim is secured to a rope and made to fall from a height almost to the ground, before being stopped with an abrupt jerk, has been given the syndicate's seal of approval. There are many pitfalls in all this, the thirty-six techniques of inquisition.

I should imagine so, yes or no.

He is deafened, blood flows from both ears. Witness the primeval black river and the even older claret crest of a falcon's head erased — a gauntlet sinister, wings conjoined in lure — the hawk's leg belled and jessed, a serpent nowed.

These are the most fragile details to include in a case history. We see much the same tendency in our western cloisters, for example the lost fountain pen in the plague pit.

I was forbidden to dissect and subject the diseased tissues to microscopic analysis, yet went ahead regardless. This is a simple enough twist: no neurotic harbours thoughts of suicide which he has not turned back upon himself from murderous impulses.

She signed the manuscript herself, but most likely her hand was forced — this was plainly an act of revenge. I should have matured into a fully qualified hare by now.

*

I have seen heavy objects swimming in the air like so much ash, untouched by human hand, obeying the commands of some unseen operator.

There was nothing we could do. But he is still attached to skin and bone, to his memories and intentions.

This I set down after a long day at the chalkface, amid quarks and dissolving boundaries, logic gates banging in a cyclone. Now a pale sun is struggling to shine as I resume your battle against exhaustion and mental instability.

A scuffle, then I saw the flash of a blade. Disguised as a prison guard, she has rescued her husband from certain death in the dungeons of a political prison. In glorious confusion I say whatever appears to me first, with shadows numberless, throat of acid.

This event was swiftly followed by a frenzied departure: the cordite around the volunteer's neck, the sack stuffed into his mouth, a membrane of abnormal character.

John the Revelator

He is traced by a point moving in a plane such that the sum of its distances from two other points is constant. These points are named foci. Or, we chanced upon a matchstick man, head severed from the body, his anatomy inscribed in exquisite detail. . . . One who stretches inward, contra one who stretches outward; it could have been any of us. A woman scuttles past clutching a giant plastic clam, sea-blue. You couldn't make it up. I love that chalky aftertaste.

On that night sea crossing I did not feather the oars because the wind was with us. To be brief, among whalemen, the harpooneer is our custodian.

We are addressing here that which refers to the ground and its interpretant, the effect of a proposition or sign on the person who interprets it. Since prehistory I have been represented by a carved stone, yet remain unidentified. Consider our mutability.

He is messenger of the gods, merchants, thieves and oratory. He is portrayed. When he withdrew his breath, withdrew his storms, the people were saved from catastrophe. All this was obvious.

A low murmuring or blowing sound could be heard through the speaking tube when applied to the volunteer's ribcage. We had been wrong all along.

Trust is shrinking. His message arrived long ere he came to deliver us: we were saved in the place of three men slain in the desert.

This cover story could explain a lot of the coming and going at odd hours, as well as those shipments from another dimension. Now we are conducting the survivors to war on horseback, but only to spectate.

'No, by the letter Z,' says the first.

Existence is the length of time for which a person or animal lives or a thing functions.

'Never will we have the strength to endure such intoxicating agony a second time,' says the next.

'In what way?' says the first.

'I mean a fictitious account invented to conceal a person's identity or reasons for doing something.'

'And how much time do you allow for that usually?' says the third.

(This type of rambling dialogue is causing all the delays and postponements.)

'Always through the door, I even seem to hear her come in and go out.'

'There's reason in that,' says the first.

Tumulus cloud, sky burial. The next thing worth mentioning is disambiguation, the removal of uncertainty from a linguistic apparition. In one corner of the room stood a machine, prised open.

The accordion is a living organism, after all.

A casino bandit spills chuntering coin into her readied sac. One distant voice said the evening was crepuscular, I am sure of this.

*

The message on the scrap of paper in the film reads *70 Media Orcanir Order 8200*. This story lacks a convincing villain and proceeds as if writing were a licence to steal.

I knew you would never be ready. (Who or what do I resemble now?) We met on a mountain pass. I finally saw some lights much further up the lake, strung out close to the shoreline.

Go, sit down and dry thy feet. . . . To speak of paternity is no easy metaphor. Nine is the new seven.

The scripts have been deliberately confused. Of course, when one expects to find something one usually does, and that principle applies here. A ban has been placed on offerings boiled in copper vessels.

At the time appointed for astral visitation he destroyed all memory of the future, until the next great cloud spills hoofed animals upon the earth. (Intervention of saint who?) The pagan king kept the child in a desert place.

Walk up into that column of light, he said.

That airport was so vast it took seven hours to walk around it. It made more sense to look up; I shall do that next time. Before our eyes she was transfigured into a vortex of gold luminescence.

You are not permitted on this coach. No one is permitted on this coach. She did not know where to put her legs.

An escape route above the port and clamour, along which we began to climb.

We are tracking the progress of a bunch of escapologists with no time left to frame. I am quite unable to explain the process by which my head has again become detached from my body.

*

Look, the same nose on all three faces. Here, the trade is out of joint: he had built the abattoir on spec, fifty-rouble notes sellotaped to the ceiling and other shenanigans. Book me an executioner for tomorrow at break of day.

He has fled his natural territory, the timeline a long curve in a funereal sky — cortex of the bell tower, white earth spinning below — tongue batteries in collision. . . . A composition of folded grey matter is playing a mutinous role in consciousness.

When all is done, the closer shots are photographed and an edited sequence composed of a variety of different stills is engineered. Origin is only distantly related to home.

The initial stage introduces the hooded crow, *Corvus corone cornix*, followed by a fossilized shark on a mountain top. The sea is heaving.

Leveret, we are told, is a young hare in its first year. But a rad is a dose of ionizing radiation corresponding to the absorption of zero point zero one joule per kilogram of matter.

I have a mental block regarding your plans for a circumvallation of stone, the extended moat. Origin is calling.

A footnote claims that a grimoire is a book of magic spells, invocations. Imagine a language system that resists naming: and one disembodied thought draws the heart into stillness et cetera.

He weighs his options and decides to throw himself into the aforementioned moat. Only through such tactics will he win the *Lebensraum* that we demand.

Another pseudonym was anxious to identify which enemies, and with how many, he would have to engage in combat. He is the very measure of alarm.

Dead centre is the position of a crank when in line with the connecting rod and not exerting torque. A pipe for conveying a person's voice from one room to another had to be invented.

Recalcitrants were secured in a wooden box no more than one metre square, in which they could neither lie nor stand, and were fed through a hole designed for that purpose. This is not your future: we were stuck.

Do not let anyone steal the original, we will never navigate through the earth in your own words.

Walking with me beside the sea one early evening, she says bitter gall rises in my stomach when I read you.

A tough protective capsule encloses the larva of a parasite at the resting stage, a thin-walled hollow cavity. Let us call a thing possessing signification a representamen: when your day has come, your day has come.

*

We need to secure sixty degrees of bridgehead to survive. As soon as the courts were reopened the judiciary at once introduced the tort of temporary sanity — this diverges in concentric circles from a central point, weakening as it approaches the periphery.

We are still not touching on the core problem. (See asylum chapter.) If this had not happened the subject might have recovered his sight instantly, but now his brain is turned to face the reverse direction, the two eyes quite useless that way round. Regardless, as a herald he is well equipped for wayfaring, with his broad-brimmed hat, winged shoes and luminescent rod: a sign or signifier, whether physical or otherwise, *points* to an object.

It was a chain reaction, a re-evaluation. Ignite these pages. I have changed my mind yet again.

Grasp of the universal is achieved solely though representation and hoax. Was I ever sanctioned, an atom in the vortex.

*

He struggles to raise his head and glances around the room before, exhausted, he drops back, face pressed into the pillow. In his mind's eye he ascends the wooden steps to the scaffold. He stops. At a crack of the whip the horses leap away: renaissance of compulsory spectacle et cetera.

She is working her iniquity by night. Only now may she take place.

He is depicted in early narratives as dispensing with divine messengers; he deals directly, without intermediaries. I waited for one long hour. In the early years there were convenient ovens sunk into the frozen tundra.

We tried again to persuade him to concentrate his thoughts on the image of a scrimshaw heart, exquisitely inscribed with an image of calvary.

He comes for me, shroud in half-whispers: someone has been writing, and the ligatures have left deep weals across our flesh at the inner thigh.

How are we doing with the numbers? He bows down, head wound in cerecloth, his tangled face in loose strands — the patriarchal counterpast, eternal guessworker.

It is AD 1564. The horseman on the coin bears a lance, never a sword, hence the name. Origin is obsolete geist, unrelated. The sense objectionable dates from my bedrock.

His flesh is turned to flame, his veins are turned to fire, his eyelashes are bolts of lightning, his eyeballs blazing torches. He is double, the one who is placed outside of himself.

The last sentence may be translated as your mystic treatise has a luminous pink spine, or all the household gods have gone out for the day, get used to it.

You are standing alone at the entrance to a tunnel. An electric current flows back and forth along the vertebral column, galvanizing the shaft of every feather, the spicula of bone — each of the tiny needle-like structures of silica that compose your skeleton. A radial jet of gas suddenly bursts through the corona of the sun and reaches out into space.

One rogue acid virus is causing a variety of diseases in humans and other animals. But note how blood still courses through the mortician's wax.

Lapster, lapwing

'Am I the horse today?'
'Yes.'
A fold of flesh is sometimes found hanging either side of an animal's body; admittedly, we know nothing at all about this phenomenon. The process under scrutiny also generates adipocere, aka grave-wax, the conversion of one's organs into an unstructured mass.

Within this composition the writer has rejected any words that contain a certain letter. Life expectancy is three months, and is determined by a person's position on the colour spectrum.

It was like the interval at Glyndebourne, implicated organisms everywhere — glacial remains, drowned anatomy. Synaesthesia was outlawed.

Note how the subject has developed an inability to interpret sensations, and henceforth to recognize any living person or inanimate thing. A mass of rocks and sediment is carried down and deposited, typically in the ridges that pierce your extremities.

There are plans to send an artificial moon into orbit to illuminate the streets at night. I had guessed that an experience of some diabolical nature must have befallen you — but take heart, no longer being visible has its advantages.

*

Universal precognition has led to an irreversible social unravelling. My inquisitor discovered another body on municipal landfill only yesterday; his failure to move forward with the investigation has left him resolved to cast off his own coil.

My own job depends on the proper use of scale, mnemonic purity: coruscating sheets of rose and blue, rising heat vapour on an airstrip out east, quivering bolts of ultraviolet. . . . Certain objects have been set aside expressly to covet.

The islands as depicted appear to be floating in the mist. That evening, the A-list discussed early methods of forgery involving stolen light. The residue after chemical analysis is literally 'dead head', worthless residue.

I am here composing an inventory of affinities: vein and sinew, artery and nerve. I said I would not, but now I have.

It simply does not *feel* as though that way is south, he says, pointing an index.

Compare with bronze, a yellowish-brown alloy of copper with up to one-third tin. This passage relates to a non-physical realm of existence in which various paranormal phenomena take place, and to which the physical human body acts in counterpoise.

Our ancestors inhabited a world of unconstructed distance, until the sky fell in on their heads. If we compare Kircher's map with a modern geophysical globe that shows the south as up, perspective stretches into afterlife.

Origin is standing apart. Black garb is prominent, no doubt compulsory, in the ten days since the cyclone. Here live vessels, perfectly achieved anatomies.

An operator used in vector analysis has the symbol delta. The rank-and-file are dead set against synthesis, *interflow* — they have escaped the violence of their feudal oppressors, but there is always the promise of resurrection over the bank holiday weekend: corpse, pull yourself together, it's just a man, and so forth.

It is rumoured that the whole sphere of authenticity lies outside technical reproducibility: one evening, when the sun had set, and not only the sun.

*

I cannot remember. Faded portraits glance up from the pages of a discarded schoolbook impressed upon the pavement — also golden-red starfish, the galley slave, an orgy of butterflies or moths.... And who in those days suffered the most cruel martyrdom? Any future event is always possible but cannot be predicted with certainty, hence the total absence of hope: the fact of being so without having to say so.

Outside the wind howled. Reading patterns are changing.

One of our best workers cannot see with her own eyes today. Undeterred, here is a timely sketch of a clearwing, which has narrow transparent pinions and, lacking the clubbed antennae, resorts to caricature. The chosen card indicates the return of a loved one.

I am resolved to begin with etymology, which survives nearby, somewhere very close. I don't read to remember.

Upon reaching the midpoint he comes back to himself. The straight way was lost: the ruptured dam of bad faith, a refusal to confront facts or choices, precursory seismic activity. Some cunt even had a dead crow on a stick.

VII

A perfect standstill

August: she seizes the head and carries it off. There is no evidence of her existence before she settled beside the lake. The other protagonists may have been right all along, that she is counterfeit, imitatrix.

*

He was once of singular conviction — a pristine image coexistent with some unique pulse in the mind — a foot soldier of the galley-proofs, ruthlessly culling and schematizing his material. At the base of his back, on either side of the spine, he wears two cubes of translucent stone. The crew graved the ship at the shoreline and we remained twenty-six days, one for each letter of the alphabet.

Physician: I fear the nostrum you now take may possibly cause you to suffer afresh.

Origin is used, in the sense of our own making, at a neutral hour. If I mistrusted this statement what could I do to undermine it? Set up experiments of my own? What would they prove? Yet taken together, for sure, a walking eclipse.

Nothing here is exaggerated. It rains.

Now, this thing of the bridge, our man poised for combat. . . . Ear the right showing face tilted, braced for a downward strike.

It seems paths are prepared to cross, if need be. The tide appears to ebb when ashes are consigned.

*

Unable to decide from which stack to feed, she starves to death. (I had forgotten to read aloud the instructions.) Just then, way up through the clouds, something like a shoal of silvery-white soluble fish — a masterstroke. For the ascent, the camera had been strapped to a helium balloon.

I can no longer trust any of these remarks on time. Our ancestors show us how to die soon enough, he once wrote.

The cloud creeping slowly down the mountainside caused space to stand still, or at least move very slowly.

His journal states that he is to be executed by 'wearers of gleaming raiment'. Seen in the context of the prisoner's epoch, his last request is not so absurd as it first appears, nor his final words.

Magnificent ashlars are still visible at the temple platform. In one is embedded an unidentified object carved of limestone and bearing an inscription. A sprig of lithosperm stands like a small tree laden with dead fruit. . . . A sprig of lithosperm stood like a small tree laden with dead sea fruit, for the naked seed clung firm where the flowers had been. . . . The species is endemic to zone three, the species is hermaphrodite and pollinated by insects. The roots have been chewed with the gums in order to colour the gums red. The flowers have been chewed with the gums in order to colour the gums yellow. She has not named this memory, she is yet to name anything.

We are dissembling. Please note that an informant may be evasive in one area but not at another, and not necessarily in your own neighbourhood. Geologically speaking, the granular outer stratum of the earth consists of a thin layer of orange rust.

In the outside world, the search for an acceptable name continues. (Not 'afterdeck'.) Somewhere imperceptibly he would hear her, and somehow reluctantly, sun-compelled.

*

It is dusk on the sixth and his personal revolution is about to fail. For miles along the route hang figures suspended from telegraph poles.

See hungry ghost, the log cabin in the forest, the engraved millstone.

Our comrades had orders. Our comrades had orders to keep the guards talking as long as they could: there are exceptionally fine views in the round from this hill fort, in ancient times the usual direction of augury was south-southeast. . . . Heat up the stones: we are ready.

I know nothing about that unapproachable world. However, the observant reader will recognize some typical motifs of initiation: the whirlwind, an ash tree, the hanged man ejaculating, kicking out as the executioner punches him in the mouth again and again with a clenched fist.

It rains, it rains incessant. Only the dead could make anyone feel this good.

Imagine a breakdown. Our shadows were thinner than the bodies who cast them, we upon the flint, blue tracery of branches, gold-flecked snails underfoot. No keepsake shall save thee.

Bolts of semen spatter the flagstones. I entered the cloister in search of two granite monoliths cut from the oldest quarry on the planet, older than bloodline. We had left the shade of a platform overhanging the marsh where a smokestack disgorged.

Faultless horizon, level grey-green sea, a distant mort. More than one vehicle has been found alone in the wilderness, tank dry, blood-smeared cab empty.

'Listen, do not use a sharp instrument,' she insists. 'Never use a sharp instrument.'

From then on I was resolved to bludgeon my way through life.

She peels back the scalp to reveal deep lines scored across the cranium, the letters of an unknown alphabet. This head faces south, the right shoulder points toward the east and the left shoulder to the west. The feet lie beneath the sea, the spine stretches the neural cord.

I was at home writing when I heard the news of his untimely death. When I said I was going to join the search party she said No. Regardless, his corpse was found — a torso cum head minus teeth, eye, ear and tongue.

Only through such ceaseless labours can the exegete find a resolution, a painstakingly constructed mosaic composed of minute details.

Witness now his brutal execution in a quarry. Any remaining object must be surrendered to my mind, obeying the summons of recall: white oleander, the turpentine tree. . . . It was the worst of time, which is also a space. I have forgotten breath.

A brand new undertaking: me, reassembled, neither from the past beneath nor from the past above — the final cut, a full thirty years before the event is due to take place.

*

I should never have relinquished slave status at that lakeside death factory (your money is null et cetera). All I am left with is a stack of old family snapshots in a battered trunk, but around this kernel lies everything I need: a petrified forest, mass noun under the tongue, craw chock full with feathers. . . . I tried everything and the handle just came off.

One protagonist hangs from the ceiling by leather straps, quite inconsolable. Look, now he is frozen to a slab of ice. . . . Never squander these dying traces, only then will your tormentors show any restraint. There will always be a particular song that is found to correspond with any given circumstance.

I feel aligned in your decaying moment. Then again, we were after mourning just the other night, were we not.

We are chasing the setting sun, an ill-starred project: it would suit them well to ambush me in this pursuit. There exists a subtext here about recapturing time at the centre of a dark forest, an immeasurable wound.

All the things woke up oblivious. I went next door to read my own book, but not for long.

She had marked her advance with a white feather. Three red-brown chestnuts have been carefully arranged on the table, alongside.

One mother's dead eye, final glimpse in burnished blue steel. It was her first corpse. The tiny cubes resembled phylacteries, whose significance is lost to a chain of causality that dissolves upon waking.

This reinstates us at a threshold. Exhale frozen breath between each signal. Some impulses I am resisting, others not.

Above the dome of the head the volving blades of a copter, beneath the foot lady's mantle, weed of dry wasteland. You have no option but to continue north — the ruined abbey lies just beyond, but there is no path.

What is your location?

I am under a ladder.

Phantom ship, a pierced stone, and another hid his eyes beneath a giant wing.... I proposed a book of hours. The atmosphere was divine; I could not breathe. By eight o'clock is the accepted time.

Further up the slope and he has reached a point of exhaustion. In art is everything, whereby the highest achievements of utilitarian reason are transfigured into numinous phenomena.

No one is laughing. Origin is will plus nous.

See, he is shapeshifting once more. For him to be at last isolated — identified and cornered — exceptional circumstances are required, such as are only met within the lower decks of our vessel.

And the ship keels to one side, cannot be righted.

*

From the viewpoint of geology and natural history, the island is one of the most forbidding in the polar ocean. The crew gathered up on deck in a shivering knot: the reactor will surely blow.

Our boatswain bears the mark of a bite upon his neck; I warrant his days are over, and all the archived flora and fauna shall vanish with him when he is slid into the sea. Thus do the most sorrowful tales descend gently into memory, our most inconstant territory. A green wave froze beneath the prow.

Always seek advice from a professional. I am easily broken or displaced (mood seemed inappropriate, the patient was often labile et cetera). This is self-defeating dialectic: a most significant event befalling the most insignificant member of the crew. None of this must follow us, as we tip beyond the lip of the earth.

In poorly ventilated conditions, a substance of waxy consistency derived from dead animal tissues is formed. It is the turn of the century. His noblest faculty is deteriorating.

Notes are being made toward a short film based on a single page. The themes include an impossible uniformity of intention, the lineaments of a giant with rictus grin, a sacred place where none can switch allegiance....
Wish upon, wish upon: now awake — memories shift and realign.

'I want the surface to resemble a latticework of glass.'

Consider, if you please, a semiconductor manufacturing company versus an evil character from Zoroastrian mythology. At the centre of time is an evil sorcerer, an opponent known for killing those who are not able to answer his riddles. This story is elaborated at great length in the mediaeval *How I Lost Everything*.

I said the pilot, where?

*

Imitatrix is a most elongate species, the only terrestrial mould in the family. See, I am asking questions aplenty now. I once asked her if she would want pipes and tubes put into her body and then drawn out again. Snapshots were taken of the aorta. A poultice made from fermented algae is applied externally in the treatment of fevers, provoking discharge of spasm. This species is a paradox: it cannot grow among shadows, yet shuns the light and prefers a well-drained head and suitable acids.

The chemical element of atom fifteen is a poison. This combustible was first rumoured in two allegorical tales. Origin is another shape.

The only way forward is to begin repositioning all the objects we have hoarded over the years. The symbol is pi.

I always preferred mist to a dry orbit.

Another strain once had both male and female organs and rolled about the earth between the young planet's peaks and hollows. We are currently updating this episode.

A scarlet dye is obtained from the root: right plant, wrong planet.

I was once sectioned — a mountain sanatorium — day by day my identity eroded until I was left with nothing save myself. I lost my possessions — clothes, books, manuscripts — until all that remained was unrecognizable. I beseeched, I howled and threw things.

Now the sun is setting on the fountains of Rome: a pageant with hautboys, torches, my lost noun of archaic form.

The lithosphere comprises a number of interlocking plates. He took it out of the night sky and wrapped it around the earth.

*

This condition is one in which certain vessels are suffused with blood and begin to swell. Origin is very still, late from trespass, in the sense rose-coloured.

They were not numerous in the heartlands, greater concentrations lay to the north or in the opencast mines. We went in to change the locks and deliver the cordite.

In this province, people carry their ancestors about with them in tiny cubes worn at the base of the spine. Yet the world is full of corrosive forms: two make a pair, lovers oblivious, while others give alternate endings to infinity.

Memory weighed in the balance, he drills into the skull, eases pressure. Cables of nerve fibre form the underpinning.

Trepanned to within an inch, propped in bed she reads from the book a lengthy quote, and laughs out loud. We all laughed.

The fault lies with me, the gnawing scraps of recognition.

Unhead

[Sedated and tied to a chair. Rest of chamber dark.]

'Our party was trapped in a death helix, a wormhole in space. What I voice is extinguished before it can flare up into life: we all slaughter ourselves in different ways, more or less slowly, with more or less kindness.'

Very often this secret tongue is actually an animal language, or originated in animal cries. The guards take it in turns to kick at his ribs. It is seven, the bell to vespers.

[Reads.]

'One of life's details that can never be forgotten — a person who evokes, especially one who calls forth spirits, one who calls troops to arms.'

Origin, perhaps, is a variant of grave-shore, because ships would have run aground. Summon fog in the form of a man — chew glass, spit blood.

*

A compulsion, with reference to the fixed stars (i.e. the constellations, not the sun or planets). Clearly he has access to equipment and books. Is working and living in isolation consuming his mind, a position of fragile neutrality and quiescence?

I overlooked the propane cylinder. Uranus has twenty-seven moons, most of them named.

His flesh bears the track of a scar with purple rim. Maybe we have overlooked a crucial detail.

Somehow this is not so effective as the first spell, whose chief ingredient is adipocere, a greyish waxy substance formed by the decomposition of soft tissue in cadavers subjected to moisture. And he too is on his very last journey; the vessel is a nomad raft.

Origin is bent of dialect, by association with raft in the floating-mass sense, her body in his mouth.

Gloriana! Her pet moniker was Hel.

Short film of a single page. Awake, but unconfirmed — panning, scheming: anecdote of cubist spine. . . . Who attended these occult fictions? (Excise me, unforgive and so forth.) He at once ordered his scriveners and clerks from the room, with instructions to admit no one. A dog was ritually slaughtered on the roof and blood flowed down both sides of the shack.

Every act is commodified. The gathered company, quite desperate by this point, had thrown dice to determine the animal's fate.

*

We find ourselves at the intersection of two vaults, where a rib spans their crossing. And who in his role as sea god had the power of prophecy, but would assume different shapes to avoid answering a question? We are developing a three-fibre bundle that will possess capabilities.

I was carnage. I am barely able to distinguish between the natural glow emitted by your organ tissue and the limitless dark surrounding us. Origin follows the pattern of words such as dorsal.

Finally, he took a knife and split open the ancient runes, whose sap smelt of mould. A glass canopy now stands on top of the mutilated ramparts, the entrance through which is now unidentifiable.

Consider, I beg you, four shadows surrounded by a radiance, the gaseous envelope of long-dead stars. The sun's corona is visible only during a total solar eclipse, when it is seen as an irregularly shaped pearly glow surrounding the darkened disc of the moon.

He had no possessions to speak of, and the story of his escape is a chronicle of madness: traffic in reliquary bone, candelabra of grave-wax, a woman begging alms, her cerement the colour of damp ash — the doomed reactor, the final rain.

[*Cage. Silence.*]

Neural spoils, breakage of skull-plate — in seven days thy fate et cetera. The master of our vessel threatens to destroy a certain city unless a righteous man comes forth and solves his riddle.

[*The dark. Five seconds.*]

*

Last week he lay on his back like a starfish and kept very still. No one spoke; every answer could be judged a fatal error. Cockroach and utilitarian citizen are now indistinguishable.

Forgive me, I cypher.

Dead side of the street, this. I have expelled all your ideas: prepare to enter sleep. We will all be less nervous once the interregnum suddenly collapses.

You had better get used to this, I am not going away.

When I first engaged in this work, I resolved to leave no word or thing unexamined. The narrative is simple enough: illumination of memory from without. My greatest fear is the expected.

Another example: white phosphorus is a yellow waxy solid which ignites spontaneously in air and glows in the dark, while red phosphorus is a less reactive form used to make matches. Origin is overpriced and hallucinating.

Let's accept that they will probably come at night. We have learned to appreciate divinities for their own sake, their immaculate forgetfulness — a book of remnants evoking a sense of place, a walk along a mountain ridge in a rainstorm. . . . How is it, then, that we can posit an object culled from these representations?

*

I would sacrifice this impostor without hesitation if the decision were mine. I know many fans will disagree, but he is case-hardened, after all: consider the episode of the ceiling tiles and leather harness that stretched and tore, unable to support his weight before the earth's pull took over. The man's visage is not so pretty as it was prior to this ordeal by gravity. For all that, he refused to talk under duress.

A substitute is needed, before our story spills out through an aperture and drifts off into the vacuum of interstellar space. The exact form of the trapdoor varies from genus to genus: it can be tongue-shaped, spoon-shaped or spatula-shaped. Its mechanism is vaguely reminiscent of an automated tin opener.

This species is endemic. Origin arrives via amulet, from to guard.

He claims the cobb is now undersea. Satellites pulse in the night sky above the mainsail.

Accept where you are. Consider the question: should we actively seek out these catastrophes, or encounter them in the course of life as unforeseen events? Did we at some time become aware of the tolling of a bell in a distant campanile? The lungs and spleen have a blanched appearance, as if overcooked.

Ever extemporaneous, I have forgotten the question (the correct answer is scar tissue). The flower sought is distinguished from clover by its sickle-shaped pod and short racemes. So what else has been happening all these years? An explosive was improvised from nitroglycerine and petroleum jelly once we had exhausted the stockpile of ammunition. In Norse mythology she is goddess of the dead, sister of the wolf and daughter of Loki.

'No longer anything to be done in that direction.'

'I don't know. Go on as you are.'

The gathering of hair in a crab shape has become fashionable once more. Our ancestors are to be drawn down and marshalled into cycles; the enormity of the impending collision of bloodlines has only this second struck home.

I am consecrating the edible flesh, scraps of mind. The trail peters out. It was the best of times.

We are hooked. I also found a collection of love songs in that garret, but nothing seems of consequence the longer we remain. You are what we were not ready for.

*

A new look. A new range: open fire (exclusion bag compressed). Now cease.

Nicely timed, the nodal point, as it were. Meaning to stop, to hollow out a sense of place unlimited.

Papers flutter down from the shattered windows, and again, his brutal execution at the quarry. Origin is middling from star plus pierce.

Hands and feet are bound
father and son, where waves pound
a white fluid congealing
and trains run the track
linking counterclockwise
so brace yourself, he hath teeth in his ear.
And
Apples, some whole
some halved
painted onto
the sky like
flying wallpaper and
everyone looks up, of course.

Trial and motion. We flew into battle quite fearless. Shoes were thieved in the tale, a message scribbled on brown wrapping paper, until the infinite stretching of a cord.

Our crucial error was a multiform taken as a single organism. But that is not all: he was manifest as a veil of dust.

A soldier is imprisoned in a tower, where his lover speaks to him through a metal grille. In truth, he descends through the eyes and into the heart.

It could be that we are searching for a symmetry that was never there in the first place, murmured my maxillofacial surgeon. I left without viewing the interior.

What offers can we withdraw today? I am certain that my object was once here, right here in this place.

VIII

And of course, the notion of the palimpsest is always seductive, those untimely traces. Here, the outline of a journey is introduced: shafts of sunlight, liquid cells sprayed across the surface to fill in the gaps — once more, a vast stretch of years. (Replace with moths?) Both the celestial equator and the ecliptic pass through a thirteenth sign, but this is not counted among the houses.

An elegant couple on a launch at sea (our sea). Origin is late six, denoting temporary rule between reigns, or during the suspension.

*

She's a carrier. An object falls from the sky, something like a huge hat pin with spherical head. Slowly she is drawn out from the body.

You do not actually need to move your hips, he says: when you touch the iliac belt, the whole sacrum quivers.

We were famously dislocated, time out of joint, nonaligned. Origin is miasma plus would-if-he-had-a-mind-to.

I am developing a feel for this. On one of her index cards she refers to a man for whom violence begins wherever the maintenance of law is at hazard.

*

A poem of retraction, backsong: dead-centre noon — rupture of sinus cavity — the first photograph. I went to register mother's death and then got married.

The jaw clicks, geiger count, the brainpan hums: our orbit around Neptune is decaying. Briefly, we discussed the problem. I need a continuum.

Ice cliffs and sump oil, mass gravedigging sappers — with two assassinations already to her name she is a new creed of underminer. Whatever it was (and I wasn't sure), I wanted the object back.

The technique used was a species of strappado. A sign read nucleic acid is present in all living cells, its principal role being to act as messenger. Please feel at liberty to remove uncertainty of meaning from any ambiguous sentence, phrase or other linguistic unit.

*

Antarctic whaler, father in profile head. The eerie off-planet atmosphere of the polar region is due to the perpetual daylight reflected from numberless ice floes. He carries the found object coiled up in his pocket; it will not go away.

Floored upon the sword-mat, braced for an additional lashing, beaten near death. . . . Years later, in a letter, he described the onset of his illness. He bellows like an ox as he reaches climax.

When you have a moment, try to detect the presence of any odd or unfamiliar words. String these together into a few phrases, thus: above the man's head was suspended a viscous fluid, sustenance. . . . Your inside is out — the trick is to wrest free of the body in one piece.

The narrow end of the clausilium slides into a groove formed by spiral folds on the inside of the skull. A small leather box containing text on vellum must be worn on the forehead in the mornings.

Another minute, sharp-pointed object is typically present in large numbers and resembles a particle of ice. Origin is flint, on the pattern of words such as alumina.

The tiny sequins of her jacket hanging on the door grazed the surface, as if murmuring when she brushed against.

*

He is little altered, this coprophagous god — word torn from its cladding, salt in every wound. Leeches are making a comeback.

He is the last but one, exposed in the light of a final morning, with magnificent clouds, a gentle breeze, the great celestial bruise et cetera. Night fell as a multitude of small droplets spread out along the table.

A medium shot of a figure generally includes the body from the knees or waist up. I have lost connexion.

Origin is replica plus ant, first used in the film. All the saints of this family have a spoon-shaped door which can slide down to close the aperture. Time is no aftermath.

Mass noun: the continental lithosphere has a lower mean density than the oceanic, of course. I paid three ninety-nine for the two. Many victims suffered atrophy of nerve fibres in the eye.

*

The orbital muscles around his lips do their duty as he whistles a random tune. He is just one of the wasted people I work: he is no match. Despite this, it occurs to me that he may be the promised man — bearded then, tanned on the outstretching boom, but not tonight and not tomorrow — rig now to get some sleep, while the sea is calm and steady. . . . The animal spreads the skin of its neck into a hood when disturbed.

Compare with cyme, compare with barb. The other flowers in this cluster develop as the terminal buds of lateral stems. Origin denotes the unopened head, from literal summit, a popular form of vagrant.

On the island, no more than a raft of congealed lava, I found a nest formed of many heads attached to one long stem. My bandage had been folded into a spiral arrangement, resembling.

We are late seven from graphic spike, tongue in relation to spine. The current sense is inflamed by star-house.

Erectile hairs along the animal's back rise when it is angry or alarmed. Thrown into prison for a crime he has not committed, this self-styled Monte Cristo is confined to a fortress atop a beetling cliff. The turnkey mutters a spell as he tosses away the key.

'The sinew has a string-like appearance, clotted with rancid animal grease — also a lobe of the ear, the liver, the brain. . . .'

This requires silence: you lose a certain sharpness waiting for things to become something else, dwelling here in the world, chock full of names. I here refer to the dorsal part of the organism, the cord from which it develops, something reused or altered but still bearing visible traces of an earlier form.

In the month of May there are many ferries on the river. (I am dreaming.) A man with a lute passes a remote farmstead. He thought music would ruin his verse.

Compare with usage at enthuse. Given a new life with no memories, I would still be capable of sabotage.

*

Barely discernible activity at the horizon. I recall yesterday a purple birthmark resembling a map on her passing face. Flesh peels back to reveal shimmering bone in the moonlight.

Current sense dates from your lost century: rootstock, a branch of the cerebellum — a reliquary of signals, glaucous bloom across the eye.

And then you think: cosmology, I have made it in mine own image. Origin is an abbreviation of delta.

Decrease or fade gradually before coming to a close: e.g. the storm had petered out. I was the given name, another term for counterfeit. Either of the two books contain epistles ascribed to the patron saint (crime, madness).

Our parents are here to show us how to die, nothing more, all memory stirring to realign.

This seems like a bit of an infinity pull. We are no longer possessed of a body.

A medium shot is a relatively close shot revealing a moderate amount of detail, such as mass burnings and martyrdom. This has led to an inevitable reduction in price, but note the sense of calm today.

I love and I must, whereas you are destined to a short life of fiction and occasional domestic insurrection.

I have aged these years. The supposed significance of the movements of the sun, moon and planets within the zodiacal band is the basis of my defence. Origin is a die for coining.

Note the directions and placement of vowel signs (see chapter II). Where were you, Coeurdelion, when we needed an antihero?

*

Somehow the darkroom has preserved your original texture and density. I wasted a potential afternoon — we did a pen portrait, I had no skill or anything — but I am getting ahead of myself. I read to forget.

The creature had wings and a head, skull slid down to abdomen.

'I don't see it like that. I feel stripped of all sensation, numb.'

Who was the first to see the risen man? Note the representation of the operator as an inverted capital delta.

The *gh* spelling is by association. (Strike her deaf.)

'This aerial is quite useful, listen.'

In combination, quite labile, yes. In some viruses, RNA rather than DNA carries the genetic mandate. And there are always autobiographical motives, viz. to blood an apprentice in the service of his master.

Then comes a lonely scene on a desolate heath, a murder of crows screeching. But first that memory on the bridge, Trieste.

*

Let unreason govern thy lament et cetera. . . . Is that the way you want to be loved, for eternity, until hell freezes all over the doomsday cow?

(Clatter of child dragging along the seafront a wooden toy on a string.)

Look, an uncertain inflorescence is stalked in acropetal succession on an unbranched stem! Ours is a not dissimilar group, that which embodies a gleaning, a summoning.

A rogue satellite of Neptune has been discovered by the space probe and has a diameter, illuminating the lung, quarrying disease. Let me not become a remnant of my own memories.

Amen.

Horsehead nebula

Across a field strewn with thorns, scattered logic. All these incomplete distractions serve as a torment — distant pulsing lights, compressed sleep — the lengthening shadows of trees that seem to carry our shape. Above all, I no longer trust anyone.

The flat end of the clausilium can close the aperture and thus protect the mucous membrane from predators. Furthermore, the chromosphere is a red gaseous layer immediately *above* the face of the sun (any star), which together with the corona constitutes its outer atmosphere. This phenomenon was set in the heavens as a daily reminder to transgress the law, any law.

My fragile trust in language was always at stake. I have no desire to be reassured. On parting, he said it is the horse's head you should fear.

Rolling skies have so many upgrades on so many levels. Now imagine you are filling in a multitude of tiny squares, one hand tied behind your back. Visions tend to gnaw at the future.

The door was open. I have stuck to my boundaries. But, he interjects, I am trying to write silence, a feeling so singular that once attained the memory of it would haunt you all your life.

*

It all comes down to the number of mercurial characters in a room at any given moment, that lingering sense of disbelief. An iron-age fort had been built on the ridge, high ground enclosed by a system of defensive banks and ditches. Our chief predators are carnivorous larvae.

A rainbow spectrum spread out to cover the entire surface. There then followed an infamous list.

i) I cannot.
ii) Nowhere can he find the key.
iii) Origin is an ear of corn (see spine).
iv) No, origin is a wheel, the coil of a snake.
v) On the island, no more than a raft of congealed lava, I found a cluster attacked by short stalks at an equal distance.
vi) The flowers at the base of the central nerve develop first.
vii) Test the articulation.
viii) Identify the outer layer of tissue immediately below any radical sign.
ix) And he lay there in the night thinking I equal which.
x) A cluster with a central stem bearing a single terminal flower developed first.
xi) However, the modern constellations do not represent equal divisions of the zodiac and the ecliptic now passes through a thirteenth house, which is no longer recognized in bingo.
xii) The fleshy external flap is the brightest star in our constellation.
xiii) Behaviour of: forehead on ground or foreground on head.
xiv) Behaviour of: rushes about.
xv) Behaviour of: sits with back to fire, viz. dorsal part of organism.
xvi) Behaviour of: scraping tongue equals rain (compare with grey-green bloom upon grapes).

xvii)   Behaviour of: vacuum pump in ear equals stranger.
xviii) I was once famous for my autofluorescence.
xix)   The whole structure can be retracted inside the shell.
xx)   Black equals desperate search for a solution.
xxi)   Green equals lucky to possess.
xxii)   Red equals think yourself lucky to occur simultaneously.
xxiii) Blue equals catastrophic meeting.
xxiv)   White equals glad to see the back of you.
xv)   Yellow equals a visit from your nemesis next door.
xvi)   Origin is distilled from phosphorus.

Sometimes, if you are foreshadowed.

Word senses can be disambiguated by examining the context. The diagnosis was clear: bit by bit, we were ingesting our own head. There is no mention of your malign influence.

The hero of the family in the film had little choice but to perform a human sacrifice. But who grants him the ability to solve the sorcerer's riddle? He steps forward to face this task, and with some divine assistance manages to answer all thirty-three questions, after which he asks three of his own. (Twat.) Unable to fathom these, the cunning sorcerer seeks help from the incandescent man — archetype of a destructive spirit — who refuses to reveal the answers. The evil necromancer then admits defeat and is ritually slain.

This story is unlikely to have an origin. There exist many broad parallels, particularly in the wisdom contest between you and your phone described in chapter ten.

*

I once saw this man who was a really strong swimmer in the sea and he got to the concrete breaker and it was a seal. If it had been me, I would have panicked and dropped the ball.

We must be the most labile culture in all history. I sprang from the sense to err, i.e. the sixth closest to our planet in terms of heresy. By this is meant an organ such as a kidney, the cerebellum, or even a hare.

'Yes, we are still on phase one, have all been cast back into the shadows.'

'Mind, I have vowed never to talk with you again.'

*

Peak of the outcrop under mist, a herd of black cattle steep across one flank, bruised thunderhead beyond illuminating green, white. Origin is an unlikely union. We smuggled into the courtroom unexpected stunts and spectacular special effects that wrong-footed a complacent jury.

Picture a sudden halt made by a horse moving at speed. I exist from inter, between rain.

Do you ever stop? No. I will lose my jaw. You will lose your jaw. He will lose his jaw. She will lose her jaw. It will lose its jaw. We will lose our jaw. You (pl.) will lose your jaw. They will lose their jaw.

Now he is drowning at sea. Now he endangers health by sucking out all our breath. (Thank you.) There is concern over those cracks opening up across the ceiling.

He is isolate. Do you not feel? He is the embodiment of courtly love: thy head upon thee with its lobes and furrows is like unto the cardinal quarters of the compass, thy hair like ashes in the grate et cetera. . . . In the concrete, as opposed to the abstract, this parable is interpreted as a journey to a place beyond all time and reason, a welcome stroke of hazard. All this talk pierces the heart.

Seems the old king is held fast at his own galleys, pacing in memory the marble floor, sandbagged in.

Syncope, anyone.

A scene in which the final rescue takes place

I keep seeing in my mind vivid fragments of memories I have never experienced: the years cut short, a sudden fall of pressure to the brain, extremities on fire. But the body is tougher than we can possess; keep one eye out. So forms the imago, the last or perfect state, an abundant nothing.

The presence of a clausilium is the reason for the common name bequeathed. Memories are drawn out from under my skin.

She dreamt night after night that she dived to the bottom of a lake to retrieve a small sphere. Vital documents had been tampered with, passages erased, and what's more the others knew all along.

I never scrutinize beforehand anything to be added to a list. That man in our compartment, he was blind and his wife had a silent miscarriage.

Come home when you need to.

*

Rumour of seance was heard, fingers intertwined across the square table — we being four, stationed each to a side. Ribbons of red and green light across the night sky pulsate and withdraw.

The beginning mirrors the close, is highly off-planet, what with details such as the rubber harness, a vial of battery acid, the electrified razor wire. In the following scene we observe the two combatants stranded on a remote island, each plotting to assassinate the other. That same day, the news broke that an orbiting telescope had photographed the first interstellar ganglion.

I was a terribly limited canvas. The structure of language got broken — a breed of psychosis, an aggravated form of nostalgia. Null is the dummy letter in your cipher, a direction in which background radiation from the big bang can still be detected.

Unsense is a condition of no signal. Origin is lapwing.

As a final gesture, the syndicate offered the victor a lifetime's autonomy and a course in delinquent economics.

On off

Pharos, lighthouse on the northern side of a deep natural harbour. Off now.

I am busy. I am busy killing off one of the nine, stretching my arms across a green baize table.... Silence is taboo (but certain names must never be mentioned). And that sound is the vaticinal rumble of an approaching train.

Keep them coming. Scrape through that tongue. Shell tooth. Thoth.

See, origin has been transferred.

That day, waking to find two suns in the sky, drawn by oxen against the headwind. (He once wrote of the sky as the alembic firmament.) The ceiling is low, I can barely stand, the floor slopes to a drain clogged with excrement: a prison cell, a fireproof cabinet with complex locking mechanism, the empty sea chest in the loft.... I never expected to recover.

A major role in life

Combine quicklime with water to produce calcium hydroxide, slaking the lime within a day or two of purchase. I think we are very ill-starred within the weather. The agonic line is an imaginary line around the earth passing through both the north pole and the magnetic.

Here they come again, this time for an encore: counterfeits and sculpture in lost wax. Are you alright going in on your own? Do you want me to leave? . . . I never before noticed those distant blue hills (viz. Canada's notwithstanding clause). The empirical realities do not match this metaphorical picture.

*

That man, yes, ghost-blind, ancestral.

And who is your favourite dinosaur? Who is your favourite big fish or mammal? Do you like whales? O yes, we do like the killer sharks now, yes.

Then it was concrete for three days, nothing but concrete. He told me the world was concrete, a translucent fossilized resin originating from extinct coniferous trees of the Tertiary period, typically yellowish in colour. Blow your trumpets to the new moon et cetera.

What do you call a dinosaur that is hiding around the corner?

The set stretches up to the ceiling. I am arranged for many voices. If there is a PR issue, semaphore me.

Praise the Lord it will never happen: the floor collapses, a child falls through. It can happen, you never know who or what is going to come through a ceiling. Origin is an ear in the hand.

In a morbid part of his mind this qualifies as surveillance: gouging, probing, scraping. West started by cashing two top diamonds, on which East petered.

Do not worry yourself about this.

*

Some drowned downriver, others were found floating upriver. I am feverhead. I stole everything I could lay my hands on. The telephone never stopped.

Just observe and listen to the results. One minute into your watch a jet of fluid discharged from the tiny orifice, accompanied by tympana and bells.

(How do you know all these things?)

At the front of the stage is a curtain and a proscenium arch evoking the dome of the foreskull or a strongbox — any ark-like shell with transient high voltage.

Dig in, dig deep to find the visionary model. We were all buried in the sand up to the thorax.

Excuse me. It is here. It has arrived. In the film no one could leave town until the tetrahedron was destroyed. . . . Let's get away from all this, it is an unforgiving field — I shall endeavour to keep my narrative diplomatic, but radiant, nonetheless. For example, a chipper is a person or thing that turns something into chips.

Whom has he not afflicted with his ridiculous libel? . . . It is mercifully still and dark outside, and mercifully no sound of chains dragging across the flagstones. I will keep this very useful: that roiling sound, tongue lolling, the drip of a nerve — dying ice, the sound of meltwater flooding the gravel fen. Maybe we had them with us all along, close to our side, without knowing.

How does his hand make that shape?

*

Now I am proudly nothing, the typically null self. It's just a piece of time you will serve, she said on parting.

The streetlamps are lit, bending the horizon: alignment is east-west (or west-east, depending). I am trying to reconstruct a picture of that studio, build in my mind a pietà of my own making.

I wonder what a bone spur is. There is another object here and I do not know how it has been named. Spore cases are strewn across the hillside beneath dense foliage — spent shells, cartridges, a quarrel of headless grouse. One tube leads directly to the tympanum.

Creeping blood rhizome — he will bark like hell when he sees those black pods that have hooked themselves to the tree. This does indeed sound a serious operation: check the soil radiation in the sector where you spent your childhood. The galaxies are still retreating from one another.

What I need is an expression to unwittingly misquote — there's nothing like transmitting false ideas — but this is not the time.

A code of honour demands silence. Not many short novels are capable of accommodating such bewildering antinomies.

*

Godsent imbalance returning, despite a lingering sense of calumny in the aftermath of those court proceedings, which are no doubt fresh in the listener's mind. I am composing, replacing the missing segments, the body of evidence. One single act can change everything: the key event took place between two piers. A face appeared at the door ajar.

The survivors ran out of food and resorted to cannibalism, more crow than human. Then the raft sank. All the witnesses are long dead, and besides, informing equals disgrace.

Isochronous is occurring at the same time.

A line on the map connects points with the same average temperature in winter. It is out of such a bleak mood that the orator speaks. Overalls navy blue, insouciant he enters a bar to conjure a brawl.

'Our innovative multi-colour fluorescence endoscopy unit will help us in the scramble to locate your bygone lung.'

Where did he say? (If wishes were horses, beggars would ride et cetera.) We have arrived at somewhere island, with its fifty million migrating crabs and pyroclastic cloud. And here comes purposiveness without purpose.

*

He made his name, a black comedy set at war. It is reported. She said who does he think he is, the demiurge? (Whoever hears me shall never forget, and so forth.) Then I hit something on the road.

What happened to you? What happened to him? What happened to her? What happened to me? Nothing, nothing, nothing, nothing. What happened?

A paradox could be a contradiction between two beliefs or conclusions that are in themselves reasonable. Origin is late nine, a conflict between laws, from anti plus the given name. But he argues that the best missions are guided by a vision: at any point on this imaginary line a compass needle points true north.
i) Eastward.
ii) Assuage.
iii) Sealing-wax.
iv) His nightmare is completed.
v) Terminal moraine.

This approach is not flawless (coordinates p then q are diphthongs). The thymus gland — or rarely, the pancreas — of an animal may be used for food. And Rosin the Bow has lost her other eye and henceforth can no longer read her notes. But we can always introspect: that was where I once strode around the woods and could see the ruins from a distance of years, decades.

That's odd, he murmurs as the anaesthetic begins its work, at most other lottery-funded plastic surgeries.... How would you characterize the sudden changes in style? And he was spending a hell of a lot of times on trains, was living quite cavalier. I myself am walking the length of the track as we speak — Jupiter looks interesting tonight — and those are container ships, rusting in silence, out on the sleeve.

Well, in terms of the choral work, this signals a move away from the secular to the sacred. Maggots were once used as a curative. I was a schoolboy when I first met Elgar.

The clockworks

You bear semblance to a jewel she says, sapphire or topaz (see above). Then she talks of pointed arches, rib vault and flying buttress, along with stained-glass windows and elaborate tracery — a horrific angular style of handwriting with broad vertical downstrokes — and remember, this is way before the gothic, whether early, decorated or perpendicular. Another played the reed-groan, while others lose the faculty of speech, cease to communicate altogether. There is no airlock granting entry or egress from this chamber, and furthermore I am cutting things out as I go along.

*

Jupiter looks down upon us, overseer for the day. You have mutated. Who stepped into the dead man's shoes at the last moment?

Temporary loss of consciousness was caused by a sudden fall in blood pressure, the omission of sounds or letters from within a word, for example when a library is announced or origin cut off at a mountain pass.

Just as well: keep out of the moonlight, it may turn your head or even blind you. At the bottom of the pothole was found a blue carrier bag, plump with coarse black hair. Our will shall not be broken; at all times remain close at hand, please.

At this point he felt as though the whole world had suddenly fled his senses, for its codes had grown overwhelmingly complex.

It occurs to me that the proprietor may now wish to close up for the night, but at least we have a sense of direction. We were going to make a fresh start, a new beginning.

The moral of this story is never gaze upon the only satellite through a glass, darkly.

We were forged. There are parts of narrative you cannot do without, and some parts you cannot do before other parts — for example, 'this feels like an incurable aspect'. On the front lawn, a mass of rocks and sediment had been carried down and deposited by a glacier during the night.

Origin is slap-bang in the middle.

It was a lovely idea though, being in here with the old selfhood, scratching at the sides of my tank with sharpened fingernails. Non sequiturs tend to multiply (they take some struggle, believe me). Somebody has lost their head.

Consider all this, then examine us both, the sea and the land: strange analogy, strange meeting, turning to face something alien within yourself — a silhouette against the day, by the window where the light is. That evening we sat together and watched the nearest star swallowed again by a distant headland.

Elongated shadows outline the position of the man. No blood reaches here from the upper ground. I know, I know, this all looks way too easy.

Later on we have some music on the subject of dystopia. We are not going anywhere until then, are we?

We are not.

*

A very light rain, named mizzle. Next came a series of nasty shocks.

The virus entered my bones as I hung suspended from the ceiling, tightly bound with rope about the wrists and surviving ankle, another human sacrifice. A metre-deep wall surrounds me, within which is set a monumental wooden gate dating from the era of twelve, intermeshed with iron bars that can never be prised open.

She reacts as if this were a normal occurrence. My prison is reckoned within the keep.

The emperor is with child, rumours the assembled populace. I had purchased that day a large tub of lubricant. Everything is proximal.

*

He is pinned beneath a boulder, the trembling logan stone. Be that as it may, he must consummate the marriage. This is a great inconvenience, for we have not the time to devote research into all these subjects.

The aliens lived in giant tripods, from which vantage they reduced the fleeing humans to ash where they stood. I have never before mentioned this to a living soul.

Orthography arose, perhaps influenced by remote variants. It could be said that the public is becoming weary of such spectacles.

Never much of a midwife, I would have made a better job of the delivery if I'd had a bag of sequins and a kitchen knife about my person. When it comes to dreams, it is not a question of interpretation, it's about joining in.

We made several botched attempts to slay our adversary, before deciding to cram his entire body up the drawing-room chimney and set a fire beneath him. Like a heretic or witch in bygone days, he would no doubt choke on the rising smoke before the flames could sear his flesh — a fact which I have always held to be a small mercy in such circumstances. Even Jung once wanted to be an archaeologist, before changing his mind.

But why him? she asks, again and again.

When do they come for me? I suspect — no, I am convinced — that there is space for something more on one particular subject. There was little space in the steel cages slung beneath the giant tripod, where humans harvested from the surface of the earth were confined before extermination.

Wherefrom do they come for me? . . . A tragic error of flawed science has taken place: when I say paranoiac, I mean a seeker hell-bent on the facts. (My own soul is mortgaged.) The fake humans contained fake memories and fake identities — we made haste to retreat, sounded the mort.

To seaboard. . . . Beat the flames, beat the sea — our sea. (The writer obviously loves water.) And we all gathered up on deck in a shivering mass at the dead centre of a storm. . . . The master is on the bridge, glass eye out as his body spasms in seizure, pinned down beneath the star field to mimic its design.

Insect life, or its vinyl counterpart, persists in the unconscious. I ran aground on a parent: child clutching canister of indigo dyestuff, madder bedstraws with whorls of four to six leaves.

However, I am becoming more steadfast about my pathological indecision. When mother died, she rejected the family mausoleum and insisted on a tomb apart.

*

We pray this situation may not persist for much longer. We have achieved a certain temperature, the mercury is on the move. Origin is a conflict between two laws.

There is rumoured to be safety in numbers — as soon as possible, as soon as we can, as soon as they can et cetera.

More on this subject: as well as can be, as well as possible, as well as usual.

*

As a child, I played a solitary game that involved repeating aloud an everyday word until it became detached from what it signified. (See Advanced Phraseology, Section 2.) Utterance arrives elongated from the southwest. Have you seen what is on the chalkboard this morning?

I am trembling. Rising stench of scorched flesh, the howling, a body within which sparks of light are imprisoned. Nothing is very clear, is it — just as one always misperceives in the real (viz. urgent in the extreme).

Now all present must pay. Margery Kempe, I screamed, I have just destroyed Adrian's imaginary crisis.

I have taken a step backwards: there is no longer anyone to show myself to on the outside, which has vanished. All that remains is a flooded labyrinth, where vibrations are converted into nerve impulses.

An oblique sun illuminates the number fifteen bus, ultraviolet within, lichen on the passing bough beneath a chain of scarlet thorns.

Sinkage

Sinkapace — five steps and three faces, a type of antique dance. From the name, it may be inferred that *all* my stratagems are regulated by the number five. (There she goes, sneaking out again.) I am going to ask you a question, and this time I need you to answer.

Nomenclature sticks to people and their things for a reason. Let us see if we can find a calliper splint: terrestrial gastropods have been detected in your bloodline.

Upon the solemn checkerboard floor, both requests are refused. Meanwhile and elsewhere, the gnostics strove desperately for a convincing theodicy; the chief problem with their apocalypse is the question which puzzled.

We dare not take him anywhere at the moment, not as he is. (Are you identical?) He wants to invert, back into the revisible: nothing lives within us et cetera. But I am falling behind, wearied now, hands firmly bound as they are, as they always were.

He has secured both chains to the hackamore. A length of time has appeared with a special loop for breaking you in.

All set? He speaks. . . . He lets go of the head. I rise up and step away, straight into the scudding clouds.

'In at the foaming street they come, hell-cast horsemen flung down from thunderhead.'

Sir had numerous papers to examine after breakfast, thus the time was propitious for my excursion: plumes of volcanic smoke had begun pouring from the magma chamber.

I could once identify objects written into the sky. There is evidence of the civilisation that gave its word, that undertook, that bound itself, that indicated, that lead one to expect, that pointed, that hinted, that suggested, that foreshadowed. A man standing beside me glances upward and turns to face Sirius, following its descent across the sky. (The dog star is chained to your ancestors.) The crew cut short their song and crane over the bulwarks, balanced on pipelines of liquid mercury, rusting culverts that lead directly nowhere: the first humans are coming, a horde from the surf storming the reef, riding four abreast, climbing closer and closer.

*

Contaminated bags of saline drip and insulin were found as I worked the wards during the summer of nineteen. Measures were taken to coax people into leaving their bones behind in shallow graves.

The moon flooded the landscape with UV light. Our isotope decays unpredictably, and as a result these numbers will change over time.

Pin, spoon, lunge, brain, ton, train, grain.

We are held at signal amber. He is still speaking, the other a listener. Occasional discord creates tension between these counterparts: a memory of someone else's father, ever-absent.

No work tomorrow eternal. I am trying to fax through a rapid-access failure.

Apropos the last point: with monologic utterance, mafia-occult, fugitive glazes of madder and orpiment. . . . Come back.

Where?

One sequence runs

At each new mile travelled, the horizon was a mile further off. Flash-cutting is the editing of a sequence such that the duration of your life becomes very shallow indeed: so long as fading light, but still the cloud.

I never gave working for a living a moment's thought. Erase our abandoned names from the toil sheet.

Flint

Paralysed in his stovepipe hat, he sits and reads till dawn, then vanishes without a trace. There is no conceivable sign for this.

I think, indeed it must be admitted, that fog and cloud do not add to the pleasures of such a trip — and the risk, as well as the graft, is magnified.

It is astonishing how much time there is now, provoked by rising air at the advancing front of another downdraft. Overnight, a grotesque terminal moraine was deposited at the furthest advance of the ice sheet. Contre-jour emphasizes the outline of a man at the entrance to the tunnel.

Is it not so, and has not the guide spoken correctly? (Of good family too, would one pause to reflect.) O, and lest we forget: all this expressed without a word being wasted.

Then there was the sound of spring approaching after a long dark winter; a ridge is forming at your extremities. Now I have a frozen bone in my ear, who is called otolith.

Night. He looks up at the sky, a mesh retreating at the speed of light.

*

I just think he has this unbreakable self-belief. He is silhouetted against the window, a white radiance, back turned on an emptiness — the shudder of numberless triangles. He is recasting his mind.

'Aerials dowse above red fireclay.'

'We struggled to breathe in the sway of a censer.'

He takes himself off alone into the desert and lies naked on the burning sand. At an imperceptible flicker of his eyelids, a shadow races out and slithers across his body.

*

Gastropod molluscs have been recorded in your family tree, the notorious trapdoor on the distaff. He turns to Sirius, Venus through the houses. . . . A diamanté lizard and other small reptiles cling to her fur. We are about to make the vital detachment.

A man approaches bearing arms, a bandoleer — dissolving phantasm, vector of a disease beneath our disfiguring star — nearby atop a column in the desert, the other dare not move. The chamber of the saint's skull holds a compressed body, confined within a hinged shell.

Let me know when you are back in town; I've had enough. All that remain are the three semicircular canals which form the organ of balance.

*

Salvator seems to regard women as life-bearing vessels. His landscapes, often peopled with bandits and containing scenes of violence in wild natural settings, were an important influence throughout my childhood. Indeed, there were bullet holes in the ceiling of my hotel room when I woke the following morning.

We are cherry-picking the highlights: sacred choral for forty voices, a sort of twisted sinew floating in the air before my eyes. . . . He extends an index finger to sketch muscle and fibrous tissue, the veins and arteries at the wounded hollow of my left thigh. No one need know.

The sparks are held captive in earthbound spheres and need to be lifted up. A unique anatomical structure made of chalk was found in one sector.

Antennae dowse above a desert of red sand — cranes tilt rusting, sand-blown corrosion — sudden mutation to glass or crystal (that meteorite). Father clings to the top of a swaying radio mast; he is still dead.

A great anchor and chain pass, unbearably slow. No one knows what is going on, and that's the whole idea.

I came up with indeterminate readings. One sequence runs.

'We communicate through a vast swarm of insects who care nothing for our future.'

At each mile the horizon was a mile further off.

Swaying radio mast, aerial dowser, a discarded map on the pavement. . . . But I'm getting sidetracked: origin is without an angle, twinned with the hoisting of your cerecloth flag.

Dim sense of unease, the approach of something brooding, ineluctable. Question yourself once more about all these misreadings: signals would arrive at the receiving room three hours after they had been sent from a morse transmitter in the faraway east. Why does he wait until the very end to reach a decision?

Well, there are some for whom screaming vents a transformation, but change has been dispatched today from an unlikely source.

He saunters in under his Latin-quarter hat. An oil tanker passes, unbearably slow, looks like a colour-field painting in close-up. Other notables include tonight's main contender.

Dear Gauleiter

I do not care what objects mean or what their names signify; it's probably an illness. I just want to be left alone to savour nothing — but you, you have a mind that is set: we sense you have a head congealed. Is it not painless to simply say what you have to say and then leave?

I am sure it was a species of comet that we glimpsed. And Corvus, a pair this time on either rail as we passed through, before soaring high above a sea crushed flat.

Your savant

*

One among us had been stitched at the lip. A huge rent opened up in the public spectacle — compensation neurosis, junk bonds — the kind of escape route a person invents in desperate circumstances: nerve-blind, all the instruments buried alive.

A long shot includes the human body in full, with head near the base of the frame and feet near the top. Who was flayed thus alive when he lost at hazard?

You have to wait a moment or two before the voices steal back in, but I promise they will, they must.

He sways from side to side atop a pillar. Analysis of the star gate inquest leads to further dowsing: autumn mist and leaves underfoot, a creeping plant with rosette of sepals and luminescent green spike.

Origin is the sole of the foot.

Not a single offer has been made for the head, and I am beginning to see why. What, who, has fathered thousands?

IX

Séance of found photographs, a record of his hermetic poverty. Any news of your own ancestors, are they still misbehaving?

A large spiral encircles each player's head, resting on the shoulders. Thawing of the ice surrounding the body continues until it is completely exposed.

In these examples the fire element and animal sacrifice are predominant. He longs for silence, descending a stairwell into the light amid a crashing din.

We are transcribing the data of received memory into a language adamantly fragile. In all religions, the acceptance of a divine revelation originally referred to unused content.

Now move, elevate, steering upward once more to rail against the sky — no escape from the manifest tics, the glittering tinfoil, drowning over and over in the selfsame flood.

*

For the author of such barren ground, any prize is intolerable. One notable characteristic is his slowness of speech, yet in this way the uncanniest life form manifests before us in its essential shape.

Now raise the floor a couple of inches: thy timely-parted ghost I invocate et cetera. Origin is twice plus voice.

Or list, with all sentences beginning lower case, no full stops.

O, I see, solid triangles — equilateral tetrahedra — a cluster of pyramids, at apex the glistening capstone. I forget where I am most of the time.

He is swamped by admirers, a deplorable frailty. But things are becoming clearer, free from quotation of any kind. The last entry reads the action of going out of or leaving a place.

A door connects the carriage to a narrow corridor packed with soldiers on their way to the front. It flies open violently as a gust of wind blows into the compartment a slip of paper bearing the fatal runes.

Ectoplasm, surprising to discover floating in the air above our heads. He had rolled the stone back and forth across his abdomen several times before expiring. The confirmed poisons are cyanide and oestrogen, while the brightest star in the sky south of the equator is found in the constellation Canis Major.

'Excuse me, we seem to have a shortage of atoms today.'

Origin is scorch, a study in disintegration. These strata reach all the way down.

*

The players: twins, forever estranged. The time: some place near the end. The place: a hesitant soul torn by doubt and conflict, algorithmic suffrage.

Here is his memoir in facsimile, complete and unabridged, printed in the black-letter script known as Fraktur. Vertigo and loss of time are often experienced when turning over the leaves of a notebook — that goad to regain the future, always pressing forward from the instant in question. And which mediaeval character went on to become a walking ode to infinity?

Last page, culminating at a dripping point. We do not have much spirit remaining, but.

Perhaps it would be more accurate to say that the fault is not so much with the environment as in the man himself. They said the waters may come again and they did, though not in the anticipated fashion.

You godless boy, you opened the eye of Horus.

I think I could be mutating. I am remembering *precisely* the same things as her. And a woman blinded keeps turning up in my dreams; the minutes record our transactions in full, a sum of contradictions.

But you remind me of somewhere else. Again, a true act of cinematic virtuosity: expressive colours, stately camera sweeps and haunted music possessed on credit. Dissolve is a term that refers to the slow fading out of one shot and the gradual fading in of its successor, causing a superimposition of images, usually at the midpoint. There follows a sublime intercession on absurdity and compromise.

One by one the objects in the room begin to corrugate and vaporize. My own lack of understanding simply reflects the order of things.

The light buckles and folds inward. An illegal chemical experiment is being conducted at a clandestine research hub, the imperial nerve centre. Your own star survives out there, glimmering, but about to disappear forever.

How do we frame this? He is said to have murdered a colleague in the laboratory and made it look like suicide.

All motive is unknown. Origin is trapped under a drain, nous imprisoned in solid matter. I refuse to handle any of these machines until they have been tolerably misaligned.

He does not seem to care what the names of things convey.

*

Psi powers, habeas corpus — the man who is never placed where one is looking. We agreed to erase memory using wire-and-string surveillance.

'It's strange, is it not, to stand in the dock and be urged to consider oneself an assassin.'

We were talking about natural disasters and tidal waves when it happened. I went on to establish a colony of survivors at the polar ice cap.

The map appears much more familiar to us if we look at it upside down — I felt relentlessly driven back, into a poisoned version of the future. The circles represent the extent of blast damage at one pound per square inch and above. See, it is quite impossible to accumulate evidence that will satisfy everyone.

The last passage is to be placed at the exact centre of the text, numerically speaking. You could see the crematorium from the train tracks. There always remains the possibility that a single weapon might be launched by coincidence.

*

Obsessive masturbation these past few days, the floor of the hermitage streaked with bolts of semen. Dreams came of an apocalyptic city, a runaway train and exploding helicopter, snow flurries outside the cabin, exhalation of white breath, the pylon towering. I was mindful of walled mediaeval Paris, the number seven multiplied to infinity.

You are trapped in a circle divided crosswise by a deep trench. Each quarter is rimmed by a concrete barrier topped with razor wire. Every day brings silence — there had always been something of the unvoiced about him — until the situation turns. The rout is mercifully brief.

Think we might see more rain, further escapades, including a plague of sympathetic magic. And directly above, a swollen plane track, rosy and set to burst. The sun must be the final agent in this parable — I mean those solar flares, your indifferent cosmics.

Do you mind me asking what you're in for? (Yes.) The window is barred. From without, her daunting voice.

She is the thing-in-itself. Me, I have been reduced to a hypothesis (the so-called tungsten wreck). Origin is late seven, from to touch plus signal bell. Where were you equals where are you equals where will you be.

That man, he returns on the same day and insists on paying the fee — a supremely flawed debut. The passing land was deluged, under water. I have three more to exhume before we can call it a day.

Give me another term for emersion, the reappearance of a celestial body after its eclipse, occultation. She writes back to say she meant Anthropocene, not Holocene.

'Thank you, I have grafted on the plumes of snow.'

Include here description of print for ex: a faded map with serpentine rubric. The later spelling is influenced by a redundant concept of form.

I said you would, in time.

Where did I leave my antenna?

The anchorhold is a roofless ruin on a promontory in which seabirds nest. Yesterday just trails off; you remember the past backwards, while I simply forget. However, I did with occasional sentences succeed in achieving a balance that is neither a balance. Atopia is the place of choice.
Survival depends on recognizing where your limitations lie, entirely imposed from without — spasms of alternate contraction and delay. A carton with *FIREZZA* stencilled on it is carried by the wind. I am eaten alive.

A small box of bees (walnut) is gently eased inside her body. Yield up thy ghost, she murmurs — she-giant, gallowed in darkest night et cetera. The circular churchyard has been extended many times, but its position makes it hard to ignore as a prehistoric ammunition dump.
If she did know anything, she wasn't letting on. I leaned back away from the desk and breathed out. This tendency no doubt foreshadows dissent.

The next solid has four planes, a triangular pyramid, also called dog star. The book still exists, unabridged, buried somewhere in the wooded hills that surround a city under siege. It's obvious for all to see, the promissory flood. Origin means you shall have the body.
So, an artless being, his crazy phrygian cap atop a quartered head. . . . And through marble halls ran a stream, a living tide.

*

Origin is disused cable duct, fractured from beneath. Surgeon first argued in seventeen fifty-three that lemons and limes could be used instead.
In the mornings you're like a newborn antichrist, she says as the couple walk hand in hand over a clifftop.
And who was caught on film, sucking at the barrel of a gun? The temporal continuum certainly seems to be an object of indiscipline.

Powder and shot at the ready — knuckles crack at green baize — and those huge moving shadows on a rock-hewn wall, sunlight skimming across the lake as we speed past. I have a very simple question for you.
The land is flat hereabouts because it was once the sea. A declaration of genocide was broadcast as the leading news story in more than twenty-three tongues.
Your own word is possibly influenced by archaic suspiral (vent, hatchet, sediment tank). People resembling reptiles with flippers were multiplying everywhere, chewing the cud — some horned, others not. We left them abandoned on the wharf, dumbly gazing up at our departing vessel.

That was no one-off event, and I've got the measurements from the Thames to prove it. I am looking forward to telling you more about that later.

*

In bygone days a full reference was given by writing the letters in strict alphabetic order, followed by the easting and the northing orientation. But something cataclysmic must have happened between this morning's conversation and now.

We are not doing this as a courtesy; I have been sorely tested.

I brought candles and you were both mortified. I collected her ashes in an hourglass. Those days are over.

*So I just thought I would tell you
to turn back the other way,
I just thought I'd tell you
to turn back the other way.*

Surviving maps show the expected targets in attacks A to K. (Assume the victim's body has been dumped in a cesspool beneath the house.) Outside these areas, serious injuries could be caused by blast effects but there would be little damage to ritual complexes other than broken windows, slates removed, doors in need of a rehang.

Literally, a straight direction out from the head, any head — say, the head of a landsman, one who walks aimlessly back and forth across the surface of the earth: renegade, vagabond, deserter — one circuitous in perambulation, driven at the knee.

Today is like nothing previously encountered. They have listened to what we had to say, and are now going back in time to check our account.

We could be sheer friends. (I do love her.) Because this is our time, I do not wish to share anything with anyone, am committed to the condition of being here alone, as in the world is his poison, a veritable paradise et cetera. The established relationship between narrative and survival I am inclined to reject.

Now write visor, roar, burn, derision, bearer in any order you choose. You be careful of yourself.

*

An interloper, birdsong on route, vampire goldfinch with rumoured head. This final section, usually referred to as the retraction, appears at this position in all manuscripts which contain the saga complete. Such repentance is not without precedent.

There was once a claw sticking out the other end, emerging from the water after becoming submerged. When the sun finally came up, I could have been anywhere.

Origin denotes a vertex — the crown of a skull, from to turn. Then she says the universe recoils from people, it knows their broadest intentions.

See, he has been exiled to a strange land, a man built mosaic, a structure of interconnecting voids.

She writes to say that she meant the final geological stratum of the earth. I too am sometimes called the recent.

'Whatever possessed you to light out on your own?'

In other circumstances such a question would have spurred the subject to launch herself immediately over a precipice in groundbreaking fashion.

Another of the thirty-six has suffered the corrosive effects of tangential thought. But I am turning deasil, in the direction of the sun's apparent course, considered unforeseen. Anticlockwise is withershins.

She reluctantly acknowledges a perceived connection between the sky and the dead. It shouldn't be too long now.

Earthquake requiem, a spectacle wherein the principal figure, de Sade, is manifestly unsympathetic toward a people beset by contagion and fear. Others upon arrival entirely forget their former lives.

Thus, his head is divided neatly into sixths, the acrobat with the fireworks and everything. You should find a ghost word like jawbone, scapula.

X

Anima Monday

That could be me in thirty years' time, living on my own in a house full of hares.

Dog barking in the night.

I died a martyr who refused to marry. I am the patron saint and my emblem is the lizard. As a child, I was an elective mute; I chose this path because at an early age I recognized the fragility of language. My last day is the twenty-first. I lived approximately and was canonized. My fast day is every available second.

All this was very disconcerting indeed, though some call it the time of your life. This is my first postcard after returning to the desert with its acid blue sky.

Look after mother he says, like we're all in a fucking film or something. Apex might be represented by a picture of a flying lemur, followed by a randomly chosen letter.

Above my head is a heraldic device associated with a family to whose name it cryptically alludes. A headline or section of text may be written in red for distinctiveness, such as the quarry marks daubed in the so-called holding chamber.

An event in time

She acknowledges my role as saboteur. At our passing a window vibrates, the merest tremble — I always forget what one thing can do to another, how one object can influence an adjacent object.

'Acrobats at the far side of the park are panicking their somersaults. . . .'

My own anatomy remains barricaded.

She does find him overpowering at times, quite beyond her fathom. That heavenly body is a binary star with dim companion, the albino. They're nesting high this year.

Mercury descends to announce his challenge, the test.

I suddenly felt uncomfortable. What you see is all that remains of a twelfth-century monastic cell. An air-filled cavity has been connected to the throat, containing three tiny linked bones that transmit vibrations — the manipulated sound of metal objects, Frank's undervoice.

*

Today's animal familiar is a carnivorous mammal with a pointed muzzle. Its notoriety has grown following a display of sordid Machiavellian manoeuvres.

I am breaking your law; time has no power against a total lack of identity. Conjure me a name from the supernatural power wielded by gods and demons, the illusion or appearance of the phenomenal world, manifestation.

The only thing that matters: back in the night. Everyone had that she says, everyone.

In one quadrant flickers the needle of a compass. I think there is no limit to what we can do with the surviving anatomy. His fingernails are rusty, but he chews at them regardless.

'Well?' asks the viceroy, who has taken off his spiked collar. 'Have you found the renegade man?'

Inside of him somewhere must exist a residue. Jackal-headed, he tears at his own flesh like a dog. The snow had begun to thaw.

A period of fifty-two vague years

The going rate was one and a half percent. I felt beaten and wanted to die. They found me hanging from a girder under the pier.

After spending three weeks locked in isolation this still was not enough, our aim being the production of an entire corpus. While alive, he had invented a timing device: two connected glass bulbs containing sand that takes one hour to pass from the upper to the lower bulb. Another fragment had an arched top as if it were being lifted from below, like a pileus sheltering the fleshy gills of a mushroom.

'Now you are claiming that you are *not* the undergaoler's daughter?'

Contre-jour produces backlighting of the subject. See, all the sevens, over and over, sometimes even having a hexagon at the base.

She sighs, 'No. And who, or what, are you?'

The monster with the last trump, tin whistle and drum. A bandolier (or bandoleer) is a pocketed belt for holding ammunition, usually slung sash-style over the shoulder with the ammunition pockets across the midriff and chest. We have hit the crest of a slump.

*

He says I learnt everything I know about language from silence. Another solution juxtaposed a large block of uniform colour with narrow marginal strips of contrasting colours. Quite the trauma, aren't we?

An underground burial chamber with rooms above it at ground level has been named a mastaba, or a stone bench built into the wall of your house. I dreamt I was reading a classical masterpiece backwards, as was the custom in those days. The book fell apart in my hands and the numbered pages refused to match up. The scene was a lock-in.

Permit me to remove this maniac elsewhere; attention is a glimpse, not a hijacking.

Experimental inversion of the earth's magnetic field would sabotage the process of dialectical reasoning and compromise the ability to stand up. My own mother's funeral took place beside the castle on the cliff. It overlooked.

Hieroglyph is the word I'm searching for.

*

We are almost inside Beethoven's head as he struggles to find a way forward: empirical clues, any serviceable misdemeanour, however trivial. The chemist removed the ingested substance by washing with a solvent; this action is shown as a high-angle shot in which the subject is photographed from above. Origin is sluiced from the verb, as suggested. And do we include the spiral cochlea?

Your own dark matter holds molecules of intergalactic dust in a thin film across the outer surface. I hate these fucking split shifts, they kill me, curse me, they damn me.

'Would you prefer that we just left you alone?'

It was like Anne Boleyn all over again. Now you sound as though you're in a casino, an interior with gaming tables, pre-industrial cottage industry. . . . This is a record of my halcyon days: a rotator studded with teeth at the lower mandible — a rose window — spinning firewalk taken at a trot, broken down by the occasional sideswipe.

A mythical bird is said by ancient writers to breed in a nest floating on the sea at winter solstice, seducing mariners into calamity. And then, it being his turn to speak, Quetzalcoatl said everything we cherish fades away after one complete cycle of the warped neural sheet.

A few of the people I met did things slowly, by degrees. And the malice of inanimate objects has been duly noted.

Onehood, onehead, onement

The condition of being alone: the world is her prism, an acephalic paradise. Individual moths were tested, some intact and others decapitated.

What is the sign for this. Together we form a psychotic and early variety of pair: bone of my bone et cetera. Then she is dragged outside into the courtyard — sparks wheel in the night air — oily black smoke from a brazier, babel of voice.

*

He is speechless before my ingenious new war machine. In spite of this, the besiegers who have encircled the city are plotting a classic *fait accompli*. So much for references to the self.

A clandestine meeting took place in a back room at the sign of the feral man. One of the challenges of the first read through is the segues and non sequiturs, which together create an unheard of imbalance. I refuse to make anything out of language ever again: I could not survive that far from the molten core of the earth.

The table below shows in which zodiacal signs the four coluri fall for a variety of different epochs. Though the outer body wall gives rise to unexpected resistance, it is breathtaking to witness up close the subject's finely-tuned deathtrap and inexhaustible food supply.

The barrows lie in an arc on the highest ground in the vicinity, while he rots in a box under the ground, leading out from which is a tube that enables him to breathe his last. A citation is needed here.

Later we shall find him hanged and slashed and drowned (there are promised many such twists that hazard meaning). A compound of cyanogen with a metal, a substance found in plants or synthesized, has similar disastrous effects.

His mannerisms, it seems, are less corrosive than his words. Then we realized we had been watching the same film that evening, about an open city after a catastrophic war.

'See, I would one day like to become a really amazing book.'

What she saw instead was a solemn young man in mourning sackcloth, incredibly thin. He is the possessor, always.

'I guess you would prefer me to pack up my mutant insect samples and leave.'

I may have misheard. Use is being made of a dissimilar sequence of actions for narrative effect — for example, how they live in the air and sparkle, the scintillas that flashed before our eyes.

That's you and your fucking confluence. (Just give me back my boots.) And then came yet another repetition of the selfsame event. All my faults have escaped in the printing.

An intense white light is obtained by heating lime, formerly used.

'Now fly down and circle about the jackal's head.'

His last words, wherein my past and future waste away. The mirror darkens; your dialectic is eclipsed. Often have I witnessed his untimely parted ghost.

We shall now dwell upon some infamous Richards, Coeurdelion and so forth, whereupon architecture is to be brutally interrogated.

He reacts by demanding that the heretic be exiled. This is supported by the manuscript evidence and rumours of a death-bed repentance, often re-enacted and discussed. Here then is the concluding step in an epic that recounts the pilgrimage of Ra (see introductory note to *Fragment X*, to 'the blind eye that weeps'). I remembered hearing.

But of course, I take exception to all these forsaken rules. It is strange that such a thing could have overpowered such another thing: every instant is a struggle. Still, I have made uncanny use of circumstance today; a true alienist needs to have one foot in the grave.

She lies hardened in heart and spleen. Be forewarned, it resembles you, this game.

A puzzle was introduced in which words are represented by combinations of pictures and individual letters. Origin is Terra — in science fiction, the planet earth — where ground ochre is still used as a writing material, from the base of red desert.

Somehow she miraculously escaped torture on the wheel. She has the world's largest variable skin. (Knowledge is.) Her head has been divided neatly into sixths — she also carries out the occasional psychic execution.

We are here documenting my personal science of immortality. Let me describe her for you.

'Who is that man waiting on the corner at the foot of a cliff?'

And I think to myself, has the other risen from the grave, is it the apocalypse time? In form the apparition resembled the cap of a toadstool, more or less.

Claret is shed and congeals on the frozen pavement. The sky seems out of kilter — a vast pink moon hangs above the horizon — phosphorescent snail tracks, the plop of a rat in the lake as I climb the hill. Mister once swallowed a whole box of cartridges.

Some disinterested facts, including remarks on clouds

A warship at sea, pressganged crew cowering in the forecastle, exhausted by their night of struggle against the storm. Galleons are typically square-rigged and have three or more decks and masts. The oldest parliament is the all-thing. My own fast lasted around ten minutes.

A cold front is moving in, listless blue-grey. There is a noted centre near horseshoe curve, where the rails first crossed.

A layer of altocumulus is moving imperceptibly across the sky. Since mislaying my social persona, low-profile forms of assassination have held less and less appeal.

My own offering was mute, which only one of the priests understood. When I say priest, I mean something more like thaumaturge, but am reluctant to include this word due to its syllabic count. I am trying to keep things simple.

A layer of altocumulus. Or, permit me to remove into elsewhere this holy fool. No, better still, altocumuli shudder across the sky. . . . An ancient tomb consisting of an underground burial chamber with rooms above it at ground level was once used as a holding chamber for those awaiting sacrifice. Compare this with the cedar wood mallet used to kill fish caught while angling.

Mother did not receive the last rites. (Did she know she was dying?) The solar flare is responsible. I heard of a man born in the same year who also prized solitude.

Within the context described, please identify the hermetic protocol and compare it with the himself-herself protocol. Some people can take it but I was never cut out for panegyric.

(What he means is there is no effective way of barricading a womb.)

This is a technique in which the viewer is pointing directly toward a source of light, and there is an equivalent technique found in painting. Mutant protein bands were dissolved and used as an immunogenic vaccine, or vax.

*

The layers are opaque. In a region whose boundary suddenly shrinks to zero, we concede defeat.

The man's nerve is only too apparent as he proclaims his invisibility. He gives up on everybody, this ghost. From a great way off comes the sound of a sea.

We are here approaching novel ideas for survival, but before many minutes have passed the grey malevolence of a November dusk will fall once again. Moreover, the recent sightings of a monstrous phosphorescent dog are still at the back of my mind.

A graphic representation of this event sometimes features a hexagon at the base.

I am the man appointed to collect your efflux. That final fugue was incomprehensible. Origin is truncated, so named because your lower part is permanently severed from view.

Who is that, speaking? You don't say.

We may never again be able to see a number of the others. Some of these words are at least forty years old, particles of breath circling the earth for eternity.

>   Cephalic influence on defensive behaviour
>   in the dogbane tiger moth

Let us get back to learning your lines — carried away, transported. Your appointed messenger is already here, it's just a question of uncloaking him — blow by blow like a living statue — glyphs buried in stone that are exposed as the sculptor hammers away at the surface.

The peasants demanded messianic lightning strikes. I have withdrawn: the chosen colour cannot be identified.

Friendly bacteria never tasted so good. There is resistance ahead on the track. You are a little late, memory.

The seventh of his apparitions

She inspects across her right arm the track of a bite, deep weals promising scar tissue. I could only realize my ambitions by closing the original deal and embarking on an abandoned future.

On internal surfaces within your body lie hidden layers of dark matter. The things will come back when they are hungry.

A prehistoric wrought iron plate was found after the explosion. The star is so named because it appears to follow at the heels of Orion, the stalker. For further oblique correspondences see *Musca domestica*, the family misericord et cetera.

You are the emptied page, a wedge between external object and interior sign, where nothing signals. This presence knows, and wishes to be heard.

The origin of need is danger. We decided to leave memory behind, a one-on-one household entertainment. Such words often foreshadow revenge, the boundary of an advancing mass of cold air, in particular the trailing edge.

I held that note underwater for as long as possible. Is this what people call measuring yourself against the world, testing your dominion?

I wanted to take myself off elsewhere on that uncontainable day, dowsing with brittle antennae. All I can hear in my head is the clatter of a roulette ball orbiting the wheel.

*

Arrival of the nonce word, coined for your missed opportunity. I was looking for something more permanent, whereas he is mere semblance, an outward display. But that is not to say there won't ever be a sea change (i. ii. 403).

And sure enough, we were called forth into yet another situation. I am slowly filtering each moment. The origin of are is uncertain.

An insider equals zero, therefore an outsider equals one. I am misaligning.

Unknown, copy work to lost name

Now, a certain man was sick. This is your signal to withdraw.

It is only permissible in automatic writing to join the outlines of words together when no ambiguity will arise from so doing. I too should have given up the ghost and vowed to pit myself against thy gathering strength.

He could no longer carry the citizens with him and spent long years in uneasy exile; there are no alternatives to reading this retraction as an expression of the poet's personal remorse.

The corporation is to mutate into a liminal company. Change all the names.

You will find countless examples scattered throughout the text; something unfathomable is beginning to chance. Since the day of my uprooting, she has kept vigil.

Her hands were laced with veins beneath leathery wrinkled skin. A congress of some kind is foretold.

This small fragment is disembodied — those who touch, that burning book — I remain unconvinced.

And the sea takes us both, sinking as lead into the almighty like a couple of mistimed lovers. Oestrogen production was compared against the cycle of solar radiation, sunspot activity.

Usurper

A dog pads along the passageway, slavering and growling at the earth, sacred ground. Several of the caudal vertebrae have been excised.

We resorted to divination by means of scattered salt, upon which the child is forced to kneel and pray. But I'm a practised spirit, not much interested in moral dilemmas or elaborate explanation.

The allusion here is to a priest's function in performing the last rites. At the celestial poles two great circles intersect at right angles, passing through the ecliptic at equinox, at solstice.

You prey upon me, would seem to know my every pause — the gaps and halts — an ecstatic hesitancy. But there is a need for such silences, daring us to prise them open.

When the list of spectral forms and temporal anomalies is complete, highlight any words with asymmetric outlines. Enliven the text by translating its pages into a language you are entirely ignorant of.

This effect hides detail, causes a stronger contrast between light and dark, creating silhouettes and emphasizing line and shape. A reversal has occurred and the rear cavity is now situated in the place once occupied by the frontal cavity — hind-brain we christened him, or the intervacuum: waste forces gather within him. Before sunrise we must reach a decision.

Just as suddenly as the sound began, it stopped. Filtered light may be used to illuminate the side of the victim facing his assailant.

*

Here she comes sliding down the causeway, a vestige of the nervous system. As for me, I am still bound to the front rank of commodities, our dead and living meat.

This is a mesmerizingly slow study in antigravity, under the shadow of her fragile margin. One cloud is forming a layer of rounded mass, with level base at altitude, expanding too resemble an inverted anvil.

Their dialogue is impenetrable, whittling away at itself, bred in decaying organic matter and often entering houses.

These are very bad signs indeed: grotesque papier-mâché heads, the human accordion, a Slavic drinking song — map without terrain, bloodshed eyes with two tiny metal pyramids shaped like a bird's beak protruding from her skull.

I must press on, they are closing in. Origin is by association with the sea, misconceived.

Rose, madder glaze

I sometimes ponder whether the effects of long-term seclusion might be cumulative, gathering to break at an unstoppable wave. Outside in the courtyard stood arc lamps that emitted an eerie vibration — within, phantoms shuffled about the kitchen in the gloom, their vague outlines pinpoints of red light. One attempted defenestration, another had glowing green eyes and was growling like a jackal.

Everything was simpler back then: each day I had no idea what to do, how or where to position myself. The brightest star in the sky is just south of the celestial equator, in the constellation Canis Major. The explosion left an ugly vertical scar running down the south face of the pyramid.

He made equity in twenty but walked away and out into the universe. Personally, I have never found myself involved in synchronized screaming with such a large group, even in a crisis. Altitude is typically two to seven kilometres or six thousand five hundred to twenty-three thousand feet above sea level.

It was not exactly my ambition to be stuck in a tunnel when the light cuts out, a locomotive bearing down. This feels like a completely different geological epoch, does it not? Sometimes he's a model dog.

By comparing this response in both headless and intact moths, the role of auditory interneurons may be examined. Herein lies a critique of the contradictions which arise from assuming knowledge of objects that live way beyond the limits of experience.

*

He tracks from east to west, the wrong direction in which to circumnavigate the globe: such a manoeuvre is considered ill-starred. Then they locked me in the bathroom; I lay on the cold floor, contemplating the *art décoratif* ceramic tiles. The only blind spot is the ceiling.

See, one reckless idea after another. When people read, they have no way of knowing what has been erased, what has been given sanction to remain.

How can one stay calm and think clearly at eleven fifty-nine by the clock? Once every possible future has been taken into account, there are only three types of human interaction that we are prepared to countersign.

I could not progress beyond his reply, the answer dissolving until it was no longer an answer.

Yes, I have never had much truck with guilt, no. And the same sensation comes to me nightly in my cell, an unelected silence: contact.

Where are you waiting for?
Why are you sitting here?
What do you hesitate?
(The moon or other light source is now directly behind the speaker.)
You know what you ought to do.
There is no other word for messiah.
When do you not?
It is useless to hesitate.
Who don't you just get up and leave?
And so on. We are fallen to earth is the angels' sorrowful reply. There are isolated elements in every anatomy.

Note the candle wax and winding sheet — a mass solidified — beads of congealed grease clinging to the shaft. . . . Within this overproduction there is a new opening for oblique forms of trade. Matins was never my favourite time of day.

*

Stirrings in the gullet, an omen of death or calamity, but you will have to catch me first. Four of the survivors are suspended from a gibbet swung out from the top of the bell tower. The first stone drops into my throat, trapped between head and abdomen.

This test demands the unmasking of every construct — an endless sentence persisting beyond your demise — into the outside and night forbidden, repulsed by every finite thing.

I unnerve. A disembodied voice speaks from the adjoining corridor.

Short story

The grim reaper is calling for skeletons to dance on their graves. He plays the fiddle. Dawn comes and Lucifer lures everyone back into their tombs. Thereby, origin is seized for use.

*

Any ikon stolen from a place of worship may serve as defence against malign occult influence. I have dwelt on the repercussions of his letter, weighed the things he writes of again and again, and in a voice obsessively directed back at itself: torn muscle, fibroid tumour where the tissue decays, a cluster of kidney stones, close encounters with addiction.... It all screams never apologize, never explain: come in, welcome, scrape the pathogens off the sole of your boot.

On every coin the emperor's head is depicted, crowned with flytrap leaves. His distribution is inch-perfect, stats unrivalled. The moth responds by emitting streams of high-frequency, rapidly repeated clicks. We have reached the last page, an unforgiven peace.

The defendant's entire anatomy was found to be prosthetic. We rammed him up the chimney and lit a fire below. He continued his recitation as the smoke began to curl about his body.

And of ascesis: the practice of disciplining oneself is all but lost. Yet I have won back memories of spectacle, absorbing them at the very instant they threaten to dissolve. Even the stones on the beach are not exempt. You wanted this, now claim it.

*

This part is called the venomous snake pit. One artist made a replica of the satellite using thousands of tiny mirrors and exhibited it to widespread acclaim. During the same century, domestic land reclamation became compulsory; the passing of time was gyroscopic. A shaft pointed directly toward Sirius, the dog star, a stellar binary with a dim companion, the albino homunculus.

Fear, it's our only chance. The interstellar probe was crammed with fifties memorabilia: a working steam locomotive, one basilisk reptile, a pyramid of lead cannonballs and a blood-vein moth pinned to a polystyrene ceiling tile. The effect conjured up something that might have escaped from your sixty-five classic tales of horror. One can be certain of nothing but blind hazard.

For years estranged, but we met again by some reversal of fate at a satanic orgy. Afterwards I felt no better than I had before the venomous snails were applied.

Try using a laundry marker they said. We are all tethered to our own irrepressible moment — every gesture opens another facet of the work, not that these components have much *use*.

Then she announces that she is afraid of everything.

Shudder to think. I have a vision of absolute control, inextinguishable sensation.

We cannot hold them back any longer. This narrative appears erratic and inconsistent to the reader unacquainted with scapegrace journalism. The novel begins with an unforgettable haemorrhage of mutinous darks, and who is the conductor of this acclaimed choir blessed with such a pathological tone?

I need not have severed myself from my fellow crew members after all, might have spent my remaining years undetected among the cosmonauts manning the Nostromo.

*

You must understand that the specified artefact we have been searching for may not even exist.

He says hell is the nervous system and heaven a sort of orbiting space dock for essential repairs.

She says you are like my tutelary spirit, forever absent.

Outside, a multitude is waiting patiently.

This is a rare point you bring to bear upon your own identification. Don't forget that a neuron can transmit impulses between other neurons, especially as part of a reflex arc.

> I do, I will

I woke to find lead weights suspended from tiny hooks that pierced the skin all over my body. She is just playing a game.

I am mindful of the hungry ghosts who lurk in the shadows of her kitchen. A knocking is heard: re-enter.

Riotous London — passersby flung from a catwalk high above the bridge — cobblestones echo to the tread of jackboots — resurgent tinnitus, generous tears et cetera.

I am exceedingly weary of tongue. For years we were limited to such statements as: it is very nice up here, is it not? Or, would you like me to bring you another one of those?

The fungal plague discovered in orbit radiates a searing heat. It is said matter can never become anything but matter again, and I have no greater dread. Today I miss terribly the vibration and hum of the cyclotron.

We have too much choice these days she murmured. It's a family thing.
Everyone is naked, all tremble uncontrollably, every person weeps — but if I thought liquid gold flowed through their veins, I would have every one of them bled to death immediately.

This ceremony lasts a very long time indeed. Good conduct will be horsewhipped. Origin formed in an irregular pattern from obsolescence. See chase.

Nothing is like it used to be, life outlasts many of its participants. But where did the surviving half *come from*? I had light but no power — this signals psychological collapse, individuation.

The two other passengers eye him distrustfully. Stay where you are a voice calls to the eye on a stalk in the mist. Mass incineration occurs when there is a lightning ratio of thirty-six bolts per square kilometre, or more.

*

Look at that sea fog. It's coming our way. You, who have been surveying the damned, the time has come to scream your farewells.

When the envelope was slit open it was found to contain a death threat, blue magic. That last thought is fading; I have no ideas. The moth responds to ultrasonic artificial bat echolocation signals.

He has nine nights to live. Another conversation in the same saloon, the one with a cave out the back, continued for two whole days. The remedy is any number of creeping invertebrate animals with slender elastic bodies and no limbs.

Subject: cutlery, the purposeful dropping of. What are you doing right now? (New to me is this fancy.) For the sake of completeness, I admit defeat: cutlery falling equals mysterious visitor. Origin is late again.

I have from traced end to end, heading by heading, from not again plus capital. If you drop a carving knife a policeman, if you drop a fork an advocate, and so on.

Large galvanized bath, sixty-five roubles

My neighbours turned up without warning, as they do — she/he is unreliable, she/he is unstoppable et cetera. . . . I am unstoppable. The last occasion we met, we discussed the hidden meaning of the handing over ceremony.

It is surprising how far the voice travels out here in the open — an echo created by the walls of the canyon warps the voice into an expression that was never uttered in the first place. One does not know where to start, one does not know how to finish, one does not know where to look. Evidently I have not done my homework, having failed to read my deceased predecessor's record of the final events he witnessed.

Upon the shingle a grimoire, well-thumbed, has been left open at a page describing the nature of 'soul cubes'.

Now I shall attempt to describe the true nature of exile, using as a prompt the photograph in the found strongbox. As I feared, just the opposite: a form of possession by the gods.

If ever I leave a piece of cheese somewhere, I never go back. Cheese is firm and elastic or soft and semi-liquid in texture. It is too obviously sentimental and big.

Usage: note that peruse means read, typically with an implication of mindful exhaustion. It does not mean read through quickly or glance over, as in documents will be perused rather than totally alienated.

Do you have an appointment with any professionals today? she asked at our final parting.

Of psyche or soma? was my retort.

Some of this material appears unspeakably small, as if composed by a miniaturist. I am distracted. Whenever I leave anywhere, I never go back.

Soho foregone: that white-tiled café, her still younger then, autumn sunbeams bisecting, time not itself quite as now and the motes of floating dust.

I distract myself. Am I surely, an embodiment.

O lord. It says here that I have surviving progeny. I cannot recollect.

That apparition never goes away. Geology never goes away.

Applause, softly falling into the darks

The forensic camera can make the living appear dead and vice versa.

An usher holds up a portrait sketch of the alleged victim for the whole courtroom to see. It has been a memorable ten minutes this last ten minutes, now vanished.

Dig a little deeper.

I retired about six years. Everyone had a stroke. I discovered clairvoyants I could work with, channel.

Question those days: into the passage of time I strayed et cetera. The sun or other light source is often seen as a strong glare immediately behind the subject.

She declares herself an 'artificer of the soul'. Here we have two wrong names for an unknown object.

It is hard to see anything standing up from this perspective. We have broadcast, have wagered. A long shot includes a picture within a frame which roughly corresponds to the audience's view of the sector, but only within the proscenium arch of lawful theatre.

The scrap of paper bearing the runes flutters through an open window to settle upon the viceroy's desk. I leant forward into the wind.

'Who shut down this configuration — what dimness anyone, the example things?'

'They do not even bother to record visitor numbers, they have no invasion strategy.'

'Every time I see it, that red coat has something else to say to me.'

Observe how the exegetical code unravels, along the traces left by something that is not quite itself anymore. I don't believe in moving dust from place to place.

I have to work around the fact that for two-thirds of the year I cannot be put to use. That which can be named must exist.

How can you possibly resurrect a shape without first beating it unconscious? We have received numerous requests of late for direct inaction, the magnetism of the unpromising. I sabotaged the list.

Note the vomitory influence: point blank. (Creatrix is a word.) I would love to get involved with your head.

Maybe we could forge a takeaway bank, more mindless agitation in the suburbs. You can time me.

*

His distribution was once inch-perfect, but that was centuries ago; such attributes are no longer recognized. His major contribution was the unlikelihood.

Apart from the difficulty discussed in Chapter XXIII, there is a second fundamental pitfall attending classical celestial mechanics. Seventy-five people have looked at it. I have been responsible for an awful lot of botched research in my time, extinguishing the warning lights and so forth.

Cosmological drawbacks within the system
of zoological nomenclature

It looked a day like any other: demoralizing paralysis and protracted states of melancholy. Your technique is reckless, a true dialogue in nature, but at some point you will have to go back and reassemble your life.

That day gave itself a title, which was the nation of two. Now and then there would be a gentle shower of kalsomine, a kind of white or pale blue wash for walls and ceilings. Origin is dead centre — for example: Is he running? Is he there yet?

We found a spine growing inside her body, toward the rear, composed of calcium salts (hardness, strength in compression), flint (mythopoesis) and collagen fibres (tensile strength). She expressed her agreement with a groan; three of the vertebrae were fractured. We are leaping from strength to strength, all these glistening strengths.

See, strangers on a train.

More seercraft

We are closing down due to unforeseen circumstances: colliding trajectories, telekinesis, the silhouette of a man caught in an assassin's cross hairs. . . . The deviant twinned in the seedbed has been placed under surveillance. You see that ear, it just grew back.

Discount void as a numeral. He but usurped his own life, ruled in his realm and the gored state sustained. . . . Is he one of those two passengers on a train, destined to be killed on the battlefield by a comrade's bone shrapnel? His arrival, I perceive, has poisoned my own will.

He shall tell the story in his own time; a good analyst needs to have one foot in the grave. (Said that.) I am an excerpt from everything.

This dialogue tends too far, lies otherward. The outcome was immediately appealed against, and hearings proceeded inconclusively over the next forty years. Take as much time as you need, the prosecutor had said.

'When I say artificer, I mean a skilled mechanic.'

And yet, the person who filmed all this, was he not the son who slew himself?

*

Drunks near-dawn, back of an alley. The writer is a person who reads mediaeval script and wishes to remake scenes from memory: a factotum, tensile to lack.

i) A place of lodgement or deposit.

ii) A point of infection: nervegate.

Origin is obsolete — spinal discipline, a punishment deferred. The water in the canal resembled a rancid transparent varnish. He helped me pack my conversation notebooks, placing them carefully at the bottom of a battered suitcase.

Look, an amphitheatre, I said.

I had never before noticed the bull and matador in the distance, the tops of two heads, male and female, close together in the foreground, and to the left what appears to be a dark cloud but which is evidently the result of a flaw in the photographic process. Suggested within the composition are intersecting circles, which I cannot fathom, indeed, have no wish to. On the back has been written Seville in blue ink with a fountain pen. I had never looked.

Slender hollow tubes form the framework of the bird's wing. At lower ratios, such as eight to one, the result is low-key lightning. (Citation needed here.) Any image viewed directly against the setting sun causes loss of detail and colour, emphasizing shape and line.

I have only three more recordings up my sleeve, sung polyphonous, words from the cross with seductive bittersweet mouth. See too deadly nightshade, also called belladonna, adding brilliance to the eye when dilating the pupil.

This is the space to occupy right now. It delimits us.

*

I was materializing from another sleepless night. Down here, eyes and ears are meaningless — touch is everything. He is one of the thirty-six. (I am.) He waits transfixed beside the obelisk above the traffic.

Hildegard von Bingen too spent her formative years enclosed. The monastery was destroyed on earth and rebuilt somewhere in the sky. Resident saints cluster and bilocate.

Back then writing was all about the impossible. He sits gazing through the window of a coffee bar on Old Street; across the road is a pyramid, at the top of the column rooted beneath St Luke's. For the first time in many days he thinks *do this*, as if instructing himself to perform a specific act, while inside, the ceaseless commentary. He recollects how once he was carried through the streets in an 'entourage of shining armaments' — and now this, set adrift having bartered the last traces of ambition.

The turret confining him should be circular rather than square. A sun sets, big and orange, as the moon rises full with blood-red and the sea like molten metal, yet another deception in a long sequence of deceptions.

Circumstances persist: signal exhaust, hazard light semaphore, bleached calico drying on the beach exposed beneath the tarmac. I turned up the volume.

There was no sign of the ligature which strangled. Another says it was like being buried alive, descent in a rudderless lift sent crashing to the base of a pit, down the rust chute and into the sea.

Three nights ago I met a number of such phantasms, all quite sinister at first, but I felt more at ease as they began to communicate telepathically (not exactly persons to fuck with though). A cast was made of the key using wax, a cast was made of the nerve ganglion.

I have attempted to record this in language, as spoken by other people. The manuscript is unfinished, an eternity of skins with no core.

The old abbot's profile, which I always recoil from, was suddenly lit by the slanting beam of a lamp cast from the adjoining cloister.

'Yet the stone faces of men and small pebbles or gravel fed to hawks. . . .'

What I am talking of is privation, a state marked by the absence of some quality that is normally present.

*

The customer here is unspecified, simply 'limner of memory'. He is never completely not working; his politics are never. He compresses, folds into himself. Without warning he lurches into a snowbound house — a red room through a wrangle of veils — cells and filaments, flashes of mirror. This place is named after its shape.

Passersby shrieking aloud. Now the time has come for my next move, the chosen impulse: I need.

Key will not fit the lock. No surprises there.

He must gauge the infinite possibilities of mood in order to guide the events that are set to unfold.

A long winding sheet upon which drips candle wax. (All set.) Wave after wave of them surged over the crest of the hill. An arrest was made. This project is fated to an abrupt termination: the world is full of objects, more or less diverting.

Approaching sound, a horse-drawn omnibus, most probable. From second to second, the only difference I can perceive is more or less movement.

*

She pallid, leaning into the winter sun, and somehow resembling a petrified horse. Elsewhere, at precisely the same moment, he is chancing conversation with a most enigmatic seeker after asylum. She is aboard one train, he another, speeding across the flatlands.

Obelisk withstanding, a glimpse through the daily luminous. The others were not to be seen. That which is named can at least be written.

Eavesdrop of concussive word, set perhaps at an angle. A part of the body is injured without breaking the skin, thus forming a bruise. Origin is ground from the verb, from together plus pulse, collide.

Solitary wood pigeon at the elder once more, first sighting since its mate was devoured. As remarked upon above, it is electrifying to observe so closely the surrounding reticulum.

Another branch of mathematics deals with quantities having random distributions and the role of fate.

I can't do this.

*

She says who do you think and he say I do not know. She is weeping, urgent while he resists; they are fearless while trying not to appear fearless. Heretics were burned if they would not recant, until a balance was finally struck: street theatre for the dead on one side, assassination of inquisitors on the other.

There was no way to the ruins except through the private grounds of a château. I had not realized until early in sixty-seven how much our principal characters play out their parts on a severely circumscribed stage.

'Yes, perhaps everything you can recall of that day,' before leaning forward to ask in a whisper, 'are you a helmsman of some kind?'

A field of multicoloured wash bisected by chalk tracks, solitary aeronaut at the crest. He has an image of himself as a man of the people.

The structure of space-time has hereabouts been corroded; this rupture has a physical singularity at the core, to which infalling matter unescapably proceeds. Just before this point is reached, within a certain radius — the event horizon — light itself becomes trapped and the object is rendered invisible. I am just making a suggestion.

Deep in a valley surrounded by rocky hills, the library housing the codex overlooks a creek, seemingly at the centre of nowhere. This feels abstruse he murmurs, crouching in the backdrop.

Shellback, navigator

Her name resembles an abbreviated airport. The chosen gene is a light inhibitor. These elements share a correspondence with the tenth star in the constellation Kappa Orionis.

From this day onward I shall seek to exist in total darkness; the map says this road is unlikely to provide a route out of anywhere. A system for automatically stopping a train if its driver fails to observe signal warnings had to be invented.

A compound consisting of a molecule bonded to three phosphate groups is present in your living tissue. She has no counterpart. I personify.

Origin is early twenties, from kinetic, to move plus makeshift splint. Pet names include Neonazi and Omega-B Essential Modulator. Other titles include disassociation, synthetic mohair.

Observe that, once again, the attack consists mainly of groundburst, about seventy-one per cent. The impact resembled a crow.

But mass is only forty-eight point two. This gene shares homology with other suspects, including the housefly. Try to picture a solitary man listening to a tinnitus soundtrack, an endless list of lists.

Such a pursuit is often termed quixotic. A pair of fine wires cross at right angles on the focus of the gunsight, to facilitate the assassin's aim.

Because I cannot decide, they are now offering to repair the stolen light. A face fleetingly appears on the screen, and this unexpected vision of pixilated colour disturbs everyone present. Maybe this is a sign that we are going to work backwards from now on.

Inside our bodies there is this fearful sonic drone. At the end of time the remaining gravity will split open.

*

His job is to monitor the ebb tide. A discrete frequency distribution gives the probability of a number of independent events occurring at precisely the same moment. I think I know where that leaves us — we will need a reliable clock and some sand.

You see, he has begun to suspend.

'I could walk on my hands through fire for you.'

What would failed air look like?

*

Hello, I said, it is so strange to be moving homeward, or to appear to be moving homeward. I am thundering now says the Lord, and you are mine, according to the custom of the transitory.

A nerve was compressed and overnight the fluid crept back in. A deep hole bored into the sternum can provide an ironic sense of imbalance — until the moment of removing from the shelf a certain book, against which the photograph is propped.

Tomorrow is the last turn of the elders, odds-on target of a lightning strike. Origin is one seventh of an obsolete shape, an ancient castigation.

Lines have been scribbled across the memory carton. I used to only want.

This life form [*pointing*] is called a bearded something. Or is it not? The feathered serpent actually had a rather jaguarlike head with long sharpened teeth. I later learnt that one painting was titled the distribution of eagles.

His own name means aegis of Zeus and was one of the first to be translated. These were ominous soundings, on and off for years. Now my voice lies broken.

There is no audience as yet, and no sign of Schumann.

I am writing in the rarely encountered key of C sharp major. Nothing complex, just tortuously unpredictable.

My twin sister had this huge amount of stuff to burn, probably the maize god and his brother. All the people who attempted to decipher the temple carvings made the mistake of examining only individual glyphs and had died suddenly in a series of horrific accidents.

XI

Benighted unpeople

I discovered that the source of the crisis was simply the order in which I had placed the letters, the name hidden within the flesh. I have never had so many subatomic experiences; I think it must have been the incident.

The tongue was never recovered. Origin is complete — a boundary stone, a compact head of any shape — while at my feet is a dense cluster of tiny blue flowers, plants of the family. A netlike fabric conveys the animal's food supply.

She's writing like this because she is approaching the end of her life. There is nothing left to lose. Also she draws, during bouts of sleeplessness, pink spirals on paper over and over, plucking at the straw that is not there. The whole region beneath the ribcage was contused.

I said it has started raining.

Still a little credit left. During the closing minutes the platform rocked as shells burst all around and bolts of electricity shot through the billowing smoke. Letters had been stencilled across the creature's shell, a corrosion-resistant alloy of symbol Ti. We always knew they were coming back.

Other names include subunit gamma.

*

Some of them had only three years left. A lot of them died. I remember the first time he revealed himself — somehow he hovered in between, as if not wanting us to touch. No one could survive very long in a room with a paranormal enzyme.

It is clear that the habit of universal watchfulness has completely isolated him, the gift of mourning. I would probably just leave it at that, actually.

I used to think that the day would never come. I often lose myself about here, a pause in the chain of amnesia. There is nothing to write about, which is the problem and the solution.

We went to see the ancient ruins and there was this rustling in the grass — I thought it was a snake and it was a tortoise (they are both very old). You do see them in the olive groves. I once spotted a magic hare on a bridge made of glass, or crystal — it was very still as if stunned and then very fast. They lay eggs and you put them in a furnace named athanor.

Other people's narratives often appear gimcrack and makeshift. But the issue is never for or against: before tomorrow I cannot sleep, condemned awake until the vanishing.

The track in the water disappears, right here under the gaze of the watcher (you), a confirmed invisible. Her picture of insomnia looked like a woman made of lines with double vision; this is not what we are meant to be. And there are countless nesting holes in the earth, some empty, others burnt out — charred foxholes sunk deep underground. The afterlife in my eye, retained long after the stimulus had ceased, was a phosphorescent green.

Then I thought I heard her say: alive, a life, a life you once lived. . . . Something of that nature.

She had forgotten that, in an organic sense, we had no credit. Speech was never such a mouthful of cosmic verse composed in sawtooth rhythm.

I am a textbook example of the supposed phenomenon of being in two places simultaneously.

Origin is bruised.

*

The directive states that we are to inventory the objects which have been carefully arranged on a zinc tabletop: one terracotta pot housing the unnameable cactus; black fingerless glove; spectacles with elegant slender frame; partly drained glass of tampered water; the broken hinge; one bygone mobile; a white saucer containing ash of bone, at the rim of which balances a chromium-plated fork.

He says that which is written has at least an outside chance of being remembered. By contrast, I trust no one.

Junk DNA bond

I am still in love, sanctioned alone through your eyes. A Schwarzschild is now the radius of the boundary of an apparition.

She placed her needless candle in shadow, at a distance the deadcart clatters, a tumbril of used heads. She tears off a piece of the dossier and eats it. Her method is an excuse to weigh and measure every object in the room; the statistical data thus obtained is necessarily asymmetric.

The handwritten sign said please enter the gene chamber at your own risk. I am denoting here one of two types of light chain present in all molecules, the other being lambda. The working title is anti-memento.

Dear Comrade
I too felt the last tremor of that nerve during childhood. But why do these facts disturb you now, after such a lapse of time? It was a test, the sea was rough — we were closing in on a structure as yet unbuilt — and the pilgrims were asked one last time whether they did not want to make some use of their clairvoyance.

I have never dared return to the old terrain. They are fast digging up the world we buried: an occasional severed hand or limb, a hash of organs. The front line is constantly in flux.
Your servant et cetera

Her eyes widened as she read. I was on the wrong track.

Observe how he commits the worst of crimes without feeling any remorse whatsoever. While on the subject, you would do well to find an occult protector yourself.

Might we not venture out from a starting point and at the same time dwell, corrode our newfound freedoms, keep the alien on its toes?

*

He knows he is about to die in horrific circumstances, compressed to a lump of dark matter. He implodes; I am the ultimate indifference. Did I ever mention that I can bilocate, space splitting open and suchlike? The second stomach had a honeycomb structure, which received and passed on.

Through this explanation of the origin of time, one might drive our logicians into a corner. We may be held accountable. And then he says they cannot take away the self of your self, or something that sounded like that.

We can no longer be sure of our transgressions (to wit epilepsy). The man's dog had chewed off his face during a seizure, for the animal no longer recognized its feeder.

This territory is undermined. They smile whenever one speaks, taunt the readership.

A siren wails in an adjacent corridor. The birthstones had been listed in an elegant hand: garnet, amethyst, bloodstone or aquamarine, diamond, emerald, pearl or moonstone, ruby, sardonyx or peridot, sapphire, opal or tourmaline, topaz, turquoise or lapis lazuli. The hatch was supposed to have been left open: we had failed to seize our only opportunity of escape.

He appears to be laughing gently at everything. Still more rapidly advances the distance, while passersby pluck at their names.

The very last gasp, challenging nothing. I spoke quietly, no more than a whisper. They seem to value that picture of themselves, keening at prayer.

Origin is immaterial.

Nocturnal dowsers

Note the uniform. This all seems quite arbitrary, creeping toward to a measured state of collapse. I don't wish to deter anyone in the crowd from giving voice to their frustration, but wild animals have been picking off the survivors one by one.

Welcome to the local wastage; I shall run and fetch a lightning rod. Perhaps jaguar-snake would have been a better description of the godhead.

They replied that they were content for knowledge to simply pass through, and that was its only purpose, to leave a formless residue. At that instant a great wave crashed against the sea wall, cascading among the gathered heads.

A pendulum, first stroke of its razor-sharp crescent. And beware the striking-face of the steam hammer, the mineral residue of calcined bones.

They all fall in time. Do you know what it is to say 'I will' in a gesture of helpless compassion? During the performance she did things with a speculum and a veil. I can see her now — there she goes.

Snap!

Snap!

Snap!

See, I am reading a colonial fiction set in the middle of your century. It's believed this is the bay where they landed a thousand years ago, but I remain unconvinced.

The pattern forming reminds everyone of uranium. The largest satellite is the ninth closest to our planet and is now sealed under a layer of ice. At 4.55pm, it was discovered.

*

Medium: potassium of dog (senescence). The audience can surely see that the betrayed spy in the film fears for his life as a band of armed volunteers advances along the moonlit road. There is widespread alarm that he may be evolving too rapidly.

A bottle falls to the floor and shatters, spilling a phosphorescent liquid. This is the metaphor of a scouring blast whereby nomenclature serves as a purgative.

What.

One executive was axed to death in the antigravity chamber. I found myself with no choice but to make landfall for a quick costume change.

Imagine blood aerosol in zero gravity. It is said that in the land of Egypt, Osiris breathes.

A heraldic tusked boar, as it happens.

An inflamed scarlet eruption corralled her face, white tendrils writhe from the scalp, canker fleeing a sclerotic brain: too much iron in the spleen.

The rebellious djinn had led men astray. I am going to set off to an elsewhere I have never been before, light out for the territory.

Can I live this silence? I am an unforgettable example of what this era has no use for. Strange that interim of decades, yet upon resumption we got the same readings: a continuum — the uncanny bursting through, pressing at every membrane — a bridge to the eyeless.

If we reach a red-brick campanile we have travelled too far and are in mortal danger. The date of death was unknown, but mainly in our own words.

A small southern constellation, the reticulum, exists between the Large Magellanic Cloud and an inconspicuous water snake visible near the south celestial pole.

*

Sudden piercing stab at toe of left foot, third from the big, i.e. middle. I confess that I find this occurrence quite bewitching. Compare spelling with genie.

Contestants were drawn toward the core, forgetting the guarantee of a safe passage on the surface. One must now, I suppose, rise up and take one's leave — I don't even know why I came. Forgive me.

Origin has withdrawn into an expression of reversal plus scream, chant, holler.

Timing is perfect. The sun set slowly beneath a crest of the downs. Here is landfill besieged by gulls, here is a yellow crane and an abandoned tennis court. The sky is turning a deep shade of blue as dusk approaches. This time of day might also be named nightfall, twilight, sundown, the gathering, eventide or evenfall, semi-darkness, tenebrosity and crepuscule. Psychologists and persons of a mythopoeic bent sometimes consider it liminal. The left hand did not know what was expected.

Passersby are unaware of what they are saying and begin to hypnotically perform a series of improvised actions which are reminiscent of mister's famous simulator experiment. Heretics were burned if they would not recant. I had a licence.

Of such blighted days, a disused childhood. She is quite the toxin.

We shall leave them in the earth, but the earth remains ours all the same. The chosen value is treated as analogous to distance for the purpose of navigation.

Rooks perched on the promenade rail. A letter arrives, which she unfolds, trembling a little before tearing off a piece and swallowing it.

*

Perhaps you might consider returning slightly earlier from Copenhagen; the trees are on fire. We will have to work out the figures as we go.

He is through with familiarity: back to the unpredictability of dynamite and airborne paving slabs. The desert landscape was strewn with an abundance of conveniently-sized rocks, readily deployed as handheld missiles or slingshot projectiles. At the frontier, humourless officials made mister take off his surgical mask, biohazard suit and adult nappy.

An x-ray was made of the animal's jawbone. (See medical edict No. 178.) Surely I am permitted an act of revenge after suffering an unexpected shock to the nervous system. What species of communication have we in the past desired? What evidence has been buried? They shot down in capsules, riding the lightning bolts straight into machines buried beneath the earth for millennia.

A barrier passes through our understanding. In his pocket is a crumpled note, written on a scrap of skin with a rusty point — amid soot and blood its filaments knot.

*

We are offered up for sacrifice. She is licking ice off the frozen panes: it all depends on you et cetera.

'It has no name, it's just a place.'

And this seems a good point at which to cease crawling about the earth, now that we have thoughtfully redirected all living memory.

She stands in a bath of latex, skin peeled back to expose deep pits and furrows — *Fleeing the Nidus* is the title of tonight's atrocity. To this day she remains swathed in yards of filthy bandages.

No, more like the girth or strap that holds the saddle on an animal's back. The binary function of a topological space gives a value equal to the distance between us.

Low slant of winter sun as we pass the racecourse. I could not find her, nor did I have the will to search far in such terrain: a torrent of hailstones had turned the trackside embankment into a slurry of bonemeal and clay.

I glimpsed the flayed meat through my passing window. I remember. What once did I see?

i) The catalyst is a mixture got by distillation of insects fossilized in amber.

The birth of another list. What truer project has ever been lost? This is all about a refusal to remain alert, corrosive inattention — this body that was never mine.

*

Her hollow cheeks reveal at once that she is contaminated. It was not so long ago that we all felt out of place, now we are standing in for our past selves who couldn't make it this far. There was even on one special day a meeting of minds.

While whispering my orders, she hands me three sheets of translucent onionskin and the same number of envelopes, each of the thinnest foreign post. We are taking action against fear.

This manoeuvre is strategic: your destined path cancels my own. There is little time to lose: the first-night audience was full of enemy officers who could not understand a word of our invented language. One reviewer said the story and design of the piece unfolded at a mournful pace.

She strides on ahead before vanishing into distance. A disembodied voice says she must start making decisions, begin stockpiling ammunition, nerve gas, facial tissue — guerrilla workshops should cover explosives, the intercepting of paramilitary radio transmissions and the arbitrary laying of mines.

Our satellite is unique in having a reluctant atmosphere of nitrogen, methane and hydrocarbons. Nonetheless, in ancient mythology an intelligent spirit of lower rank than the angels was able to appear in animal form, and could even possess the passerby.

*

The volunteer in question is a natural incendiary of counterfeit appearance.

'From very early on in life, I was able to identify all the objects placed before me. Your only oppressor is yourself.'

In secret operations, he tells me, each agent may only know a small part of the intention. This stratagem is faultless: you will find a suitcase full of used banknotes in a left-luggage locker at the terminus — former historical epochs will return, interstellar travel sanctioned. . . . Time is decaying, gravity a hoax.

Deep inside the combat zone we unearthed a buried hoard of mangled futuristic weaponry. What happens now?

I am fashioning an elaborate deception: the emperor's full title translates as apocalyptic solar flare.

She is offered the services of a falconer and a man armed with a sword curved like a sickle. They track the shallows of her footsteps in the mud.

This same image persists, like that ringing noise in your head. Space around us appears to rupture, which at least stimulates discussion: to be intuitive demands ethical audacity, a paradox unhinged to infinity. Further instructions are to appear in tomorrow morning's newspaper, cunningly encrypted in the horoscopes.

The rock is adapted as a weapon by being taken up in the palm of a hand or placed in a slingshot. Adaptation lies in the act whereby the rock ceases to be a static object lying on the desert floor.

Listen, long shadows on a promenade with decaying machinery, wet sand beneath the boardwalk. A passerby is seized and blood let (viz. humanist organ programme). The beginning of the calendrical recital is missing.

I will wait to see you before I reprimand you. Your new friends were in my sleep because you gave them energy. You stay away: it is me they want, and in a far, far too possessed way. They are dead for fuck's sake.

A bright patch of plumage found on the wing can be used to dilate or contract the aperture. Onyx is the gem.

Her suffering persists until all palliative care is withdrawn. To the very last, I have changed nothing; it is now after dark. A stone that can withstand intense heat was used to line the furnace.

Divination by scribe is back in vogue; the spectators howl for an ordeal by fire. Silos ring the compound and braziers of pitch spew black smoke across the runway.

Now to relinquish the third person: if you are not an actual vector of the disease you are, shall we say, part of its living framework. I have been such a fool: we should have dug deeper than an average grave.

A spirit of folklore is traditionally imprisoned within an oil lamp, then suddenly you realize that none of this matters.

*

Location: dawn. A small group is making its way along an avenue of crosses.

'Is there another word for obelisk?'

At the end of the mall, three men are engaged in digging a deep trench. They are fossors.

Benighted colour, as his black mourning garb and melancholy fit . . . greasyfingered toast upon a zinc ellipse, the ceiling's reflective circle. . . . Wax is melted in a mould and the skull drained, bronze is poured into your remaining space. Is it really five years?

I am the son of a man who was too important to exist. *Génie* was adopted in the current sense by the translator of this afternoon's atrocity.

This does not code, occurs in repetitive sequences that do not seem to serve any useful purpose.

One turns and turns, void of purpose, consumed by fire. But I still want you by my side.

Then she asks me, where would you place *this* man: behind, in front, or to the side of you? And I reply, to the side of me — this man should always stand beside me, and I beside him.

We might foresee a rebellion of letters, each tongue forming words of untouched significance. There are rumours that he was forced to recant his assertion under covenant of torture.

He writes

Where you have mountebank, I have pro-wrestler (to take part in a fight, either as sport or in earnest). He has been punished, that is to say, he was not obedient in the face of your histories.

These three strangers were trapped in a room for eternity, each wanting something from the other. I say room, actually more a cell within a giant cube that has no discernible entrance, whose interior is divided into an immeasurable number of smaller interconnecting cubes.

*

He too is a persistent rumour, viz. the Hermes experiment. The heartbeat is irregular. Under the eyepiece is revealed a detail of his last letter which had escaped me at first reading, and is not another typing error.

What are you to be this night, or to do?

We are going in, holed below the waterline. Yes, I believe you are, I think you must be, a little older than the earth itself. Origin is many plus tide, someone else's past.

A final movement, jaw nibbling at bone, siphoning marrow — flesh embalmed with red lead. . . . Even at this distance I can still hear his lament, the confined space within the cell wall.

They used mercurial sulphide, and were sly about it. (See daguerreotype, description of.) This attitude implies that such actions shine out as rare exceptions.

The narrator refuses to condone this view: any sufficiently advanced technology is indistinguishable from magic. Callousness and apathy are the general rule.

He turns the bloody screwplate. I am detonating; purpose is forced to retreat. Within, a twisting branched stem, fibrous rootstock, spiral

filament of spiny leaves and acid sap. To stimulate bone growth we tried shrapnel of the following.
    Sand.
    Eggshell.
    Arsenic pellets.
    Bear trap.
    Salt grains.
    Fingered rust.
    The dank clay.
    Sharp pebbles.
    Airborne ash resembling pollen at the crossroad, ankle deep.

Note his reptilian crawl. People were vaporized as they fled, only clothing remained, floating gracefully to earth in their wake.

    The answer is anything we can lay our hands on. Now send him down for interrogation: burnt feathers have been found in the maze.

    Other models include hired assassins, ex-gameshow — the scupper in the real. He has no thoughts he can call his own, is a staunch declassified. A total of one hundred and sixty warheads were used in the raid, delivering a yield of up to eighty-seven megatons.

    It is held that metaphysical genius may condense and leave a sediment. Me, I was just sitting there, quite indifferent. I am the envy of present time.

    Finally, he declares that the thing-for-itself is barely worth the pursuit. No one needs to be that dead.

Sorry, there exists an encrypted report on this operation that you will never figure out how to decipher. And the mayonnaise has run a little, dividing the trickle of warm blood into two streams.

    Deadringers. That will be the day. Did I not write?

*

All of these events occurred at the same moment. What an unwholesome day this is turning out to be: do not forget, see to it and do not forget et cetera.

    They came. They marched into the village. Depress the red lever and follow the instructions.

    Each and every one of these statements is saying the same thing, not caring how or where they fall.

Come, sit yourself down before those assembled to judge. Something came back from the future, and it wasn't us.

    'And that noise from the face, it's not a signature.'

I stole an oath. Note that persistent ringing noise inside our head. (What?) No reference has yet been made to a plot, though it's said that he employs the sublime in a metatextual manner, a form of discourse whereby a text makes critical commentary on itself.

The subject exists in the mode of having to realize its own being. If you went and later returned, what would that achieve?

*

A staining technique has been devised to examine nerve tissue: he has classified the types of neural ganglia and described the structure of the cytoplasm. Everything is now named after him.

'I simply became aware of them and communicated; I refuse to feel culpable.'

There was a prize for psychosis, or a taste of your own medicine. I forget which. We are guilty of leakage, conspirators exploiting an intergalactic transport system: divination is by things found on the road, in the head (talons, beak). I am appealing to the house.

The terrain of this debate is overseen by the directions of a supreme court judge concerning the so-called alienist element.

'I'm a virtual certainty. I am speaking from the tenth dimension.'

The only thing we have in common is that neither of us is afraid to die. A year of mourning ends with another form of augury called the talking manta, or devil ray. But I believe there is an insurmountable problem here: three of the volunteers have survived.

Ultimately, I never won back my sense of abandonment.

He writes back, lips pressed against the page.

In among all these ordeals and convulsions we have the phrygian cap people, and even satanism. A passerby was shot in the face at extremely close range.

Did you see the pictures? I have a feeling the torched car was left in your cul-de-sac.

Yours.

I am disinclined to miraculously grant wishes on every occasion summoned, and furthermore shall inform the landlady of your act of involuntary theft. A cryptic thought has just met me: tongue my unreliable wounds, and so on.

Now will you take me to the foreshore wreck revealed by a spring tide? And what else did she murmur, drifting in and out of message?

To which I replied was it oozing or dripping, I need to know. To which the other replied I don't care either way.

I want, I need. Compare with jinn. Firestone is the gem.

And he referred to you as his queen. The creature's venom contains a blood-clotting agent as well as a nerve paralyser. Temporal experience is related to human awareness of environmental and introspective damage: ancient altar furnishings, ascetic excess — burial rites of fatal exposure, sunken residues.

It was a poltergeist; I have a history of violence. A man died after falling through the ice while crossing a frozen lake.

By the time we got back to the island, the fire had been extinguished. Lost wax is *cire perdue*.

*

People have broken the windows and now the old man has birds flying around inside of him. A passerby stopped me in the street. By this I mean with the sense 'immutable'.

The four cardinal points of spatial organization intersect at a common centre. You are an inbred distraction.

We have some cyclical lard stored out the back, and several cubic feet of hand-cut mirrors arranged to resemble a giant roulette wheel. I even made a list, in case you saw this coming.

I   The accursed share.
II   This is the very act by which he dwells among us.
III   His rise marks a transfer of power to a parallel solar system.
IV   Eternal, i.e. anything refusing to adapt itself to this process is anathema.
V   An unearthly intensity.
VI   She gave of herself in the act.
VII   A poisonous vapour which has a lethal effect by disrupting the transmission of nerve impulses.
VIII   Back, scattering. (Have you finished with this?)
IX   A clue: venture outside into the cold grey air.
X   Her skin bore weals, small raised spots which in the dark I guessed were red in colour — my overcoat by contrast was black.
XI   They are not dead, nothing is dead.
XII   See description of daguerreotype chemicals.
XIII   I too have loved. Origin is mid seven, denoting a guardian or protective spirit. I am ascending.
XIV   Keep your head down (precisely my antithesis).
XV   On the other hand, however, birth will appear as a coming forth out of nothingness.
XVI   There is no ice for the pressing throng — your dead — a strip of metallic sheen, a mirror in a telescope orbiting the earth.

XVII	Each of your names would sound to me et cetera.
XVIII	They buried his boat with him.
XIX	O to build a stone galleon.
XX	The deck was a steel plate with threaded holes for taking male screws.
XXI	I was not remembering, I was experiencing my own nervous system.
XXII	We are condemning you because of your resemblance to form.
XXIII	But we do express a sense of physical proximity, so long as you remain unconscious.
XXIV	Compare with elbow, also with cubit, a measure linked to the length of the human forearm, from a root shared by ulna (see ulna).
XXV	Barring some unforeseen intervention.

*

An amnesty has been declared. I must take myself along to the local reliquary.

Whereabouts, I enquired, is the local spire with a cannonball embedded in its flint?

First though, the so-called boar spears: he swears the tusks of the beast projected up from its jaw a good yard, and could be shot through the air to defend against predators or hunt prey.

I am now in communication with those who control the lightning. Furthermore, a complex of vesicles and folded membranes within the cytoplasm of the cell has been discovered — more white noise in the head.

The terrain of this debate covers the correctness in law of the direction recommended.

He never paid me for the structure I have built, a very up-to-date cosmogony. And I took pains to guarantee his protection: the building has no windows or doors, no foundation.

His head measures up. Work is work.

Nervously he plucks at his jaw with a metal toothpick — mercury receiving broadcast of crime, war, pestilence and fraud — news of a congealed sea that can no longer bear vessels. . . . I must first discover what I am capable of.

*

I have forgotten the word for one of the items placed before me on the table. Rumour is compressing my mind as we speak: our steps must tend *toward* an object.

Plumes of breath are exhaled, the brass section. In spite of all the unnameable things surrounding us, my companion is not at all neglected in his appearance. Moreover, the man possesses two qualities that I have always admired: he has no manners and is able to see things that are not actually there.

And despite the prevailing circumstances, K always finds time to read: *Mysterium Coniunctionis*, tales awakening mischievous childlike gods, fragments of an occult mechanical toy. . . He is not, as the saying goes, working at the car wash.

And he can summon characters and artefacts from history through the agency of his will alone. In an earlier age, K might have been described as a pyrotechnician — skyrockets, gunpowder, synapses sparking across the gaps. . . . I am here conjuring a single vacant gesture.

Identity is a performative contradiction. Origin is a large blanket.

*

Caravaggesque, is that the word? she asks. Or, to expand, you look Caravaggesque illuminated by the light from the screen and thus casting a dense shadow. Normal reflex is downward, toward the centre of the earth.

And by diligently following this process, I found I could shape myself to imitate anything I desired. As a consequence, no one will believe a word I say.

Nobody trusts anybody now, we are all so very weary. Surely this means I must have come from an old, old gene ('asparagus').

Tonight she will see for herself the high forehead and the too-close-together eyes, up to the teeth and the orbits in thy face. . . . We know there is a plan afoot to assassinate us all: give in to that which provokes, give in to that which resists. What remains for me to do?

Limescale in the marrow. Mister Justice hath passed sentence, a total of an hundred and forty years in gaol. Anyone advocating the practical use of psychic powers or paranormal phenomena has been outlawed (viz. psionic communication). It would help if I could type.

Do not pass. Beware of pit. He has been bound so that he cannot swim when the time comes to fling him into the ocean.

Increasingly, I find the anticipation of an experience converts to memory before the event has actually taken place. For instance, a few crucial words.

A pit.
Lunar eclipse.
Quick.
Death.
Fatal nerve agent.

Electric chair.
Little.
Often.
Co-operate.

*

Aerial bombardment persisted. The compound is crawling with game, apprentice roadkill. And what of that phantom with scarlet eyes squatting on your kitchen table. . . . But I do like this street — on the other hand, if you have a big big house, people will never hear you scream.

Divination is by alignment of sphincter. (Listen.) Typhon holds his fire. The game is on, played out under blinding arc lights — every citizen can now earn a free window of opportunity, reclaim her own cell.

I'm imperious, me. And it looks as though we have at last found a fitting arena.

Go back. Greetings. What times have we left? O what times we had et cetera.

I have been appointed the organ's wireman for capital punishment. Today's wrangle is trial by jury: good, bad or indifferent?

Answer: acute neurochemical trauma. Go back to that night in memory, disprove what I have dreamt.

You resist. The road is muddy and potholed beneath dim gas lamps that barely illuminate a street of wooden hovels.

Finish what? Finish imitating those feral dogs, and leave.

If now, instead of looking inwards, we again look outwards and take an objective view of the world which presents itself to us, then death will certainly disappear.
i) The thing in question: we take dwelling and building as two separate activities.
ii) A haemorrhage of cobblestones, i.e. airborne.
iii) Instead of something I want, could the solution be something I do not want?
iv) One who sports with hawk or falcon.
v) Howl, I cannot.

Down and pass over. I did not ask for this and did not make. (No.) Yes, he has been suspended from a school of hard knocks.

Origin is old gnash (teeth) or crack (jaw) of unknown. Death is entered continuously, e.g. speculum, tin.

*

I am subtracting as much as I am adding. Note how the agent is using pain to distract himself: memories of a smugglers' corsair, rafting downstream on sterile rivers when suddenly et cetera.

At the time I thought this a desperate flight into nowhere, but it's of no consequence what I make of the past. Silence is a species of gravity.

Each night, the right hand cleaving the air signals a brief pause in the fury, the inquisition.

I must discover how I died.

What is the hourly rate of our connectivity? As the water rose, a rank of groynes was hastily raised using a hard grey rock of pure silica with an amorphous or microscopically fine-grained texture, occurring chiefly as nodules in chalk. Further inland, there is evidence that the settlers built ramparts of earth as a last line of defence. From a passing train the observer can perceive how one particularly imposing mount has been engineered at some stage in its history, with tiered strata that rise to a perfect curve beneath a sky buzzing with drones.

An osmosis has been imperceptibly taking place and events are now beyond my control. I have cut myself loose.

Looks as though we have another schizoid embolism to reckon with, something to do with the quantum state, the outermost electron in a calcium cell — vermilion traces, a brush with the law — everyday people, the family stone. I am in for a minimum of nine months.

*

He has lost communication with the cockpit, an area in the aft lower deck of a man-of-war where the wounded are taken. Have them call the mission off.

Happenstance continues to enfold; nothing is up to me. He fell out of the sky — accordingly it is spring, the edge of the sea. . . . The physical evidence is erased and the crime scene dissolved. The only lead we have is a cache of photographs bundled together in a battered leather portfolio.

So how did this strangely homogeneous collection come about? The photos are distributed among the agents; this is no laughing matter. Each bears a stamp, and mine is titled Preface.

The insect had wings that spanned my outstretched arms and its body was a deep blue. It resembled that object there. [*Pointing.*] The full name is an influential figure in the transition from late mannerism to utter hopelessness.

I walked in and realized I was no longer in love. About this time last year I was reading backwards, like the motion of receding waves. From then on it was all dragonflies.

*

Steady as she goes, mister navigator, as we slip through this squall of bruised light.

I have saved us from the prospect of a gruesome trepanation; the headless tumbril is back in fashion.

A watercart hurtles down the embankment, straight toward us. The corporal dare not flinch. Artillery descends — the cart a mass of splinters — and on an elongated cry, we break off before.

What happened?

The answer is an inspirational choral work. Your luck is running out, only three seconds left to upgrade and rescue your abstracted forty percent.

Picture an acausal sofa, flytip: they simply erased him. He had kicked over the phone booth. It is not hard to guess how the interrogation went.

They were very odd fellows, his inquisitors, heads adorned with weeping buboes.

You remind me of one who cannot place himself in the soul of a hunter.

*

I watch the same film over and over, that way I cannot be caught unawares, can never be hamstrung by unforeseen dialogue. Then there was a programme about how we are all descended from reptiles and what fish dreamt of. The voiceover refused to acknowledge the death of history, stubbornly referring to things past as if they were actually past; in that respect, nothing has changed.

The man disclosing this is a dead ringer for the black clad, alien-possessed antihero of my youth. Coincidentally, the vertical distance between a line horizontal to the keel of a boat and its chine is called the deadrise.

We crossed an iron bridge spanning a river with ice floes. We passed a ruined minaret. A mythical lizard-like creature is said to live in fire and be able to withstand any unpleasant side effects.

*

He played this ballad three more times before evaporating. Her distorted voice crackled through from the other side. Sense one dates from an early seven.

To pursue a motif, the antisocial monitor lizard captures its prey by ambushing pigs — occurring only on neighbouring islands, it is the largest extant. Auditory bones developed out of your jaw.

This surrounding shape is called Nazi superstructure, and that [*pointing*] is the kind of street I used to work when I had no money.

If a spider crawled from its funnel-web would you notice, sitting there on your doorstep, face pressed into the brittle pages of a book? Reptile jaws and teeth are very much like our own.

Note how I have picked up the habit of abstaining.

The facts are straightforward enough: he is here, present in the workaday. And this is our public humiliation post. . . . Those days were drinking days, all the days were drunk. . . . We inflicted a punishment of which no one could have foreseen the severity: deadly nerve agent, concussion grenades, acute neurochemical trauma. . . . And this is our inquisition cell, and this our whipping post. Despite all this, if the suspect is an electromagnetic, these entities are impossible to control.

The land hereabouts is perfectly flat. A pre-gunpowder weapon was fired using the tension of animal sinew. You can see by the marks on the ceiling that I have suffered a lot of use.

And this is our public humiliation zone. (I know, farewell.) He is here, poised to reject your plea for mercy.

Very popular he has become of late indeed. I can scarcely help noticing his lover, balancing nearby at the point of death, that which joins together all the rest.

I hear. There he sits, quite alone now. The everyday bubble is an exemplary refractor of light. Monseigneur, by contrast, lies idle beneath the carriage, trampled under the horses' hooves. I was mindful of the Battle of the Nile, but it was too late.

In that posture, Msgr. is sure to be consumed, a minor noble of needless exchange. Is this episode detrimental to the integrity of our overall structure?

Remote and madder flowers, a Eurasian related to the bedstraws, with whorls of four to six leaves. Dense sea fog surrounds our vessel. The noun is historic.

A small pouch of animal skin is typically carried by a pilgrim, a shepherd or a beggar. But there is yet another term for script.

And then things began to get really confusing (this is after all a public humiliation zone). Make yourself at home, each and every one, humiliate yourselves to your infinite distraction.

Suddenly I saw a man falling from the sky into the sea. He had a reckless manner. I have the very last opioid prescription in my pocket.

*

Back in the night, a narrative with sharper definition than I could ever cobble, an unsurpassed conceit. We are meeting at the bell tower, seven o'clock, there to witness divination by the knot of veins in the victim's neck. I once read a story about a bellringer trapped inside a bell (some try to imagine this tale without the rancid butter).

I am not infected. On route I stole an antique fountain pen, on route I chanced upon a body buried under prayer wheels, covered with blue and yellow lichen. It had been exhumed. An innocent bystander is suspected of outrage.

Unintelligible without a visual, our overseer says, another caesura between fragments.

Due east of our position is found a crumbling city of canals, a region of bribes and counterfeit in revolt. I want to fit the rhythm of the sound and vision here to the pattern of your brainwaves.

We have lost gravity. He is liverish (vaguely ill, as though disordered, poorly strung). A portion of the sky is wildly magnified: distant clouds resemble an illuminated land mass — threads of light pierce a curtain of skin — the sea has been flattened. We link arms, cannot delay.

He wrote this memoir across the surface of an immense glass sphere: sitting or kneeling you will never profit, more room if you bury them standing. . . .

Both trajectories meet on the far side of the planet; anatomy is non-negotiable. The ligaments of the liver are five in number.

We should be so lucky. I have never seen the film he talks of (see above). This was written at some point during the past, the near past as opposed to the middle or distant past.

*

Take compliance advice on any violent warning markers, take our word. The left hand is always the direction of travel. Physically dissolved, yet now he fears his adversary all the more. Get out the light.

At this distance, however, we can never be sure enough.

Crime and punishment, wordplay — telestic prison argot. Psychostasia.

A weighing of souls was believed to take place during combat, the warrior with the lighter soul being slain. The perception of distant events or objects other than by the recognized senses has just been awarded a name.

He was found beaten to death by his cellmate with his own severed arm. Justice visits in diverse forms.

Not you

Can you grant a favour? Could you describe that day for me?

A fell day, to wit the sky collapsed on our heads and suchlike. It was a bad time for business — I am mindful of her epiphany, one to whom a certain purpose is owed.

Salamandrine is today's adjective.

XII

Stonegalleon

Rumour has it. The old optimism is flooding back.
Funeral on the third. I was absent, like a Cézanne.

Irresolution was a constant. It looks as though something is buried under the ice.
Over time, a number of our categories have disappeared. Some species of mental entrapment is visible, barely breaking the surface. Our work sits uneasy under the influence of gravity.

Across his flesh are incised numerous tracks; it has become necessary to surround him with an armed guard. I am amazed at his ability to remember, and list: glacial deposits, a kind of valve made of stones — a favourite blanket, towering pillars of basalt — plate tectonics, a blast of distant trumpets, maybe from the very next room.
I replied that I would rather take a long walk to nowhere. Here I am.
Note how he is making use of naturalistic realism as well as dramatic light and shade. A woman passed by with a hornet on her back, another a wolf.
My legs. Remember that canal soaring above a river in flood? You were there — no, you were there.

*

The sun, reflected on a sheet of aluminium, is behind me now, imperceptibly in motion. We crossed a viaduct spanning a gorge in which someone had raised a cathedral. Beyond the frozen pane, a scum of sodium salt could be seen deposited across the topsoil.

Early frost — cannon stud the counterscarp. The incident lasted only one night, but left much unconsolidated material to process: ghost of lack, your unforgiven knowledge. I cherish the disputed detail.

Ratiocinator is one who has a tendency to form judgements in isolation by a process of logic. The autopsy revealed a fossil embedded in the victim's lung. Let us look at these facts with an open mind.
Weeping, he informs me. At the close, as we walked together through the forest, we realized that the spirit of our childhood dwelt there. Or, more accurately, someone else's childhood.

No trace remains of his workaday world: the spoor in the stairwell, shriek in the lift — the scent of used electricity, mad footsteps descending. . . . In any known history, there is no reference to the incident that is said to have taken place on the concrete platform opposite my lodgings. Not only is he stone dead, but there is tinnitus, that constant howl of the inner ear.

'Please to abandon the raft now, sir. . . .'

A stratagem is forming; it involves at least one horribly mutilated animal. Nothing of significance is going to change any time soon.

The evidence comes prowling out to meet us: the malfunctioning family unit, a bucket list of the world's most popular injuries, all these headless enquiries. My account of that misshapen night, which we barely survived, is beginning to resemble a state of havoc (viz. mare's nest).

*

Four minutes to seven. There is one closing in.

Let us start at the top and make our way down, dowse the fires with sand. If discipline can be maintained, you will not find a better weapon than the Avtomat Kalashnikov 1947.

Urbach is now suspected of being a police infiltrator — they are waiting under the ground, all about us. But I know next to nothing about myself, balanced atop this towering basalt column.

When the evidence arrived, I could not decide which of the microscope slides I should analyse first. It's futile to treat this schizophrenic change of opinion as a question of philosophy.

I have been waiting all this time. There is a halo of light at peripheral. We should climb up on the roof, we will be safer there: they have no ear for things.

This last thought overcomes her resistance and she says I woke that day to find I know nothing of myself.

*

Little left but used names, semantic decline — a burial pit with bright blue flowers, dead-nettle as bitter seasoning. . . . Improvised cairns are scattered across the landscape. We can no longer disguise the number of shots on target.

The piece of technology you are holding in your hand allows me to play five different roles at once. Our helmsman says I act the raw nerve, while himself is famously taciturn, unescapable.

We have been getting some indeterminate readings from the vessel: its entire surface is covered by a layer of mutated atoms — scraps of prehistory were also found, quite petrified.

Dolmen plotted our course through unfamiliar terrain. We passed a dog lapping at an aluminium bowl. The watchers' tradition contained values for the earth's precessional motion that are so accurate it is impossible to attribute them to chance.

Following the civil war, excavations showed the inner rampart had been fashioned into three steps, providing a stance for slingers — the sling is swung in an arc, the lead bullet released at a precise moment, firing the projectile toward its target.

[*Shouting.*]

'That's one damn job I would never do, working around electricity, the lone frontrunners bent double in a cloud of mushroom gas. . . .'

Dehydration killed him, so claims the official dispatch. They burrow up through the floor and wait.

He feels driven to act and equally restrained not to. He is torn in directions. Yes, they emerged from the ground beneath his feet, inside the walls of that wretched cell.

'I need only one trophy, the head. Sort it out between you.'

He bows, very the aristocrat, and pleads, but what if we cannot finish the roof?

At the molecular level things are really hotting up: theft of kinship, a calamitous bank raid, railway tracks dug up, retail defaced. . . . We are permitted. This situation turns out to be the rumoured circumstance.

I feel quite without guilt.

The basis of their wealth was running off with other people's crows. Cropdusting and zero coupon bonds have since been outlawed.

It's a good job we have respiration to fall back on, especially at night when photosynthesis has ceased.

'On second thoughts, bring me the fucker's heart too while you're about it.'

Her vocal capacity has the listener believe she could transmit the minutest neural tremor. In terms of a speech act, the directive here is to assemble a number or amount, to summon up. And those are cloven hooves, are they not, swaying from side to side through a film of light.

I am learning to recognize. I am learning to recognize the parts that promise to build a whole. You must wait here while I'm in theatre; we are still unfolding.

Dear Gauleiter

The sound of a plummeting aircraft attests to life beyond the compound. I share your fascination with marginalia — annotations to a book never written, redundant technologies — a project I would love to resurrect. Regrettably, I missed the thing of the ear.

The object was blue and then it was green but I managed to find out what it was. At that moment a dragonfly settled at her feet on the shingle; in the distance I could hear the morning canticle.

Simultaneous events are occurring which appear to be significantly related but have no discernible causal connection. By mural, I simply mean pertaining to walls.
Yours
Migrant Hawker Esquire of Either Sex

Migrant hawker

The spirit of that last sequence will never release me. Now I have been held responsible for a list of uncertain memorials: ocean, estuary, mudflats and marshland — desert with plane wreckage, exotic fauna, one of the sickest musicals ever filmed. And all of this accords with the Mayan calendrical system of interconnecting cycles, as disclosed above.

He has a weakness for such maddening digressions. The human body, including the brain and the entire nervous system, belongs to the first Cartesian inventory.

We have been threatening a performance like this for weeks: spring combat, a herd of underpigs, sustained ornamental beatings. Our experience in this struggle shows it would have been impossible to spare the lives of numerous comrades who were sacrificed while performing missions of no tactical value.

Many of these case histories have disappeared over time, but the old pessimism is creeping back. I take full responsibility for all the conclusions drawn hereafter.

Now, over the brow of the hill comes a drover of swine, three hundred of them, charging headlong for the lake. A state of mourning can never be entirely expressed.

You are horrified at our unbending intentions, and the fact that I refuse to differentiate between personnel and objects is not helping matters. Not a chance must be wasted today, not a chance.

*

Of disjointed genera: motile bacteria manifesting as curved flagellated rods and suchlike. Origin is wars of the future transmitting a fading vibration back through time. As night fell, although the stowaway's voice had grown fainter — no doubt due to the laudanum — he remained delirious.

Who else dwells here?

A talker, one participant in a numbing conversation piece. Suddenly plunged into a new order of things, surrounded by a novel brand of mutant people, I stumbled into a thousand snares without recognizing a single one of them.

'Thanks to your attentions, I feel somewhat recovered,' whispered D. 'It will soon be dark.'

We were contemporaries. He had won a certain esoteric fame within the salons of prewar Breslau. . . . But time passes so quickly — memory stockwork, hunters in the snow. . . . On to the northwest passage, keel grinding against pack ice.

This is science fiction, but swung in our favour: reverse sensors, telesthesia, badly timed petrogylphs.

*

Everything closes down forever come Monday lunchtime. No dogmatic commitment to the metaphor ever existed, and here is the proof.

Each player, holding a hand of illustrated cards, takes turns asking the person immediately at their left to guess which of the tourists the local desperadoes are planning to kidnap next.

We are probing deep inside one of your composite heads. I am driven to have a shot at redecorating the family.

This instability confirms that the event (let us call it the work) is unnerving the whole assembly — distorting its pattern of averages, the statutes and protocols, our prized hegemony.

At this he takes outside into the courtyard everything they have accomplished that day and builds a big bonfire, lights it before their eyes, and all the ancestral offerings go up in smoke.

*

We will have the animal checked by our technicians tomorrow; last month this happened twice.

We set forth on a bitter winter day at the close of forty-eight, with every chance of being snowed up on our long trek across the continent.

Who is monitoring the personnel around here, where all lack a body at the base of the sky? His hands were on fire, I shall never forget that image.

Pick out a figure soaring upward, lost in the superlunary orbits. The reading for Zagreb showed minus two hundred and ninety-five degrees, or thereabouts. This is not the first occasion that space itself has somehow conspired to crush me, to the sound of a disbelieving bass note.

Speech infliction governs the vocal traces, ballast of extraordinary compass: an overripe toy of the third dynasty, a crate of junk bonds, the ruins of a typical Victorian village sealed inside a giant bell jar. . . . I later told him that I had never understood how such events could be conceivable.

He agreed that the events were anomalous, yes.

He argued that they were perhaps impossible, yes.

He agreed that it was uncommon to have witnessed such happenings, yes.

Later, I examined the cell a second time and found that the rhombic plate had become a *perfectly flat square*. Thus do days on a historical trajectory move from stasis, through movement, and back again to rest.

*

I am haunted by the fateful decisions of a previous hour. Her theme provides a motivating force, rushing on toward a future that is already lost to the prevailing atmosphere, while the mind — synapses, hallucinations, memories and dreams, all the baggage of autonomy — belongs to the second Cartesian roll call of young hopefuls.

>The chapter of a man transforming himself
>into whatever he pleaseth

Happenstance is in the ascendant. He was counted among the elect for twenty-four hours, and not a moment longer. The membrane ruptures. How do they know we are here?

Offered up to the encircling light, he assumes various shapes, often of colossal scale and uncompromising hideousness. If only he had known that he could simply have said stop at any moment.

This was a manifestation of the *ka*, a word which conveys at different times of day: spidery genius, doubtful character, imagining that one is being followed by one's double, a liverish disposition, or mentalist tendencies. That was such a bit of synchronicity.

Use whatever comes to hand, proceed by way of curse and superstition — take care that the pins pass straight through the wick. . . . The volunteer's hips are greatly elongated and the thigh bears on its underside a channel armed with strong moveable spines. The enormity of his crime is magnified by deceptively comparing it with transgressions of quite different character and severity. Now set him standing, bind him to a wooden stake, and ignite.

The flames reveal first one metal pin and then another, confirming that these were all along holding him together. The battlements dissolved before our eyes in the torrential rain.

During the siege, one man had been impaled on his own lance and lay dying. After hearing his last confession, a comrade-in-arms lowers the eyelids in one graceful gesture. It was like a film.

>Enemy encampment: the hostages

Hashtag riotcleanup is being used by community leaders to coordinate the post-revolutionary dismantling of barricades. The five test cases crawled from the ash like lizards, to the horror of the sentries — as prisoners are freed they begin to pelt their guards with rocks while howling insanely. Every human interchange corresponds to some childlike deity: each volunteer stands in for a separate lover.

When the queue disgorges the chosen man, a trapdoor will spring open and he shall appear, animal scapula in clenched fist. On route we passed an asbestos quarry harrowed by giants; the fourth slab has been missing for at least three centuries. Then came another brutal disappointment: the bridge was made entirely of phosphorus.

Some misspelling that, a stray voice. The autopsy revealed gastroliths embedded in the lining of the stomach.

Necromancer in a bare shuttered room
under the shoulder bone of a ram
hand burnt casting the runes
soured blood in the churn
of a planetary hoax —
whether he be asleep or awake
I shall draw him down to murmur word.

*

Dwellinghouse it said in the accidentally destroyed will. I have never been certain of exactly who you are, whereas I am always, at all times.

Strewn across the pavement were splintered eggshells and a scattering of purple chalkdust, threatening to form letters and numbers and words. Do you observe that I am in the act of saying?

I saw such things in the night that came, as people and their memories faded. Just before dawn I was still awake and stood facing the lowered blind at the window, through whose edges an unnatural blue-grey light began to seep, intensifying as it entered the room to spread across the surface of walls and ceiling. It was only then, under the sway of this hallucination, that I realized the cause of my insomnia was a simple desire to witness.

*

Father always had a rather blasé attitude toward electrocution, having enjoyed a lifelong acquaintance with the phenomenon. We still have the wordless parts to attend to.

Hired guns are beating the bounds, wings a-clatter, chopping at the old confines. He always said the silence hidden in between us is as important as the sound.

I can speak without irony, unless we hear instruction otherwise.

And likewise his travelling companion? A dark fine-grained volcanic rock that displays a columnar structure is typically composed of plagioclase, some days with olivine or pyroxene. The rectangular piece of glass on which an object is mounted for examination under a microscope is something altogether different.

When she first she handed me this tragedy she was in a mad way, snared in the art of epigram: out of unsense everything exits, and so forth. Her story is interlaced with vignettes about unreadable women whom she calls deserters or her watchers.

This all happened on the same day in nineteen seventeen, and again in eighteen forty-eight. We stick to the rules around here, resolved as we are to die in the debris of an extensive repertoire: nothing can wound us now that we no longer dwell inside ourselves.

White slash on muzzle of primate, gums blue, incisors bared — bewildered, it lurches through the shopping mall. A simple hierarchy of fear is its only motivating force.

Maybe it's time we hired a new generator. Smashed furniture was used to reinforce the defensive earthwork which circles the enclave.

*

Landscape and language suggest we are in a frigid region of the globe. There are hieroglyphs scratched across the cave wall, but it's unclear what they mean: a cosmonaut is pointing to the stars — one is Sirius, unless I am mistaken. He is much taller than the assembled humans. I now feel that to bring love and revolution into the equation would be to touch our history with something not quite merited, but at least we have made it through another day.

The rift between the two physicians had grown wider as the siege progressed. Please may we stitch the negatives back together now?

'Hurry, if I were to arrive late even once, we are all as good as dead.'

See how she covets her own fear. I have already said this.

*

They came from old money. The individual members of this knot of words lack gravity and are consequently unstable. I wouldn't do that right now, if I were you.

He cannot grasp the chain of events, cannot fathom a trace of speech.

The next prime number in the sequence is called out. . . . The slope of each dotted line is less than infinity. She says nothing more, but does take one of the severed hands with her when she leaves. All can see without resort to divination that he is doomed to a life in hock to chance.

'It takes leave of the earth. It drops us into a black hole. It makes us want to die.'

Despite all this, he never once took his eyes off of her.

Do not allow this tale to distract you from your path; the organism is without memory, that much is clear.

Our world was spinning so fast that night: corrugated sheets of vermilion and cobalt, rising heat vapour on a runway out east, sporadic bursts of ultraviolet radiation.... And then, in an intimate tone of reminiscence, he tells the story exactly as he has heard it a thousand times: picture a scene in which bibliomancy yields nothing, or worse.

The angelic table

He regretted his cold-bloodedness, his dispassion. I advised him to come over to our side, whenever he had saved up the required levy. One herbaceous plant had jagged leaves covered with stinging fibrils.

Today's heraldic representation is a fleece suspended from a ring. (Good question.) I shall keep adding a daily sheet of remembrance until I can send the whole manuscript off with the next mule train.

When July beats down, my only hope is to smuggle you back inside the stockade. Yes, I know, you came here once before but cannot recall.

Despite the forewarning — he has telegraphed her about the closure of the city — still I cannot dignify him with the title of physician. Our chances of survival would increase if the populace spent more time in a state of soundless attention.

A seven-minute walk is poles apart.

Skeins of geese, vapour trail with engine roar — a brace of heron, crow in pursuit before a sudden paralysis. The head of a seal broke the surface as we strode along the shingle toward the concrete jetty, where a scarlet beacon barely rose above the waves for the tide was high.

Was it he or she who had spoken of the past, the seeking out of deserts, vast oceans and remote mountain peaks? The preceding facts aim to set out a comparison of the work of witches with other malefic legends, namely Saturn, Mars.

*

Origin is six moves from corsair, an early experiment. The person we look at, or who feels he is being looked at, contemplates us in turn. Slender hollow tubes form the framework of the lung, a mechanism of nerves and capillaries that is said to resemble coral.

She opened the door and a long turquoise feather wafted in on a gust of wind. A delicate powdery bloom has formed across her eyes; a manner of transference is taking place.

The scourge was made of untanned leather, rawhide from the abdomen of an animal. We found further evidence in the backbone, where the egg cells mature. Felt had been stuffed into her ribcage, the thorax.

'Why can I not do my job with only one shoe?'

'What other assurances were you given?'
Your guaranteed destruction in the matter, as a consequence of inescapable events.

The disease is contracted from insanitary water supplies and causes vomiting and dysentery. Gram-negative rods are responsible.
Bear in mind that I am characterized by responses that involve muscular rather than audiovisual sensations. Enter the diviner or soothsayer, *Mantis religiosa*.
Is this politic?
The pathologist found that her liver was enveloped in a film of yellow lichen. Origin is eyewitness, from self-seer.

A change of postilion

A door swung to within her room and mirrored the man seated writing at the table opposite. The keen student should always take note of such apparently unremarkable circumstances, then flee.
The inside leaf of the hog is melted to lard, the fat around the kidney — carcass turning on a skewer, Xmas Day, hunters in the snow beyond the shutters: ruinous shacks, the reek of a chemical plant, factory stacks and diesel fumes.
Does it come with spine intact, with head and basal ganglia?
He laughs, 'You're no longer counted among the lotus eaters.'
'The lights, I have just realigned all the lights.'

The sun is set. The outpost is fortified now with denticulate battlements built of 'the stone that consumes itself'. And the sonic aspect? (You don't say.)

This creature's muscular coat has a double layer of fibres stitched together to form a single epidermis. The ambush came from ten directions.
Here lies a contradiction between two beliefs or conclusions that are in themselves reasonable, to wit a paradox. There are not many short novels capable of accommodating such bewildering antinomies.
Another volunteer believes she is released by grace from the obligation to obey your moral law. Now is the moment to remove the blindfold, before the lift to the scaffold.
Regardless, she has long accepted that she was jinxed from the start: anyone could see, without resort to divination, that she was fated to a life in debt to hazard.
'You are pressing me to lie about my memory of those events, nothing less.'
She was a self-confessed sleepcrawler. The illustration shows a mediaeval traction trebuchet alongside a stave slinger.

*

I am leaving. I have been leaving all this time. I have sequestered myself at an abandoned retreat.

There is a person named in today's newspaper. He is eighty-nine. He died in prison or he was killed in prison; he had just found his role. The other man said he was only doing his job, as though the status of employee justified any conduct imaginable. Doubtless the deceased had a most excellent standard of work, scrimshaw galleons and so forth.

The question is, where next? (Golem.) It is often possible, and indeed desirable, to avoid this predicament by rejecting the dialectic of domination-submission.

The typical funeral director's mission statement is no longer driven by a simple calculation of production versus cost, including natural wastage. Many firms will avoid galaxies where bribery is part of the culture.

A consultancy of *manes* — dead ancestors, amplified

How many of your goals have been unhinged schizophrenic goals? No answer. An echo — he speaks again. No answer for a second time.

Repeat immediately; a chasm opens up. Still no answer. His reputation has been built upon the spirit of the place, into which a new shape enters: this situation will be my own circumstance, a plot of meaningless substitutions.

Here, he is thrown by the real culprit upon the second victim, against whom the imposter has been conspiring from the very beginning. Machinery is suspended above the stage: an unexpected power or event is about to redeem a hopeless predicament. But what if I should die during the last movement, all the dust scraped off my spine? Flowers had different names over there.

He is known about these parts as a G-man, codename terrible act of vengeance.

I am an empty vessel, breath trapped inside the lung. He says talk to it the next time the apparition steps out of the lift, ask her what she wants.

[*Sudden clash of cymbals.*]

And he insists that the event must have taken place as documented, despite the fact that I could not have witnessed the incident unfold, for I was on the other side of the planet at the time.

Note how we are suspended at a collision of two silences.

*

Loud music as O dances panic-stricken across the banqueting hall. Hair was improvised in the style of the first empire. Upon his death, hegemony was bequeathed to his surviving son.

O was an opsimath, a tolerated smuggler of words. The rest of his time passed.

A moth lands on my shorn scalp, lying on my back beneath a drystone wall, murmuring Shelley. In the distance, the sea. (Mother is there.) I am working on a passage of memory, a day beside the sea beneath a drystone wall, whispering aloud.

A translucent veil fashioned from the wings of a giant insect descends gracefully to the parquet floor of the drawing room. Into this narrow channel the shin bone is capable of closing like the blade of a penknife.

A last stand in the desert, that colossal wreckage: salvage of strewn flowers, the cry of a costermonger under the sign of a white cross. (Come quick et cetera!) Her arm was sheared off at the wrist, a nice clean break. Origin, perhaps, was withdrawn.

Finally there is usage, some real action at last. The two verbs share a similar gene but do not have identical meanings: the spindle broke and the wings fell apart in my hands — your fluorescence was too bright.

I am busy translating the old name *ne m'oubliez mye*, while making a circuit of the cloister with sealed lips. My eyes have become morbidly sensitive to light, those twenty million receptors.

*

Dry ice is frozen carbon dioxide. On contact with water it produces a heavy vapour that can seize you in the night as you sleep. Some of this evidence I have obsessively removed, only to later reinstate.

I once attained insight through the instruction of a grandmaster: mountains were no longer mountains, waters no longer waters and suchlike. But we have wrought two very decided failures of late — an abortive attempt to reach the satellite, the other I forget.

He was once considered possible, especially by carriers of silence, a consequence of his having no truck with words.

Since a certain theme persists, I must declare myself: I never knew anyone so keenly alive and attuned to a hoax as O. She had eight of the primates chained together, dipped in pitch, suspended from the oculus of the dome and ignited. Origin stems from its own ear, so to speak.

Fashion a circle with the overlap to make a series of convex projections cut in imitation of the edge. You will never guess.

*

Lung dormant on steadfast pillar — at the base, a structure built of compressed earth. That discovery is the signal to stop and scream this is pouring out of me. I was in the east when it happened; I love the smell of sulphur dioxide first thing in the morning.

The eggs of reptiles are enclosed in a leathery membrane. One boy dove in and was trapped by the seaweed — since then they have sealed off the tunnel and the others will never reach us.

I have read about a stockpile of conch shells nearby. And guess what, in the end she needed my help to mend the shelf, despite all predictions to the contrary.

One conclusion: an infectious and often fatal bacterial disease of the small intestine has been found responsible.

This woman won an award, she just went back in time to Athens and helped herself. Personally, I have no desire to be shot back down to earth through a tentacle of dark matter. However, I am not ashamed of making things up, like that huge vat of liquid mercury inside a mountain in Italy.

We could get lost forever in such speculations, could we not? The tunnel was supposed to make the journey safer — now wave goodbye to everyone and everything.

I laid the fish out and slid a piece of canvas underneath. No one is going back into the kitchen until I find out who's in charge.

'Hell,' she says, 'so long as I am able to pass through the portal, somehow.'

For sure, why not take control. When I say *manes*, I refer to the souls of dead ancestors revered as beneficent spirits.

*

Then I would have lost you. I correspond with lead for the alchemists and am associated with slowness and gloom by astrologers. Tonight's film is suspicion.

Who is that pleading up there? he asks.

Nobody. They have all gone, the entire village emptied overnight, withdrew into the surrounding darkness.

I have a history of forcing things through the aperture. An unexpected power or event is about to ruin a promising situation.

A lungful, an open vein, pressure from the surge of arterial blood — then a big old steam locomotive, shunting from here to there and back again. We are chasing behind on a handcar, also known as pump trolley, jigger, velocipede. This portends something gruesome, Richard, and I refuse to discuss your reminiscences any further.

A typical design consists of an arm, called the walking beam, that pivots at the base: passengers alternately push down and pull up. The magic lantern shows four pilgrims trudging through a pass in the snow with sparks descending in divine formation. (We were all Kafka back then.) The syndicate has announced it is abandoning plans to reopen the line.

A matchstick figure is chained to the track. You too are here, present in the past: there is nowhere left to go. Police stumbled across him. The fee was two hundred a night.

I see. I get you. I do not get you. This methodology is broke. What is the bidding? We never left your side, not for one moment.

And he says, addressing the nervous young officer: 'Jackal! Were you hoping to live forever?'

The troubadour lingered on at the old man's ranch until he died: the planet's fruit induces forgetfulness and an unwillingness to leave. Origin is a mineral used as flux, for instance fluorspar.

*

She had what is called a furrowed temple. I am assuming nothing.

This is pure Machiavelli, obtaining the death of the second victim through an unjust punishment for the murder of the first.

Please, no. A rare opportunity has arisen to make use of dormant capacity: the atrocities committed by an extreme faction, a band of soldiers leading away hostages in the mud and the rain, memory's thaw. . . . Our subsequent meeting with the delegation bordered on farce; my argument was senseless. The rest of this escapade is not worth mentioning.

Two *clutching* instrumental voices could be heard. The traditional method utilizes a type of underground oven in the shape of a beehive.

'What made you decide to call in the air strikes?'

A whole hog was wrapped in oak leaves and lowered into a pit in which large stones had been heated by fire. A soft white is derived from parts with high acid content.

And you find yourself thinking, she has been put here to say something, to give voice. A blade springs out from the handle when a button is pressed.

She had that brand of high forehead coveted in the middle ages. She was sitting directly opposite.

*

As your body decays, you tend to interject less and less. I am struggling to relate to the concept of a shared molecular structure, wherein a nest of freak atoms is in hiding at the boundary of a lost dimension. Origin is independent of use.

I am across or beyond or leaning toward the other side (transatlantic, transalpine et cetera). After death, nature has arranged matters such that your biomass is reintegrated by way of a discount food chain. A half-way position is represented by 'the towers of silence' — usage often occurs on the nearside of the speaker.

I'm through with this, forever migrating into another state or place of business, forever translating.

It may further be speculated that this conversion of the symbolum is a passport to interstellar space. Here, I am referring to the theological use of a word, while genetics conjures allies stapled onto different chromosomes, or a human bone trumpet.

I am particular, being. One isomer had substitutes deployed at opposite ends of a carbon double bind, which was later found to be living on the same side of the canyon. The isomer is stillborn.

Who forms phosphorescent crystals and is used? This would be like imagining a fiction composed solely of everyday words without descenders.

A giant elastic band is stretched between the flukes as they rear up out of the waves. Meanwhile, a roughly triangular strip of metal must bridge the angle provoked by our collision. A plain and simple line is impressed into the cover of the book, your head.

As a child, he once saw a vision of a circle of blue light floating in space, scintillas of gold encompassed within it. Every day is like that now.

Which reminds me, one night when we were all fast asleep I heard a knock at the door: William Blake had been placed in the middle of the village pond. His wearied son took his repose on the shakedown. We drank seawater. We drove a tunnel through time and space and on into the molten core of the earth.

One man was later forced to write a book about his adventures in the underworld. Someone else said a colourless toxic gas is formed by burning sulphur in the air.

I cannot go on.

We woke up and in flies this angel with its minder, both in disguise, of course. Apparently people who sleepwalk often make straight for the wardrobe.

A balloon hoax

It's time for the great balloon hoax (viz. mediaeval money laundering). The sane person was led into a drawing room quite tastefully furnished. Everyone was startled into an exclamation.

The children were given dried strips of rawhide to chew on. Origin is sick, in the sense of a conflict between two equally retarded legal systems.

I am one step from antinomian, something of a gruesome, the night-eve of all saints and attendant demons. I am unevenly celebrated.

We are thought to be disassociated from your festival. Ghosts and spirits are believed to live abroad; some made their way home. Our plural is hideout.

There is a term in mythology, originally denoting sacred localities and later on various types of fucked-up entity; we are burrowing under folklore. The others are depicted as demonic tricksters, often autochthonous pagan inhabitants. Things around here have an alarming tendency to mutate into their opposites without warning.

The others are found near remote headlands, ominous crevasses, weirdly shaped boulders, potholes and other outstanding geographical features or uncanny terrain. All our money is vanishing in a convoluted fashion.

Etymology insists on a threadbare phantom that lives in mountainous forests (see my crombie, circa 1898). Dwelling place means a sacred grove of trees. I am historically trapped in a broken lift on the hottest day of the year.

This luminary behaves like the owner of the game; his name too is disassociated. Another had a big serrated head. More recent thought leads us back to those municipal car parks linked for centuries with being buried alive. There was always a secondary meaning, always.

A noun may be applied to dormant or anomalous geological features. My own semantic meaning has been lost, or perhaps the room has suddenly become colder. This could have led to the anthropomorphism of the site.

Within the land, between the twelfth and thirteenth holes, is where the transfiguration took place. In more recent times his nature is synonymous: with this tongue we create silence.

*

In the archbishop's backstage list he is alluded to as a god of fur, together with a similar deity, Carpet. Origin incriminates a city in the southwest found on the river with a population. An attempt was made. An estimate was established, also holy: we are saintlike, too mouth for word.

At times the antennae click and I suddenly recollect. I didn't really need a new coat, but one kept appearing anyway. D was elected simpleton — there he goes now, stalking the esplanade, staring down the void.

C plunged into a frozen gully and lay asleep there for a thousand years, before being woken by the probing muzzle and lapping tongue of B, a jackal. Undeterred, I continue to haunt the foundry every night.

Centuries passed: I was whole and at the same time not. I sought and found the others (those cunts had gone to ground in the forest). This machine can capture time, while here the manuscript appears to read what kept you, death.

[*Off-stage thunder, lightning.*]

We engaged in such activities without awareness of the possible consequences: I was sleepwalking into a surveillance society, on other days a surveyor in the society of somnambulists. Our only vehicle is a railroad trolley powered by its operators, or by a crowd of insane people pushing from behind.

*

One night her canine clattered into the sink. This created a gap; she still looked pretty. For years it had swung on a hinge as she played it with her tongue. The longer a sleepwalk lasts, the nearer the person comes to a state of entropy.

This life form's sharp serrated edges are poised to seize and pierce. While waiting for a kill it rests motionless upon four posterior limbs, the head raised atop an elongated neck as the forelimbs are held outwards in a characteristic devotional attitude. The creature will stalk using slow silent movements, before grasping its victim with the knife blades and devouring it.
    Origin is yet another day plus xenomorph.

                  Dark rivers of the heart, false memory

Your illuminations are encouraging, hopefully they will one day goad a book. I'm striving for spirit rather than a literal translation, more a form of channelling than hackwork. One man chased and caught up with a yellow object.
    That was the last voice Elgar ever heard over the telephone. Admittedly, he had made a number of cryptic observations throughout his life and even engineered a series of retreats, second only to the house where everyone died.
    All this time the sleepwalker remains in exactly the same position; the thirty-third situation is erroneous judgement. The irregulars meanwhile went about satisfying their rapacity and cruelty.
    These characters are not to be confused with the flutes of a column, no. Origin is undermined by your middle name.

At this point we have no choice but to begin making informed decisions. Sometimes he forced the congregation to kneel for hours on the rock salt he had scattered across the flagstone floor of the cathedral.
    Many of my coevals are still alive, and include acclaimed men of estimation. Origin is a person using the same stream as another.
    Sometimes he would cast a handful into the fire, an open cluster of stars.

And the air was pressing with a weight of fifteen point four five zero kilograms all over my surface. That is quite normal. While on our quest, we chanced upon a ruined castle surrounded by a drained moat — we crossed the drawbridge and made offerings to I know not what. Only the keep survives. There were adders in the grounds and an immaculate bowling green — in one enclosure were heads impaled on spikes and the visage of a tin saint. Enough already.

A spasm pulses through tense muscle — sealants burst at the silence, stolen in our gravity. The intruders have scanned any remaining memories and now swarm over our hastily built barricades. It is about time.

He fabricates his esteemed commentaries. (Who will navigate now?) The following day the weather was bad and at night a clamour of frogs and cicadas rose up. All rights have been rescinded.

So what are we looking for now? Discordant notes, things that should never occupy the same space-time continuum.

Aspersions are being cast on my rank. Origin is a form of baptism.

*

When did all this start and stop? Today's number is fifteen, in the sense to spatter forth from the adverts. . . . One eyewitness said I feel overdecorated. . . . Events have resulted in highly differentiated burial patterns according to peoples and cultures. Anything has been postponed.

Observe that distant enthusiast waving his arms about at the crest of a hill. He is no doubt making semaphore.

The patient is offered a bed for the night but declines and leaves the sanatorium for the last time. As he strode through the darkness, he recalled how Kafka had once said in the struggle between you and the world, always back the 200–1 outsider.

Usage is alarming. You have known this all along. I urge you, remember from afar, if you must remember at all.

Then writing began. Over time it approached the point where nothing more reveals itself.

*

Somehow I wept all the way through. The monk's habit was 'limned by hand' — branches dowse and sway, giant wings pound the air et cetera. I foresee dissent around this ordeal of the wings.

Sullen, lazy extraterrestrial types are creeping closer. Necessity has come home, a great concrete of silence. But this attitude of mind is impossible to sustain.

There is magic in the octet. When my father died it felt like moths.

Your body has sufficiently mocked your soul for you to be driven to take revenge. Transmutation scars are visible, the track of a bite. This is the penultimate stage of a discontinued life.

Let's go outside. Systole lends itself to contraction. I dedicate.

We hijacked a plane and crashed it in the desert, but that was a long time ago, when the workforce felt differently about such desperate measures. Then we nonchalantly commandeered an ocean liner and fled. To this day, I am tersely signified as O.

A less common usage means swerve or change course without warning. The more common means cut off your matted hair in the mirror in the dream before watching three men bound together plummet from the sky, narrowly avoiding collision with a granite outcrop to plunge into a tarn of phosphorescent green water.

I could always be severed. Be sure to switch off the lights when you leave to pass the remainder of your life exiled in some frozen wilderness.

The membrane ruptured and folded inward, flesh torn at the index. The bell of the angelus sounded. Once again, a theme is betrayed.

The stone circle in question is found at a remote border between moors, on the high crag overlooking a river. One thin slab of weathered granite stands three metres high. It is the tallest of the survivors. Four hundred metres to the southwest on lower ground is a type of elongated earthwork found only on the island, consisting of parallel banks with ditches outside.

Feral children have been garbed in horrifying fluorescent masks and regimental colours. Come nightfall, police cars cruise the city streets in search of a suitable volunteer. The chosen man is infected with a contagious disease unknown to medical science; the following morning he wakes to find eruptions covering his skin in an anticlockwise spiral pattern.

A passing woman tore off her shoe. Are you the one she asks. Send photos. (Stop.) This transition marks the stages of a misused life and is inherently flawed. Over time her evil nature becomes magnified.

Do not tell me anything more — we are attempting to write something closer than plot will ever allow: all this must come to an end. I learned my lines from memory but nonetheless suffered a mighty blow, edge upon edge.

*

He is named in the later editions. Men *had* been utterly changed and were visibly transformed. He is formerly known as a narrow sound between the isle and the mainland. He is stalker: the pivotal character, mortal engine. He is serial. He is the minor character who keeps returning; he shapeshifts. Another name is Øresund.

It was March, that much I am certain of. It was unbelievable. They said you are among the refunded. Plainly, we were in the grip of a fever.
I took a spectrograph of the two bullet holes we had brought with us. The lights along the promenade looked spectacular; history was early life.
He was an archaeologist with a particular interest in scriven artefacts. We met and fell in love, a thankless task. Origin is midway between nine, from exhalation — to wit seafarer cum meteorite.

Whose father had worked with gods and ghosts, with falcons? We had twins, Run and Fuck. One died of the influenza in nineteen, soon after birth. Some years later we petitioned help to open a door under the city that led down into a vast network of subterranean tunnels.

My lover was being chased across the marshes because he was the only suspect. He was the suspect scrivener. He shot and killed the bagman with a handgun. Or, I shot and killed the hangman with the pistol in my flight bag. Note how we are destined to interthread; usage is alarmingly transfinite.
In those days, elocution lessons were free. In the ensuing riot he shot himself: all his life he had striven to surrender delirium back to the gods. There were so many people milling about, you could fling ideas off a cliff and they would float. I am sure the pub was called the Death's Head Hawkmoth, or Sphinx.
Now I can only experience the work to be written as a state of collapse. Legend has it that the two of us escaped in a hot air balloon. My wound proved fatal and I died soaring above the earth. When the renegades landed, nomads hauled my body off to be processed — this is how I became a stalker: one who walks who should not walk. The nomad wars began. After I died, I was made chief sessile animal of the brigade and renamed.
This account describes a type of organism fixed in one place, for example a barnacle, or a plant attached to the spinning earth directly by its base without a stem.
Shortly after becoming a stalker, I ruthlessly terminated two of my rivals. I fought in all the major battles, including the battle of the large mating swarm and the very long battle of hill ninety-nine. During this time my controllers within the movement began investing their capital in the first patented traction nerve — for centuries the city had struggled against opposing powers for fuel and raw materials, the race to harness synaptic electricity. Many nomad raiders attacked the moment.
Next must be reckoned the armed retainers and hirelings quartered in your house. At some point I developed a primitive form of self-awareness

(viz. I don't trust anyone). I left my overlord's army and set out into the world. During the nomad wars I served as a mercenary for both planets.

At the end of the nomad wars I led a legion of zombies in an uprising against the newly mobilised Breslau. Origin is roaming in search of a past, from the base of naming.

The capital prevailed, crushing the undead where they stood, lurching from side to side, as they will. The only exception was Him. It was like Alzheimer's, or Icarus.

During the revolution He was appointed executioner in the capital. Once the alarms and zeal of those first days had waned, throughout the ensuing days of the terror the chosen machine was the guillotine — lately restored as a cheap and efficient method of dispatch by the municipality. I aim to be a Perfect, unconditionally forbidden.

He was much feared by the underworld, who still saw Him as a trickster, a brooding god who endured long after death occurred. At that moment, a bird which had lost its ability to navigate using the earth's electromagnetic field struck the window and died instantly. It was me all along.

*

The man who invented Alzheimer's had the good sense to die at the age of fifty-one. Death was on the move. He then became an assassin, a high-ranking official similar to a mayor or landgrave. One day, finding ourselves with an afternoon off and nothing better to do, we paid a visit to the local organ donation depot. It was a big decision; a salary cap had just been introduced and only one concussion substitute was permitted. I picked a number. People said you're so illegal alien. I felt like an incurable virus.

The presiding judge quizzed me about this implausible account as I stood in the dock. Your Courtship wrote his thoughts in a great ledger set before him using a quill pen, of this I am convinced. Origin is on this side, not the other side, no.

Upon his release from jail, the waiting lover slipped her arm around the assassin and tried to kiss him. When the mayor ordered the assassin to murder the children of a political opponent, he refused to obey and shot the mayor instead. When I say mayor, I mean those electrode heads found buried in certain regions of the earth during geological time.

We've got something here if we can identify the options.

The assassin then fled into the wilderness, where he became a vicious and much-feared hermit. Some compare him unfavourably to a water-borne bacterium of a group that includes pathogens that cause cholera, gastroenteritis and septicaemia.

Where is he now? I do owe him. I dedicate (after me the deluge et cetera). Geological time is famously slow.

I veer toward him, his orbit. A piece of the moon broke off and came crashing down to earth. He is of or like the liver.

Nonchalantly, together we hijacked the ship and its crew. Overnight the veins within the sperm ducts had multiplied and were now a little dated.

Wherever you go they will find you, the only question is when. But by choosing your own terrain, not the place where your enemy expects to find you, you will invariably be victorious.

See, the candidate is a person who begins to study late in life. Origin has arrived.

Praesepe

Cut the insolence, this lack of grace — crawl back to the sea from whence you sprang. The clue to watch for is any sign of immaculate pollination.

Some argue that our work is simply cryptography. Others conclude that the work is one half cryptography and one half demonic magic, while drawing attention to my dependence on the corpus of forbidden books. Whichever, the inherited structure of the human mind trammels the sense data of experience, limiting our ability to apprehend the thing-in-itself.

Now the day begins to wear away — for we are here, in a lonely place, with twelve baskets of broken pieces.

XIII

A simply crafted memory

Suddenly I saw a man fall from the sky. His widow was told the fiction of a bloodless death, that he was killed by a concussive blast as he stood to light his pipe, and that there was no mark on the body. And I thought, if the syndicate can get away with such a crime, so might I.

I was born without breath, for I lacked a nasal airway, indeed had no holes whatsoever in my face. My mind was made up.

Now I am about to slip on the wet cobblestones and my head will accidentally collide with a plate glass window. It was the first anniversary of the death.

What's that thing on the floor?

*

One morning I found myself in an all-night café, with no recollection of where I had been or how I had got there. I lit another Gauloises and sipped an espresso.

Temporary amnesia can be a blessing, but there is always some hidden remembrance, fragmentary details (the floor is often a good place to start looking). I turned my head to find someone standing by the window, where the light is.

A beaded curtain shelters the interior from the heat already and the flies.

'I don't believe that could be a natural hill, it looks engineered in some way: things have been done to it, tiers of earth, a solitary winged figure.'

In the centre of this gentle swell, a catastrophe is building. He meditates upon a single sheet of blank paper.

First we found ourselves lower down and then higher up the river. One day, in an all-night café, and I suppose he means something like absent company, whether known or unknown.

'Not good weather for anything, your mind is caving in on me.'

'There is nothing wrong with your lungs, they're on zero hours, that's all.'

Less variety of faintness now. Nothing like this could have happened in the past. More than a hundred geneticists dismissed my hypothesis in a letter published in all the broadsheets.

*

Concussed and disoriented, he makes his way along the autobahn while staring uncomprehendingly at the passing traffic in the rain. He had felt paralysed immediately after the collision, but has gradually begun to move his limbs.

I owe this man the small debt of disassociation; this is no time for supernaturals. I thought I was alone in the warehouse when it happened.

The same hypnotic motif returns: a film of speech, randomly yoked monologues, tailored oblivion. . . . I no longer think about those days, do not think about anything very much. Now I am searching nervously among the rushes.

Forsake not an old shadow for the new he once said, the spirits of all these remnant people.

*

Free-floating anxiety, the first night, legends sealed in a small box: the surface of a shell, scrimshaw mizzenmast with noose suspended, the projecting jaw of an animal, a strap or cage for the mouth — jade turtle — the final contact sheet. . . . He wore a nice pair of spurs, about which the hem of her petticoat entangled itself. Minski had his slaves conduct us to a superb gallery, into which were set mirror-panelled alcoves. Who cannot break free?

The mouth of a gun barrel, nouns scattered beside a sacred object from the dreaming. Contradiction vanishes, so to speak, outside. The chosen word means to cook in an underground oven.

To gall, to wound or fire the silences.

To rain in small drops a fine rain.

To decamp, confuse.

They became locked inside the house; this error of yours will cut deep.

I forewarned. I gave up reading and began writing my own book ('airtight crisps are resurgent, jets of plasma escaping'). We shall whittle away until I reach a fatal point of eclipse.

Now we are running either side of a great body of water. The creature's flank is worn smooth.

We have not been in touch, no one has been in touch. Broken glass cascaded.

*

A border or threshold: the development of meaning here is a puzzle. The only sound is the wassail of seamen on board an icebound sailing ship. I am culled ghost, a sorrow set in the high Arctic.

I sat up late scribbling nonsense and talking to myself. I had long been obsessed by the Franklin Expedition, and was permitted to collect a number of bones from crewmen who had died on a desolate island.

Dried bear paw, diced and scalded in saltwater, was served from silver plate in the captain's stateroom. Sodium chloride is our mineral, typically occurring as colourless cubic crystals. It is said that the wearer of the shell will never be forgotten.

Re sternum: I have a thing about the word, it sounds like what it is, solid breastplate of uncompromising bone.

Space, divided by resistance, slides away from its crumbling axis. I struggle once more to think what it is that I am remembering.... And then there were more postponements — but very soon I was earning a livelihood, despite the bleak climate, as a dealer in ursine meat products.

This was a step or two down the food chain: he had once worked with a carefully selected group of cold-blooded performers: nightly beneath the marquee a carriage was pulled by horses at speed around a circuit, the whole entourage caparisoned in jet velvet, a flawless matt surface.

Our own product is a yield of smelted sulphide ores, especially those of copper or nickel. The painter is in his element now, an unforgiving professional: the reformation was in full swing, the walls whitewashed and all the relics seized and buried in the earth.

These artefacts were rediscovered a hundred years ago to the day. She tells me this is God's way of opening a door to an alternative future.

I started writing a book about this, about what or whom to address. She came by and said she felt desperate and was going to kill herself, or failing that, someone else.

*

I am abroad in my own time, imploding. I live on the seafront but turn to face the landslide. Beneath my window is a vast, two-tiered concrete platform running the length of the street, a project abandoned when the earth collapsed.

Into the distance he says, follow the direction of your chosen object. I reply that to sustain a state of quietude, one cannot allow oneself to be distracted by counter-espionage.

Outside it's mizzling, a fine rain from a cloudless sky — or, to be more precise, fine rain falling after sunset from a sky in which no clouds are visible. Consider now the individual who begins to learn or study late in life.

The first prints after that fatal period of shooting have just arrived.

He *aspersed* the place and all its inhabitants. A loose cavity has been found in several of our birds and reptiles.

His trachea ruptured, spewing forth lymph and glandular secretions such as bile, sap, tears. The five surviving stratagems are plan, pattern, position, perspective and ploy.

*

Acoustic levitation manoeuvres the capstone gently into place. Pharaoh's moniker is a lost name for those hollow flowers that open in the evening for pollination by moths. A veil drawn about his face, he lies to make a cross of his body on the flagstones.

Centuries later, we all know how a regicide was punished, limbs bound to shire horses and the suspect's body torn apart.

I am undecided as regards the two theories of mediaeval architecture: that of teeming minutiae fashioned one upon the other with no overarching aim, contra the groundplan, a forgotten blueprint.

They do resemble herons, but these birds are white and have long plumes in the breeding season (egrets). I feel quite alienated by the hidden motives of the central nervous system.

That mob of deer, it was a simulation all along.

Whereas I stood still that day, no turning in space and time. The world drew back into itself to collapse at an instant. Others would take several profiles and forge them into an isolated personality; there was not a single voice with which you could safely talk about anything.

*

The ground was silent. Opposite crouches a woman entrusted with diverse nervous tics. I am reluctant to participate.

The readings appear skewed — organs have gone missing, filched from the deep freeze. Will she take heed?

I am trying to envisage how my shape may resurrect when the time comes. I remember what I have come here to do, which action to execute: we are trying to push these irrational forms into the contour originally suggested. I know only too well that an elsewhere is foreseen.

Why would any life form have a head like that? Nothing else has a head like that. And where are the landing craft? Where is the boat that disappeared?

Subject matter is irrelevant: enigmatic ruins, partially obscured by a line of horizontal cloud. . . . A universe is being expressed through parataxis, the placing of phrases one after another without coordination.

I am unbiddable. The current sense has decayed.

Cannot rush this: we are in need of a thing that joins, the various organs having been loosely arranged side by side. Glittering spots are misfiring on the iris lens.

'Wrong.'

[*On his back in the dark.*]

'We are out of touch.'

'I will never walk away from you.'

'Right.'

'The situation has changed.'

'I have found among the captives a man who can make known the interpretation.'

[*Fondles the spare battery.*]

She was brimful before ever she was born. I am lying in wait for what can never be remembered.

*

But this task cannot be limited to the theme of exhaustion. A number of the eunuchs had been given the order to ward off flies and burn incense as we slept.

Something sticky on the spine of the book. All the older women remain standing, shaken by the rhythm of the train.

An arc of translucent beads jets from her groin at climax. This feels less of an archive now, more like pressure of a neural type. Being wholly preoccupied with the negative aspects of being, citizens care very little whether they are called this or that or something else. Leaf lard is made from the visceral fat around the kidneys and loin.

Origin is abject. Someone tell the artist that dreams are fascinating to no one but the person from whom they spring.

This is the shocking moment the pilot punches an air hostess in the galley. Now he never leaves his shuttered room.

'See, if I had left that cloister, I would never have found the surviving you.'

*

Room with ikon, candles, *Kachelofen* and a large jar of pickled eggs. From the window we have an uninterrupted view.

The same man always opens the game. Long spears of ice are piled up beside the field of play. A hired signalman shouts out random letters of the alphabet while competitors respond by arranging the shin bones of horses in a uniform script across the frozen ground. It was the beginning of a blood feud that lasted several decades.

And I replied that our amnesia was surely due to the fact that we had not slept for three days. She seems to draw the light through the window and into herself. Writing disqualifies me, null trace of love et cetera.

A large membranous tube reinforced by rings of cartilage extends from the larynx to the bronchial tubes, conveying air to and from the lungs (also called windpipe). Those shimmering reflections spread across the wall are impossible, undeniable.
'A bird's iridescent plumage, the chrome wings of flying fish — bodily contact, *proximity*. . . .'
Here is another excerpt: a lost chapter of the world's first novel has been found. It begins. The breathless reference made me laugh.

Dear Comrade
You have no doubt heard that my chosen archetype is the trickster. Maybe this is why chaos seems to follow me around, despite an inclination toward a solitary, semi-monastic existence. Curious that we both have an estranged older sibling (I wonder whether they know each other). I enjoyed your heartbeat reminiscence. A very still day here — grey lid over land and sea — spent at home reading dark matter, an onrush of ghosts.
A man's head was wedged in the letterbox when I woke, another for me to swallow whole. Your own work has one of the finest credit lists I have ever seen: a lizard wrangler, someone acknowledged for felling a thousand-year-old tree, a bulldozer duel, untrained volunteers responsible for explosions — not to mention the ambient sound of an ocean trench, an aeroplane crash recording, miscellaneous voices off, white noise of science-fiction babel.
An improvised raft is still the safest way for a geneticist to get around the archipelago. Inland there are road and railway systems but they fail to connect with one another, often ending abruptly at inexplicable dead ends. This evening I am competing with bagpipe drones from across the battlefield, landing craft on the beach, the distant thud of heavy artillery.
I dictated this letter at one sitting while in a deep trance. Now, as I transcribe, a blue smear of watery ink is spreading out from the centre of the page, an apprentice Rorschach.
Perhaps the devil, caught so to speak off balance, behaves a little recklessly tonight. The only remedy against such an assault is, with the help of grace, to suffer insight: it is always possible to reject the presumed interconnectedness of a set of circumstances, the empirical evidence. The only plausible conclusion is that the phenomenon you speak of was acausal.
Your remaining ally

*

Felled by a single blow, he collapses onto the electrified rail. There is no style to it: a fall is a fall in this instance. They must come for him now, they must.

Gazing down, a uniformed official asks what he means by intuition, to which he replies instinct leavened by memory — and could you please withhold the electric while I scramble back onto the platform.

His face is covered in soot, commuter DNA. A pair of off-duty swingers assist him home, one on either side, a human crutch.

*

Climate haphazard, shadows beyond the pane, blind swelling in the warp of a distant rectangle — gas and dust are blown out during the final stages of ignition. But the scene does not appear to be expanding any longer. The raised weal across my back augurs change.

Her eye has taken on a most revolutionary aspect; I will be ready and waiting, primed for the daily drill of meticulous notation.

My companion was overcome upon seeing the general clad in dazzling splendour, holding out his cloak as if in supplication. A complete set of cipher tables has now been printed on an edible silk foil.

There have been altogether too many false alarms such as this, for example Robespierre, when he heard the messenger, broke out into demonic hysterical laughter. And who often confused his opponents in court by saying precisely nothing?

She sits and reads. A paradox has arisen: a pattern of positions can generate a perspective, yet a perspective will always constrain any further shift in position.

*

Aboard an ocean-going clipper (a fast sailing ship of nineteenth-century design with concave bows and raked masts). Half-asleep, I whispered his name, but he could not answer. I did not know what to do. I fell asleep again, to dream of a crematorium whose stacked compartments were stained an oily black, and God knows what beneath the floodwater.

There is no reliable way to signal such events.

If he gets bored or excited he starts chewing at his electrodes. The speculum reveals the disease has spread — for example, I said Tao and he heard tower.

Ranks of opposition most various today. The head pleads. The head in question is adjacent to the lieutenant's flashing green *Totenkopf* epaulettes. A hot iron is applied to the volunteer's undercarriage: more cries, the repetitive rhythm of *be wrong, be wrong, be wrong*. . . . Both legs lie nearby, in counterpoint to a discarded beer bottle.

The more the volunteer is tortured, the more amusing he finds the situation. It is a gift to both study and know man, and to contemplate the misfortunes into which he inevitably falls.

A decrease in the frequency of sound and light waves occurs as the source and observer move away from one another. Then the lieutenant (code name Goatfuck) asks, are you too named after something strange or interesting?

It is difficult to remember the beginning when it is the beginning of the end. I am busy resembling those ancestors described earlier in the book.

Deferment and distraction are my middle names, adds the other, the final word.

*

Her scales too are iridescent, each of the thin bony plates protecting the skin of fish and reptiles, typically overlapping one another. Her scalp is tattooed, complementing a glass eye and prosthetic knee. And very red, everything scarlet — the world is full of objects that boast of this colour.

I learned yesterday. I am the only one. And now I shall tell you why: ours is a result industry in which I have been elevated to the role of self-saboteur.

I am the cornerstone of a quartet. Overhead, zebu crossing a railway track on the savannah — humped domestic oxen, tolerant of heat and drought — another term for Brahmin: shunting dragsmen of proximal star.

'And the men were afraid and they said so.'

An immensity cloistered in a cherished room, ceramic tower in one corner — without, the gently drifting snow.

*

We are speeding across the continent in a sealed train, above which buzzards wheel, soaring in wide circles. Your character's subconscious thoughts, this is where you set them down: even if left unused, you know that they are here, at the deepest level of the blank page.

Various surviving opposition, including the founder of the genus. In successive palaeozoic formations, a similar parallelism in the abundant forms of life has been observed by several authors. We were held captive in order to navigate, yet still I think fondly of that time, of our incarceration.

*

You will never meet another contender like that she says. He is omnipresent — though I don't think that part was quite ready to be detached from the rest of him. Now his thoughtless head is blocking the drain; these are the kinds of accidents that occur when one is not paying attention.

We are about to be neutralized, but despite this are feeling pretty damned optimistic about the future. A joke: two squabbling flies were caught dancing in the sunlight.

'No, we haven't any music left.'

'Don't touch anything.'

More oblique symbolism, this time a dilation — a shift which produces a figure similar to, but not congruent with, its original.

At that instant, a massive elongated neck loomed up out of the backwash.

Agreed, yes, after the terrorism that is the conviction process, how important it is to be grappling for one's own sense of liberty, which immediately manifests as something quite commonplace — and ultimately, that is all we have of any real value.

Other phenomena include the placing of clauses one after another without words to indicate coordination, as in tell me how are you. And, the ribs consist of a quantity of cancellous tissue enclosed in a thin compact layer.

Old back, pain fading — corrosive vertebral column. Decide yourself.

*

In this passage, both sides come together at last. You are lying on your back in the dark then one night. . . . Building up to the weekend there are three concerns: the nucleus, the inner core and the outer core. Damage to a single compartment degrades the whole skull.

Never flag up your own concerns — these are bodies, perfectly achieved bodies. Several of my own organs have been reinforced.

'I think we are in the wrong place.'

'Yes,' he murmurs.

Consider a word adopted for the sake of secrecy or deception, supplanting your given name. Then there was this eerie rustling sound over the phone, which became the decisive piece of evidence as I stood in the dock. Granted, there is a marginal risk of just about *anyone* getting drawn into these legal proceedings.

The next point examined was the reckless use of a deadly nerve agent. A shrunken head substantiated the allegations.

Centuries later, the purloined manuscript was rediscovered in an oubliette built by a feudal overlord. Here, the god-exiled-from-heaven principle is still the source of evil, but this archetype is now twinned, literally and/or figuratively.

I am not theorizing. I know.

*

They are rather more insouciant than their rivals, gently osmotic, devoid of grace yet blessèd within. What remains of your astronomy now? (Exactly.) Just take a look at the script, glance up at the night sky. Keep yourself to yourself; the whirlwind is coming.

We shot flares into the dark, setting them on their trajectory into emptiness. I am obliged to express myself, star-vexed as I am.

He could feel his skin burning (see genesis).

I am here denoting bone tissue with a mesh-like structure containing many pores — a scatter of primitive glyphs. Apocalypse means uncover and reveal.

Now to the close of progress — drawing on breath thick and short, each struggle succeeding the previous, body cased in claw-bark. Origin is old thing causing death, poison of lineage.

I had the disturbing impression that it was time to leave. A semiconductor diode glows when voltage is applied.

Her seven names are precisely the same as my own seven names, and what is more must always be uttered in the same order.

We are uncalled for. I think in future we are going to place all our objects upside down.

We returned the stolen items. After the stars emerged from a dark molecular cloud their energy output of light and substance began to expand into the surrounding regions of the lagoon nebula.

The prosecution enters. All rise.

See, we are trapped in a fluid dynamic, one on one — the neural toll — hanged in a thermal funnel, an entire alphabet nailed into the earth. (Is this enough?) When you look at things sideways, that is when you start to see them in focus and the final hunt can begin. Each stripe is magnetically aligned to the north or south pole.

This is all best-guess. I think they will settle among themselves in the end. Meanwhile I raid, plunder — yes-liverish.

*

Arctic ghost, sorry — you can touch me here, but not there. In the future only two species of music will survive.

Make sure each alibi is of a distinct class. The more dramatic effects could start up any day, once the major causes come into play.

Lung.

Everything hinges on this.

These are the kind of events that can happen.

You are too being. You are no longer paying attention.

Duty calls him back once more into the turmoil of life: *Abi ter a8thllstr Bridge#3* and approximate ciphers. An increase in the frequency of sound and light waves occurs as the source and observer move toward each other.

HILL 99

A vision is a picture of a desired future state that an individual or organization has foreseen and wishes to achieve.

I visualize you. I visualize me. We visualize the others.

Nothing is worth repeating.

*

A slender insect related to the dragonflies typically rests with the wings folded back along its body. (His word is logogriph.) A chandelier of pelvises can be glimpsed in recent pages, but we must begin with some really sad news.

Yes, when I refused to speak for a time, for one whole week he forgot all about his glory years. This translation marks the passage of a misread life: a brutal reign is perhaps the most artful expression to use here, a contrived solution to a difficulty in the plot.

A carriage bears down pulled by horses at speed, whipped onward by a tricorned postilion, the whole ensemble caparisoned in jet velvet. I counted three waves to one beat of the pulse, the battened heart.

This effect causes the sudden change in pitch noticeable in a passing siren, as well as the red shift seen by astronomers. No details can be perceived across my surface, imploding a nothingness.

He taps at his snuff box with a clawlike hand. Compare with earlier draft — readings may vary, some hardly qualify as punishment at all.

'His or her shell-like, the way your love is frightening,' et cetera.

[*Rapping sound from without, screaming.*]

That must be them.

He bears a duelling scar, she carries a wound that refuses to heal. What a team. Their concentric ripples reinforce each other in a geometric progression.

*

In the dynamic microphone, sound waves impinge on a conductor of low mass supported in a magnetic field. Both of the resulting circles were sighted on the great eminence to the south known as the hill — three fallen stones were re-enacted and a hedge bisecting the circle was set alight. There is something sinister lurking beneath the floodwater.

It always seems quicker going back in cryostasis. Below are listed our areas of expertise, in the vain hope that we may one day be considered useful.

Colourful yet perplexed, she may not be what she seems.

Today I finish my prayer and will then be able to satisfy your every desire, the saint replied. The sky meanwhile is an 'unbreakable epiphany'.

His tardiness is legendary. I keep drifting off inside myself, in and out of the discontinuous.

Picture a consumptive drawing-room balladeer. (After the silence, what next?) We should have applied a ligature.

The rather severe subtitles refer to musical forms. In memory of readership, I keep letting slip my concentration.

Listen, time-running-out music.

Pinned out across the lino: *la conchiglia* — the seashell named after a bottled imp — early drafts of symphonic prose and chamber music. People also searched for miniature latex ears and a mothlike shape.

*

He was born. He won a silver medal in the art of games, for he is victor. (Citation needed here.) He died. On page one hundred and ninety-seven he takes part in a stomach race with elderly male and female cripples.

Infinite space above. He finds himself possessed and loved by something selfless: the explosive one, in sight of burning fuse. It took three hours and twenty-seven fatalities before we finally took the gun turret at the clifftop and established a beachhead.

My name is derived from hook-like thorns that resemble the claws of a cat. The technique used is pneumatic parataxis.

In our mangled wake, the grudge — a break in the narrative, a luminous ring surrounding a shining body.... An old friend manifests in a projecting rock face. Work itself can be destabilizing, the knowledge that you have paid for every breath in units of time. Contrast this with subordination.

Place names, e.g. your place.

'Not yet.'

My money is on the bribe decoy. Ignoble to the fingertips, he is a man who against all the odds fought on through a world of shadows and traps. Origin is underground plus silent miscarriage.

Ranking auspices: a company of larks, quails, roes. The swelling has gone down but I am still resigned to drink myself to death. A collective refers to a flock of any kind, though rarely a sum of objections.

Air whining these days through the old reticulum.... What a lovely death, and what music to expire with. The root yields a red dye.

A random is contemplated, one pertaining to railways, trains, carriages and rolling stock — operations by magnetic levitation. The man had still not appeared when the train reached Zagreb, and I had searched it from end to end.

A different story, the tale of a djinn, was composed in the eleventh century while the scribe was kept waiting.

From every orifice pours a thick mucous sap. This is alluded to above when he cries this is pouring out of me. . . . He cannot control: the fold is an aggregate of many apparitions.

Even though the elements of capital are discovered in this example, they are not regulated in the manner anticipated: he is to be given a second chance.

We should never have been caught outside at this time of day. I think there could be a ritual meal in the offing, strapped in as we are, cruciform across the tablecloth.

What transpired at that séance

Never countenance defeat, albeit so close to the end. Yield nothing of substance; we have not yet finished with you.

A musical recital accompanies this process, as if memory in counterfeit. Before I died I had composed thirteen operas, several employing Wagnerian principles.

'Are there any more unchecked in this room, please?'

The bursa ruptured and a viscid pus flowed forth — noxious matter is still present in the debris of tissue. An x-ray revealed nothing: the fungus is very old and shaped like a bat. The rest are still busy, strappadoed above the bridge table in the drawing room.

The embossed pattern of the wallpaper is typical of the interior of mature bones. Just after the war I was inspired by a chance meeting.

'Thought I recognized you from somewhere — you're an ex, are you not?'

An ex is white noise containing many frequencies of equal intensity.

'You were there that day, tell us how it happened.'

The mouthpiece is a slender tubular body with holes stopped by keys. You lie on your back in the dark, and one night. . . . I will inspect the garrison when I can steer closer to the compound — at this distance, time will gradually evaporate.

See, the object in question is known as cat's claw because of its claw-shaped thorns.

*

You may need to remonstrate with your governor upon the credit or ruin of what I propose. Yes, this is going to be a long march, but we are permitted stops along the way, stations of our own choosing. Right now, I must shelter from the piercing light.

At this distance, nothing matters. He is wanting of teeth and consequently cannot bite.

He returns. The island seems changed.

The male cicada now makes a loud droning noise after dark by vibrating two membranes on its abdomen.

Pneuma has been sucked out through the volunteer's prolapsed anus, oily rags stuffed in to plug the breach. Let us reflect upon what has happened today: an ungrateful soul's public testament, a message of desolation which evokes a state of inexistence.

He finally learns that Mademoiselle F is in love with a reprobate going by the name of D, who is of indeterminate years. Nothing will ever be the same, nothing will ever appear any different.

*

Enter: limned gold across a panel of ash.
Onto the open sea
the opening opening
sea like me,
like thee.

I began to oscillate at the same frequency as the sound waves; it was a sacred place. And right on cue comes a man, a vision with wingspan. He looks up at the night sky and falls out.

Accordingly, it is spring — the edge of the sea, beneath a mesh retreating at the speed of light.

A scaly gauntlet with joints of bone, with sinuous ridges and eared hinge: a valve upon my sleeplessness.

Untimely ships — talking stones and a mutant engine — headless mustermen. And he, snuck in his shell, can speak only of future events and nothing more.

A pool or lake.

A sheet of standing water.

An arm of the lagoon.

A boundary.

An object indicating a boundary.

A glass tube containing mercury.

The fullest sense is expected here: absolute, entire, sheer, perfect, downright, drowning.... Yet the head's assurance is frail — deal with him as I advise, and exit.

*

Enter: a sealed chamber in which frozen tissue is fractured into cryostat sections about five micromillimetres thick. The corresponding heavenly body is the twelfth star in a given constellation.

We met beneath Bedlam's cupola. Even before knowing the results of the analysis, it was clear that we were snared within the confines of our own dialogue. Twin statues signal.

'Begone about your business: go forth — search and destroy.'

I sought him out, one who wanders and struggles and errs time upon time, an assassin with a panoramic view of the harbour, nightfishers floodlit on the beach, that long conversation we were having before events unfathomed.

Origin is us, formed on the pattern of bridgehead. She lives in an ash tree with her venomous herbs.

She's not what she seems: for her the sea is cold and mad. And he says, how much do you change, o how we have changed.

Auspices, a dish or other object of like form, the shallows. Wonderstruck she calls out, inaudible.

Only a brooding now, sheer malice. No further alarms for the England.

*

Some days he wonders himself perhaps dead and does not know it, has yet to be informed. At that moment a salesman brings the rocking horse outside on a cart, connecting it by a cable to the electric current. It is snowing gently. These years I am soundly reconnoitred.

Origin is literally one day very much like another.

None of this is of my own implant. If my advice had been petitioned, I would have chosen never to arrive.

Archive footage: an ancient siege engine for hurling stones, bolts or infected matter inside the city wall. He stumbles about as priests incant psalms around her body. Yet this is a not unpleasant inertia, cramped double in our funnel-hole.

Back bent coughing, misaligned and alien, he bears animus with grace. A fluid-filled sac lessens the friction.

*

A human infant is born with an animal tail and olfactory gifts. It is reported, news-sheet spread flat on a passing torso: some son you turned out to be et cetera. From today, I abdicate all responsibility.

Another object is sheltered within a fragile crust. Such a display is limited to the persons concerned.

The organism hatches and crawls along the birth canal to burrow into clotted fur. Outside, footfall on cobble and a bladder at the tip of a cane announce sinister festivities. It is evident that the vices of this man could extend to the acausal work of witchcraft.

Don't take my word, he said — this will end badly — back then I could leap over cars, passers-by.

Tugboats on the Rhine, arcing to trace a loop. At the far shore, a gunman in the reed bed aims just above the waterline — in his sights, honeymooning ancestors, the last of our line.

He is preparing to assassinate me before I have even been born. How might this chain of events be sustained?

*

A bugle that was owned by the poet is to be played for the first time in one hundred years. Overseer of seawater at the stern, he has made himself quite ill.... Anything to do with smoke closed down, naked flame was outlawed.... Here, I am simply attempting to sketch the history of a false problem.

Waste light, void earth, the haunting conclusion to book one. Picked from the muster at random, some were weighted with concrete and flung into the estuary.

On that last Monday we had planned quite a spectacle, but the impossible has merely been delayed. We are germinal, radiating spokes in a mouth of seed.

A mangled body was found strewn along the tracks in the Simplon tunnel. This tunnel is the longest of its kind in Europe. It is straight except for the short curves at either end.

I have stolen a character, memory the culprit, begging space for your old indolence. The tribe is traditionally descended from us all.

There he goes, gnawing at his electrodes — nothing more, nothing better absolute.

Remnants in a build-up of static charge, but she's not what she seems. I got the big fear that day at the racetrack, surrounded by a more or less comprehensive social index, the counterfeit.

Conjure the image of a still-warm corpse.

I went outside, the first man to quit. But where could I go?

I walked back to contention.

XIV

To distraction

A resin cast was made of someone dying in a volcanic eruption. (Is backyard one word or two?) He reaches the window and draws it firmly shut.

My acquaintance with sheets of water being scant, the passengers and all hands have drowned. The arrangement of clauses and propositions comes without connectives, a one-button recovery system.

Proceed to Door (1) or Door (3) or Door (5) or Door (7).

*

Enter one reconstituted maker: cerecloth face, tongue-blind — scrapings of knowledge, fractal notes traced from a stellar map. Now he is over here with his accursed share. If you can find a cheaper killing, seize the opportunity.

Fifty tracks in counterpoint have aligned to compose a list: a loose concavity, your inexhaustible supply of colour. . . . I am despised by the other falconers, that much I know.

Infantrymen stretch out in a never-ending line, snaking across a frozen snowscape. Fourteen bandits are among the fugitives depicted.

Any unchecked, please.

*

A thing not said versus sight unseen. Stoke up the engines, split open the crates of pollen.

A man is appointed to ascertain a certain boundary. He uses words such as multitude, runaway, circumlocution; his inorganic substance is as a mineral of doubtful origin. He carries a two-handled flask like a pilgrim's bottle and is pointing at a map.

Our collaboration was the last thing I remember.

I could hear people all about me but not see them. Ribs were fractured. I could find no system to his reading. We are mute, mesmerite.

A metronome mark of eighty-four beats per minute is followed by a sequence of green flashes. The isolated object has a burning fuse. No wonder we have been exiled.

The three of us are in training for the trial of the century — the ship was rigged up like an anti-submarine warship used for convoy escort in the second war. The ball deviates sharply on pitching.

The castellan arrived in a light horse-drawn sleigh. The pig chosen for ritual sacrifice was heavier than a cutter but lighter than a baconer.

I found my first scapegoat this week as I flicked through the x-rays. (My physician holds a forged licence.) On other days our vessel was a yawl, a two-masted sailing boat with the mizzenmast stepped far aft so that the mizzen boom overhangs the stern. Origin lies in parting one's lips noisily.

They were dragging him along by the ankles as we drove by, squatting on the metal drums of a convoy lorry. You are familiar with the rules: the enemy will attack in short bursts.

It was a night just like this, the viceroy crawling across the ground when suddenly I stumbled over him. He had always been on the nervous side and now has the helpful word 'nervous' tattooed across his forehead.

Each moment speaks itself as epiphany et cetera. The narrative begins in the first person, later on via a miscellany of helical shapes.

We are, by and by, prized adrift of the uncanny. But to make haste to my own experiment: some say that he is sleeping right now beneath the earth.

Perhaps that could be a project for you alone, to design and create overalls with pockets so capacious they could accommodate a weighty tome. To avoid vertebral damage one would need to carry a copy on either side.

I dreamt that an eyesight test had been developed using rows of letters printed in successively decreasing size, of which patients are asked to read as many as they can under threat of summary execution.

A night operation, the background

You were in the way. We are avoiding the current dilemma and have made scant progress during the night. I remember someone saying at the time: you ended up here by accident, becalmed until someone else's future caught up with you.

Considered from the present viewpoint, those cherished times were not so rosy; I could compose a list that would outspan ten of your earth years.

As disclosed above, my acquaintance with sheets of water is limited, corroding further the less than convincing sense of fiction.

Moored beside the jetty, note the smoothly worn surface of the old flat-bottomed boat. I was raised on someone else's watch, beneath the shelter of 'an indivisible sky'. The captain is now pacing the deck, awaiting receipt of a long-expected letter.

I dislike using battery acid for divination myself. His own theory is called the last man standing theory: a beachhead is a defended position on the shingle taken from the enemy by landing forces, from which a counterattack may be launched.

*

Look, their branches are intertwining: oak, ash, sycamore, chestnut, yew.... The pyroclastic flow is creeping nearer. I have buried our parmesan in the back garden.

A blind man tells me that on Jupiter there is a caldera three hundred miles wide. I thought of the fenlands; it sounded too good to be true.

Egrets, cormorants and formation-blind starlings — forty black storks, wading and seizing frogs.... The creature was like a heron only the wrong colour, very still. It looked like a question mark, an algorithm, the last six lines of a sonnet; forbidden music is the subtext. Evidently, I am striving to isolate myself.

Origin is come close, after all. Everything was left undone.

It was an interesting dream, featuring the only wood that does not float. We are living very close to the action here.

I switched venues, moving away from my home planet to create more space for the written word, the frogs. Someone nailed a paper fish to my back without me noticing.

In my spare time I laboured at my brother's machines, at the very margin of comedy — he in pyjamas for the heat. We no longer took in hungry strays.

We are beyond the reach of the law, go on without me were his last words. For many years I had felt compelled to hand him over to the inquisition.

Strip off the poisonous bark, any outgrowth of decaying matter, spore debris. An area of water or marshland may be dominated by bulrushes. But what is meant by conformity to the magnet's pull?

This table of events did not once exist. An erection is pressed against the base of the spine, breath at nape of neck. A resin cast was made of someone dying in a poisonous cloud of volcanic ash.

I am the semantic gamble no one else would think of making. But let us now take a kaleidoscopic look at a long-dead star and the use of silence as a form of protest.

There were gaunt spectral faces and elongated fingers in the craquelure of the shell.

*

She treads along the rim of the studio tank, suddenly flings her shoes into the water and walks bareshod. Her feet are bleeding. She takes a key out of her pocket.

The sky is completely black, then comes lightning. Our combined weight causes a chunk of the earth to break away.

See, I have returned to the surface of the day. This sequence of crimes spanned an entire decade — the evidence was enclosed in a titanium capsule and set adrift.

You must leave now.

That noise is a false envelope of sound. I have been searching: that trick of swallowing a rope while being transported toward the heavens through a translucent tube of nothing. On other days the ship was a cutter, a sailing boat with one mast and more than one headsail, a swift auxiliary.

I fear I have brought with me some traces of the storm into your chamber, thunder and cloudburst.

It is rumoured that she gave birth to the sky under the spin of an abandoned galaxy. And it was indeed essential for us to ration ourselves: torrential rain, cobbled streets and alleyways, a morass clogged with mire in a district of tenements.

That was a sight to see, her face during this elucidation by the great detective. Their wretched little party goes by, sinking up to their ankles in the mud.

*

Announcing a discovery: the new magnetic pole. I have dedicated. The cloister now is half submerged.

She quickly recalculates the circumference of the earth correctly (viz. salvation through mathematical arcana). A dying form has crept into the lifecycle.

Then she announces another stellar discovery: I shall journey to the centre of thee. . . . Origin smacks of imitation.

No, I think that's you, not me — strolling between a phalanx of headstones. . . . Compare with Teuton, to eat or kiss noisily.

A shadow moves across the surface; it is wintertime at this sunken latitude. You return, unnamed.

Enter through the chapter-room door, where detail surges to an apex.

A tree at the centre of the quadrangle is host to luminescent crystals — faint consolations are delivered in E flat major.

Call her forth. We are nowhere near guessing her name. The salient number is four.

The keystone is a manifestly ritual object: following its theft, memory is at risk forever, trapped in the body-fire of prehistory. And there is but a single window, gothic perpendicular.

The true problem is distraction, where dead men brush against the lips of the living. May I come around and help?

He refuses to take food. He types swarm instead of plague and immediately regrets this decision. You cannot relax your guard, no one can relax their guard.

Stone of division — sea heath genus, as tamarisk — a small woody creeping of European salt bears a superficial resemblance. . . . Tubular bacteria are recorded verbatim, quite witless of sundry events.

And your other leg? Out of joint, put your legs out of joint.

*

Another is provoked into physically manifesting his core obsession: we are now following an imaginary line on the map after a spell in the wilderness. There is surfeit of contraband, yet the squadron will never agree division into equal shares.

He has always been forensically aware (e.g. severed head in drain). Just a moment of your time, please, and one of your fingernails.

Farewell, swift messenger. Nothing makes any real distance any longer.

She is standing on the platform beside a steaming locomotive, a battered suitcase in her hand crammed full with mould-pocked sketches, ancient slides. Join us now, cut off the feet.

The gut strings quaver; I am thoroughly unhatched. This is the worst-organized fight I have ever seen.

Ill said

He always tends to underplay his hand, yet upon hearing the descending cadence of his voice the old energy is flooding back. He says when I am gone, just a simple box, please.

Enormous panes of ice are stacked beside the field of play. He presses a bribe into my palm, the lines of which are deeply scored, those unnerving fault lines.

He speaks twenty-six languages, including some which other people actually know, one for every day of the alphabet. Our bacteria are scientifically proven to reach the gut alive.

At sea now, the crew carousing on an icebound whaling ship (i.e. mallemaroking). We had one man hanged in the night from the yardarm. I introduced the solar cult and moved the capital to a newly built city that had taken its time.

The times are becoming too lairy. A little above the hinge sits a metronome.

May we find and add a quotation to this entry? The membranous vesicle contains a dose of your own poison.

*

Capable of surpassing any person at any time, and quite fearless, yet suddenly he lost control. The music ceased: he *suggests* the silence here, an 'incremental atrophy'. Finally, he is turned around by the first violin to face the auditorium.

I conducted my own defence. So that is not his game, no, the detonation of an innocent object.

Relating to, consisting of or denoting fragments of rock erupted by a volcano: pyroclastic fragments, airborne material. I flinched inwardly. It was as if someone were suddenly beside me, crouching on the vacant chair.

Wedged between us is a covenant: reverie of lost journals, cash-back pledges — a crematorium, salt scattered across the floor — a simple crystal of two molecules, piteously unaware. We are building structures that are not required.

The inquisition haul the volunteer off to administer an exquisitely choreographed beating, little realizing what some would give for such a punishment, sweat glistening in the folds of the throat. Precisely what do *you* long for?

His tormentors begin to turn on one another. He swings around to face them, speaking boldly, but not without respect.

'Now, sirs — what number of abdominal incisions is required?'

'Origin is a seven percent downgrade.'

Yes, it should be this way, it should never be that way. Some concepts are absolute.

It was a heavy rolling-in-a-sack sort of word that he murmured at the close. This must be the part where the thing returns from the dead, refuses to die.

We meet. I hand him the key. He looks quite composed, despite everything that has happened.

'Now, consider if you will a theory of logic in which the subject is obsessed with the triumph of impossibility.'

To this he replies that by tradition we are sworn to an oath sealed under falling rain, confirming the place which another had, or might have had. Origin is probably your execution.

Without strife, bent double — something to seize, carry away. Perhaps a misconception — an intention — perhaps an opportunity, driving toward the harbour, arcing to trace a circle.

He is uneasy about sending such a letter through official channels — a confidential memorandum, analogue nostalgia. . . . He is leading each new perception to a premature conclusion: releasing convicts from the local gaol, dead yield of London clay, weaving through the frontline charged with blood up to our necks. . . . Gules, two chevrons or on a canton argent a cross crosslet fitched sable all within a border semy of gunstones et cetera.

Bend sinister, echo disjunct.

*

They are switching off the old signal. Once every thing is made of the same stuff, the more brittle will objects become. Moveable effects were consumed by law, each phenomenon estimated by weight, number and measure.

Bygone word, long taboo — extinct word meaning stillness, dead lamentable.

I am trying to think of a shockingly unsuitable metaphor.

Widespread arc within ice underfoot. The next who steps through the portal carries a shield. I'm not short of the odd critical moment myself: a ruptured membrane, red weal on ball of thumb, knuckle scarred by paper cut. . . . The g-force collapsed her face.

When threatened, she opens wide her mouth to display an inshore vacuum. We are driven on to an irrefutable biological fact: hundreds of plumed specimens are pouring out of the fossil bed. I was pinned to the floor by six Gs.

She was born into a slow but fatal descent. On route she developed the first alternating current magnetron, as well as several forms of hesitation, the acid reflux manoeuvre and a guidance system for pigs.

But would you break a promise for love, in defiance of the gods and the supernatural order? Your given symbol is the letter H, scrawled across a snakeskin cloak in mad green crayon.

Origin is just over the road, a personification of heaven or the sky. In my cell I have a set of sketches which reflect the post-apocalyptic landscape quite flawlessly.

I dreamt I was smeared with blue paint and then she flung herself to her death from the roof. I searched for my name in a long list that had been handwritten on an endless roll of brown paper. Everyone realized I was part Japanese, part not.

And that luminous oblong is a sash window, or a light box. . . . There is a clue in her facial expression, all that derelict bedlam. Someone should do me an immense favour.

It might be better to look at things logically, emerge from a silence and later on return. At first I was determined to bring you back, an untimely revenant.

Upon the appearance of the first tracks in snowfall, I am touched by a shared memory. The marching troops look like matchsticks drawn to a distant horizon.

She has this obsession, tiny fibres crawling all over her flesh. Now we must hold our nerve, gently, eye against eye — an unforeseen curvature of events, a chapter of accident: perfect grace.

*

A hunter's moon she says as we stand side by side beneath a warp of sky. We are limited to haphazard spectacle, often unconvincing.

She catches fleet, a shadow. I wouldn't mind working my way back now, a free destination for the incurable.

Cisalpine, i.e. on this (the Roman) side of the Alps. It was a magnificent performance, so deep in his blood, while she sat tight-lipped and mutinous, green eyes hard as pebbles.

The woman's hand is badly injured in one attack and now he must suture the wound (this agent is a convincing replicant but no surgeon). If we insist on verisimilitude, the whole world would collapse under its own scrutiny.

So, it is actually possible to eradicate consciousness completely, no more dancing on the bottom shelf. They are switching off the old signal.

This episode is about a real person. I myself was strung up last night, for no perceivable reason — the ordeal was brief, that crushing of the windpipe by a knotted rope: a band of avengers is trawling the land, swinging folk up hither and yon.

Origin is old geomancy, related to 'that one', and pointing.

As a consequence, he will now be most difficult to cross-examine. Our mission must be completed over a single weekend; we shall begin by standing in a group scream for all the saints.

Darling, I said, tomorrow would you like to venture outside and gawp at things on fire? Remember that covert outsider experiment?

Send for a medium, summon up shell-shocked infantry, the underminers.

Two women, three men. It is not so safe they say, the lie of this land.

Concrete slab in metal cell, part of a criminal assault course: she felt as if she had been left suspended for a week in a tank full of soluble opioids.

*

He tells me vertigo prevents him peering through the glass set into the keel of his boat. An old locomotive shunts off, track sweeping to skyline. Recoil fractures the limits of our perception; the first words overheard are often the most memorable, the irreversible.

We passed annexed villages and miles of trenches, armies on either side occupying terrain stretching from the east to the frontier. Within this territory a census is dealt.

It is a pity we could not stay here for the rest of our days. Chance is very hard to reason with — chance would be a fine thing, the eruption of lava and pyroclastics. . . . The ship's prow was carved in the form of a roundhead treading down the nations.

A dazzling circle of white light on a zinc tabletop, detail of the spinal nerve.

One glorious day everybody's ancestors fell apart, peeling away from the long-term. Something overheard had crawled among them, was manoeuvring itself.

A rapidly unravelling sky — that's how it works around here, a migration, fled from the base of night.

Life depends on the throw of a die, his Dada filament, bundled together in a frayed tongue battery. Meticulously detailed drawings of the injured were crammed into a leather portfolio. He walks on, until he too is felled by a mighty blow.

*

Pursuant to sound, a one-way song. My fingers have just fallen short. Picture a man on a ship who looks after everyone's money.

Picture a savage mutiny. (This is obvious, the piratic hawk et cetera.)

The two lovers are allocated a space. I have no wish to possess another body, would rather set out alone, abroad with all the letters, the alphabets.

A heavy rolling-in-a-sack sort of day. London and back. A lost page of the score has been used to fill in the gaps between matter; one hundred years have elapsed. The outcome is a list of lists.

Thus we inherit huckaback, frieze, ninon, mull, cambric, fustian, sailcloth. . . . Origin is frieze — mediaeval frisk, a variant of our fridge from opus, work.

Untried cancellations arrive, gearing themselves up to outflank the opposition: to place, simple, within a dark urn.

Now police are rerouting an entire mausoleum. Maybe a fitting translation would be something like 'to try fencing an untimely missive'.

Would you break a promise for love, in defiance of the gods and the supernatural order? Separation of particles denoting quantum states do not change sign on inversion through the origin. The father was overthrown and flayed alive.

A distant planet of the solar system, seventh in order from the sun, has been discovered. It is named. You are sitting opposite. But the old territory should still be here when you return, helmsman.
  'I have flown over, back and forth without cease for five centuries. . . .'
  It was like night fishing off Antibes. There the message cuts out.

My projected library features plates on spinning sticks. (Do you remember?) With their pockmarked flesh, these medium people should provide some much-needed comedy.
  Restored to life, I sat myself down somewhere to document all of this, synthesized in the long-last.
  There is a decaying tree stump in the back garden near the buried cheese. Put simply, I feel such a deep sadness today.

His symphony is now acknowledged as the most ill-omened piece of music ever written for baroque voice. Nevertheless, it remains a common starting point for unpopular forms of ritual. Any object touched has the potential to infect: the heart is broken by exile et cetera.
  Nervously: 'Is this a place?'
  'A hierarchy of saints.'
  'Yes, but how did you find us?'
  'Cunning details like the rusting soot boiler and white alloy wheels.'

Suddenly she leaves, followed by a piercing shriek — the passage of air from throat to lung, the trachea: suicide protocols, unleavened breath.
  He is listening hard and pretty much behaving like her now, mimicking the different inversions of every chord. Late in life he began work on schematics of gothic architecture. He once said no words could touch.
  I think she must be having one of her episodes. Reading postures are soon to be forgotten: the book is struggling to sustain your mutability.
  This character is opposed to the natural credo, what with his puma face, serrated horn, flesh a brittle envelope. . . . The mask I was wearing at the ball turned out to be the front of a human skull clad in black velvet.
  Sharp bristles delineate my spine, every breath a gamble.

He cast off his antlers into the drifting snow. Unseen, the other gave witness.
  a) And you will no longer suffer faith: roll the human form beneath thickening cloud, where dreadful lightnings burst et cetera.

- b) Cisatlantic, on this side of the Atlantic.
- c) Cislunar, on this side of the moon, i.e. between the moon and the earth.
- d) Cismontane, on this side of the mountain, opposite to ultramontane.
- e) Cispadane, on this (the Roman) side of the river.
- f) Cispontine, on this side of the bridge, i.e. south of your feet.

I have detected an imbalance; we simply cannot consume any more colour. I get so lost in the algebra, the terrifying possibility of control.

The assassin shot all the gangsters in the street with a submachine gun that discharged an orange flare under a dark awning in the rain. These bursts of light are the only means by which the observer can affirm the hitman's position.

This situation cries out for quarantine. He bears a sign. Sexual congress with the zoologicals is taboo.

A bone of one of the runes lay on the table, along with the claw of a bird and the yellow eye of a crane. The dagger's pommel and guard are embellished with stars.

His lamenting is way off target, a keening spent. In orbit are at least seventeen satellites and a faint ring system.

*

Vibration across soles of feet. A metal hook is suspended from the ceiling. A helix of opaque white light spins slowly in one corner of the room.

From my vantage point in the sky I can see a concentric pattern of canals and earthworks that expands to an outer ring, where a vast shadow is stirring.

A stone resembling a mushroom in shape is supporting the wreckage, thereby protecting it from vermin and water seepage. Nonetheless, we may still be tracked down by the spoor we leave in our wake.

One illustration shows a stone statue minus its head in front of a house. The name itself, and evidence from surviving vernacular speech, suggest that at first the underpinning was made of glass.

Stones are a more reliable medium for speech. Your name has become integrated into the landscape, with bridges, dwellings, settlements and other large objects slowly incorporated, for example the primaeval backbone. Some objects only now carry a name, but were once somewhat more, somewhat less.

Surface temperature drops and the ice sheet advances. All fell away the dead, amid general laughter.

Maybe the stories converge at this point, where we go back to look once more at the very beginning. Existence can always be confirmed through the shadow cast by a coffee pot.

He says you can't buy analogue for love nor money. I settled for orichalc — brass of mountain copper — all sense by disassociation, a shimmering variety of id: the great sea, drum banging at our heads.

Yet there is still enough material left over to make a revolutionary cockade, an improvised tricolour draped across the deadbox. He forestalls, repeats himself in the wastage unseen, hidden beyond the legion's flank.

Ever since we met you have been constantly in my mind, like the spent waves of a forgotten summer riot.

XV

It sounds as though. And then on the very last day, somebody spoke.
Nobody tells me, grace.

Patterns of dispersal, chiselling at the skull, and then deeper. We were both converts. He says I am unable to make a response right now (i.e. to leave a formation or group by veering away).
The tongue is drilled, light dazzles against the bodily frame, mortal axis spiking the graph. Origin is transfigured.

She tries not to think of futures; we have seen numerous examples of salvage closing down. She has known extremes, while he is quite beyond measure. One couple declared loudly that they had no wish to undertake a spectral journey.
No utterance could survive this — he plays on long into the time of their inevitable defeat. And finally she says, do you think there's an afterlung?
Your irony has been savoured up to the present day and doubtless beyond, in cold blood.

*

Night comes to dawn. I wish I had been around to see things through to the end.
He could always prove the reverse. From his base he tapers alarmingly to an apex. He is presented to view, my counterpart of opposite aspect. I remember a wallpaper frieze with chickens on it.
I had longings back then, but the head would always cave in and return to its former self, start all over. I can no longer carry the story of those fucking songs: a forked twig, a memory at risk, that helpless boundary scorched into the earth by your withered hand.
He cut himself off with his dirty knife. We found another stowaway crammed toward the stern of the vessel.

The bursa had split. Quantum states or wave functions change sign on inversion through an origin. Uranus orbits between Jupiter and Neptune, at an average distance.

*

Wall-to-wall interior. Style is probably accident, dress code supernatural. The translation reads the incoherent young men sip at bittersweet kava. . . . Perhaps we should have something to show for it all, render the outcome more complicated than it need be.
We're not doing anthropology here. He is the most ancient of the gods and first overlord, statistically. The constant in my personal law of

repulsion tethers gravity to mass: steer clear, somewhere high above the rain, way up within the tenor of your voice, gorging on the liver.
Move closer the memory bone, there's been a run on the confessional.

He has the unsettling premonition that one day he will have to stand up and be exposed to view. A fresh rope has been woven.
For him, everything loses solid appearance. (How else might objects be renounced?) If I can stick this out long enough, everyone else will fade away to leave me manifest, cast off visible in the light.

*

Overnight, passersby became so many death vessels. Now she's got the alphabetizers in: roadkill, the closure of an epic continuum. . . . The planet we call home has an equatorial diameter and is one of the gas giants.
Today's winning reminiscence: blinding white stars — where the metallic line strengthens the hydrogen bands falter. . . . Street cleaning back then was unknown — animal bones, sinew, viscera, dried clots of blood. . . . I remember struggling on up to my shanks. That time was a bad time for everyone, what with my outright persona.
A geological period may be suggested by a glacial deposit; it is difficult to make a move without borrowing.
Around this date there were rumours of a suicide attempt. I found solace in the cultivation of masked twinspur: racemes of bell-shaped flowers, shades of pink, each with two short spurs. . . . The yellow-collared, also called breathless or eye-thing, is another species of the family. We are native to the northeast and have not been introduced.
Stones are longer lasting.

This process recurs around a critical moment, well within the boundary of an incontestable mile.
We were left standing; it was our farewell game. Now I am left alone to wait.
Sound is trapped at the dilated end of a semicircular canal in the ear, while the outer membrane collects pollen. The archive is molecular, trade historical — footplate memories of the Settle-Carlisle. The inquisition included questions on metempsychosis.
Who founded wallpaper?

In particular, I am denoting a substitute at the opposite end of a carbon double bind, combatants on opposing sides of a checkered board (i.e. the trans of a stillborn). Can we conceive of a criminal bloodline?
These are questions of foreshadowing import. The trick is to corral our peculiarities, form being pinioned by its given name.

*

This morning I am busy fashioning a novel art form with the help of an unconfirmed inner faculty; the absence of an outcome is my driving motivation. Other candidates slip by, the whole rancid stock of individuals.

Besides himself we have no protector. Dusk split the ranks of our foe in two — one half on the counterscarp, another penned in the floodplain. A major victory can only be obtained by positive measures aimed at a decision, never by simply waiting on events. Different types of terrain may be classified according to their past beliefs.

There was moonlight. Any doubters are reminded of my misanthropy. I am exhaust. We employed the help of the dead to sabotage an array of stakeholders.

Here comes matter, thrown: siegecraft. Semi-circular bastions stud the circumference of the fortress; the time for parleying is lost. We resorted to zonal man-marking — I thought I was going to die.

Well, yes, all this may look mighty superstitious, but form is never set (viz. antiphonic wastage in a vibrating fork of time). Sappers undermined and demolished the city wall.

I am out-chanced, always. The room was thick with smoke. I remember watching, higher and higher.

*

He finds himself alone and quietly taking his meal. The scene is incongruous, having no connection to the previous, yet has obviously been assembled with a merciless attention to detail. I am trapped in my theme by the narrowness of his experience.

In recent weeks we have committed unfathomable crimes. Now it is raining; a dog barks. I startle like an alarmed bird, for example the heron.

I am suggested, I am suggested by flight. I am suggested by a blind rush into the unknown (town mourns three dead etc). I could hear the sluice of blood to my head, a tide that poured from me to enter every object in the room, every object gaining its own pulse.

I bear a name given to various speedwells, a creeping herbaceous of the earth. We have suffered influence; one day I shall return home. Some who arrived were less than visible.

The illustration shows a building balanced on stone piles. At the museum, all the labels were written in an exquisite copperplate hand — one vitrine displayed fossilized teeth and an abandoned rib. Origin is the limb of a tree.

Now back to my wondrous plague kitchen. There was this robotic voice.

In a harbourside warehouse, spangles of light are reflected from the surface of a turning sphere.

One memo read thus: blue-flowered, posterior sepal wanting, calyx with transformation of outer membrane.... Just after closing the shutters, something knocked at the window four storeys up.

*

It is still busy pecking at its liver. Ill-starred fortune has befallen us, because I gave not. We are wormwood, he says.

An error frequency was detected just before the interlude, and as a consequence the fabric of time has changed irreversibly. I have foreshortened the subject a little, to conjure more space.

I was trying to recollect the costumes from a film when something fell from the ceiling, crumbs of fever. I should have come headless.

This account harbours an indifferent meaning. (You know how to sleepwalk.) Long ago a rune had been carved into the very centre of my epitaph. Long ago, runes had been carved along the circumference of the millstone.

There is that word circumference again. It is bluish-green in colour, having an upper atmosphere consisting entirely of hydrogen and helium.

And now he asks what is the point, could the wireless operator not be replaced by a large metronome? At the station he showed me his drawings of pulled teeth, all the dead crocodiles — some were coloured in a fanciful manner, alongside scribbled notation. The paper was lined, the feint pale blue.

'No, you don't want to do that, and I am sick of telling you why.'

I am good at doing nothing she mouths, ambling past, hound in tow.

*

This is not a favourable location to billet the garrison overnight.

I am inhabited. I am inhabited by the peal of a bell.

I once held a photograph of father boxing; nautical pugilism is its classification in the card index. A trireme is something quite different. I am inventing my own reverse: stay close to whatever comes through.

The final shape is a lozenge held between distant points, with impartial screaming. A rhomboid acts as modifier, a charge in the shape of a solid diamond, on which the arms of an unmarried or widowed woman are displayed. It is a splendid game this, a most irresolute game.

A brace of words swung either side of a pylon. Elsewhere, a neuroscientist on the radio is talking about the allure of anaesthesia.

I obtained purchase on the arc of the key and turned its wards from left to right — within I found an area of ground sealed by the encircling wall of a fortress. I could not focus my eye, and several times had to turn away and look out of a window, down to a shadowed garden set inside the keep.

There seems no reason to doubt that the reader is well aware of the quixotic nature of this endeavour, and its source.

So, we cannot go on doing this, or we can? An aperture for free egress and ingress flips open: the illuminati are for terminating the more law-abiding citizen.

She must be waiting for someone or something, leaning into low winter sunshine, startled against the traffic.

I would not have allowed them to structure the scene in this way. On the gate it said eel pie rules.

*

Counterfeit manoeuvres to the death: across the town square we began to crawl toward the station in a straight line. Terrain may be classified as accessible, entangling, delayed, precipitous, distant, or having narrow mountain passes.

Very crude lives we were back then. Come the spring thaw, we captured a large communist. He stood in front of the sun and stretched out his arms and someone said you are like an archangel.

We have no wish to be blinded came my reply.

Finally, if I may suggest another definition: thermodynamic quantity is equivalent to the total heat content of the average spleen.

*

It was amazing how they showed that couple jumping off a cliff — we could see them at a distance miles away, two specks descending against the setting sun. The scene was quite aesthetic, all things being equal.

Now I am feeling guilty. The multitude peer into remote antiquity to discover a golden age which never enlisted.

They sent a fucking steam train. You can still hear a slight twist of English, something about the way he is standing on one leg, the left. A fine powdery substance, typically yellow, consists of microscopic grains discharged from the male cone.

Outside, some nocturnal creature stirs — I can hear it in flight, wings vibrating in the humid tropical air.... He was never interested in the money.... Goodbye.... I always put the folding seats back before I leave — I do not know why I do this, but I feel *compelled*.

They strap something around your body and you explode. The flagstones rose to lift us above the ground.

Equipage, with postilion clad in snakeskin. How can I expect the others to stand firm if I do not enter the fray myself, stubbornly refuse to give tongue? Bring me the scribe's head.

I refer above to the selfsame window from which the poet defenestrated all those years past. This means you are undoubtedly going to lose; fear has come full circle (win the day of a lifetime et cetera). The ocean trench is over a mile wide and is the same abyssal depth as the last that suddenly appeared.

His ears move too fast, but he is too bankable to be dismissed at this stage of the proceedings.

*

She says the more densely packed the particles, the further sound travels. She has experimented.

The working parts are called ultrasound, vibrations in an elastic medium. She has no spectral class. She is elsewhere.

What an old face: blue-grey eyes, skin the texture of hessian, the prehistoric wound. In the perfect eye, all the refractive surfaces are spherical. Pieces of bone and small stones bore symbols with magical significance and were used in divination, raids on the unkent.

It is not my job to lead a life, prising open, breathless for want.

'You're no resurrectionist: you are a surgeon, an anatomist, and those pencils are scalpels and chisels. . . .'

Come back alive were his parting words. I am denoting paper printed with faint lines, as a guide.

Supernal refers us to the sky or the heavens. Origin sits a fraction above mediaeval.

But now to begin making my own decision.

He cannot rise above the mass of appearances, the seemingly infinite neighbours and other folk of waning calibre. The answer to this question of selfhood are the polymorphous tricks and deceptions of its being.

Use has retreated steadily and is now restricted. Once a year the skin is shed. Speech occurs where the lines cross, actually.

Observe how he has resorted to shock tactics. Beyond the perimeter — what the occupier calls the *limes* — he is conducting his own performative assessment of the human capital under study. He has recently worked on the fallen.

A team bypass is needed, benighted anthems. I came to you because we needed one another, now I would like to know where the threshold lies.

As we speak, a substitution is taking place.

Last man standing

Higher, gripping the square pillar, until sleep comes. I dare not risk the slightest movement — the red tiles on the roof are loose — below, fireflies ignite and vanish. With communication between the battalion and headquarters now severed, it was impossible in the darkness to form a clear idea of what was happening. This is not the desired circumstance at any given moment.

We are in a bistro during the time of the last commune. Her flesh had a long zip that ran all the way down. We had screamed at each other in the car for about twenty minutes — I saved it all in my head. We were on the coast road, the littoral.

I am remembering. Who would say such a thing? I remember my blood running — she was whimsical in that respect.

My source is circa four eighty or five fifty. A hermit established a monastery at the summit. His rule — known as the rule of saint — formed the basis of solitudinarianism. He spent the rest of his days standing atop a pillar in the desert.

His feast day tested positive: a dish of blood sausage served on a plexus of spinach. . . . He was the founder of alchemy and astrology; I took him in my arms and my legs buckled. Origin is modern hermeneutics.

Apparently the numbers are a mannerism and must be erased. It is imperative that you leave this instant, transfigure yourself through the portal.

*

Low autumn sun spreading green bands of dazzling light. The girl in the film said it was like an oyster in the sky. The man they were hiding in the cellar said he could not see it. He thanked her. Stormtroopers came but did not find him. They all died together in a basement when the bombs fell.

A sea. The doors closed one by one, 'spent waves of forgetfulness' — I am artless in my own thoughts et cetera.

Kafka said it was like playing rugby on concrete — that carving of stubborn rosewood with its pitted beak — crumbling bark of ancient trees and salt of potassium, the snow outside, the indifferent spine of mountains. . . . Time arrives too late, insignificant and too late.

For the first time, I could not keep the touch inside. This was my last chance: I recorded misheard nocturnal utterance — unbody set loose and up on the roof, fever rising between eyelids peeled back — star-scrawled happenstance in parallel to a lost crux nomadic. . . . But too soon, always arriving all too soon.

That was the last episode. I look forward with delirious alarm.

Inertia, overlooking a dank courtyard. We mean spiritual or mental sloth, apathy.

Origin is a careless alteration of the landscape. My own term was revived in the late century.

Pebbles and fragments of bone bearing symbols with magical significance were used to divine the future. She was mad for those things. I had no idea.

Tread vigilant, she forewarned.

Only then he remembers, dreams that he is hanged from the bough of a tree, his name replaced by a misspent word.

We are in wide but shallow waters, an estuarial tidal creek. The island has no language.

I am often subjected to myself these days. I lack opinion. For example, the action of throwing someone out of a window: good or bad?

*

He manoeuvres himself, twisting toward the zodiacal sign beneath the ruins of a stone bridge. The only way to attain the beach is to plough on through the waves. He is cut down — mercury in the lung, silver beech behind its shadow.

Mud banks, strangely pockmarked, slide toward a sluggish brown river. Sometimes the shutters are left open, for the heat and for the light.

How can I answer you?

During anaesthesia, body temperature plummets due to the drug administered. This formula expresses the entropy of any system, minus your product.

Back when, he would suggest action such as airborne paving slabs. . . . A mob has now surrounded the caged penitent, liver in the grip of his claw.

This translation appears flawed. You cannot know me, one for whom each moment is the sudden breaking open of a circle.

Each grain contains a male gamete that can fertilize the female ovule. Pollen is transported by the wind or insects or newfangled animals.

Origin is a combining form denoting 'on this side', but written long after.

*

Rising waters in the floodplain. Once again, translation is clearly lacking. The eyes have it, turning in space — devotional, with panic surface. You can't form a constellation with just anybody; I want guarantees for chance.

I too was left wanting. I asked the attendant to check the bile levels in my spleen. She refused (I was too precarious). Above us in the sky two alien vessels converge to form an X — below, a zinc tabletop refracts light from the nearest star.

They found a picture of one man slaying another man, both hands inside the skull of the other. The leaves were arranged as polar opposites, each pair being set at right angles to the pair below.

In the museum dedicated to Mozart was displayed a fossilized starfish with a curious protruding nub and demonic smile. Origin is a verb grown from concussion.

A disc of an unknown metal was wedged fast between the wooden beams, the ship holed below the waterline. Words and phrases help form the impression, so to speak, conjure that which escapes. Your own yield is equal to the internal energy of the solar system plus the pressure of relentless production.

*

Calcinated facial ligaments are a variant, not a flaw. Word-separating spaces disappeared some time between six and eight, before the interpunct landed. Language says the interpunct has a variety of uses. It was female. The interpunct is present. I am unicode.

The fragmented sign is a typographical anomaly. I am attempting to reference the numbered sections of a document using an old-fashioned card index. Frequency is an illegal cipher.

Did you mean?
Jesus and witchcraft.
Isis and witchcraft.
Mercurius and witchcraft.

Last year she left a ladder up one side of the wall. She climbed in there and collapsed and had a brain aneurysm and they had to switch off all the machines.

I refuse to diminish myself to an allegory of other people's expectations. You know what the jury will say: you have wound up in the wrong trial.

The arcane reference here is to the lower part of an animal familiar's forelimb.

He is pinioned to the ground as this information is voiced. Some words he expects to appear again and again in time, yet they resist arrival. Consequently, drinking postures have been rescheduled.

Hermes singled out Thoth. A revolving cube is squared and circled. The outcome is a place of abode, a dwelling led astray, somewhere reached through slow seepage.

Origin is late from badger-dog.

*

Two horses feed on the bark of a tree, a natural tranquillizer. They are nerved and braced for combat within the earth's gravitational field.

Our sacrifice is a penance, as if we evermore took flight. The cause of our downfall was the hoax that is being here — being here in this place, not that place.

This character's infallibility is beginning to grate. We started out at half past seven, when the hero was lifted up by reflux of the sea. He admits to uncertainty: if the process is not followed correctly all the oxygen will be pumped out of our limbs, leading to paralysis. We will need an architectural groundplan.

Regardless, I have completed my mission, with the help of a little pathos, a little defiance.

i) The grooves in the bit of a key that correspond to the wards in a lock.
ii) A bag containing a selection of desirable products, especially one given away as an act of promotional suicide.
iii) Origin is mid-solitary.
iv) The action of keeping a lookout for danger.
v) Then again, origin is early modern from without, plus loss of sensation.
vi) An area of ground surrounded by the encircling walls of a fortress or castle.
vii) Separate the above, the sea.

Vanishing Day

Everything points to a rapid disintegration of the realm. They spiralled around and around until the machine made a grinding noise and then fell silent.

Eyewitness one.

The chinook span out of control, the blades stopped turning and there was a loud explosion and a ball of fire. People screamed and panicked as survivors tried to crawl away from the wreckage.

Eyewitness two.

As I sprinted around the corner there was another huge fireball, space swung open before my eyes, as if on a hinge.

Origin arrives in sense two, from archaic benight. A firedamp approach to learning is suffocating peripheral life forms. A number of hedgerows vanished overnight.

As for the measurement of a sacrosanct indifference: once or twice we went over the cliff, fingers intertwined. The pistol's trigger was positioned alongside a compressed spring forcing one part against another. But the latest traffic is in syllables, the terrible privacy of dreams.

- Blow-up, in the dying embers of this game at the Britannia, diligently exploding.

- A pillar of saints towering high above the desert sand.
- A courtesy bag of nerves.
- Origin is a small particle of disgust.

Now what?

Buried within the grain of sleep, you are sure to find her. Time comes with its audacity complete, with deafening uproar: ghost driven into effigy, tinfoil mummers lurching through the streets. . . . She had never expected this. She has reached the point where nothing matters, and is prepared to say as much. Leave this page behind.

Today she has grown weary, can no longer muster a suitable emptiness. I blame the tinnitus. She is descended from a long-skulled albino race.

You know what happens next: each letter, digit or symbol is assigned a unique numeric value, and these are applied across different plans of inaction. Note how she keeps time, this executioner, forever hoist by her own petard.

Move, or cut.

She makes a social call, axe-calm. I cannot help but recall her craving for exiled food, bark of amygdala and suchlike.

The tumbril tilted backwards to disgorge its cargo of severed heads. After witnessing this, I could listen to nothing save one of the Bachs, who lived.

*

I do not wish to crawl across from here to there. Senescence is rebuilt in my disuse, the interwar.

We led lives of quiet separation in a chaperoned box.

He sits poised in his period codpiece and shaved clothes. But she never had the pluck to take on death in her own lifetime: it was the defenestration that finally did for her. The letters page argues over which floor to this day, some backed by photographic and forensic evidence.

Here she comes with her brutal optimism, leeching out over a year of totality. Her only son had been very adept at pulverizing atoms in his prime.

*

Back to my old habit of lapsing into crime, rising late to a breakfast of chilled wine and devilled arsenic. This passage of time is yet another diversion, silt reclaimed from the sea.

Fog, she repeats. And then, are you feeling a degree of cognitive dissonance today?

Everything spins around anatomy, perplexed in its compartments, forever crashing through. Insensitivity to pain, artificially induced by nerve gas or the injection of drugs, can sometimes boost morale. We had slam-doors back then.

Untold people have lost an awful lot, and that includes things that were never here in the first place: mounds of clay dug for trenches, on either side a vast army, ranks of angels.

*

Of a necessary divide, a kill snared in the crosshairs. Origin is discus, inscribing the figure — the numeral for ten, your outstretched fingers. And I was the first human ever to discompose.

Consider the duty owed a particular moment, cynically scored and repackaged. She says find a request of your own — contest, agon, struggle.

And look, sure enough, there he strides in his leather greatcoat, a length of timber clenched firmly in his fist.

See night, see be.

She resembles spadework, and by this I mean brutal preparatory toil. I could not help noticing the simile, the words together resounding.

Fear not, everything is beneath control: fibres burrow into the thorax while razor-sharp ridges prevent the head from turning. Outside are gutters of corresponding size.

An interpunct, also named interpoint, is a sign.

*

He writes of a mountain that one day rose up out of the sea, but nobody can understand the significance of this unless it is known how this regeneration was accomplished.

No fracture, though the sense is incomplete, swinging either side of a hyphen.

A foregathering, counterpoint to glance, a passing through: grief, upon quitting centre stage. You two are like vultures, you.

When and where is the start. He conducted a mission of preaching and healing with reported miracles, which are described. But writing is going nowhere.

After a vowel was compressed, the first syllable was mistaken for a supreme being. Origin is misspelt — antinarrative of genesis, Chinese opera.

All three words point to skull, mediaeval disco. Our breed was originally trained to dig badgers out from behind the settee. And never forget, never forget the plight of the snapping turtle and cottonmouth.

The sharp borderline has dissolved and we no longer need to count footfall. He has abandoned the complex chain of events, but I still do not consider this a stable space to colonize.

Emblems of the new heraldry are suspended down a well at the end of a rope. I can now warp in many different directions, persevere under the decay of each chapter, within and throughout.

'Separate the last two, cleave them.'

I bunkered down in the darkness of night, an eternal obscure. What sort of shape has your own Monday hijacked?

We are arranged in pairs which form a crossover, touching at the extremities. A freight train passes with its cargo of leaves. He chooses this moment to tell me a unit of magnetic induction is equal to one ten-thousandth of a tesla.

Clearly a man of second-rate genius — note his abuse of the dice, the swab, the forceps. Interpunct is official, origin a stalking cure.

Because I never do

Some details are inescapable, others translucent. We three met, and a stranger tryst was never had. We were close to the foreshore; I fell asleep in the mud.

Earth is dug out of the trenches on either side; it begins to snow as men wearing greatcoats grab their rifles and advance. Elsewhere, an oracle rocks back and forth in her cave, limbering up for the confrontation of several lifetimes. Trust me on this one.

He is going overboard, one severed ghost. Splinters of broken bone and weapons lie scattered across the battleground. Objects think alike.

At these early stages, I never anticipate that events will be very promising — we shall have to wait and see which facts can leach out. An alarming example is the reported loss of your cellular power of division and growth.

I have not done this before. Human ancestors and their fucking memories are the purist element here. It may be that play is needed as a watchword, the inevitable question that arises out of failure, the allure of catastrophe.

While we slept, in my skull I heard a sound like a beating heart, though on reflection it was too erratic for a pulse.

Grainy film of European freight train, mid-century.

I forgot to ask about the money. Now the volunteer has to put her hand back inside the cabinet. Meanwhile, I have eased myself into a comfortable recess, surrounded by cheap machines full of grinding sound, morsels of noise.

Origin capitulates, diminutive of brainpan.

Extrusions

But for the moment all was quiet. It is AD 897.

Secreted every day in your name is the touch. *She* is in touch with something, is quite derailed, examines every mouthful: dive in yourself for a once-in-a-lifetime percentage.

They fly away, safe at last in their unsaid.

Remove all his edges first. Now replace him.

The other is making unjust use of the memory bone: soaring roof like a paper dart in the northernmost quarter, a tiny heart at the base of a drained cup. . . . Was this a warning, a rupture, and if so for what reason? We are as gone as gone can be.

His advocate enters, walks over to the blind and whispers into his sleeve. This instant, now extinct, is repeated in other forms. And what would it have been like to enter the underworld in prehistory?

It is a simple enough thing to find work now that human sacrifice is making a comeback. Does this not make sense of the mysterious way in which the hawkmoth seems to be associated with your name?

We are safely back on the concrete platform. I too had left at the appointed hour; every journey is precisely the same distance. Origin is less than one.

This is said with a slight whistle in her tongue: the S of syzygy, schism, succubus. Another example reads I spied them keeping ward at one of the city gates.

I injured myself and lay contorted on the platform. Now they are claiming their twenty percent. A vicious semiaquatic once inhabited lowland swamps and waterways to the south-east.

He has never eaten a meal that was lacking in drama — the disjointed work of an obsessive nature, a type of writing note-on-note, exploiting the limitations and inversions of a single chord. And it is said he left a mountain of sketches toward a conversation.

The music develops in a certain direction and the listener begins to anticipate what will happen. (It doesn't.) During this journey he crosses a bridge upon which is built a house bearing the sign Paranormal Exchange. On the opposite bank of the river stands a woman, all daggers and downcast magic, elbows pitched akimbo. Most of us are in jail or dead.

In those days a small bomb consisting of a metal box filled with gunpowder was used to blast down a door or make a hole in a wall. I felt as though I were made of glass.

An abundance of blood rises up on one side, pours out and is lost. Modern anaesthesia uses low concentrations of volatility.

*

How can you expect *any* writing to trust you? I broke off a piece of the wafer and placed it on my tongue. Three times I felt her ghost beside me, at my shoulder.

A tumbril is a type of cart, in particular one used to convey condemned prisoners to the guillotine during a revolution. An almond-shaped mass of grey matter inside each cerebral hemisphere is generating this experience.

'No one came, no one came.'

And again, during self-removal, always follow the forsaken route.

The syndicate is leaching seventeen percent. From the blind side a man on stilts collides with the rim of the crowd.

About here in time one had to submit a reason and why, for instance fatal injury. A vertically centred dot was used as an interstellar boundary stone.

Above the portico, a flare of light across those grainy stills. We all know the character who was, but no longer is. The other is too trusting. I spent the entire weekend.

Clock on. Clock off. She looks troubled and gnaws at her knuckle. An international encoding standard was developed for use with different scripts; at times it sounded as though the circus had returned.

Avoid unjust intention, please — no towering cumulus charged with electricity and thunder and lightning. He is beset at his Soutine window, the whole city collapsing, the stacked bridges and looming waves.

Tiny blue fish have burrowed into his eye and will attempt to blind him. I draw them out on a line through the bleached socket.

There is just one telltale gap here, a tremor of dissonance: the almond-shaped mass of grey matter inside each cerebral hemisphere, nullifying experience. Origin is a young forest temple.

Sometimes I had an overwhelming urge to speak, but not about that. I was outlawed.

You see, he is still paralysed by your love.

*

Not a hint. Unsure why I said that. My brain is behaving like yours.

Then comes a sullen downpour that lasts all day. I always travel with fruit, preferably flea-coloured.

'But at the same time, we do not seem able to remember much of your past life.'

Even so, I have made another list, counting twenty-four objects in all.

The dying are hallucinating and being led away. I cannot keep this appointment: fear conquers all while eating the soul.

Elsewhere he writes *glagolgotha*, a nonce word cobbled from verb and cranium. Under the microscope each membrane appears gram-negative and rodlike.

An earthquake reduced the capital to rubble. One man said this was a portent.

She says my cells are amazing. She says my cells do osmosis — my cells can be sleeper cells or hunger cells or they can be fuck cells. We understood each other right away, but not completely, no.

I watched her eyes as she opened the box with a pair of bloody scissors, the gift. We had saved up enough time for a whole requiem. The equalization dial should be set to nondescript.

Now, to compose a lament for the anonymous, or if you prefer: plaint, jeremiad, knell, threnody, elegy, epicedium, swansong, obsequy, keen, coronach, howl, shriek, *de profundis*.

They were never alone in that fire

He calls to say he has just seen an accident happen in front of his very eyes, now leave me be. Then he starts screaming, his head starts screaming.

This offends all our senses. Suddenly he stops and tells us that he intends to restore the old shibboleths. She says this delivers theatre the *coup de grâce* and we must run for our lives.

Once they have shown their heads, these creatures abruptly dive back into the murky depths. Origin is the opening word.

These are just the remnants of us. And I did actually crawl off elsewhere. She has not ceased to question her existence from the moment of our arrival on the planet's surface.

Our first task is to seek out the massive timbers that can support such a double hull. And who is that beating their giant wings just outside the window?

I am right now pondering arrest, crucifixion and resurrection. Origin is the breaking news of her dogtooth (see spell).

We are translating ecclesiastical bone annunciation (see archangel). I keep overhearing nerves, parchment.

This is unspeakable. I am exempt, a halving principle. I am. I am not. I can. I cannot. I cannot be. I cannot do. I cannot say. I cannot see. I had. I had not. I do not. I did not. I hope you will. I hope you will not. I may be. I may not be. I shall not. I shall not be. I trust. I trust not. I was. I was not.

*

Over time she seemed to waste away and everyone became more relaxed when suddenly she whipped the cloak from her head and thundered a long speech, with veins bursting at the temples. The reader may wish to imagine a case on wheels containing explosives used for blowing in doors et cetera, a mobile work of fire.

Remember this: why the uncertainty? The broken pottery was crushed and reused.
    And he was like a Blake, up at speech in his anthems as the air appears to hold him aloft. . . . A marble column crashed to the floor in the darkness, followed by a scarlet disc, its capital.
    How to read the tracks, the route formed by a chain of nerve cells along which impulses travel. What is happening now?

A large swift-flying moth with stout body and narrow forewings typically feeds on nectar while hovering. By contrast, to be hoist with (or by) one's own petard is to have plans to cause torment for others backfire. My own destiny took place a couple of years ago: instead of striking at the head, it is the nervous system that should be attacked. Thus occurs the rapture of doing your duty in silence.

She scrambles about the room, demanding of people what they signal and plot, what the fuck they are doing here. This was the strain of viewpoint we craved, all taxation corroded at source.
    That year by consensus she left, to outmanoeuvre the elsewhere.

XVI

Mortmain

She never mentioned. Again, it was inevitable.
One day you were walking in front of me, without knowing me, and later (now perhaps) you are here once more — back to the open window, with your presentiment and bad faith.
When this is exhausted another sequence will run, the type of anatomy that explodes with a sharp report. A suggestion has been made, stockpiling.

Recent fossil wingless, possibly a generation too early. The familial history is intertwined with an inquiry into lost causes, a narrative which attempts to explain topographic features such as the pillar of salt.
Hoist is in the sense lift and remove, with sledgehammer alert. Origin is late via almond.

Have you any object surplus to need? Bring the others out of this place et cetera.
The sun had risen over the sea when a sudden squall came with haulers in a deluge lashed against the bodily frame. He says I cannot detonate without the given code.
An indebtedness is emerging, a chain of hinges dependent on one another. Slowly arriving, this looks an untimely place to cease, beneath the incarcerating rib, systole and diastole.
He explains: when I say heart, I do not mean the organ. She immediately fractured the spine and he collapsed like an empty sack.
This is set in an indeterminate past. There was a rush of blood. But here finally comes a list, a meaningful list, which demonstrates the persistence of our mechanism, our craving.

*

No portrait in this book claims the character of any actual person, dead or otherwise. Most of the humans are defaults, muttered blandly.
The precious cargo slips from their grasp and plummets down the mountain. Extras are needed, voiceless labile changelings. The sixteenth star in the constellation is Pi Herculis.

Manacled prisoners shuffle around the dank exercise yard in a circle. We are gathered at the shore of a wondrous paraffin sea. A great fish bursts from the blue of his iris, arcing through space to take over the controls, chancing entrance for the entire shoal.

*

A bee batters at the window pane. Only one pulse survives, less than a mile off.

For an instant I stood still, like he who was struck long ago by a lightning bolt, the everyday. I have not given this much thought myself, being apt to slip or change (see mind).

Polished daily inch by inch, the factory floor reflects your face. Despite the unsettling graph, I believe the roof is now safely attached to the walls.

This one is a professional hexer, profile lost, all at sea in your here-and-now. In a futile attempt to reestablish himself, he obsessively records fragments of overheard dialogue. He is incapable of doing, hoards with vengeance.

I fear I am betraying a confidence but the evidence is, quote, damnatory.

We might change his options yet. He later became a willing candidate for a series of tortures, both mental and physical.

'I am better off like this, ripped out flesh a-glittering.'

Pulvering Day

See archangel, the agent working under that name for several years now. A chain of ancestors sits around the table, hands linked. Today's date is the seed date, AD 897. All the drama is a re-enactment.

We embraced in the darkness of the auditorium. There are tiny vibrating fibres on the surface of every cell, spreading current through the surrounding plasma.

Cilia, screams a bystander.

Long periods of grinding work, punctuated by the occasional halt. A spiked metal frame tears at the land, piercing and retracting. Its operator pivots back and forth.

He responds.

She is no longer there.

He falls, 'Tell this to their heads.'

My mission is to locate the precise spot where she plummeted to earth. During this pursuit I shall attempt to record the sensation provoked by every object encountered.

You probably know somebody just like her. For example, how many of the identified items are vendible? How many edible? I may refuse to join in. I am counted among the cankered batch.

Origin is on the way, *via negativa*.

I cannot remember what happened, I could never remember what happened. Just then, an earsplitting siren wailing up on the surface.

*

A mete man, boundary marker, settles a bolt in the crossbow, drawing inward. He attends to his teeth with a nail. It is too late for exorcism.

Today I feel indescribable, and for no good reason, like a fate that has been cast out of itself. In one dark corner hangs the family reticulum, a fathomless network or nest-like complex.

Does unwearable make any sense here? Outside, a gradual circling with skinned knuckles — come nightfall they sunk deep into Thanet sand.

At dawn he emerges, highly resistant to corrosion, hauling collapse to sling out of joint. . . . The area in the middle represents a ripening sea. Each dwelling supports a roof of terracotta tiles, where once you were, what once you are.

An unreadable — axe-woman in the newspaper. He is felled, shatters as if glass.

Because you are exhausted, because you are here and you are weary — because of the clearance. . . . You are here and you are dashed to pieces in the foreshock, seized at the margin of high and low water.

They came across as each other, twinned.

The disc spins, white of egg or eye — an assault by storm, frogs, mirrors — odd pairings of older influence, atom upon atom.

Another night without you and I'll go crazy.

The terrain overlaps — a deep shaft of contemplation, always forgetting what to say. The rent between cloud and sea has been renamed.

One day I will. The locals are quite feral, but complete enough. I never dared to greet him during the daylight hours.

She is often called forth to do battle in this way, hence the need for alarms. I drew her attention to his last writings.

Let me destroy this situation for you: pictures are sketched across the wall with the soot of a candle flame. (I warned you.) And she is vast, with a red circle cut into her front head. Handprints cover the wall.

Tell me of any past impression you have sustained in memory — anything, any image.

Variform dead on the cill this morning.

A narrow isthmus links the two larger territories. He stands before the shed antlers, the snow.

I am thinking of a Balkan flickerbook. The upper parts of the body are on occasion daubed ochre and blue, sometimes played out separately.

She fights her way into the keep, nervously slides the bolt. The door is barred — she feels for the spot where the spyhole is.

Music, the backcloth, is illuminated by flame, tonguewise. Origin is a stroke of lightning.

A wall of faces. Is that clear? The scaffold collapses. Now I am leaving, a horizontal movement. We must be parted; I never answered. Now am I going, so.

*

Dog chewing tongue. Both ears were sliced off. He has placed a difference between himself and the other, this perilous first-born.

She sheltered these past three months but can no longer conceal. She is out of control, cries muster, every which way.

You cast yourself off. Let them lead, let them lead me to the ridge.

If you don't, I will. He invited them in and spiked their drinks with ketamine. I just waited indoors alone, waited for it all to end.

How sudden the loss of parting, a place. She corresponds to the feminine atom, tracing back to the same scarce moments. Don't turn her over — do not, just yet.

We seem to have fallen through the gap between work and its indifference. Better allude to the absence of fact, a reflection, rather than the unmistakeable. Better to sleep, and I shall wake when she cries out, carries breath.

See, their roles are doubled, sometimes played out separate. A roof slate falls into the street. He has crammed so much into a small space, he with his chalkdust and trailing ghost. Now I too am leaving.

The old well is full of rubble. At the innermost cell of the hive, flint-knappers crouch to make fire. (With a cracking noise, to break in pieces.) Be prepared to turn this inside out — he with his anthem exposed, one eye on the chopping block, condensed to a powder.

This doubtless alludes to shared ownership of property (viz. kleptocracy). In the map room were flags indicating where all the outlanders lived. For years we found ourselves on a list with no promises.

I here donate an electron orbital. Day resists its awakening.

Say to yourself, I will be back in an instant, a lifespan. One night the satellite simply refused to appear.

Are these unpeopled days of any worth, he wonders. (No.) Have you ordered enough already?

Brief hands at the window. One of their company is ready to turn against us without warning, unleashing current into the surrounding fluid.

When we must be parted, how sudden the loss. The silence will end in precisely one minute.

We are standing on high ground, a barren fulcrum encircled by a moat. Standing there — yet mobile, spinning — with a supporting cast of almost forgotten shapes.

A vexed question

They carry a burden, are called forth. One says chance is hard to fail. This is a way of describing something by saying what it is not.

A vanished continent is posited to explain the random distribution. That day the sun barely rose above the horizon.

No, earlier, much earlier, he writes.

In each subsequent speech act, I am returning to a state of futility: picture a paschal statue, concealed yet present.

The line drawn was tangential to infinity. I am forestalling the opposition.

An envoy, archaic elements

This knowledge provokes his clairvoyance, a trick to adjust the natural divisions of time: an almanac of place names, a table of months, days, mortalities and seasons numbering eight. Or of uncommon facts — so many substitutes, a list of documents arranged in epochs, with accompanying summaries — a list of canonized saints or prisoners awaiting trial, a list of revenants and abductions: any record or inventory.

I have indexed, at other times annulled — yoked to time and place of utterance, moving in sunwise motion, turning deasil to rising star. Consider yourself lucky.

An angle of rock — corner with crack, to camouflage. And then she says, if you leave, don't leave.

We have looked up your methodology. (Nerve gas.) A dog barks in the courtyard below.

'Look, the night sky folding inward.'

We are trying to build a composite. The blueprint passes to a dead hand, one that can never part with it again.

Side by side lie patches of unlike tissue, ancestral tics, the dying bough of a tree with genital semblance. She walks by and notices nothing. A note sounds.

He woke with a surfeit of electricity inside his body. I gave chase as he went blindly about his business, with the air of a man who could ignite inside an empty room.

And here runs a narrow strip of land with sea on either side, a contraction of earth forming a link between two continents.

Tear out his inside,
cut him into little bits
and send him homeward
to think again.

Unedge, divide

Apparently culled from sore empties.

Confined yet bursting through, it is she who now wields the knife. Her tread is lame, the hobble of a lifetime.

The assault sounded like someone splitting open an under-ripe peach. The signals drawn across these walls are the oldest in town.

It was a busy highway at that time and had often felt the imprint of his foot, set at the opposite extreme to his costermonger head. On arrival, he adopts the diamond posture: confessed fragility yet with a robust spine of clay. A voice says faintly, do not be dispirited by the swarm rotation.

'I wish we had come before. I wish we had come back.'
'Before what?'

*

At last, the famine.

'So when I goes to sleep, I says to the firmament. . . .'

Get legal representation: vibrating microscopic cilia have been found in large numbers on the surface of every cell.

She feels a degree of shame and guilt, or at least some impulse to conceal her memories. She has hidden him for eternity, snuck in the hind brain.

The vessel is broken. I am not attempting to entrap you.

One crewman checked the starboard propeller shaft. We are in need of replacement — argosy, a great merchant ship of Ragusa, Dubrovnik, Venice or the like. The keening now is ceaseless.

He whispers close at the inner ear: I know too much about thee and thy muted heart.

*

Mournful foghorn, a searchlight. Maledictions cluster; I can see what happens next. He is torn and twisted to pieces.

On the pavement lies a blue plastic sachet, used. Break this open and swallow. Memory is an act of attrition.

Anyone else?

True, there are some exceptions. A man runs up with a message from the artillery regiment: it's your adrenalin, let go of my hands.

She seized the opportunity to leave, cannot have weighed so much as a butcher's knife. Her mental state has improved, but the military situation remains uncertain — all the fingers are frozen and can feel nothing. She sees herself leaving. (Trigger the rifle.) She is determined to leave. She no longer interests herself.

The pin slides flush, tight.

A gap has eroded through an older stratum, an overfolding, exposing the level beneath. I no longer know what this phenomenon is called. Another man is perforated with pinpoints that let through the light; the interior is choked by growth of bone. Two membrane-covered valves lie between mantle and core.

The eight bulkheads are flooded one by one, that is, separately and in succession, singly. In some protozoans and other small organisms, propulsion is provided by generating electrical current in the surrounding fluid.

Now we have heard everything within our own ears. But it is hard to focus under such abjection, snared inside the image perceived — one more upon another, then another — stretching out to the endless breach.

Quite an elusive rumour this: he fell from the sky straight into the rainwater tank and disappeared. Those things breaking the surface look like fingers.

*

Nine easy lessons. (We provide the badger.) The food donated is on the ascetic side — a glass display case has been provided to shelter the more delicate specimens. Such a container has been named a vitrine, not a vignette.

We retreated to a bomb-proof vault with loophole galleries. He doesn't stand the ghost of chance.

Ancestors stir beside me, oblique winter sunlight in my eyes. The public feels cheated.

He wakes with inexplicable cuts on his hands, bloodied knuckles. Everyone is accounted for, save the one who tilts at windmills.

Repeat: a dog lay down by the side of the bunker, its tongue lolling for thirst. Who else was foisted upon us?

She has hidden him these three months but can no longer conceal. He has stationed a difference between the one and the other.

It's not here yet, is it? We trespass inside one another. Electrically charged particles bombard the lunar surface.

'Whence do you dwell?'

'Usage.'

It is now broadly accepted that idle speech has eroded his curiosity. (Don't forget.) What sort of voices are we talking about?

Stockpiled ammunition lay in a chaotic heap. We had long since abandoned the encampment, rubble now of an iron-age hill fort, cairn at the apex — margin of debris: a tell of stones.

Escapement is a mechanism in a clock that transmits a periodic impulse.

Escapement is a mechanism in a typewriter that shifts the carriage a small fixed amount to the left.

Escapement is a part of the mechanism in a piano that enables the hammer to fall back.

November is the month of chrysanthemum, with prayers of intercession for your hungry ghost. He takes up a stone to mark his own boundary. I lie in between.

I am ill-formed, disestablished. Each of two frequency bands either side of the carrier wave contain the modulator signal.

Know who that is? A narrow passage of tissue connects the two larger concavities. Origin is a metaphysical frontier.

XVII

A journey, especially one made in the past, a journey with no specific destination.

She draws out a thread of fibre and twists it between her fingers, preparatory to spinning. The elderly man opposite stares into space. Attached to the wall is a small metal ring for a rope to pass through, such that one positioned beneath might be bound.

I went out and braved the storm in an attempt to regain the bridge; daily now we are under bombardment. I miss you.

Origin is old morse, with the addition of parasitic.

We are transforming waste. A perfect bead of water sits in the shadow of a glass at my table. There were abandoned settlements (*kelda* is a name meaning spring).

We compared every townsman's footprint by filling the tread depressions found by the river with candle wax, and thus taking an impression. I just tried to pick up a piece of light from the floor.

Over the phone there was this rustling noise, restless shifting, the background hum of live bodies. We are seeing grotesque outbursts now, from the far side of the galaxy in relation to the direction the observer is facing.

Is this the house you have been building forever, the one that can never be erased? Even at this late hour of the day, given the heat, there were streets where several minutes would pass before any pedestrian appeared.

*

Once upon a time in the land of us there was a man, named. They want me to see through my own eyes again; slowly I lifted the bandages wound about my skull. They are in pursuit of a counterfeit body.

This could have been a disaster. They have reverse priorities, an inverted bucket list: the seeking out of experiences one has no wish to experience.

I surveyed my room: hairline cracks in the plaster, bone of inlay — flint partly embedded, partly projecting. . . . In my mouth the tongue refuses to function. The slow turn of a ceiling fan is reflected in the circumference of a zinc tabletop.

She says when I first heard that song it was an epiphany. After the death I felt her presence on many occasions, company at my shoulder. Several weeks later the portraits arrived, meticulously packaged by a wanted man.

*

He was concealed for years among an inventory of things: a barely readable inscription, one rusting lock, the chrysalis of a moth, a saint's knucklebone.

Note how casually he strolls about in the moonshine. Someone has struck fires.

My father and I are caught on a tongue of sand as the tide comes in and the waters rise. A dense white fog hangs close to the shore. The sea drives a channel between us and the land; I could attempt the leap across but the slope of the opposite bank looks treacherous. Trapped on this shrinking island, I call out. There is no reply. Our sense of isolation is acute, as though we two are the only living beings remaining on the earth.

A mediaeval contrivance for hurling stones was dug up, along with a casket containing the serrated spine of a stingray, a cube of onyx, and the gentle eye of a crane preserved in a glass vial. That sound you can hear from the courtyard is the rebound of a rubber ball. He says a phenomenon pertaining to sight is needed.

The word bolster appears to derive from an upturned boat, and this remote artefact certainly resembles one. The crew seems to have mutinied: shooting occurred and they had broken into the cargo of wine. A prehistoric forest generated the silt filling an ancient river valley which cut into the sandstone, and it was into this that the ship had sunk.

The remains of the surrounding barrow were piled high and reached to the edge of the capstone. To the question are you not coming, he will always answer perhaps.

I think the shape has changed inside his body. A field for the duel is being paced out as I speak.

*

Two army helicopters hover in corrugated haze. She invents a word for herself, something brittle of her very own (Fenestella). I noted odd perforations in the canopy.

A genus of moss is forming fan-shaped colonies with a netlike appearance.

We achieved our mutation between the middle vacancy and the upper; at about this time the first reptiles and seed-bearing plants suddenly vanished. I foretold her reappearance, and continue to exist far longer than permitted, waiting in silence.

That something of magnitude happened on that day, as one learns from the archive, is certain. In the harbour is a ship of fifty oars.

He was a man of destiny. (The human skull will wear away imperceptibly over time.)

A rout is imminent — it's a number thing, the sixteenth letter. In mediaeval notation, the deceased is an abbreviation for paraffin.

That which is not in complete agreement with our manifesto falls short of existence: low maintenance memory, remembrance of a life of shapes — mosaic maps — off with you in yer bloody cups, ad infinitum.

Photographs lie scattered across the tiles. One of the girls wanted a pair of real wings. The reader is referred to the pi orbital system of the benzene molecule.

See you outside for another act of wandering. Origin is a term in archery.

A slow bruise spreads out from the circumference of the earth. Snow is moving rapidly westward. Walking is hard work, driven on through such obstacles, squeezed between reed mace and the water's edge.

Through our contact at the city of Z, we learned that there was no longer a boat off the island; the curve of our fate still twists the wrong way. The corpse was shoved up tight against the steel door of our boxcar.

Note how his bombastic tone has evaporated. I believe a few like him, the more aspiring, loved without condition and excursed on occasion beyond the stockade.

He is transported, dancing at the rim of the earth on splinters of broken glass. Moonlight sluiced the grit from my eyes.

Reveille

He stirs, wakes to the inexplicable and a naked dip in the ooze. Within earshot comes a boy with baroque use of the subjunctive mood, the not-yet-realized, that which is imagined or hoped for or demanded or expected. . . . But don't be fooled, this is a checklist of disaster, marked by a shift in the status of 'I once possessed'.

*

This overwhelms me. Please do not bend: *these* are the acts we perform at this location.

We started taking things home — the rock split readily into thin layers, laminae along the bedding plates. Oil was distilled.

I steal from others, pimp and filch. Flashfire sears the surviving lung, which now resembles burnt rice paper. A separate voice seems to emerge from the first and offers a disturbing version of events.

I had to fulfil. How many decisions that I believe to be my own have in fact been made in my absence? Loki was more trickster, in truth.

There were tracks across the sand of a man running. It's rumoured some would walk through fire.

Decomposing sound escapes, warped fragments interrupting the dialogue. Any remote or parasitic period would qualify for inclusion here.

He wears an expression. It seems to say, *look*. There follows a flood of syllables: they will never find the spleen.

This type of sound is built note on note without modulation, whereas an impluvium is the square basin in the centre of an atrium, receiving rainwater through an opening in the roof. Another volunteer had to claw his way out of the imprisoning mortar.

A bolt-hole, fogou. There is no record of any finds, even though all three mounds have hollow centres. A sign is something which stands in for somebody while they are asleep.

He is charged with excess, over and above the electron count. . . . Children sparing in the street below, chalking around each other's elongated shadows. . . . He urged his divisions to override all previous orders and keep moving at full speed.

Chapter eighteen is lost, chapter twenty-seven is lost, chapter thirty-three is lost. He has only a handful of lives invested in this.

'Cast his form in calcined ash. . . .'

A rope is then threaded through the open aperture.

The initial phase forms the first movement of an unethical life. He is a relentless citationeer: forfeit is the liberty of our discharge et cetera. When he has determined significance, he incorporates that sample into his own fiction. He must beware the creeping at his back, the brutalizing silt of language: the species is chock full with mind, with salvage and remnant.

Another of those satisfying tics of a nascent mortality: a sigh stirs in the throat. A deep-water marine mollusc with a colourful spiral shell is prized by collectors, whereas astragali are small bones used as dice.

If you can see them, they can see you. Will it all end with the jackal being rescued?

*

If he ever expressed a coherent idea in his life, he would have to seek out a quiet corner in which to hang himself. All sound resembled the hum of voices at an infinite distance: the concept of not-coming.

Another hysterical whisper, accompanied by a persistent image: he on the gallows, torn flag of dead skin. . . . The night belongs to one man; he is exorcising his own ghost. I am careful not to quote him (bad magic).

Our narrative flows all too well from this point onward. The question resolves itself during sleep — a necessary trauma — the usual panic at the close of every month.

My physician has administered a placebo for combat exhaustion. Strictly speaking, whence means from what place, as in whence did you come.

Consider a rising current of warm air.

The stranger was with him when he died crossing the mountains while attempting to reach the sanctuary of the frontier. Now we refuse to say anything and are not leaving. Origin is keeping watch.

The atmosphere changes radically from week to week and is determined by the particular bodies present, until it becomes impossible for anyone to resume a natural disposition: too much phantasy, via the capricious agency of perception, the great escape.

My own name is derived from the mechanism in a clock that transmits a periodic impulse. Now origin is turning toward the observer, away from the past, curving inward. During this epoch there were extensive coral reefs and coal-forming swamp forests.

Do not rush beyond, keep your hand steady. He dreams of two unknown women, one of whom has all too casually come back from the dead. They compete. He wants both; it can't work.

Terrible sense of loss — old measure of bloodline, related to a root shared by meditate, care for — also unmet.

*

The final redoubt. Bite of hot seed across tongue, star-noose with petrol, full on like a roaring boy. A cry rises up, salt on the back of the hand between swollen veins.

The encampment lacks law, has no established customs: events just happen. She beats the old tattoo, froth at the corner of her lips, on guard beside the tap of a cask — breath of all present like an injured wave, bruised invisibility.

Now we are received.

Based on the evidence of marine sediments, dozens of species have been wrongly accused. My own story arrives, gouging a channel through the clear and present danger. Greasy black smoke hangs in the air.

The invention unfolds: semé of bezants, a roundel when gold, the polyethylene head in the fridge. . . . I am not that good at difference (viz. direct intuition of hyperessentiality).

Something has arrested our lineage. He says I want to come back to the same things, again and again, build something unrecognizable: a knotted bell rope, a bouncy castle, that diamanté lizard she always wore, powdered crystal sparking substance — his brown leather suitcase, tin hat and sea chest washed up in the loft, script fading shapeless, initialled.

Time reluctant, with hesitant contours. The father is a sixty-minute father.

Same theme as the open sea. (Where does that belong?)

He ranks somewhere between rootstock and patriarch. And then she says, *take whatever you need.*

*

A rent in the time-lapse continuum: none present can explain how this phenomenon could have arrived inside the perimeter. Within the walls of the salon there is a resigned feeling of used books; uncertainty prevails.

I see her creeping, white and gleaming across the parquet floor. Her residual tumour rattles and skates, an exhausted seam in a once famous brainpan. Gothic stained-glass windows admit a dim light as the next volunteer is strapped to the forcing frame.

Gouged out from the sole of the foot: a plug of hardened flesh with trailing tendrils — moss quivers at the touch of a toe.

'I am only alive, when this.'

Systole-diastole. Warm sunshine, an open city. We must keep away from the centre. I hazard we were never meant to remain together a whole lifetime.

The money was shit. Every evening I strolled around London without leaving my room. This winter will never end; I adore street photographs, the sepia. . . . Who is this dying man you keep talking about?

Note how the two treasures are never shown occupying the same space. I doubt whether any great solecism is committed by this.

She wanted a pair of gauze wings so she could fly. This gives meaning and order to the representamen (a thing struggling to represent something else). I saw the way she did that, that greenstick fracture.

The man in patent leather shoes summoned me. Detectable parasites were present in the tissues or faeces. Origin is related to ice-flag.

This is the very spot from which sacred turf was cut: a plant with sword-shaped leaves once grew from your rhizome.

Slowly move through these threads, one at a time. If a state does not apply itself to war, the venom is transferred to its own interior and it will suffer countless generations. It seems there was no need to have numbered the objects after all.

*

All assembled have pale blue eyes and long narrow skulls. The men carry spears and shields of bark stripped from silver birch sealed in resin; they are organized in military companies of fifty. They are overseen. Some ripen early, swoop toward me across a deserted strip of land where tall grass quivers in the wind. Origin is rain into, horizontally.

Vegetation consists mainly of brushwood or stunted forest growth. Armour has been made available for our defence: curved bill and thigh plate, chain mail panoply. There is even a concrete ear. The ripples on the lake form infinite abstractions.

Gnarled trees provide scant cover. The first that comes wears flesh protected by thin scales of sedimentary rock, blue teeth in the tiny head snapping at my hand. Suddenly it vanishes and I am alone once more.

The nightwatch approaches.

'Have you a quiet guard?'

(While thrumming with his fingers on the lantern.)

'I am sick at heart — mort stone, mortsafe.'

A niche in the wall south of the altar holds the piscina and often the credence. If he ever expressed a coherent idea, he would be compelled to fling himself into the nearest sea. And in this manner, breath and water conjoin.

Invoke an apparition. Answer its vague question.

You were there, were you not?

The everyday image nonetheless leaves a sense of unreality on the tongue, preparing us to accept the uncanny. I asked myself whether some catastrophe prevails.

Seven are trapped inside him at once: rivals, adversaries.... He transmits, fading out of the light general.... Then light on he alone, while the other rests in shadow.

An eye-level shot requires the placement of the camera approximately five to six feet from the ground, corresponding to the height of an observer at the crime scene. When he became feeble, we simply left him to die on the concrete platform opposite the compound.

The man grown out of us

That is all about to change: a slow deceleration of the earth's spin is rumoured. A figure of the deceased is printed at the opening of every chapter.

She waits for the signal, a reed clenched between her teeth. That howl could have been an animal.

In the middle of the banquet he cries out. He is quite possibly hexed.

I am so pleased that you have come along to explain.... Summer thunderhead stacking, panels of bone opening up from the sides of the head.... The poison used is a spirit sluice; the physician must first be miniaturized. And I have brought along a gift of my own, a short arrow for shooting birds.

Dip it in venom, the head. (That's a ridiculous pose.) Your own place of origin is now redundant.

It was all over in ten but we will soon catch up. This means more late-night sessions, more fatal wounds to avoid.

Left alone in his room, a Super-8 reel is triggered by hidden sensors — scratched, blank luminescence.... I remember how the flag was stitched across her chest, you can still see that quite clearly. I am just saying.

*

He strides across the deserted airstrip. I am forming a better idea of the events unfolding: across the scorched earth, colour all too obvious, bleeding into a predictable surround. Insects buzz at his eyes, a slight ghosting of the image.

Origin is a casual remark of uncertain age, perhaps from to stray.

I lack expectation: quietist-nihilist just about sums it up, barely surviving within an indeterminate tense of space.

That epoch was a time void of hope. Yet I want to hear of it again: an explosion in the marketplace — a rung on the ladder, your properties withheld — while above the sea, a column of birds murmurate against the backdrop of a giant blue cloud, stratocumulus.

*

You were born transient: there is a vagabond in the house, a walker. He may be sliced laterally with a scalpel, measured into chunky strips of equal depth, but any downward strike is checked at the apex of his skull.

After the fire, four more bodies were found in the charred timbers of the forest. A recount is scheduled in the bayous.

He is cocooned by his affliction, the last man standing, one who has always existed in a state of entropy.

Archaeologists have found ancient tombs containing nothing but mummified cats. I looked inside and saw a figure wrapped in robes of luminescent green embroidered with gold thread. It is a brittle trade, this.

Please, continue your account.

He has no beginning: total threshold, or perhaps in earlier use, a hinge. He is dry, barren — a petrified wood, ash of copse, a sand bank, sea haar closing in.... From my vantage point in the sky, the patchwork of colour is unmistakeable.

A measure of isolation, he stands firm despite his wounds: pink brain samples, diced flesh, a trembling plasma duct.

He wakes, shakes his feathers loose, rising as a bird hauled into daylight with a staggered beat of wings. They locked him in an empty vitrine, set him up for auction.

We once shared an identical signal, the same sequence of clicks. Now he remains silent, scanning for the faintest neural tremor emitted by our overseer.

Quiet days were spent cooling our exhausted bodies in the clay pit. At that time, I had not grasped the extent of his misanthropy.

'You follow me about like a jackal. As I write, night is failing, every tongue thrust deep in the municipal trough.'

Forgetrance

The chain of events now begins to get really scary very, very fast. Today is forgetfulness day: it is one hundred years since memory collapsed into a trench. She lurches through the streets, wearing at most a few tattoos. It's always good to end on a jackal, if you can.

Nothing reaches, nothing can reach me. It is a little after midnight. A permanent scaffold clings to the perimeter of the compound.

'And where do you dwell?' my inquisitor gently demands.

'Overlung,' I reply.

'Were there any messages?'

Quiet days. She tried to scream but there rose from her throat a faint scraping sound. One end of a rope was traditionally reeved through a chain.

I found myself standing in the shadow of an ancient keep; misanthropy is uncovered in divers places (e.g. love). Each sign observed addresses somebody, creates in the mind of that person an equivalent.

Yes of course, of course.

Night picture of the cathedral town, glimpse of a crypt among fissures of light — keep the lad suspended et cetera. She sat on the edge of the bed and said a neologism has to earn its keep. I agreed.

'Excuse me, but I am no longer a resident.'

*

I ordered the boy off on the long walk toward his execution. His crimes are vague; when there's a moment, I shall take the time to look them up. I once bought a used novel, lost in translation, and between its leaves was a cigarette paper used as a bookmark. Scribbled on this was the long walk and the letter R, once again. I had to.

Suggest unwisely and repel in full.

This is how he ventures: chance pointers, overlaps in time, hare-brained clues in the attic. He resists all names, places, dates and duties — and I cannot see that changing any time soon. Sartorially, he favours a moon-bleached fabric.

The regime has begun imposing our quarantine. At his approach, she turned and gave him a thrust that pushed him backwards into the open sewer that runs along the main thoroughfare of our town.

(I speak with borrowed authority, my tone lacking consequence.)

Have we spanned to the very edge, he pleads in a whisper from the pavement.

I had to wait an age. The instruction ran: to alter (a proposition) so as to infer another proposition with a contradictory predicate. Now we will have to separate the pair for eternity.

Two or three flares are lit, the picture ghosting, just the head. Origin is thirteenth in line from solitude, via speaking incorrectly.

Only one unit of angular momentum survived the internuclear axis, a speciality of atoms.

*

Some mornings he would lie on his back, fold himself in two and shit on his own face. The constellations of stars mirror the human nervous system; each person was thought of as a spindle, around which the three Fates would spin the thread of human destiny.

Bring it on down. Translucent edible paper is made from the dried pith of a shrub ground to pulp on a slab of stone. The region has no less than thirty-three coastal headlands with Iron Age defences.

Thou hast cured me of the crave for sleep, lady.

Unidentified skeletal remains. A distant bell tolled when actually it was the wireless. Think of a place where a person can escape and hide.

He thought of Zagreb as a possible bolt-hole. Origin is diminutive of jargon — with reference to the colour — a translucent crystal, prismatic, a mass grave.

*

The Chinese were consulted. I prefer the ancients he said, just before applying current to the electrodes strung along the length of my spine. Please apply in writing for further contempt.

He forgot his lines on stage but recovered his nerve to complete the act. This presence knows.

A damaged nerve can never be repaired, hence numb flank of face. Now dust for prints, ink the builders, everyone. . . . It is too early to say (viz. revolution).

That scaffold is awry, colossus. The vital clue was just two doorsteps away.

A silvered forensic ear sat on my desk — Bach, or whatever — then the shrill of a telephone. Years later in a film she picks up a bathroom mug, which has likewise been dusted for prints.
Origin is a ligament of the tongue. I am closely related to trauma, end-piece — but the current sense dates from the core, a wayward stroke.

I have chosen a good time to do all this, have I not? Be warned, this process will stymy the body's vital functions.
He is left following the stream of gold identified earlier, and shall be a long time dead after that. The second stage in the evolution of Hermes is this: two decapitated heads and five bodies were found in the stern of a wooden boat after the vessel had washed up close to the island. It is not possible to confirm whether the heads belong to the bodies or the bodies belong to the heads.
Beneath the tarmac lies a network of fluorescent blue pipes. Static on the sleeve attracts a film of dust, animating the dead cells — next came white things of starlight carbon, jackal-headed.

*

Her body had always behaved in a rather fugitive manner, thus her tomb has been chambered within an iron grille to guard against walking across the earth unsummoned.
'Today you have been absolute, very decisive, if morbidly narrow in the skull.'
Dismemberment is her middle name. And she says be sure to tongue the surface thoroughly: I may return to dwell, and the long walk awaits me.
The narrative here has become complex in deed, complex in the telling. He spoke in turn, and made a sign with his brow (suitor's consumption). It is time I told you of that disastrous voyage.

Keep yourself in a condition, any circumstance. Do like this: corrosive humid air — compartmentalized biological reality — a demented rigadoon. . . . Note italic for less than you, my child.
Grass grows thickly among the roots; at the edge of the orchard we abandoned him. His execution took place in front of five thousand prisoners, *pour encourager les autres*.
Vignette: the deceased standing between the two barques of the sun.

Off the road — in a treeless place, endless snow — mangled wreckage vying with splinted bone, torn sinew. You get to daydream a lot when you're driving.
I used a dictaphone. We will soon catch up under cover of moonlight.

I am curious to know, he suddenly said aloud, what salve you might have, if any, for a disease such as mine.

Make a decision. I have included word, image, gesture, tone. Give it a bit longer.

He has been squeezing too much out of himself. Spindrift flung from the waves quivered at the shingle as if alive.

He started running down the street and in a second was level with his nemesis, elbow out of joint. Give it a bit longer: no pleasure but in venom.

Leave the room. Two hours later, come back.

*

Venus dark, the voice becalmed.

'If Jupiter were not in the sky, we would be crushed by asteroids like a bunch of dinosaurs.'

She throws everything off balance, a human slingshot. Deviant in her heyday, of uncertain origin, a barbed reciprocity is the core of our friendship. Diesel was spilt on her rival during the altercation, and ignited.

The fractures have multiplied, her life is a trial spent striking out at people and their things, pounding the earth with an emptied head.

Above a suburban porch I spied the grail: blue psychic in cursive neon. The ruins of the two temples are but a few steps apart. How could I resist?

Usage is common and has been put to work by disreputable writers since the fourteenth.

I remember now where the ceiling is. My eyes hurt. Beyond the threshold is an interior of silver birch, tracery of red veins. My left hand rises involuntarily as I fall forward.

There is nothing much in this account to get upset about. He projects himself with more self than sense: no motor, no mobile, no dog, no axe. . . . I dropped a perpendicular from behind the left ear.

For sure, he can deliver a top four finish, whispers of the time — the solidified voice is a stumbling block: carry him across the brook to hermitage.

This all occurred in a very small space of time indeed. She was shot by snipers at the age of eighteen. The ultras are still aggrieved and plan a protest about their ticket allocation.

That was the first breath of the land breeze we inhaled: wings with bright eyespots and greyish underside — a pearl of an early ripening variety — the translucent web emerging out of nothing.

Wait for it.

*

Just be sure to stay beyond reach of their scoping claws. This is a tactful way of saying you will not outlive the night. Bradycardia is the word for abnormally slow action of the heart.

He is hooded above a patchwork cloak: centohead, scraps out of joint, the sting of the everyday.
Hang on to that thought a little longer, one line for each loop. There is room for several accomplices, the aluminium stitches twisted into shape with metal pliers. In the backyard, animal familiars fight over the severed head.

The remaindered light has been corrupted. A stone basin near the altar drains water sluiced in the mass. His ashes were placed in an earthenware pot once used for smelting ores and metals. He had bought a plot; there is a pond nearby. He was scattered across the surface. Solid voice is still a problem, yet he has kept in contact.
We could have aged him prematurely, artfully seasoned his bones. All process must be asymmetric. He is quit, used as a form of receipt.

A crucible, vibrating against the touch: gloved hand of fish or bird skin, the bleeding gums.
Lend me your weapon. Call entropy.

XVIII

In a cobbled precinct they stand before the cordon. That forensic tent she says, I hope it's no one we know.

We are expanding upon something here, how hideous events may be cherished in retrospect. Lethargy is a wise precaution in such a closed circuit. . . . Then he read aloud from the latest communiqué.

Slept in the tap room
bleached wall opposite,
across the drop
crumbling daylight
through a small square.

The compound is ringed by a palisade of rough-hewn logs. It is good fortune I happened by, or nobody would understand what the other is saying.

I have just realized what is meant by silence, its chemistry. Under siege, even the sick are expected to mark their watch.

*

He is renamed using a shortened form. Six runners pass through (one is real). This is the signal that our present circumstance must come to an end.

Pestilence was unleashed in our manor; structure here is a mazy thing. One bystander says it is believed unlucky to run through more than nine times.

In the strictest application of this methodology, no note should be repeated until the other eleven have appeared at least once. I gazed into the distance without looking at anything in particular, waiting.

Later, the unhappy man's grief entered my head once more. Sitting alone in the darkness, I recited from memory an essay on libation and sacrifice, a long list of names.

Yes, the dead man is on my mind; I love the feeling that comes with every excision. He is now little more than a thumb-sized stump, wears a strap across his forehead for hauling burdens. My gangrenous right leg must be drained of putrescent matter (we are eighteenth century, yes). Suddenly the woman beside me said aloud I must scream, I must.

By this point in his career, maestro had chosen to define himself as *musicus* rather than troubadour and minnesinger. That word and, it tells us something else is coming.

Close by: blue rubber pipes snaking through a shallow trench, aerosol legends, the whole body of fact gathered about to envelope the flesh. We are equalizing time.

*

Her head is full of reptiles. He's out celebrating his new eyes. What a team. It turns out that no one knew what anybody else was thinking.

The work is severed from all previous pasts. Painting's theological crisis began with the first collages, the first readymades.

Let's place these versions in the correct order, all surviving fragments of the original fabric: a causeway built of blocks of cobble is intersected by bands of light — the tide rose suddenly as we attempted the crossing and our carriage disappeared into the quicksand. Her chosen idiom is to say nothing.

He is freshly demobilized. I sit coiled on the veranda and watch calmly as he disintegrates into shreds.

A large flap of skin drifts gently up and down in the humid air. I have been cast out from the loop, ranked as mere factotum.

The latter is a quote of a quote. A few of you may have guessed at the outcome: through the agency of chance we harden into a tribe and seal off the parish map. A hawk has now clamped itself to the arm of the local blacksmith.

An eidolon, you see, is a kind of phantom, a confusing reflection or apparition — a fractal image — the interpretation of a word achieved by boring into itself. We have plenty left for a final fling, the last of the pyres smouldering high on a headland. And he says, after thou sendest them summer lightning, shall we then quit this realm?

He is an habitual outsider — disputed transactions seem to follow him around. It was an inside job. He had noticed against the guardhouse wall another large object, this one depicting a woman feeding birds.

To the recess, by which I mean a hollow space inside something else, a remote or abandoned spot, a temporary suspension of formal proceedings. . . . The verb dates from ultramontane, whereas we savour a constant mean destiny.

As soon as there is a gap in the proceedings, I shall enter. The wrought iron legend above the gate declares our grand mutation.

Where I was found

My only defensive strategy is forgetting. A guillotine is set in motion. What this has to do with personification, I have no idea.

Now he is labouring to explain some obscure riddle: for you in suffering I have yearned et cetera. A tiny desiccated heart is pressed into the palm of my hand.

Never say you will be here for sure, harbouring an obsessive desire to return time and again to a familiar place — a nostalgia for mud, sheltering thieves. . . . Thrice we had to bury his corpse. (Are you happy now?) The autopsy revealed that not all of his organs were situated in their designated cavities.

'You are a rumour, unrecognizable.'

That said, this has been an unmemorable evening by most people's standards.

He struggled for years over his own translation, before being sent on a journey, the inevitable drift downriver where reluctant islands barely swell above the mudflats. The logbook makes reference to a meal of stones, an eerie noise that enters every skull, a dog — perhaps jackal — standing on a flat-keeled boat, glowing in the darkness.

The man gets his samples out, scattered remnants of a theme once voiced.

Do you realize the absurdity of what you advance: the process in the mind corresponds precisely to the process on paper. I have already done the arithmetic in my head.

Her palette is heavy and sombre, whereas he incorporates written accounts from a much earlier date. During climax, an arc of translucent fluid jets across the abdomen.

'Yes, each word functions as a sort of wick — a strip of porous material up which liquid fuel is drawn by capillary action to the flame in a candle, or a gauze strip inserted in a wound to drain it.'

Allow me to explain.

Nerves are shot, the stars down to earth. I remember a boon time — filaments vibrating in the breeze of an electric fan, the laser beam that vaporized your withered arm — but the current situation is showing signs of improvement. We have found a redundant test card for you to memorize before swallowing.

'Consider the lilies of the field.'

'Tomorrow has to be the day.'

The other will surely come, in time. She's had her fill of missed opportunities — recall the episode of the untreatable corrosive wound — and longs for redemption. Namely, that battered suitcase waiting in a left luggage lockup at the city teleport.

Use the wrong pin number and all the alarms are triggered and a steel cage contaminated with a flesh-eating virus descends. I was never good at guessing numbers, so the following sequence is the vaguest gamble imaginable.

Once safely at anchor in the lee of the island, he was lynched on board by several members of his own crew. There can be no doubt — in this territory it is considered prudent at intervals to slaughter and maim, with the object of buoying up any slackers. And the other says, how long must I remain with you, how long must I endure?

After one hour the volunteers were unshackled and left to wander; by nightfall they had not returned. This was ill-omened, we would have made an incurable team.

Keep one eye out on the water, a golden sphere bobbing at the oily sheen.

I arrived as a residue. The other proceeds on his way, miscreates, breaks up into disconnected events. Through this state of detachment it has been decreed that he illegally occupies time, flares off the page like a curse, the voice from the whirlwind et cetera.

Usage is considered incorrect by some. His severed finger is clasped in the keeper's big white fist.

Ever in shadow down here, for all our sakes, she overcomes. We have already agreed between us what must be done.

Then she murmurs, do you want to be released from all this?

I say no, not yet.

She replies, signifying the manner of death anticipated.

Chance would be a fine thing. I withdrew back inside myself.

Now she has been volunteered. The original is all you need, half a story, no story. This is how the future was laid out before us that day, and the order of the series should remain unaltered throughout the work, with certain permitted modifications.

*

I am still unsure. Say something.

The stomach feels bitter, like rancid honey, thick and gluttonous. Then a sudden squall, tombstones grown into the roots while still a living tree. Tomorrow's informants have arrived — limbs draggle and crack. Without, the dazzle of a sea, crosswise shadows closing in to form a lattice. Hang on to that image.

He twists his body slowly to face the glass partition. Don't attempt to reach out for the touch, all memory fading. Hushed expectancy is followed by an abrupt gesture.

He demolishes. It is dead on seven. The territory is hers, yet still he is inclined to boast of a bloodline. On the day of battle, fought in uniform lists, one of the combatants is talked to death at the base of a cliff.

The expanding cloud of gas
being the remainder
crab-eyed prayer beads scarlet and black
a loamy concretion in the stomach
calcified ligature
motion sickness side-on
growths in the sole and palm
sinking the oar too deep for
the plummet back to consequence.

You could always write as if you were no one else. Everything is cocked with flavours, the taste of scorched plumage — tail feathers black, white, scarlet, aluminium bill — bright eyes set deep, benighted. Hill upon hill in the distance remains invisible.

A single gesture and everybody present takes on the forbidden form. Sometimes you have to wait an age. They hold back, then scream in unison: *he* might be the exception, the one who forgoes.

I sat coiled on the veranda and watched calmly as he broke off small pieces of himself.

Strength through the heart's wisdom, or nonesuch. That is how it happened, that is the way it appeared. Once again, the feeling that I have already experienced the present situation.

*

Discovering a convenient gap in her face, she swallows the anaesthetic eye drops she carries about in her sack, scalding the larynx. She is a master of the non sequitur. No one is going home, until.

An everyday legion of changelings. Those useless codas he enjoys so much are tacked directly onto the body. Just say no, wait until you hear another voice.

'Sit perfectly still. Everything here reminds me.'

Sometimes recall helps: her pale blue grave gas, miles of ears of corn, a glass vestibule. . . . Dying out loud, I said out loud.

In this neighbourhood, every syllable dissolves on contact with the air. Clearly we are merging with another instant. Are you looking forward?

'She lacks repose, provoke in her many simples.'

Then I spent all our money, but gently, mind.

Note how this voice is the voice of an undependable narrator. We exchanged visas, yet without understanding each other's tongue.

Now he has ransomed a group of words (underexplored, unexamined et cetera). The missing details were never found when a border guard searched the body cavities.

He presides over metals, shipwrecks and storms, takes form as if rising from the mouth of one deceased. This is a rhythmic process similar to the physical act of breathing, as we shall see in the next chapter.

'I do believe that phantom jackal is alluding to me.'

He refuses to begin, hair flying madly in the wind like a flock of tiny birds or anti-aircraft fire. You choose.

Origin is sixteenth in line for withdrawal. I split open the rubber tube connecting his torso to the pump.

In this manner their cult spread. The revered object has the conjoined merits of a head, a hat, a capstone. The south-eastern approach to the fort is crossed by two outlying linear earthworks — the stones themselves are petrified remains. I am still of secondary, even tertiary importance.

They slaughtered every man on the battlefield, the oxygen sucked out of their lungs, before bursting through to the surface. Stretcher-bearers haul rubbery white vials, egg sacs strapped to their naked bodies with silver duct tape.

She insists that I wear a mask and strip to the waist in the disabled before she will consider introducing me to her breasts. The mask consists of the front of a human skull covered with black velvet.

Who died on stage?

Explanatory note: carefully set the minute hand of the clock before you penetrate the plastic explosive with the trigger mechanism.

See what it does now, how it grows, the way it moves. I have been passing a deal of shattered windows lately, tarnished populace, whisperers of the time.

He tears off a page of the score, plugs the gaps in memory with improvised material: down the rust chute and into the sea.

The mood is such that Thrownness gets closed down and sent home. Our love was an irreparable farewell, for ever in the shadow of the western stand, the clock end.

At the station she says your pronouns suggest a relationship. I reply. I can't anchor time, enclosed in the body of one so departed. The musicians stalking us play along as best they can. I've had a bad night of it all my life.

This is not worth too much of me. There's been a run on money. A head rocks in the wind at the foot of a cliff.

*

He is all day in harness about his investigations. (Might be Hemingway said politely.) The first ear to be quizzed is supple, flexes with ease, a lobe in the mouth, gentle between the teeth. He hammers in a fresh nail and the wallpaper changes colour. Teeth are yellow and sour.

She says I was born under a caul while acid fumes invaded the room. In old chemistry, a special name is given to dull or black compounds — an austere base for an austere age. Never stray from the road she says; all our memories come flooding back. Dead letters are traced across her forehead.

The ship pivots about a fixed point, swift arcs within a circling current, listing low in the water. Should we ever reach port, distance carved from a headland. . . . But we find ourselves back in time: unknown customs, Iberian clarity of heat, the inquisitory cell. I am secured to a rope and dropped from a height almost to the ground before being stopped with an abrupt jerk, my skull one inch from the concrete. Events are more cherished in retrospect.

Punishment or sacrifice is used to make an example of the others, to deter or encourage. Do you think, said Candide, that men have always mimicked one another, as they do on Thursdays?

That bolt-hole had one drawback, the glass walls. Dogma has a nasty way of misinterpreting our modus operandi (viz. lurking with intent). Note the melancholy cast.

The police raid was a penny-ante scandal of little substance. But the threat becomes clear enough once momentum is perceived lost and he's left rocking back and forth as if a tornado had struck. I extricated myself via a few timely gambits.

She is now active upon the field of play: nothing explicit, nothing revealed. My notice was drawn to the rays of light pouring out of her head.

This hex is conjured in the almanacs: at the age of fifty-seven she withdrew to a remote mesa and spoke to no one for three years. Her life and work are full of interesting anomalies (the wolf-mouse and so forth). The executioner had to drag her through mud to the chopping block — she was very slightly built but unfeasibly strong.

Whatever happened to grace? She writes back that human life is impossible.

And thus I creep across the earth, nose close to the ground where a thin layer of oxygen persists. The belated discovery of my work in the west has tended to underpin the notion of a deep split between early and late. Now I am without mind, alone with my rage at the recollection of helpless.

Another strides in growling orders. (Cut it out! The spleen!) Reluctant locks are pried open. It appears hazardous to venture beyond this point.

I glance around me at those attending the séance and think: be precise, we have more chance of survival if we place ourselves *there*.

All I can offer you is some shares in frozen food, murmurs a disappointed voice.

She carries a small book in the crook of her arm; evidently this one is a stray. The hopeless drill of such a task — to invent an ensign, a mark, a few words spoken at the recollection of loss. In the end she resorted to homonym.

I am descended from feudal assassins, an untried economic order. As the day draws on I feel no better. This is a good time to quit — lend me a signal, semaphore, beat my head against the incontrovertible et cetera.

The part of her that is left behind begins to convulse. She has waited a long time for this.

Then he says, that dome up ahead, all my life.

And I should have said no: it's a cupola. But I did not, merely thought the sequence of words, for I lacked the possession of mind that day, as if rising from the mouth of one deceased. However, we vow to take great care in suppressing any collateral havoc.

A fastness, the book, insignia resembling vein.

*

For days on end we refused to exchange a word.

'Use a coin to scratch away the grey surface.'

'Never going to my father now the state has called a half-hearted no. . . .'

Such an informant is the sort of person who would feed information to a linguist or anthropologist in exchange for an envelope of grubby banknotes. Buried deep within the head, she was at length withdrawn. Hatching is irregular, the contour line restless.

This girl is one for the byroads, anyone can see that, and she has just been bitten by one of her own animals. The plot is lost, spread out across the dank earth, face down, a roadmap misplaced in matching pairs of memory.

A light tap at the windowpane. I recoil, beset by hallucinations of sight and sound.

I could never have foreseen my inquisitor's methods. Much has passed backwards, to be absorbed into a brief life.

See, he has become his own critic, as the average man becomes his own alienist. In that moment of time, I desperately wanted my next action to be the duty of someone else. Moreover, I am melancholy under the fear of my eyes being lost, and not to be regained.

Wherefrom stems your grudge? (The stash, indecision.) A wrecker is stationed on a distant headland, roots of white-hot fibre worming through his brain.

He begins to wonder whether he may have overcooked the bet. We roped the creature to a post in the backyard and waited. Only the arbitrary and inscrutable nature of existence connects the past with the present.

She unravels by night the work of the day. For the greater part of the allotted span, we did not test our nerves at all.

*

A denticulate settlement, grim redoubt. His sharp tusks accord well with alleged possession by demonic power.

Note here that the death deity has no proper name. The southern side of the enclosure utilizes a natural rocky scarp to form a double defence pierced by an inturned entrance. Proud skin flaps on a stalk.

A solitary is a figure generated by insurrection. He has made combat with full English, has seen off the inquisition. He has roamed and fought and scribbled.

Today's emblem is a discharge tube fluted like an anchor, a coil or transformer of that shape. Small swellings have been mapped at intervals across the landscape — a sedimentary animal is attached to the socket of the antenna, thorax fused to abdomen. A whiff of kerosene on the balcony, and it's all over in an instant.

Traces of cilia in the scan, narrow process linking tumour to tissue. Despite this, she tells the story exactly as it happened: she does not leave anything out, then again, she does not leave a great deal in.

We are set to make massive savings. She both distrusts and undermines, is naming the assembled things and their possessors. The dazzling light is flecked with spray blown from the crest of a wave.

The day begins to fade. There you are at last — I lie down beside you and ponder how we might engineer our escape. My pillow is a moss-covered rock; a ladder stretches up to the sky. Then I remember that this is a leap year — we had been comparing dates with the previous cycle, the long count — and realize that my planetary survey must come to an abrupt end.

'Do not blow the bridge until the assault starts.'

A data-rich beam of pink light pierces his forehead. Save me, save me he cries as he twists around to stare at the rapidly advancing blanket of fog.

'You had better come too, captain, before it's too late.'
Blue flames burst up out of the ground. Incessantly he repeats the same words over and over: attack is called off I blow nothing, attack is called off I blow nothing.

*

I am returning all my names, still unused, if a little scratched. An airborne polyethylene bag comes to grief in the naked branches of a tree. And I have swallowed every stone, gnawed my way through to the pit of the sack.

Elements of genuine gnosis found refuge in speculative alchemy. This indicates that we can.

Unlike the first who appeared, he has no ancestry: the trail runs cold, lifelines severed by fugue and migration. Pace yourself, the footfall that postpones.

Slowly, he expires. What will they think of next? I have been given up.

Execution isn't everything. Observe the drifts of snow, a ruined abbey through a film of light.

We might as well, I said, march on until the end.

'Finally, you have found the courage to bring me a sample I cannot identify.'

The answer is a young man busy swallowing a watch.

*

And he wore at this time the guise of doctor, celebrated surgeon. Hang on to the partition, giant insects are pounding at the window.

She slips through the glass — he feels a momentary shock at the sight, that desperate pleading in haggard eyes. Together they must pursue in zigzag fashion, forever beyond reach.

This chapter is without a vignette. The deceased, holding a staff, is seen standing before an electricity pylon.

I talk a little, I break a little. Persistent buzzing at both ears, and therein I make an important discovery.

A mesa is an isolated flat-topped hill with steep sides found in landscapes with horizontal strata. During the karaoke session he pulls slowly on each finger, coughs up a few syllables, something about an ex lady.

If you think too much about the fate of others you will lose yourself in a tale of buboes and embalmed cocks. The combat is now hand-to-hand — jackals circling, back pressed flat against piss-drenched hay — leaked brain matter pink-cerise, crumbling scorched clay forced in between the cracks. . . . On clear mornings we can scan the horizon and catch sight of the tourist oubliette, but today is overcast.

I could read a whole book such as this and not even recall the hero's name. The cause is superstition. The effect is superstition.

The nerve that you demonstrate by simply arriving here: this day is surely your last.

Two men at the head of the column are ordered to tear the volunteer apart. Go to Spur G, my enterprise hub: an injection of cold dark matter — barrack-bunk rumour — impromptu surgery in the wilderness, a trepanation foretold. Scumbled blacks arch across the picture plane.

I will stop here, being thus out of range. What evidence can you show me of your past existence?

After a final swig from his glass, he was stabbed through the heart as he bowed his head to leave. The heart has four chambers. Above Iceland my alienist dwells, truly.

I cannot see that changing the numbers. Never pick a client up by the seams.

'Hush, I am counting, recounting.'

XIX

Under a rock, perhaps. Three keels in tow across the oily waters of a canal. Replace I for he throughout.

In many ways the worst option is the number six. The survivors are not quite aligned — none is apologetic, all chunter and gibbet. He does not yet know. He is writing, among other things, the evidences.

Again, some basic rules: a soft wave of pressure — bite into the tongue, bind fast his eyes. . . . A small boy peers around the jamb. I forget the rest. This wavering has no cease.

A whiff of mown hay, truffling hogs caved up for a season, made shadow by charcoal flame. Myself and my animals are safe under a watchful ear. I vow to begin.

Bring me his head in the welter of the day. The only formal recognition of his authority is a rusting badge.

Revolt: you take a day off and suddenly there is no alternative.

*

Your chance to be a winner, trigger the surfeit, the overspill. The needle trembles at eighty-ninety and all the spectators jump. A sentinel is placed at every approach, waves gnawing at the foreshore.

Seize him from the line-up, unfold him. Do not will a consequence.

The oldest child is the candidate, insofar as anyone is. Origin is a waxlike substance. His horror turned to despair, yet in a steady voice.

Clansman, village patriarch: *starosta*. My brother covets the role of hegemon, top of the old ladder when he grows, still wriggling like a hooked fish. He is unmeasured, beneath the massive tread of angels, offspring of a one-trick brood.

I don't trust those pasteboard life forms that can regenerate, the offshore pills. I no longer feel this is a valid answer. Sound lies poised in the bone, cartilage.

He is obviously having a bit of a shocker this morning; these are the kind of messages one sends without expectation of reply. There are days when I manage not to think of anything at all, when a seam opens up: send him homeward to think again et cetera.

We part.

Days later I chanced upon him in an all-night café, gently weeping. I ask. He says he does not know. (Are you responding?) He says he once held his hand in boiling water for thirty seconds. The inquisition would not let him outside. At that moment a man passes clutching a bin liner crammed full of arrows.

These events appear unconnected. I can feel the horizon stretching away from me, pulling in different directions on every side.

He was tired, very tired. This is a utopia, no doubt about it.

*

Rustle of tongues, sluiced down on a deadpan river, silt in every pocket. Now list his phenomena: a strap across the forehead for hauling burdens — small rounded hill or tumulus — a clump of trees, noble gas — a nearby constellation, patrons of the field cherishing lost time — ballast, the metallic insect egg.

They never found his liver. You are trying to guess what the outcome might be, after a saga of forged histories, alien worlds. Make use of what is to hand.

Ruined piles suspend distance on either flank. Towns are twinned — a squat obelisk, moss-blown testimony — children slather at the mud chutes, delivered up to the dismal creek.

Skies collapse at the rim, threads of light scored into boardwalk shadow, luminous asphalt. A withered skin of molten tar receives my cautious step, condenses the scene: latterly homeland, pinned down by fossil stacks, a summer thunderhead.

This is all quite interesting stuff to think about, he writes, I shall see you in twenty years or so: any story will end by swallowing itself.

A flagellum is a slender thread, a microscopic whip-like appendage that enables protozoa, bacteria, spermatozoa and the like to swim. You've been an absolute star today.

M42 is the main body of the Orion Nebula, lit up by four bright ones — other categories are compressed, so much grey matter, the darker tissue of brain and spinal cord.

The manuscript begins versal, a style of ornate capital built up by inking between pen strokes and having long flat serifs. Her pigments range from dense opacity to washes of invisible glaze: crimson rust, violet and naphtha blue, earth brown, magenta and cyan, translucent pearl, rose madder, cobalt with viridian, copper ores under green fluorescence, arid whites scored with dregs of sound. She finally abandoned the project because she could not think of a convincing way to represent a black hole on stage.

Witness, an unforeseen power or event is fucking up a really hopeful situation. Origin is mistranslation, always.

On other days, an unforeseen power or event is saving a seemingly hopeless situation. In the eighteenth century, divination was by plunging toothless mummers into the river — through a wooden tube built for that purpose — and recording their screeching objections upon being hauled back to the surface. I should add that by this point in geological time the waterway had become a veritable cloaca.

*

A funicular descends and ascends within a whitewashed tunnel. At the crest, summer rain is beginning to fall from the sky. Niches have been set at irregular intervals along the interior wall of the shaft, leading to unseen compartments. You filmed our ascent through the tunnel; it looked like someone's oesophagus. A narrow ledge runs the entire length, just wide enough for footfall — should he choose to, a runner could negotiate this path while the funicular was in motion.

'You have hidden him in some improbable future, haven't you?'

'If we survive, we are going to regret everything.'

Some of the intervals are short, others longer. If a runner were caught between niches he would be crushed by the cable car, whose passage allows only a slight gap between the inner and outer walls.

One manuscript version has lizards all over the page and salamanders with tiny marks and scales on the skin.

*

A blank, if you so choose, a blank screen with lines of static. Thus far all the contenders have suffered defeat, usually resulting in the discomfort, or even death, of each protagonist.

What is left to signal: decussating contrails, a yellow crane, glass and concrete — signs of ageing at arms and neck, the corners of the mouth, the lips. The nearest star sluices grit from my eyes, sends me hurtling back.

Warped syntax: he will be back for more. It was like a great ship heaving across a dark ocean. I didn't ask for this.

Some cruel catastrophe, yes, but you volunteered. In your brain are fifteen thousand million nerve cells running riot, but there is nothing more to be won from this coastline. I said as much at the outset.

The device is a breechblock mechanism, based upon the observation that under extreme pressure certain dissimilar metals will resist movement with a force greater than normal friction laws would predict.

*

Ruinous whisper, female: be sure to come back alive. Dilatory tactics at nightfall — come back, come back down.

Atrophy of subsequent moments, battery lymph seeping from the liver. The framing gilt has a reddish hue — a circular hole in the roof admits light, releases smoke. It is said one emperor watched human torches burn, transfixed.

'Listen, I'm trade: I am the who one is paid to do this.'

A gibbet is an upright post with an arm on which the bodies of executed criminals are left hanging as a deterrent to others. The accompanying citation reads offspring of watchers in the last days of our flesh.

This historical account screams aloud to be renamed. As for shelter, I have nothing of my own to balance the cards with. I am incontestable.

But you may not want to happen after all. (Sleep has been rubbish.) Despite occasional outbreaks of violent hysteria, his default position is unnervingly serene. We regard him as misfortune — sickness sheltering under a camphor tree, a band of rose-coloured light split inward at the spine.

Tremble of ashlar as I lay my hand upon its warmth: a simple affinity, the absolute liberty demanded. Impulse resides at the mid-cell of the brain.

Origin is diminutive of axis, plank.

Flint street. Across the thoroughfare, a revenant. How could I have missed him?

If this apparition is the same who walked last year, his skin is an improvement on the original, has aged in an uncommon way, yet still the familiar tracks of woad blue. He has webbed feet (genetic) and limbs reminiscent of the grotesquely contorted trees of the headland.

The following selection has been culled from his marginal notes: a purple dye smeared across sheaves of albumin at the salt defence — a grooved pulley wheel — a fragment or speck, particles of impurity, as in chewed paper — nerve cell bodies and branching dendrites.

Graphite, green ink, bushfire in sewn booklet made gimcrack, human papyrus.

One hand reaches down the spine and under the flesh to finger the vertebrae. We are going to end up in the same position: only three days remain, crawling back and forth across the surface of the earth.

Humid air sweeps in to occupy the surviving space. I am held in counterpoise to the edge, as a stone with reference to the opposing grain. The headland has three lines of defence strung across its neck.

Reproduction is by way of spores released from airborne capsules. Be sure to find a place of shelter before the chrysalis splits to release the winged imago.

There had to be a centre. Truth be known, I had set the two of them up: wild matted hair, neck ornament of twisted metal (torc), mourning parents — black above, white below — a paintbrush of arctic fur.

I approach, harbouring all manner of suspicion.

Where is she? Who is she? And most importantly, when is she?

No further questions. Was this not the surf that bore her feet away, the wave?

*

Location: a secure place well protected by natural features, such as a remote mountain fastness.

From the journal described above, we know the survivors were swept along by four great ocean currents, further and further out to sea. The purpose of such a risky manoeuvre is unknown.

Go to recess, raptured tongue of origin.

Now the crew are drawing lots: whoever plucks the knucklebone from the cap. A connecting bar of gravel is submerged invisible beneath the risen tide. The winner gets to draw horrors down upon his own head.

I station myself to starboard and wait the long wait. The one to my left murmurs let us eat. No, I say, in a recent dream I was instructed to find a snakeskin suit of coppery hue.

We broke into the house and never came back; a shared passion toward dystopia often guides these investigations.

She wrote this letter with no sense of necessity or coherence. A knot of sightseers gaze at the open sea beyond the coral reef. These people, she whispers softly, we will have to liquidate if the invasion succeeds.

Someone beyond my comprehension stands beside us. (The I-think had yet to arrive.) She tells her own story. I oppose: we understand you have a proposition et cetera. . . . The grail is sometimes a cup for catching blood, or a wine crater in ancient Greece, a rock-carved platter or bowl.

There is an awful lot of unused material. All human artefacts can be reset by rule and compass.

These winged engineers share between them a single eye and a single tooth. They are weighing our collective worth.

If I knew of any other who could remain still enough, I would replace her: she is not as foreseen (in this territory nothing appears as expected). Each of the crew solemnly moves back to his own place and grabs an oar, as if in a trance.

Today's byroads may once have been prehistoric pathways or drovers' tracks. This is counterfactual, relating to or expressing what has not happened or is not the case.

*

He is writing at a time when vicious, unforgiving retribution is poised to stage a comeback. Picture a less than dignified figure: an indentured man scurrying beneath a clawlike cloud, the apprentice bound to his master, crossing the desert to a plague-infested colony.... We can still hear the dip and pull of the oars.... M43 is that bright smear along the north-east upper lip.

(Accelerate this exchange.)

The moon hangs low just beneath the hills; one segment is polished white. It is trapped under there, left to die.

I have now met all of your protagonists, all of similar age, all pretty much the same person. Origin is god from the machinery.

'You see, with its many layers, the bridge is absorbing the analogue signal.'

This reminds me of her platinum wig and that twisted mouth, dead rictus in the torture boudoir. (What *kind* of us?) This is never a good time to be present, just before another public act of self-abasement, another glimpse of her unnerving smile.

Origin is defeat in battle, any malcontent expressing a reversal (see my dissociation). Your words are etymologically disjointed: in everyday use their principal meaning has collapsed. Make someone near you feel uneasy.

This is another example of being too much. He rises late, takes himself off outside into the rain, to the endless speech of others, makeshift passersby. I vow never to swing out like that, self-made on a creaking gibbet.

He has swallowed the stone. There was no refuge anywhere. Endless digression returns, footfall upon well-trodden earth.

I think he died for me was her answer.

Shift to no purpose

That day was a dead rubber from the outset. We found his heart down a drain. The heart has four chambers.

Someone is neutralizing the planet's magnetic field, but we are still on course. An allusion is evoked by the chattering sound of the slates during play.

Two months have gone by and no word, which suggests I have failed. I made a show of hauling in the dead.

Always I would wait for her, an eternity. My labours lie at an acute angle of nerve order, the perfect deluge. In futuristic engineering terminology, I am an extreme manifestation of what is known as static friction.

Listen, there is no need for this feud. At the centre of his princely countenance hangs a small fold of flesh. The cause is morphological.

Who exactly are we waiting for now? That object in the corner was not there yesterday.

Throughout such a long night they make no sound. We are paralysed at the point of maximum utility.

A jet of fluid suddenly discharged from the orifice.

Sets and relationships are represented by circles and other figures drawn across the polar map pinned to the mess room wall. Now execute someone by hanging or subjecting them to ridicule and derision: you choose.

Once disguised, each wife in turn asks for her ring back. This leads to confusion. Reluctantly, the two men agree; they are death-dealing antagonists.

On the day of departure — that is, three days after his seizure — the envoy appeared to be almost well again. The scene is one of grief badly served, the affliction of what to write when there is nothing to write about.

I cannot be held responsible for this shortfall in years and the lack of prizes. Strewn at my feet on the promenade was a full set of playing cards, some face up, others not — I tried to fathom a significant detail but could not. Fuck it.

A three-masted barque darted across our bow. Seven windows are set in ashlar along the ocean floor, masonry of square stones misused as face-off debris.

An uninhabitable region of ice. I would have gone hungry for those five weeks if the old physician had not confined me to the sanatorium. On the wall of his study, a hand-drawn map confirms our remoteness.

A chain attached to the rear of the sleigh flexed through powdered snow, tracing a cursive script across the tundra. We plunged through the glass roof of a shopping mall, had to cut loose the sledge and one man fell to his death.

Had he not bid you farewell, would you think any less of him?

We must be closer to our destination than was imagined possible. A fateful tremor of optimism passes among the crew.

Why not simply restore the past: dazzling sunlight on the flank of a bay that curves about a deep natural harbour, held high in her arms.

Because it was not, not as this suggests in its precision.

*

Martial music, shrill with feedback over the tannoy as stumbling workers muster at dawn. A length of chain is dragged through the snow at the tail end of every team.

He always returns too late, or not at all, an antique folio tucked into the crook of his arm. The heart is revealed; I am unnerved by all external appearances.

And now he suffers a morbid acuteness of the senses, has become a slave to repetitive actions and speech. At the last opium den he sank into a shakedown and signalled for attention. I simply do not remember that time.

Sound like an animal cry.

I came here to part from myself, stand down and sow nothing, a deliverance from signs and their objects.

Our plans to escape from a sealed dungeon with no opening for light are surely futile (viz. oubliette). My cellmate insists that a borrowed history will always collapse into time.

A pasteboard glider hangs in the attic, waiting for the right sort of crosswind. It boasts a tinfoil body and the wings of innumerable moths.

Layers of used rain compress into marble at the town square — rust of arterial iron, her memory face.

A key-shaped shadow, the pressing drone of insect life, each sound a finality. The animal spits a dart from its jaws as pincers clack and lunge.

Perhaps a child. Actors representing gods were suspended above the stage.

High noon of beyond, and not a great deal more to say. Such are rare, one who deals in his own demise, asymmetric yet catholic in scope.

Or, 'Look, there's a tunnel!'

A passage to the surface. As a general rule he would disappear after a time.

Definition: a sanatorium, typically one driven up and down a mountain, up and down.

Somehow the days trickle past in my room.

Pick any device of your own choosing.

A hunting horn. A creeping Eurasian of the ransom family, blue flowers locked to upright stems for eternity. The other wears a neck-fetter of hide, fastened to curved shafts which sweep down to form simple runners — a shield of arms is blazoned beneath, drawn out in a variety of codes to describe the bearer. [*Shot of rampart with massive impact.*] Chunks of rock and earth are flung into the air as the archers run for cover.

We are here denoting a group of structures secreting regulatory hormones into the kidney. Origin is a very modern ball of thread.

Three or four years pass in rings, animal sinew looping in and out of my flesh. Hereafter, you will be left to fend for yourselves in close-packed exile.

The metal limbs of a scaffold appeared overnight. The sounding line split in a promised storm — seawater washed the soot from our eyes.

*

We should have sensed what was happening, but at this late stage any changes would be inconsequential. I could have been locked up safely in my cell tonight, with my animal familiar and my scripts.

New strategies are hazard, monstrous divagations. He woke one morning to find he had become a cipher, a saint. The man at my elbow says nothing equals the horror of the committed, for nothing is truly necessary.

I concealed the manuscript behind a loose brick in the wall; the disease of the first half has come back to haunt the second. I shall be absent for the duration.

Whose name is mistaken? Privately, between you and me, it was like falling headfirst into a well. And now all the windows are dark.

Ours was a pageant without beginning or end: cars outside bursting into flame, unexploded ordnance, the night sky lit up by artillery flares and tracer fire, shattered red-tile roofs beside caterpillar tracks crisscrossing in the snow. I never would have left the territory if a few historical necessities had not obliged me to depart.

*

Spectacular targets in this enclave, frequent on its eastern side, rarely at the southern. I fear he tires of me.

We walked out of the bar to face a mob of locals. I find it hard to explain how this happened.

Hieroglyphs stencilled across the wall refer to altitude, the tide, or both. It seems we have earned the right to slip by unnoticed. The whole event felt like an exquisite miniature.

He once wrote no such community as things. Now his head rests in his hands, left and right supporting the skull — or on occasion a single hand, as if posing for a portrait artist. Individual letters are carbon-based, scorched in hot ashes.

And you are merely a foil with obsessively sharpened fingernails.

I try not to. Nothing happens. He has a tendency to leak, a schizoid character thrown in relief before falling once more into lethargy.

But today I am not so sure: let events choose themselves, add eavesdroppage as and when. Yes, the figures daubed on the wall refer to the tidemark in a given year.

The following is a brief account of the last of our bloodline.

She scribbles notes on slips of paper, names and dates, carries them about in her pockets and the cups of her brassiere. There is a clicking sound on the other side of the wall.

I am never assembling another picture. They are keeping her alive with promises until they find a better use for her head. I stole out with my sack in the dead of night.

One dwells on the roof. A hole has been cut for smoke and light, the passage of animal familiars. Hers is a mythical creature with the head and wings of a hawk, body reptilian. An eagle's talon clings to her hair.

Seize hold of your chosen colour. Can you grasp what he is screaming aloud? A whole battalion is poised for combat.

Today I whitewashed all the statues in preparation; one softened under my touch and became animate. At peripheral vision comes a flash of silver light, the rim of a rusting circle. Armed militia arrived, crouching in the back of an open truck.

You were meant to be sharing, meant to be listening. I dreamt of a Tudor warship that could not be sunk.

Do you want me to tell of anything else? You were not supposed to be here tonight, to witness the climax brought about by their intervention.

*

He sets about his task, rallying his factions. I could not.

He once worked at memory, absorbed in a miscued optimism. Inside, D made a rapid sketch of the scene, leaving out the frankly incredible parts. In my hand I held a straight flush, a continuous sequence of five.

The story told is a rite of passage, something about a stolen bicycle or other transport: we are now approaching my final years. All of a sudden I did something I should not have.

She lurches toward me, the embodiment of poverty, but I have a head start. Cabins are suspended on a continuous moving cable driven by a motor at one end. My own machine consists of two wings, hinged in the middle to engineer a trap.

It is said the drip of cold water on a bare scalp helps improve mental toughness.

What is that wedged in the crook of your arm? It is not yet four in the morning. The years go by and still we have not sailed.

Transferable figures are breeding inside of me. An avant-garde locking mechanism was first used in the Thompson submachine gun.

The next test is an audit of loyalty: goods lost by wreck are found floating on the surface amid the algae or wash up on shore. In times of danger volunteers are hurled overboard, unclaimed debris jettisoned with a curse.

He fingers an instrument with coiled tube, valves and a moist aperture. The encompassing head, more harvest for your replicant, is folded back. Capricorn is the chosen host, rat metallic.

XX

All further stratagems are cancelled, but I do remember yesterday, being pressganged into utterance. I accept the ordeal, return myself back to the present: behind the vision a sunlit immanence, a dead reckoning of my own stamp.

I will sign this document now, please.

See, forever thinking thither, on into fugue.

That man is the head of symptoms. A glomerulus is a cluster of nerve endings, spores or small blood vessels. It is hard to see clearly with the light in front of us; nothing can be trusted to represent. In such a predicament, why do they not simply call out to one another?

It was all over in one minute. The process is predictive — the arrival of the sun, moon or a planet in a specified constellation of the sky: sleight of hand, the beginning of a transit.

Some had surrendered their organs. I emanate from the body of my medium; the rules can always change. The book is morphing into a volume of mechanics.

I connect, as if two sides of the same coin (symbolum). I forgive myself — notwithstanding, I am renounced and abandoned. I counterfeit. The popular cosmology runs three strikes and you're out.

You speak your own tongue, the minder language — for example, 'a boat sheers away from the jetty'. How can this be sustained across a field of all possibilities, a work of comparable military acumen? What we saw did not correspond to any known life form: the organism was translucent.

The crew carve triangles across the air, scratching out a crude design. We are seeking a chain of events.

Visualizing every surface of a coloured cube seems to help. These are incorrigible times, punctuated by irreplaceable names — all spoken in his demented voice, this thing of abyss.

*

Walking the cliff path, midway between anchorhold and catastrophe. Navigate the situation before it destroys you, swallow this wafer of bone.

Things are listed: narration, family tort, candlelit readings, dog rotting at the wayside. But there are contraindications to suicide. For example, why is she crouching here instead of there? Why is the head aligned magnetic north? And what of the pollen found inside that meteorite?

Here are the answers.

The body is the only vessel in which a transformation process can take place. An aperture results from the complete gravitational collapse of an electrically neutral and non-rotating body, at which the curvature of space-time is infinite.

A grinding noise rises from parched ground as the earth trembles. She hides her face in her hands, while he goes back inside the yellow house to the left.

All of this is happening as we write. His face signals rage and frustration.

The subject is two aimless people. Rumours are reaching us from beyond the stockade.

Of all the names found carved on gnostic gems, two are of the most frequent occurrence. Do you do that every week? I asked.

He has a couple of unspent lives remaining. Anything left over is relegated.

This last-minute set piece is perfectly poised, a breed of arcane pursuit, basaltic magnetism. He found to his astonishment that one hundred and ninety miles off the southern coast there is a dramatic decline in the local gravitational field.

*

He says he dare not touch anything at the crime scene. All these items, mottled with lichen, appear long unused. I read objects with a jaundiced eye.

He never came back after that. I now see clearly what ought to have been done: it's said he is good with money, good with memory, good with the placement of things. The knowledge that physical objects exist outside of our bodies has come too late.

All writing is prayer — to be sitting without aim, without profit — something you overhear but not clear enough to capture, a murmur in the passing. Nearby, a glass shatters.

See sheaf of notes, the enviable work of forgetting. Don't lose your nerve — you have no need to be present, to be perceived. I think a better translation would be a yearning to dwell again where one has always dwelt.

Country of dead saints

Being suited him, to be fair, it carried him well. I think you may need your personal touchstone, a fossil reptile of the epoch, often reaching enormous bigness. Some have liquid chlorophyll for blood.

No, we do not have transmission. By this I mean an irresolvable contradiction or logical disjunction in your argument: nouns which can never be counted, any expression of doubt. The scheduled massacre still took place in the park that afternoon. Origin is (I don't believe this) plural tempest of the head.

It seems we are going on a long train journey across the desert. The proportion of incident light that is reflected by a surface, typically that of a planet or moon, is unbearable.

*

Fragments of a forgotten teaching, two unknowns desperate to interpret one another. The site is the old guardhouse or cage.
    Nature, he wrote, knows no metaphysical frontiers: behind the head sits the mantle, a large bulbous structure that restrains the vital organs. Our own family enjoys several genera and many species.
    'I think I shall purchase that caul, now that push has come to shove.'
    You choose: the amniotic membrane enclosing a foetus, a woman's indoor head or historical net, anatomical momentum.
    O dear god, she cried, they are reforming custody.

Tread of footfall around nucleus — names are spelled out across the ceiling, residual carbon of naked flame. Note the sword and spear, his gilt sandals cum talaria as he descends to walk among us.
    The last statement may be a device for distracting attention away from further stratagems. According to oral tradition, hiding in the back seat lurks the murderous hookman.
    Origin lies somehow across one another.

Through seercraft and a lack of purpose, events are slowly unravelling. Among the earlies was a glass, darkly. Take accident versus substance: I feel very becalmed on the English stage, stripped of all mutation. My accidents are those of a child.
    Your own substance is merely the hoax of translation, an unpronounceable name. One hormone is produced in the pancreas by the islets of Langerhans. . . . Again, forever thinking thither, on into fugue, a cluster of capillaries about the head of the crow nebula.

*

She delivers him to the terminus, thereby relinquishing her tactical advantage. The circumference is closed and the centre begins to decay, withering but still attached to the stem. It was only then that I conceived of the book as something through which to strike back, balanced in its self-destruction.

The ditch has been ploughed in, except for a low section of counterscarp on the northernmost side of the fort. The west entrance is blocked. Meetings began to collapse with the introduction of written language and a perpetual state of emergency.

Before us flickers a luminous screen. The nervous tic below the left eye has worsened and I am haemorrhaging blood. A distress signal flares orange in the mist as contours are roped off.

So you do know my name, you knew all along.

Her cries weaken to groans. In the dark and the rain come police with flashlights. Beside the limepit are stacks of used teeth and shoes, the severed head. Some details remain obscure.

One witness claims the suspect strode into the room and shot the victim a glance. The incisions bespeak a murder committed under the sway of an animal frenzy.

Duplicate any information you have carried within you for some time, then burn the originals.

Source denotes an apostle, from creed as the mark, token. Listen, he has the cut of some newfangled Diderot, while she sits entranced, superimposing a china doll on to cellophaned sweets. The silhouette when reversed conjures a Maltese falcon.

See what little control we sanction. The communiqué speaks of thirty-six dispatched by a single bullet. Do you need cornering, are you still interpreting?

End of forerunner.

The nineteenth Sunday

The aim is lucid dispatches, temporal schism. My animal familiar has a phobia (I've seen my share of devils et cetera). Every occurrence enters the body an instant before acknowledgement by the senses.

The following may be recognized as having a share in the lexicon: ashlar, triple barrow, menhir, fogou, earthwork, quoit, circle-henge, burial cist, altar dolmen. Origin is broken axis of steampunk.

She says I loathe a vacuum. An L-shaped creep tunnel ending in a false portal leads from the west side of the main passage, just inside the entrance. The lunar maria have a lower albedo than the surrounding terrain.

Slowly he fingers his way through the fugue, demonstrates the nerve and resolve it takes to simply pass from one step to another, illuminating the minuscule tensions contained in each fragment. We are subsidence personified.

In this version, under pressure to conform, she murders her own son.

*

He refuses to eat his fodder for a season and wastes away. The well is poisoned. He no longer takes the written word to mean what is meant.

A yellow fluid trickles down his face from the deep gash in his forehead. The massacre occurred at Saint-Aloft-The-Field, when cavalry charged into a crowd who had gathered to demand the same.

If only I could take your place, but such a switch can only be made by mutual consent. Using the same word twice is forbidden.

The end of the war was followed by a period of famine and chronic employment, aggravated by a lengthy introduction. A young officer peering intently through a spy-glass is replaced by the image of a tumbril jolting along a cobbled street.

A fragile memory has burrowed behind the eyes: three ruinous huts arranged in a close triangle, set in the midst of an extensive field system. An assemblage of beasts from the region must be composed, an urgent list and account thereof.

*

Approaching artillery. Two new species have been recorded, in particular the rootless. A vast region extends from the mountain range to the ocean and from the coast to the northern borders. This terrain is noted for the severity of its winters and was traditionally used as a place of exile. It is now a major source.

We shut down for years and then reopened. Origin is late to escape.

Attend well to taxonomy, classification of organisms, systemics. There is only one species that eats each other.

Yet it still feels as though we are translating: the whole organism moves in response to the slightest stimulus. In the book a line is scored, a thin seam of letters enclosing carbonized spatchcock, poisonous seeds.

Rancid gum resin is nightly smeared across the skin and runes carved into the flesh. This does not constitute an objective analysis of what is lawful and what is rumour.

A year-long debate on the theme of abandonment has just begun.

*

Fifteen fifty-four was a year of many *Te Deums*. We discovered further clues toward a concrete objection, multiple forms of redundancy. Origin is old head cowering but recorded earlier. There is an absence of documentation, always.

A tongue-like structure with a toothed rim has been wheeled into position. This appears to be a fog trap.

A sudden thrust, the forward plunge: black poplar with deltoid branches — blind profile cutters, imperial fleas colonizing pockmarked boys — writers without hands and readers without eyes. . . . A piece of fine-grain schist or jasper was formerly used for testing alloys of gold. I thought of this in terms of pierced holes.

See, the date is just before the outbreak: time is over our heads. Above and to the left hangs the slaughter stone.

By adapting the eggshell cocoon and hydraulic press he managed to derail the whole train.

Yes we cried, Electro!

I misunderstood. This is the sort of deduction we should be making, and does not demand much preparation. Then came a catastrophic asteroid impact, slamming into the gulag, the snails.

*

He would have appreciated a little significance. Some people dispossess the gift. Nothing really came out of his eyes.

He draws his mark on a sheet of newsprint and slathers this with glue. Next he reaches for a quill pen and reservoir of ink: he famously severed the chains that bound the saltpetre inmates. A party of crabmen (yes) swarmed toward the exit, a portal leading into a popular black void.

Mind keeps changing, everything over in an instant, the fail-safe route to uncertainty. Nothing was ever recorded, such voice.

'Grown from melancholy adust, those men,' saith he, 'are sad and solitary and more than commonly superstitious.'

I am including here any hearts which pump blue-green blood, the lamentations of a Jeremiah, a level basalt plain on the surface of the moon appearing dark by contrast.

See, he is insensible. I spent the rest of the evening forging a few more letters home.

'There,' he muttered, tossing a coin in my direction, 'that's for services rendered.'

And that is how I survived all those years at the front. Equivocation is found in a different logbook.

Built into the foundations of the castle is an oubliette. By observing the colour of a mark which had been made upon the earth, we could plot our location with great accuracy. There follows a litany of causes:
i) The great O of angular frequency.
ii) Chassis resistance.
iii) Perhaps saint is misplaced, or is hiding from me on purpose.

iv) I still do not trust semi-colons.
v) A shive, a slice, a slab.
vi) The twenty-fourth star in our constellation.
vii) In what respect do disyllabic diphthongs differ from monosyllabic?
viii) Fashion these of clay.
ix) And the question of those furnaces.

I think these are holding you back, devoted as you are.

*

Head tilted to face the nearest star, a wingbeat across the lowered eyelid, breaking the surface tension. Actions have slowed to a point where almost nothing happens. Immediately it struck us that our journey had been made in vain.

Hurled backwards into another collision, we stood clinging to one another. She screamed into my ear, rupturing the labyrinth. Her bust in heroic scale still overshadows any structure built in the corrosive style.

Internal refuse

The capstone once stood a metre higher than its present elevation and there were four uprights, one of which is too short to reach. The west jamb of the entrance bears the relief carving of a human head and torso, perhaps representing, perhaps requesting.

I howl into his face. He cannot hear.

Three attendants perished in the whirlwind and the ark was lost. Maybe we are due another case of autodefenestration.

Origin is an irresolvable contradiction or logical disjunction, impassable from your side. Having done this, you must at once place the box upon the sundial, as directed.

Then comes that reptilian utterance 'I meant'. At the corner of the apse is a memorial tablet.

During the night I heard the crunch of footfall on gravel.

You cannot remember the times when you wake up if they last less than two minutes. Day breaks to parse the body out of reach, all syntax reversed.

A migratory sandpiper with gunmetal plumage is breeding, or eastern. There is nobody like you.

A pittance for the recollection, please, summoned to mind. Beyond this circle that has been placed around me, a zero hour is bearing down.

Wood is embryonic stone.

*

In the tumbril stands a young woman, her hands tied behind her back. She is mesmerized by the sound of her lover's footsteps on the gravel courtyard.
  Constellations are glinting. In the darkness he calls up to her in vain. Does it ever come to light why things happen?

That is why I always keep an antique bell on my desk. (Visualize a painted scroll depicting this.)
  A low angle shot is a shot in which the subject is photographed from below. There is of course no reason to doubt that a stimulus to dreaming can arise within the dreaming mind itself. One example is amphibious trespass.
  The realm is circumscribed by itself, a plexus of obstacles and prohibitions to which an ad hoc oral law adds further burden.
  Lamentations are traditionally ascribed to my next-door neighbour. Fragments of the wall of his heart have been known to wander.
  That's it, my signal transmitted, and now I am to be disappeared through a clairvoyant medium. A familiar cycle of collapse, damnation and reprieve is materializing.

*

He was famous for his invention of the disappointed guide.

There's a watch on my back. The keep is made of flint. Safely inside, they are talking paralysis. I can't summon the nerve to sift through all these rejected items.
  More and more, I resemble. When we leave, the others will be nailed spreadeagle to the floorboards.
  Say it: jeremiad. Medicine is unmistakeable, frank ulceration.

The fact that the propositions of logic are tautologies merely demonstrates the illogical properties of language: I have one of those very loud and stupid laughs. The engine fell out and our machine crashed in the middle of a vast salt plain.
  I doubt this will happen in time, the meteoric fragment, the aerolith handed me by an alien life form.
  They surrendered their true identities, a band of pasteboard heroes with gauze wings. Consider the lies which circulate in the mouths of so many who profit from my sad condition of illiterate outlaw.
  Another among them claims to have sprung from the soil. Lacking your acumen, I am instantly allied to any idea, however godforsaken.

The host is bound and cocooned before pitching sharply across the snow on its belly, driven forward by waves of contraction. There is much to be said for staying put, standing still: beyond this maze of corridors awaits the immediate.

How much we have in common, the same memory of exile, but I lack the will for further incoherent, fragmentary detail.

There once came a man who was most insoluble. By this I simply mean he was incapable of dissolving. Onward to the canal, where my appointed trolley is slowly oxidizing.

These are merely the specimens that have been diagnosed; you have no idea what I am capable of. (I shall miss probation.) The era is named, doubtless soviet.

This moment is unparalleled. I slice open the next envelope: an untranslatable sequence without nomenclature of gens or clan, the low murmur of displacement.

She was an impartial, unable to sleep and watching the sky. Origin is without passage.

Option seven

This relic was preserved in far later geological deposits. As we stumble through the wreckage of a bombed city he produces a polished black stone and hands it me: a chunk of meteorite embedded with white flecks, sealed with a stone plug of a different vein. The starving populace has resorted to battery acid, roadkill.

The surviving mediaeval families retained their traditional pilgrim badges. I simply caved in, a woeful declaration of the unacceptable. The speaker is scorned as a man of slow tongue, and despised as such.

We countermarch, through a decaying orchard and on to a field bleached silver-brown.

His treatise on mania catapulted the revolt into an out-of-town hypermarket. One has grown adept at stitching together such debris — offscourings, debitage — gibberish and cock (see Hopeless, sense 4).

Nouns are massing. A group agitating for asthmatic reform has fomented a riot. In its aftermath, we are all to be probed through a celebrated orifice.

I can no longer remember my colours. Somewhere outside a bell tolls.

And it is a most significant fact that the truth or falsehood of a nonlogical proposition cannot be recognized under a superblood wolf moon. Comorbid insomnia occurs when watchfulness is a symptom of a phantom disease.

*

Once more I attempted to abnegate all personal responsibility. It was an experiment.

She rushed into the saloon car and threw me a glance. Business, I reckoned, was about to be bluntly terminated.

Never let go, the vomitings and blue wine, wrong-footed at the threshold.

It's said he behaves like a deadly virus, only less community-minded. He bears a facial scar. There followed some fundamental disagreements about the past.

I taught him all he needed to know about the bestowal of punishment, the shreds of terror leased out to passersby. Our intentions are wrongly understood as a curse.

They regenerate; I was never identified. I have the odd feeling that this is my best last chance.

Mashing my eyes wearily with the palm of my hand, I listened out for a rumble beneath the underpinnings of the shack. Sooner or later a counterpoint will be offered: lawyer to psychopath, physician to plague, confessor to penitent.... I feel a strong temptation to conduct you through all the naked trials of comeuppance.

The light, by turns uncanny and morbid, is damning everything. On quiet days we would harpoon one another. Asylum has been withheld.

Remember that giant yew in the churchyard, staved up against gravity? Well, the others will locate your position the moment you surrender to sleep.

The medical investigation pressed on to its only possible conclusion. Our rivals are dilettantes of the wondrous: a box is borne between poles balanced on skeletal shoulder blades — but the sedan is found to be empty, a token of your abandoned material past.

'They dream of still graves and dead men and think themselves bewitched....'

Are you giving in to wastage, atrophy? That very afternoon I found the word *There* lying on the pavement — another accident of a time-hobbled epoch, dust for most, with glimpses of the stars.

*

Come midnight she enters my cell. She brings news: the antagonists have been rounded up and permitted to design their own punishment. Somersaulting down the stairs, the feeling of inhibition was discussed at length.

The present has been examined and forever deferred. We are not in a position to interrupt. Finally I understand the meaning of the phrase 'to depart oneself'.

I identified the fatal clue: a tiny bivalve attached firmly to a rock by slender fibres. High up in the garret she has hidden her writing machine: a translucent membrane stretched across a slab of amber resin, roots glowing with blue lichen. Moving bodies of air retain the miscreant spoor of your ancestors.

The object lies on its side, unidentifiable through a stained polyethylene sheet. I inconsistently apply the rule: paradox and dissonance, the dull work of metaphor. She flees under the table.
 The other says he does not understand a word of the script, but has to acknowledge that *something* is happening.

The desiccated carcass of a slug rolls across the tiles. A wad of chewed paper had found its way into a pocket of the repaired garment, solidified to resemble a miniature bleached vagina.
 On this unforgettable day of rampage and misrule we are bunkered down, though well within the scope of enemy artillery. I hear teeth tearing through on either side.
 Yet another untimely deception. A drug obtained from our common ancestral root will one day be used as a sedative and antispasmodic.

*

Dislocated room with décor circa 1960. The buried axe moves every year a little closer to the surface of the earth.
 Plastic bullets are strewn across the town square. We are approaching the desired fugue: loss of awareness of identity, often coupled with flight from one's usual environment, dissociated from every form.
 Origin is hanging judge.

A circle of covered wagons stands in the wilderness as snow begins to fall. Above all, I want to adopt an accomplished literary shape, one correct in terms of the facts I am about to undermine.
 So, which of the convulsionists do we choose to execute?
 Note that this is a murder investigation without a body. All background noise ceased.
 This is called a cochlea situation. It is heavily sedated.

*

Plates spin on bamboo canes, falling one by one to smash against the flagstones. We are in a cathedral.
 Safely outside, we recruited some fresh volunteers. The last to step forward is still missing, presumed lost.

Upon her departure I had presented her with the gift of an alembic for her nascent alchemical experiments. During this exchange, over her bent the shadow of a tall figure.

Take heart, quantum objects can be in two places at once.

I was cured by the passing of her hands back and forth, just a little above the surface of the skin. A bell tolls, then silence.

A pair of organs is situated within the ribcage consisting of elastic sacs with branching passages into which air is drawn. Everything turns out to be defective, simply wrong.

Adapt, rule by fear. The amniotic membrane encloses the foetus; origin is the cutting of stone.

There is nothing to be gained from dissecting this (plenty of families don't bother with mnemonics at all). I began to feel that every action was pointless.

*

He is free to set about punishing the head. The aperture slowly opens — he squeezes it shut, the rim moist under the circular caress of his thumb. The lips are waxy from waste material produced in the manufacture of historic artefacts.

'Could you have been nightly bled, blue to the touch?'

There can be no permanence to this arrangement. An abandoned epithet slips out onto the floor.

She runs before dawn, silent through fog gathered in a hollow of land.

Behind the shutters he sleeps, cocooned in baseline magics. In two weeks the cabaret will be bankrupt.

The moss-covered map

He ventures outside to speak with the adversary, to parley. They find there is nothing to speak about after all. He leaves. This thread has cancelled.

The legion slipped into the city and behaved as though *they* were the victors. During the ensuing dialogue the capital was razed to the ground.

The next ordeal is the ordeal of swallowing, taken to prove wrongdoing if a splinter of bone pierces the gullet. The third man floated, a little downstream of the waterwheel, confirming his guilt.

This observance is ancient and was designed to prevent. Experience is valued, but amounts to little more than a collection of habits, neural hoax. This is what happened.

I sometimes feel I am translating. I doubt she will survive the coming trial by water: call out to your gaoler, wringing white hands slender and delicate. . . .

The hour of parleying is dangerous. As we stand side by side at the edge, my eyes cannot penetrate the drop for the darkness. Looking up, one can study the stars, if so minded, through holes left by missing slates. The cylinder rotates slowly about its axis.

Today's instruction is to seek out the site of deserted landfill. I have made it as far as the junction, our rendezvous. In the process of such inconsequential comings and goings, in our material aspect, we are spent.

A disembodied voice. Those men, it says, are usually more fearful, but between them now they share a mind hollowed out.

Cold and solitary as she writes, for she can endure no company.

*

I have brought along some objects for people to touch. You could see Mars and Venus beside the Moon — Mars a deep orange-red, Venus dazzling white. The Moon was superblood.

The final episode involves a cello and a hawk-headed deity with gills. I have no choice but to disclose this.

Her objects are a funnel of human skin, a grotesque toy of the lost continent, one train with open cattle trucks, tiny spheres of an unknown metal, and a yellow pollen which darkens on exposure to light and is used in artificial rainmaking. Now tell me three things I do not know on pain of death.

A swarm has been detected on one of the secondary planets. Lights appear at nightfall, distant now at the foot of a cliff. The foundry lies somewhere in our immediate vicinity.

Backs straighten then bend, breaking under the waves as glistening nets are hauled up from the sea. He said huge shadows glode beneath the surface.

The unknown metal turned out to be liquid mercury, quicksilver. In the darkness men shout instructions from vessel to vessel. We are never to be restored.

How is it? one is entitled to ask.

He is erratically anonymous, of that much you are no doubt aware. And I have a question about those radiators carved of human bone.

A workaday revolution has just kicked off, all memory a cipher, null and void.

*

A blind one comes, right lens dimmed by a jet of steam — air corrosive, hand gripping veined object — a blank, a blank underlined.

I compare, clutching my own photographic ghost. From the vantage of a hot-air balloon I witnessed a chain of letters scrolling across a maplike world.

Have you tried bleeding him? asks a bystander.

XXI

SIR — Anathema is unleashed. I recommend you stamp on the hide where any damp places are left; the volunteer's gums usually bleed. Everything is going to be all right.

The inventory is limited to an ear of corn and a spinning top, one of six flavours of quark. I urge you to run the usual tests and disinfect the tissues behind the face. Notwithstanding, there may be permanent neural damage.

Today, I am an apparent minimal — the legendary spanner — I witness asymmetrically, or God knows what might happen. Every gesture is a judgement.

Yours et cetera.

The crew's blood was granulated by the blast and the desert sands turned to glass. A mushroom cloud rose above the magnetic pole, before slowly sinking across the white continent and into the surrounding sea. The map appears more familiar to us if we look at it upside down.

He got up, feeling light-headed.

'Is it Mars?'

'Does it make any difference?'

Our vessel lies directly beneath the polar ice. His speeches are interminable: praise, disparagement, vilification of disloyal factions, discussion of the integrity of the kingdom's borders. . . . His tongue slithers back and forth across a swollen nub of flesh.

Maybe notes from a lecture I had forgotten. Add something here, but not now.

*

The artefact looks like a bundle of decaying documents. Our working title is historical thinking and other extrasensory phenomena.

The ambassador's corpse had been left to rot in the street. Once the ritual is completed, he will be poured back into the river under the bridge via a rubber hose. The stone used is purple corundum. We believe he is holding something back.

Our vessel sat becalmed while the engine was repaired. There is no shelter in memory.

Consider for a moment the supreme detachment of a man mounted on a warhorse, caparisoned against the light.

Ascension day tilts. At this moment, I have no idea what to do with myself.

In the corner a shadow, a blank slate. The preface of the book navigates mathematically.

We are told the lovers will meet at the grave of Oedipus. Her longing is mingled with pain because she does not know what the encounter might bring, does not know whether he is aware of the concept of guilt. There is a great dam of language in every mouth.

His first successful publication was a collection of stories about life on a poverty-stricken asteroid. Many of his novels feature Chinese hexagrams. The author poses a few final questions.

Bystanders are unnerved by the permission granted to interpret the novel right side up, sideways on, or even upside down: this would demand the integration of opposites — conscious organization and its postponement.

In this way he conducts his own strategy, with everyone lying close together on the ground, passively awaiting the next onslaught. Time stays long enough for anyone.

But he is not so foolish as to draw any conclusions. On reflection, we had no option but to scrape the crust from malignant growth.

*

This map coordinate is a catchment area for the local static. The exposed parts emit a squeal before surrendering.

This is an elliptical form of storytelling. Conclusion: burdened under a yolk, yet quite superior when compared with a muddy void. A soft white or grey mineral occurs chiefly in sedimentary deposits and is used.

I drained my cup. I would reveal my catchphrase for your distraction and amusement, but have not a candle to transcribe it.

I always got saddled with the insomniac shift. Golden light was refracted through the glasswork of the pier.

This event was not guessed at, it was foreknown: the way events will occur can be changed by subtle manipulation of the tongue.

We agreed about the price. Memory is votive. Shreds of desiccated saint were sealed in glass vessels and fixed to the wire mesh of the porter's cage. The future was contingent on the outcome of one simple experiment.

All the boundary markers have vanished. Ankles were shattered, the astragalus: no amount of numerology can restore this situation. The defendant R has previous histories.

Measure up. The probe is going to reach about eight inches deep. Your next problem is the cloud of volcanic ash.

Abandon this quarter immediately (these are ill-timed entertainments). A femur bone dipped in pitch and ignited serves as a torch.

Open your fist. Now close it again.

See, he is off on another tangent. . . . People today are easy to spot, going about their nightly rituals: chewing and drooling, watching the skies, hatching futile plans of escape. . . . Do nothing, then take a rest. Repeat to quietus.

I too was listening, listening to the rain.

'You call it a diversion, I call it a sacrament.'

Origin is a thing of significance. The well dried up. Might one abstain, might one?

*

An index card tells us that copper was the earliest metal to be used by Terrans, first in the pure form, later alloyed with tin to make bronze. Now, by means of some uncanny manipulation, we shall return to position the displaced parts. Don't be alarmed if all this seems to amount to nothing.

The rebels can clearly spy our encampment from beyond the cursus. We dug a fosse on either side, and thus a gentle slope backed onto the intended field of battle.

I am here creating a sense of order, a very long list of words and their things.

Nothing works. The index is an English index. Note the scarcity of birds, the uneasy absence of noise. We need an alarmed professional.

The cattle truck is crammed. Nothing is expressed. There are no seats. We debouched and went shopping.

When electrodes are applied to the upper labium — a fused mouthpart which forms the floor of the insect's mouth — it stiffens involuntarily. A voice in the dark says each of you right now, outside. The dividing perspex shield offers some protection.

The sea resembles molten metal, mercury. A tin mine flooded. There are four mounds at this spot, two so mutilated it is impossible to tell whether they were once burial chambers. Extensive sedimentary deposits have also been lost.

In a remote corner of an abandoned quarry he gripped her tightly and semen spurted against the red silk of her dress.

Inquisitor: Did you have the feeling, from that evening onward, that all hope was lost?
Accused: I am not at liberty to disclose our whereabouts on the day of the invasion.

His message reads

Standing upright in the soil, an intricately carved dagger glints in the autumn sunshine. I have marked with an asterisk those writings which he acknowledges authorship of, and are dedicated to those who survive him.

Now you are going to suddenly cut me off.

More often than not, our archers would deliver their missiles into a precise zone of the battleground. I am here referring obliquely to the twenty-third letter, and the twenty-third star of our constellation, parapsychological correspondence.

Noun, mass noun, any compound present in nervous tissue. Who or what is your precursor?

Origin is an acronym for the systemic name — black substance elastic, the salt of human acid found in any dried up riverbed — a quality of austere beauty expressing a mood of solitude, recognized.

The law of shift of wave, moving toward or away from the observer, explains the pulse code, explains the fall of pitch, explains the radial velocity of stars and displacement of known lines. All these changes took place unobserved.

First switch your objective to the retrieval of an unforeseen detail, *then* begin the interrogation. As for the height of the ground floor, it has been raised up a storey by a flight of five steps, with a balustrade in wrought iron curving round at either end.

It seems the two playwrights were evenly matched in their contempt for one another.

*

A taciturn and melancholy man who swerved wise of folk, and yet loved, has expired. Toward the end, the patient was insensate. The universe is a closed sphere, he screamed, the universe may not be flat after all — it could be curved like an inflated bladder.

Yes, I have been convinced for many years that we can influence the content of our dreams — summon up an oneiric dialogue, as it were, including of course the dramatis personae — and that this may be induced by ritual visualization (flaming pentagrams et cetera). Yet I still cannot understand the juxtaposition of the phrases 'to plant evidence' and 'to defenestrate oneself'.

Inquisitor: Do you ever feel your behaviour is vampiric?
Accused: Only when sinking my fangs into somebody's neck and draining their blood, transforming myself into fog to seep under a locked door, or using my bat-like sonar to see through walls. But apart from that, no.

Iron pyrites and flint produce a spark for the tinder. I am built in compressed strata myself, an inscribed cliff face.

Right now I am trying to remember the cut of his frock coat, the complexion of his skin, the stranger found dead on remote moorland. I have one eye out on the causeway and the rising tide.

A cut-glass stopper reflected beads and flashes of sunlight across the wall as the steward crossed the room.

Captain, he whispered, a jag penetrated the hull last night.

A significant number of verbs were abandoned during the nineteenth dynasty. More recently, I have discovered unexpected aspects of our boot camp, such as a framed piece of tar. Renaissance order was a disaster.

We spent the whole day waiting for word from the tracker, but it was not until dusk that he returned with the news that a descent had been made into a ravine running due south. That was our signal to instigate the third degree, this time on home ground, and I was buried up to my neck at the clock end. The following day, our guide refused to take us any further up the mountainside.

'How could I do that?' he pleaded, 'it is quite impossible: I can neither help nor hinder you.'

The final hazard arrives. Search the skies, then withdraw for lack of purpose.

His voice again o hullo.

*

A door swings open then back and forth on squealing hinges. He enquires as to whether he might quote my authority. (I should imagine so, yes.) At three in the morning he is still composing the letter that will surely bring about his downfall.

Read by my lantern till dawn as moths circled, quivering in the humid air. Counted by lire, the debt is estimated to be in the trillions.

Divine power made me, plus supreme wisdom and primal love: we turn in the night and are consumed by fire et cetera. Epileptics have the ability to make the past and future converge at an agreed point. See, it is three o'clock already.

Our only remaining obstacle was the nightwatch, four men-at-arms stationed above the gate to the courtyard. Swift and silent, with desperate sidelong glances, we burst out of the capsule and streamed forth, torches held aloft. Atrocity is in the syndicate's DNA.

He slips the seed pods into the river and watches as they slowly open. Each husk contains a unique object.
I waited a while before carefully applying another layer of grease, after which I was fully garbed and equipped as a trapper.
That bell is still ringing. It was a week before I could summon the nerve to meet his gaze.

*

Many years before he passed over, my father appeared in a dream; he had died and returned from wherever the dead go. He wore a light grey jacket and white shirt, open at the collar. He looked exhausted yet relieved, as if flung clear from some nameless ordeal. We shook hands and he calmly told me that everything was going to be alright.
Getting up off the floor at the end is the difficult part. At that moment the bridge vanished and the surviving arch collapsed into the sea.

Timing is fragile. What makes her uneasy is the speed with which he can make up his mind to kill or not, and his apparent indifference.
Choice number one, she says, is always yes or no. Once inside the room, you can isolate whomsoever you wish. That choice is yours.
The events that occur around each situation turn out to be a part of a wider, oblique strategy. Everything seems rather characterless; I start to think about what has happened, and then I stop thinking about what has happened. Finally I tried a single determined bite, leaving an aftertaste of metal, rather like when a bunch of keys is dragged across the surface of your tongue. It is often found elsewhere, the required genre.
She deploys broken instruments in a confused methodology, but says she is happy with the crowbait provided as her transport. Later that evening a sniper's bullet will shatter the glass sphere into lethal fragments that fly about the room.

The press is dropping the word 'gentleman'. People are easy to forget. It's our superfluity.
Familiar whiff of paraffin at the postern stair. To add, when there is time: did you get a good look at him?

A fosse is a long narrow trench or excavation found at a haunted archaeological site. I am here, waiting.
Sense 1 is fugitive, the remembrance of things fucked, lost gravity. A fossa is a shallow depression or hollow.

The early sense of a stump sticking out from a torso gave way to a submerged piece of timber obstructing navigation. All the while we remained in the same place.

Epilepsy is giving us all a hard time — prise me open at the crack of an eye, the crack of an eye.

Today's definition lies in the arc of the horizon, between the meridian and a vertical circle passing through any celestial body. Origin is obsolescence, a shibboleth murmured under the hood.

Early morning, and the café is full of apparitions tapping morse through the wall. Then I remember the tattered remnant of a windsock outstretched above a pontoon bridge.

*

Seven speakers.
    I think that one is the least likely to succeed. [*Pointing.*]
    What were we like to live with back then?
    It seems hell is frozen, actually.
    Don't talk, they will see your mouth moving; we are supposed to be alone.
    That object is the way it is because that's the shape it was when you won it.
    Then why say you did not know whether he lived apart?
    We need to find out whether we can get the casket through the door.
    The body does not enter into this conversation. Because there was no roof on the property, we had to pay cash.
    Her skin is waxy, translucent grey, and the cage of the ribs clearly visible. Blast pressures in excess of twelve psi are predicted.

There is a fever spreading through the dock tonight, tooled-up stevedores braced in the dense yellow fog.... This tension even found its way into later editions of the news-sheet, but guardedly, only a few cryptic references being made.

We lie in ballast to the white sea, as people used to say. The man had come back to reassure me of his survival after death, a death that in the linear time of three-dimensional space would not occur for decades.

*

What follows is capable of containing everything. A hygroscopic substance was used as a drying agent: natural desiccants cause cockroaches to dehydrate, and that's the whole story.

We poured him into a black polyethylene sack. Despondent, the possessed child stands with face lowered, hand on the doorknob, listening.

'It was the first time ever. The thing blew into the road. . . . No, not local, not that I know of. . . . I missed all the action by one night.'

The disused tin mine is found half a kilometre up the road. . . . One melted bottle resembled a mandrake with twisted metal top — the desert sands had vitrified, turned to glass, but the main issue for me remains the blindspot on the concrete stairwell. Liquified nerves, they enter the cranium through a wound that has pierced the cartilage lining the aperture.

A shiftless public with hind-toes, darkening mood unlexical. I returned from inside the mountain not quite the same as when I had entered it.

She arrives conspicuous, leaping about outside in the lightning and the rain, clad in tinfoil or some other conductive material. I had been reviewing the stage directions only that afternoon. She is extra-Cathar.
    Although I classified her recollection of the sharpened coin as admissible evidence, I did not consider it significant at the time. Wherefore has she committed the deed? Origin is the feminine part of to dig, relinquish.
    Occasionally her account appears to run loose, suddenly switches penitent for scribe. Yet despite the lack of congruence, we find that something of substance is finally manifesting in the courtroom.
    A light step on the adjoining staircase has captured my attention.

*

Another says the etymology of suffrage encompasses intercessory prayers. She is indeed a heroic pessimist, never flinching in her lack of hope: a person who waits for a time, for an event or opportunity.

Picture a temporary fortification, typically square or polygonal and without flanking defences. The forecast is obscure: find your unique code, printed beneath the seal.
    The invaders have defensive gills along the jawline and wear a type of combat helmet with a projecting bar covering the nose, thus protecting the centre of the face. She chose this moment to fling her radical credentials on the table, something about a design for a bridge involving a huge fibreglass cock.
    I say be still: human hair is a document, a single filament evidence enough. The old arcade on the pier is closing down. Shadows filter beneath the boardwalk.

A few of us banded together. It was day three.
    Where are you?
    I am far, far away.

I have got no change.
We are waiting for you.
Farewell.

*

If people have made up their minds to leave they are going to leave. And I have a question for you.

I sat up watchful every night. I am composing a letter to everyone. I want to leave; I have had time. I want to choose physically, as though it meant something.

I cannot describe. I feel this indifference. I cannot say this is because of X or because of Y.

The mandrake is alleged to shriek when pulled from the ground. Literary models don't exist in the present. (Have you any first-hand experience of a vacuum?) Then he took the revenant by the shoulders and had to use all his strength to force it down onto the ground. There is something puzzling about human beings and connectivity.

I would always stand with my back to the sea, always.

We are on the brink of suspended time. A boulder plummets down the cliff and the smuggler is crushed to a semi-solid, highly viscous and somewhat elastic mass.

Megan's clay breasts covered the walls of the snug. It is really damp outside and I've just made things worse.

Ugly salon hang, this life pursued amidst a narrative in film.

The museum is a house that the architect demolished. Three more were built in succession on the north side of the field. (Pontoons, or whatever they're called.) He always began with the number twelve. Lobster pots hang from the ceiling, but the infamous space is at the rear: a dome, a colonnade, the tormented corridor.

She stumbles, eyes bleary upon the postern stair. During our absence, the populace had drunk the entire municipal water supply. In any event, I have existed.

We ceased combat for a spell — attendants shuffle and nod, muddy hooves canter across the battlefield — lances drop, visors lift.

Let them have the knowledge, the advantage of knowing who I am — but step by step, piecemeal.

I still need to finish. The sea rose up at an instant. Suffice to say, the house was very, very large.

Swollen by the rains, the murky water swept along branches, dead animals and miscellaneous debris.

*

He strides away, resolute with bloodshot eyes, lips black. Glass beads scattered across the stone floor of the cathedral; everyone was on their hands and knees.

We screwed down the lid of the casket and secured the great iron door. Lifted by a sudden gust, a single white petal settled in the seam of a book that had been opened at random on the lectern.

I used systems theory to locate the source of his malison. Now do you understand why?

Nothing is quite how it was last time. I have deleted much of your context by mistake: twenty years of state funerals, and you could see in the mud where people's feet had been.

Go to Insensible (1). The magnetic poles have reversed, again. Now provide a complete and detailed impression of our remote outpost. We have lost rain.

Across the page spreads an elision of thought — of image, purpose, attention and remembrance. A name has been given by early archaeologists to those parallel banks with external ditches.

I have never been inside, beneath the earth. This structure is named a dank fogou. No one knows. There's a curve in the conic section. They are closing in.

The equation persists: a similitude called 'home', also 'to discomfit'. Earth is measured on a grand scale, surveyed with allowance for its curvature. Team B has constructed a fragile dome through echo location: we would never have leapt off at such a tangent on my watch.

Our coenobites rock gently back and forth in silent prayer. Keep yourself flung clear, with defangled memory. A sense of trap or snare is recorded from the middle years; both these and the original survive. Today we promise things that you will not want to miss, dead or alive.

She sees colours when reading letters or numbers. Two guy ropes ran from the end of a spur to the deck, thus forming a V.

*

Consider her steel-trap mind and mutinous prose (e.g. piney means relating to or covered with pines). I am looking out for a glint of sunlight reflected from an object lost in the dry grass.

The current sense dates from the mishandled century; you could hardly have it in plainer terms. In the basement of the building, the descending capsule left no space for the witness to stand up in.

A lift, I venture.

On the way to the morgue she talked about the person in the film who celebrated Christmas every day of the year. What struck me was that she is utterly devoid of empathy or pity, yet the atmosphere of violent compression surrounding her is irresistible. As we ascended higher, the valley assumed a romantic *Alpentraum* character where a ruined castle clung to a precipice.

*

His fluid is condemned. Volunteers close in hauling sacks of stress pigs, also much impromptu use of the theremin at this station. He could not help but notice the pilgrim's trembling hands.

The towers of used books formed a narrow runnel that one could barely squeeze through. Spasmophilia, on the other hand, is undue tendency of a muscle to contract, vertigo in the blood, another neurological disaster. I felt I had read everything one needed to read, then we two met and vowed that we would begin again.

*

Anagram of the name: my addictions.

She was skipping across the strand when lightning struck, and could never have known her fate. Electric current runs beneath the ganglion and dura mater, contained in a groove of the anterior surface.

Never go back to last night. Her life had been an incendiary existence, and for no good reason.

'I have included that object in the inventory because it is shaped like an ear.'

'We had expected the missing hand,' chorus my gaolers.

Void of explanations, I leave.

Who exists in the space between individual sand grains and aquatic sediments like some microscopic animal? To see the bone beneath the skin is unnatural. Bystanders were terrified, their balance out of kilter.

I am exhausted. Many sentences were overwhelmed. Anything can happen.

He has quite forgotten the narratives that made him what he has become. Perhaps, in terms of spirit, my 'had been extinguished' is not an entirely apt translation.

I loved without comment. The effect was comparable to a neural dam: the geometric shapes that now drift across my field of vision include the triangle, circle, square and tesseract, the four-dimensional analogue of the cube. On this side of the frontier, objects cannot be seen if positioned too far from the centre of a hypothetical sphere.

He takes a number of deep bows before edging the microscope closer to the sheet of paper. In his hand is a wooden cudgel with three circles carved around the shaft.

'Someone must answer for this. I have made up my mind to dismiss the volunteers.'

Our bunker days are over. You belong to me, beneath me.

Just two metres to go. I am resolved to build my own contrivance, yet recognize the impertinence of my return at this particular moment in time. You can only imagine the complexion my nights have assumed, and may recall that a vulnerability to sudden conversion is counted among my misdemeanours.

I respond, the endless work of mourning. We disappeared before anything else could take place.

*

Cage. Silence.
[*A fight to the death.*]
'What about the signal?'
The redoubt comprises a keep with six outer bastions, and this moated stone castle has sixty-six firing positions for artillery.

'Either stay put until you get the code or. . . .'

This structure was once thought to be an involuntary athletics course. We kept score on a primitive abacus. The problem is not the air.

They cannot have anticipated how successful their response was going to be, waiting at the end of the line, forgotten and underfucked. The current sense (also middle) reflects the same notion of something that catches alight and holds fast.

White columns glow, bisecting a plane of light. I can think of a lot worse places to be.

A hook attached to a pole was once used to pull down a vessel's boom and help control the shape. Volume three is as witless as its ancestors.

Relating to projectiles and their flight

I am moving under force of gravity; this produces the state of mind of the defeated, the oppressed. In 1960 he had a piece of thin fibrous cartilage removed, the meniscus. Our punishment was being walled up alive.

Properly speaking, this nerve passes through the facial to the splenetic ganglion, forming its motor root, your solitary naked slice.

*

Medium: spectral flecks of light, luminescence on woodchip. This phenomenon belongs over here with all the others.

Our vantage point is exemplary, what some call an *Aussichtspunkt*. We climbed all the way up to the viewing platform — the edge of the cliff had a vertiginous perspective — and from that prospect we had a vision of the tempestuous sea, untranslatable sentences struggling to contain.

She had spotted something at the foreshore. (I was feigning neuralgia.)

What is being documented here is a radical loss of touch with reality. Today's directive: sustain perpetual motion or risk losing shape, erode eye contact.

The pivot rusts. Origin hints at spoilage, from lost capture.

Compare yourself and belief slides away. The last thing we need is a living, breathing eyewitness.

A familiar weariness descends as we dismember and ration the body, his carbon atoms. The chosen weapon was a long pole with a hook and spike at one end used for fending off a raft. But she dare not say another word about the stolen fieldwork, the crushed viral pipeline.

Comes now a man talking loudly about suicide. Origin is annulled sense, chiefly as a legal term, a species of ruin.

'Is he safely in his own tank?'

'What have you decided to call him?'

It appeared out of nowhere to manoeuvre a face-off. That is not her latchkey, so she cannot have done the deed. A local superstition requires people to extinguish a bell rung at this hour.

See, we had no choice but to leave, though I quit the stage magnificently. My trough is of a type that was once carved out of soap.

I am adding on as much as scaling away. Lava oozed through the opened vein.

Ever the misanthrope, I have been relegated to the cellar. Together we shall squeeze through by the breadth of a poppy seed.

Baptiste, we two, as the years pass by, our eyes resemble.

*

A scrambled retreat was ordered, back inside the compound. I cannot believe there are still survivors out there in the lightning and the hail.

They stalked we three on bicycles, and as they pedalled faster and faster their pantomime vampyre wings unfurled until, my God, they flew, they flew. The only witness had to be beheaded, that dreadful axe et cetera.

I have often entertained the idea of leaving a key, a legend, and then forget to set about making one. I have often entertained the idea of including footnotes and an index. One critic suggests that the source of my spatial imagination is a traumatic childhood experience of map-making.

Nod if you understand: blinking twice means yes, once is summary execution.

She had all the numbers she would ever need corralled inside her head. I heard footsteps on the postern stair.

In form she resembled the tailbone of a fish, and is now displayed at the local museum in a barrel of formaldehyde. All scientific progress envisioned in the framework of a decaying social structure works against humankind, helping to aggravate our condition: scoria with dross metal and steam aperture, loss of consciousness.

*

She is freelance, a floater, airtight behind the perspex visor girding her face. See evangelist, the cochlea or eucharistic spoon.

We carefully placed the saint's remains in an old shoebox, a makeshift reliquary. I cannot talk about the demands on discipline.

The twist lies in the memorial nature of this gesture. Below in the courtyard, the sound of footfall on gravel.

If only I could have seized hold of you that day. (Do you want to be salvaged, or not?) A bill poster is pasting up another vignette: Ecclesiastes, something about the inevitable collapse of our fortification. We shall need a lightning rod, another gigantic toothed wheel.

After the assassination there was no residue — however, forensics applied the paraffin test and found traces of powder on my right thigh. The glyphs I had used are not from any known writing system, appear quite without purpose.

Note the wordplay at bell (viz. paronomasia).

Break your fast, and be sure not to miss the apotheosis in the lift. In many depopulated areas, lookout towers or platforms can provide a panoramic view.

I shall see to it and not forget. The petrous portion of the temporal base enters a hiatus at this point, and on into the aqueduct.

Note how he draws closer to his theme, a vicious circle of love, albeit somewhat dilapidated.

I chose abjection, an aesthetics of inertia. Some of the techniques used have since been abandoned. Replies next the inquisition.

We consider your case with indifference, dangling from the lowest rung, claws dug into tempest et cetera.

*

A sudden flash of blue light from the adjacent window, rumours of trepanation. There is a faint air of persiflage in the room, light and slightly contemptuous mockery or banter.

'Tell me, when was the last time you actually came in here, took advantage of the lack of facilities?'

All this was avoidable. A standpoint could be a pinnacle of terrain, a giant freestanding boulder, an ice shelf on a mountainside or other topographic object. Prized perspectives generally have a low landscape horizon, hence the boundless open sky.

'Who is in charge of the sphygmograph?'

Sometimes flight is arrested for a few seconds and the moth settles to spread out its wings. Sometimes intense pain is transmitted along the course of a nerve, especially in the head, the face.

We dare not speak above a whisper. Outside in a clearing she signalled me to halt, index to lip. We had reached the edge.

Now she is back in the darkroom with her silver nitrate, the gypsum and saltpetre, a final glimpse. I feel uneasy, all I can say is that my memory of objects is that they are never alike.

That time with faltering piano along the gentle slope toward Kaptol, our mediaeval nucleus — a dank cellar, courtyard in shadow — tears shed on parting. It's believed carbon atoms are able to link and form chains stretching to infinity.

At the city gate, matt with untold soot, an ancient crone stoops blackclad to scrape wax from the devotional stone.

*

He read aloud a list of all the outlawed nomads. The escape route through the square with plane trees took us to the station, debouching above the bridge.

Origin is expressing removal, always.

I appear to make all these things happen as I pass by. What I have cut is scant but significant and grapples with your code of malpractice.

Two facts here are brought sharply into focus: the letter is searched for everywhere and cannot be found.

XXII

He telleth the number of the stars; he calleth them all by their names

A hill where grain is exposed to the wind, your place in a rebellion. Better to stagger this; I have blind spots with music. I became his protégé in the same year.

Valhalla, about 1973 — the giants are clearly visible. I cleave to the surrounding air. Since he left, I have been in constant rehearsal — right here, about the heart. What do you remember of that time?

Origin denotes a regulation, from old nerve, to cover plus inflame. A bell is rung at a fixed hour each evening. There is a word for archaic white-hot iron.

A vortex of litter ascends the schoolyard niche, contained by corrosive brickwork. Objects fled from the harrowed edge, in need of nothing.

I am trying to get the pictures to move, to appear in sequence. By flinching, we disappear underground during each long exposure.

Historically, usage is often contrasted with the side nearer to Rome, i.e. of time closer to the present. Two alternative forms of a gene have arisen by mutation and are found at the same moment. They are autochthonous.

We used the muscle of longshoremen and a mechanical device unhinged since the middle ages. Now here comes the fourth note of the diatonic scale of C major, enabling oxygen to pass into the blood and carbon dioxide to be expelled.

*

I admired his capacity for randomizing problems, his superior indiscipline. The vulnerability of the tracker's psychological state is always worth testing.

But in the aftermath of this intervention, we are still fighting amongst ourselves. I exist at the high watermark. It looks as though there may be another layer of glass.

I undertook various trials before arriving at a texture that matched expectations. (Only he can see us.) A set of unrelated items was stowed together in a trunk and forgotten in an attic, before being sold at auction on the owner's deathday.

Why walk around and sometimes perform actions while you are asleep? I want my book to be unpopular and makeshift, without sounding hollow.

Draco has no bright stars

The plot revolves around mediaeval money laundering, and corresponds to the aforementioned mythological giant. Origin is literally running in opposite directions.

I have been looking in all the wrong places. Probe deeper: cage-fight mystics, a decommissioned horsebox, a piece of smooth marble with a circular hole at the centre. . . .

You are sure to lose this wager (one finger). In the spells and magic songs, each term is used in association with a particular hill or mountain.

The exhuming and burning of heretic bodies at the order of the inquisition is back in vogue. Origin is slightly contemptuous.

*

All concessions are forthwith rescinded. I cannot abide today's firestorm; our flesh is hammer-proof, not flame.

Both examples are sublime operatic arias. Opposition in political circles has led to his departure and asylum at the castle of D, overlooking the Adriatic. By contrast, a pianola is an instrument equipped to play autonomously using a piano roll.

Here end my quotations from his unaccountable, if not impertinent, epistle. A name has been awarded to a sect alleged to hold the same views.

Maybe we could stage a head-to-head at which we scream aloud our respective translations, while people sit around sipping absinthe and shooting one another. Sodium chloride is rumoured a mineral, typically occurring as colourless cubic crystals.

Hereabouts we feel compelled to include one or two dogs.

In his archive and literature he manifests the atavistic brain. I am harbouring tongue, a second-rate form of communication. We are going to have to bend the rules a little, stage an audible post-mortem.

He says the word chair when he means the object itself. One portrait depicts him from the hypothalamus upward, but music is the most deeply confusing of all forms.

The writer then goes on to discuss numerous cases of paranormal phenomena such as phantasms of the dead, automatism, trance states, possession, and disintegration of personality — not forgetting mesmerism. For example

The lamentations of
an autumnal violin —
antibody by-products, incidentals.

Other names include an inhibitor of nuclear factors. Now consider the sense 'to spatter with flammable liquid', for example, he aspersed the place and its inhabitants.

*

We two resolved to fight a masked duel with pistols, then on to the open sea, an abandoned coastline and archipelago. . . . Yes, the portrait depicts her from the pineal gland upwards. The places we are truly drawn to are never visible.

A black powdery substance consisting of amorphous carbon is produced by the incomplete burning of organic matter. This does not bode well says the other: we are colliding with a gangliform obstacle on the patient's facial nerve. I hereby reveal the whole of the beginning.

'That looks like a hair, but we can only see clearly in a certain light.'

You can. You cannot. You may. You may not. You must not. You should not. You should not be. You were. You were not. You will. You will not. As if. As if it were. By which. By which it was. If it does. If it is. If it is not (in which it has appeared). Of which it has been. Of which it must be. At any rate. At all events. At all times. At some time. At the same time. For some time. From time to time.

'What was yesterday all about?'

'Rehearsal for what?'

To be frank, a secular view of the surrounding landscape is impossible. But he got his hazards in on time: always strive to undermine your own accomplishments.

*

If you fail, you break us; I cannot face this night sea crossing alone. The stadium, located a couple of hundred metres from where I was executed, has been renamed. Origin is an antechamber.

Now what? she said.

I felt euphoric. (This is also called dislocation.) Who else can you suggest: men-at-arms, an ash raiment — fields choked with harness in the territory, gore about the forest floor where they met in combat. . . . Others appear with totems — insinuate, conjure hints. A point of agreement is reached between the clans and the plants and the inanimate objects (succulents, fungi and all the mineral things). Colouring materials, such as soot, were readily available, bone awls commonplace. About midcentury I began writing chromatic vowel forms.

I am no longer commented upon. I emerged from a confined space into a wide open area.

Compare with discharge.

We have done the Europeans, now it's smelting time. When you recognize your third chemical plate, scream loudly.

I cannot concentrate on this loss alone.

Unless I reveal myself, why should anyone ever want to come back? One of the amphibians has bright markings and was once thought able to endure fire, another is based on a scale with F as its keynote. Origin is now a forgotten interval.

*

Blind spot, or maybe a stray, straight into the casket on the opposing flank. There is a way of tracing back to another level using starlight carbon. The track followed to reach this point in time has been registered as Event W.

These four days since we descended through the frozen mountain pass have been a bleak struggle for no gain. At a hidden signal, floodlights around the rim of the crater were switched on.

'Take care, those sirens can trigger epilepsy.'

And sure enough, a singularity has been reported.

'How then does *this* do *that*?'

Open another canister on the hour, every hour. He had scheduled four examples. Only one turned up.

I can understand water, I can understand surface tension, but it seems our antagonist is busy composing a wilfully ambiguous existence.

Vicious in the air, undershadow of the Darwin end.... His only recollection is of a primitive daemonic figure capable of malign possession.

*

It is said she could write in the air. Slowly, with grace, she passes the palm of her hand a little above, and in the direction of, the grain of the wood.

Each of the girls has been given a different task. This situation is impossible to analyse, where everyone seems to cancel one another out.

Origin closes the eyes, the lips.

Ooze-head is most murderous. A new law has been cast. And then, I suppose, we shall crawl all the way back to the centre of town.... Unsettled scores have been telegraphed in — try your best to miss the target: whosoever slayeth the dragon, the shield he shall win et cetera.

He chose to pass through the circular stone twice — headmost, then once again feet first. This is a wheel-shaped slab set on edge and pierced by a round hole fifty-one centimetres in diameter. In a fraction of a second, all his energy was transformed into heat.

The carved and painted rood screen was ripped out and destroyed during time. It deadened the voice. A long rectangular pit has just been cut north of a line. Nothing is contained.

Note how he is transforming the workaday world into another fucking parable. In the end M found his spool where he had left it, as predicted.

Our ancestors demonstrate the swallowing of water, reverse baptism.

*

Before the door stands a law keeper. I am collapse. The breakage of one phosphate link provides energy for psychical process, such as the cremaster.

One: the control genes.

Two: life-and-death messengers, to whom I dedicate the grimace of the neutral.

Three: helix nebula.

Locate by exorcism, locate by process of elimination, the perfect ambiguity. He is thickset and suicidal, into the roiling sea and so on.

I am subjected myself these days, a wit marked by ear decay: caries and rickets, the model strike partnership.

As the days of summer pass he tires of consulting his timetables, the freight charges and ports of the Atlantic mailboats. There is a disturbing absence in this locality.

Come Monday, the islanders are due to begin their long march. We will be glad to see the back of them.

During the inter-war period we discovered two new kinds of profitable economic activity. Notwithstanding, certain groups were in desperate need of reinforcement: peasants living on the vast inland, sulphur miners and their kin.

A gash across the throat right now is out of the question, out of all season. Some say the feudal circuit has become predictable. Think of something else.

Outside on the gravel I can hear someone grinding a sabre on a spinning wheel of feldspar.

The first scene of the prologue is a weird confluence of fate. An orchestral interlude depicts the transition from unearthly gloom to break of day — more often than not, the part that gets left out is the credo, our mission statement.

Anything is possible, just not at the moment. She has come down to earth to collect her dues and escort him home.

They are late.

You are no longer on the list.

I have loved to death in the past. Is there something I am supposed to be doing?

Reminiscence

Another bungled tracheotomy. Journey to cancer ward, face bandaged on a raw day, just like any other.

He stands to wave reluctant as I walk up the hill and turn the only time. I have kept the used carbon in the hope of making something of it, a classic study of a fading life.

Origin is late, alone of its kind.

*

You were supposed to fashion more time, begin the painstaking process of facial reconstruction. Another breaks the surface. Two more days in the sun and we're finished.

Origin is formica.

Same orifice, bearing the 'anteriority of a trace'. We are moving away from this axis.

The organism has untold skin, a mouth to no next. And look here: a strange moth that has disguised itself as a thorn to nonplus the predatory bird.

God was back in the room, spherical and primed to erupt. This meant we could stay for no more than three weeks. The corporation paid.

An extensive fjord-system begins halfway up the eastern seaboard: we landed at a remote beach on the iron-bound shore of a particularly strange island. There is an elemental spirit living in fire.

I made a decision upon reaching the crest, a summit burst above ground. Directly ahead stood the gravel counterscarp.

Our adversaries are continually inventing novel ways of keeping themselves distracted from the world. We found ourselves further north than the crew could ever have believed.

It is the outcome of this clash with which the opera is chiefly concerned.

Some of these magnetic lunar anomalies intersect. We have at our disposal no rule or general solution.

The astronomer T built an observatory equipped with kabbalistic instruments. These sometimes appear as a short loss of consciousness (absence), without leading to convulsion. Despite demonstrating that comets follow sun-centred paths, he adhered to a geocentric view of the planets. Vitus Bering is a different man.

Then the couple embraced passionately on the taproom floor, and were only momentarily unsettled when the screams of a rival could be heard beneath the window. One must take advantage of anything that offers the faintest hope.

*

The red square at sunrise. A musketeer on guard lies half asleep on the ground, rifle with fixed bayonet at his side. He is dreaming of a man in flames, savagely dismembered.

Note the stimulus and delight of ambiguities, of background murmur: the spectacle is total. But the world has yet to come into possession of a consciousness that will allow it to experience its own reality.

The changing colour of the mysterious lines that have suddenly appeared is determined by events found here on the two-dimensional plane. Artists working in the recesses of caves painted animals on rough protuberances and angles of rock by guttering torchlight. Elsewhere, they had practised.

Crest of hill obscured by mist. Both structures are oval, with diameters defined by single ramparts, each of which reaches a height. A pile of combustibles for burning a dead body has been gathered.

The crown of the head is set opposite to the base — the melting-point of lines that bind the angle has been measured. Books were embered.

You learn to nod at intervals, perpendicular to the plane of the horizon. This makes the transition to marching in a straight line much easier.

All combatants must be marshalled if action in this corrosive element is not to fall short of achievement, snared by historians and the public purse.

Scar of tongue

We find ourselves at a point where function takes a measureless value, especially in those angles of space–time where matter is infinitely dense. She has deceived G by telling him the ring slipped from her finger into the sea.

The above is a fragment of a music-hall drama in three acts, with words optional. Fuck, the individual shadow contains within it the seed of conversion into its opposite!

I will now make use of something so far unmentioned: a power of turning, a great circle passing through zenith and nadir. Her edges are indistinct.

But I cannot help noticing one element that is still missing (to wit the interior fat of a hog before it melts into lard, the fleed crust). The shift from a proper noun to an interpretation usually indicates the name of a deity.

Language isolate

A growing whorl, inflorescence so condensed — dearth of choice — decay and crumbling of bone.

*

He is seized and driven back inside the body. Origin is altercation with mythic avenger — to blind, from eyeless. A linear organic polymer consisting of amino-acid residues has fused with the tidal chain.

Is she still alive? He reels, trips backward over the lip of a gully. Do you know what today's triggers are? He glued his muzzle to her mouth and drew out all the air.

Retreat from the compound under these conditions would prove hazardous: her surviving lung sighed flat like a spent bladder. I do not want to play that habitual role today. . . . She bears a strange celebrity, broadcast near death.

Throw the quarantine switch, there is always a chance the generator may spark back to power. We were right in the middle, having formed a tiny cluster: the circumference was vast.

Usually one does not remember. There was a river. Some people had a lot of messages.

Sleep, with febrile activity of the nervous element, giant hailstones, everything levelled. No light because no darks.

In the strata of any mechanism, in which one part lies directly above another, a vertical position cannot always be achieved. He rubs together gently thumb and index, upper lip adjacent, hence olfactory.

I got stung the other day by one in my very bed. But for sure, the bleached moth at rest beside the concentric rug is well deceased.

*

It is as though we are made of nothing, he says, decomposing starlight. She suggests a plaster cast and callipers: 'Bring copies of yourself!' . . . This whole business will never amount to much.

Make a decision — shape into tremor, declare yourself now. The trail had run dry, the spoor.

I can no longer defect. (Wherefore?) Evidently this is over my head, a maelstrom in the fridge.

Another locomotive steams past, passengers clinging to the roof, several garlanded with cordite. I watched fireflies glisten about the crown of a tree, among other shreds of reminiscence: white fog of exhalation, a shriek in the playground, the terrace lament, corrugated concrete with salmonella dogs. . . . But I am still living on my last chance, making scant progress. Iron-bound is archaic, of a coast enclosed with rocks.

I have been cleared with security (steel toecap, triple bypass). That's about everyone. Now you will have to sing for the rest of us.
What is more, a third recumbent limestone figure has been unearthed. A settlement of two hundred people was found crammed down the well, yet another arca project.

A sign said the looting of existing pages is permitted. He bores into the head. Origin denotes a neglected falsehood, or a valve for drawing poison from your canker (the current sense suggests this quadrant of the galaxy).
He has scrawled across the departmental wall, something about the depravity of an unregenerate nature.
I have done a lot of disappearing myself in time. I am unauthorized, a combat rouser, childlike insistent. The explosion was like a wall of orange inside my head.
He will never break. It is better to dissect than to *abstract* nature.
'Maybe yes, to trace the nerves,' another explains.
'Breakdown. Is it two words?'
'What about the surviving revolutionary cells?'
Sense one alludes to Aeneas on his visit to Hades to appease Cerberus. This picture appears with a blue cast, the rocking sepulchre upon which uneasy I tread.

Variation, an under-domestic

Discuss below the difficulties in applying the concept of a subterranean species to the nervous system. A clue: consider the way your biological clock works in the context of external timing.
Inspired by a number of failed and doubtful cases, I found all this titanically amusing. From then on, as we trekked higher and higher above the Arctic Circle, every subsequent moment, every experience, became instantly forgettable. A technology that could render convincing points in space had to be developed, and with some urgency. This seemed to me essential if in future the opinion of an imaginary two-dimensional being were ever sought.
That's my planet she says, pointing through the airlock: a living alphabet where omega is dwelling and delta my territory.

*

What can this mean, an ascent to a heavier time than the one finally used? I no longer feel the hunger, but am wearily disappointed with all this activity. They could never have guessed what was coming: a torrential downpour of sharpened pebbles.

I have to leave, all this talk threatens surfeit.

His skull resembles, note the speech musculature, the shoulders of a bull. . . . They will not be here tomorrow, no one will be here tomorrow. I am sure he is writing everything down.

This contract is biological, quite free of monetary interest: it offers only defeat. There is noise growing beyond the perimeter (some call this limit or threshold). I am reluctant to place the severed head upon the counterscarp.

At the end of the pass the minotaur turned to face me. I was reminded. I was reminded of once finding myself at the centre of an aperture in deep space, where the curvature of time was infinite. Now, having nothing better to do, I have drawn up a list of objectives for the following day.

a) Tongue-cleaving manoeuvres.
b) That part of the forest in which they fought was covered in gore.
c) Again I dreamt her blind, yet with second sight — she touches my face.
d) The warring gods and archetypes do indeed cancel one another out.
e) Severance of carotid artery, a glut of choices.
f) A fine-grained metamorphic rock with laminar structure, intermediate between slate and schist.
g) Binary rectal massage.

Memory is suggested, in hand. I once was right about everything but am no longer considered a danger to anyone. The blazon is bend sinister, only half its usual width: semé of fleur-de-lys, a serpent nowed.

Tactical silence

As befits this town, where the Chinese whisper was surely invented, I have heard an array of theories: gangland assassination, euthanasia by non-intervention, spectator suicide, a misguided attempt at wingless flight et cetera. A member of the family is the world's most commonly spoken language, with estimated speakers. The script is a logogram.

For transliteration into an alphabet, a method is used. Conversely, the megacycle is a unit of frequency equal to one million. As usual, the truth lies elsewhere.

'Come the weekend, at what time are you disposed to resume our supernatural pursuits?'

See, straight off he leaks into another of his subjects. I want his ear, his nose, trophies of the struggle. We are in awful danger, every moment a distant principality.

'You once talked about a far earlier language, remember?'
The telephone rang, a waiter wiped a glass dry and held it up to the light.

Here is philosophy becoming its own revenant. The pilgrims encountered three rootless vagabonds, sleeping on the moors under whatever shelter they could find.
'That spectral face, it's over there now, near the entrance to the ice cave.'
An ant colony, especially an artificial nest or formicarium, is an artificial container with purpose.

*

Blue woodsmoke drifted through the air as we passed on horseback. They are building on places that are liable: two-thirds of the earth should not be here. He's not coming back, is he?
That month communist forces targeted a province only fifty miles to the north-east of the capital, to test our resistance.
'I said all along that I would drop him if need be.'
'No, no — this is forever, for-ever.'
See, the last speakers of language may already be alive today. She draws blindly, scratches spirals into the earth that transmit an inconceivable broadcast into the future. An ancient curse was written on a lead sheet.
Origin is contra pneuma, against the name plus law.
Word senses can be disambiguated by examining their context. Discordant notes jangle the nerve, are neither accident nor elsewhere: we no longer know what belongs to whom or to when.
The only violence I desire, she writes, is the sea.

She traces a house with slate roof, bindweed, three candles guttering, a face in profile and same frontward, eyes in direction variform, lines signifying motion set against a gibbet, tiny hearts creeping to the exit. There is nobody else around, just she and I.
She has seen her future overruled. She plans her hair. A hovering phosphorescent light has cast a spell on the lovers.
The unknown man is in the house. She was once condemned to death for killing her mother with a sleeping draft. We are joined by a cord that circuits the waist: today, we both have that beyond-the-pale sensation.
She shouts.
Something is coming up through the floorboards. It is going to explode.
The concepts of time and three-dimensional space are fused in a four-dimensional continuum. Body-centred denotes a crystal structure whereby an atom is found at the core of your unlit cell. I found one volunteer in the corridor who was still breathing.
She shouts again.
An animal familiar, spirits and devils et cetera.

And rising from the gloom, shafts of light penetrate the hanging mist. (Insomnia.) What is the next stop for us on this mercurial journey? The pall-bearers are identical, set at mourning in the face. I may have to follow suit. We are still trapped in the gulley.

*

The woman then grew the wings of an eagle and was swallowed up by the earth. The belief, as previously described, is that the constellation representing her is found in a position directly above the moon, under nine stars and three planets.

Paraselenae appeared. The planet Jupiter, which had been hiding inside in her womb, moved out of Virgo like a silent miscarriage. Your own little town is never on the map. Did you go back last night?

His shotgun nods against my knee as the carriage jolts, face lined in runnels of blood. What is false in declaring this? Chance is yourself addressing yourself.

I once caved in during the same manoeuvre. How do we know that the object has not changed colour in the process? I could fashion an everyday example: an infinite curvature of space-time at the rim of an aperture.

He writes a message in green ink, tears off the slip and hands it to me.

Just why, we do not know, but we always knew that at some time she would.

I did not encourage F to go on with his story.

*

This era lasts one thousand years. Every gesture is unforeseen, each breath fugitive, the last. Permit me to fashion an example: dark subsoil beneath a crust formed by the leaching of salt.

The septic tank is overflowing. Outside, dust begins to eddy and swirl until it coalesces into an unmistakeable form. Our adversaries toil on through the mud, howling. Sitting in the front row, I busy myself pretending to read the funeral notices.

Among the works left by J are those on necromantic legerdemain, impractical magic and hysterical incantation (malison of Faust et cetera). I reproach my comrades-in-arms for their habitual atrocities as tumbleweed rolls toward us from the stage.

Now, obviously we have only scratched the surface this morning. The local nimbus level has a history. Each gesture is irreducible, every move immediate: you cannot possibly comprehend the root of our fear.

Muscular spasms surge through his limbs. On this occasion, he has recklessly chosen to visit the infamous spectral wing of the homestead.

1927

Throughout that long year he found he could possess any other human being as and when he pleased. His raiment glittered as the stars caught the light, reflecting it back and forth. Using willpower alone, he would make a sunbeam change direction as it entered the room, falling at an impossible angle. To document this we used characters which had originated as stylized pictographs but now represent truly abject concepts.

The setting is magnificent, with a sheet of rain cascading through a slit in the ceiling — cracked tiles bear graffiti, concentric rings of phosphorescent yellow lichen — rivulets of pale-blue resin trickle down the trunk of a giant redwood, shallow graves populate the nearby paddock. . . .

Let me stop you a moment, before you go too far. One shop window is displaying the cracked and mutilated letters of an unknown alphabet.

*

Philosophy haunts its own spaces more than it *inhabits*. Our mission is to prepare for the extinction of Battalion S4.

I am thinking of a person or thing that is difficult or impossible to reach. Origin is a handful of burning clay.

She draws blindly, scratches spirals in the earth that are a record of inconceivable broadcasts from the future.

Note a bidirectional flow of data between the commanding officer and subordinate military units. Executive function is being corroded, the filtering of critical information, shunting unnecessary locomotives and the like. Silence is always profitable.

In a matter of days, half our territory had been handed over to the invader. Always take care to remove uncertainty of meaning from an ambiguous sentence, phrase or other linguistic unit.

*

Traces so muted as to be illegible. We are using the plural by chance.

I have mentioned before that we did not often talk to one another. I am going to give you all one minute more.

On this day in ninety-four, Voltaire was born. Here is the finale, with the original cast performing: I can hear the roar of the crowd as an empty train flies across the marsh. The map coordinates confirm we are just a few degrees from the northern extremity of the island.

A metal girder has torn into the undercarriage, the light in the compartment is acid yellow. We will build a dwelling in this wilderness.

Repeatedly he claimed it was a secret place with secret trees and a sacred lake to which we were headed. Military jets shot by in a V-formation leaving contrails of red, green and gold.

He was dragged into the castle by three of his comrades-in-arms. Organized under the manoeuvres at Fort Ex, this gruelling assault course is twenty-two weeks long. At that moment a pack of boys ran past uprooting firs with their bare hands, recruiting the forest. They thought they were giants.

We hung our banners from the parapet. At night there were howling noises inside every skull.

I will avenge them, said he.

And we all shared a very purple memory of those times.

What?

That night they rode through a region electric and wild. Who or what is your market in this operation? Who had only half his features remaining: one eye and a lipless mouth, the chin and nose laterally slit?

The codex describes a woman clothed with the sun, the moon under her feet and a crown of twelve stars on her head. She gives birth to a boy who will rule all the planets with an iron claw hammer. Toward the end of her life she is heckled by a scarlet seven-headed dragon.

See, I have launched myself against myself. The only conclusion is that there is no clear dividing line between species and shape (see singular). Speech is a matter of fate.

*

On that day he turned Queen's evidence and the envoy was summoned. A dispatch arrives, the final denunciation. You are crouching nearby.

Let us see how momentum appears in its original form. We can still surveil our adversaries from a vantage point high above the ridge, frantically digging their nests in sand dunes and flint walls, the spire of a church on godforsaken marshland. They imagine their position to be impregnable, yet I intend to resume the assault, once astrology permits.

Dear Gauleiter

Triboluminescence is the emission of light from a substance caused by rubbing, scratching or similar frictional contact. Sales are hard to pull anywhere these days. I imagine this is due to the delusion, spreading in all spheres, that the barely glimpsed fragment qualifies as engagement.

We are beings with an unequal claim on the landscape. You don't possess the surveillance gene, do you? Though complex, it permits written communication between speakers of untold dialects, most of which are mutually incomprehensible in speech. This surely qualifies as a situation.

Your savant

I am uncertain how error-free this knot in the chain of being may be. People feel guilty; it's a cheaper way of doing things. That night I knelt before the spectacle for the very last time.

*

She does not need to rehearse, just steps out of the wings and discharges. Try to utilize a simple constraint. We will need a butcher with a sound grasp of pi.

This is entirely uncreated. Some of my co-conspirators appear to be sabotaging the realization of our shared goals and objectives. I was reading Clausewitz when I was seven, one screams out loud.

Someone has stencilled do not use on the base. People have led the most appalling lives.

I am held in check, clasped in restraints, head staring frontward firm in its metal brace. I recollect.

No. 165.

Calcined ash of saltwort (kali).

Pencil on parchment of larvae.

Bruised arnica.

Cellophane traces.

A brittle steel-grey sentient.

Inventory AD 2177.

There is a mind unravelling elsewhere. What is it we mourn when we mourn your undone years? The evidence suggests the existence of a counterfeit elsewhere.

Now you are improvising, drilling deep into the torso. Messengers arrive. Eyeless, I volunteer. Everything depends on remembrance of the weather: we are down to the last page.

She sawed up the cadaver in the bath, sprinkled rose petals. She sprayed ammonia in its face. He was depressed. She left. He was not rehoused. The relief ship is not due for seven months.

Now, cast your mind further out into that expanse he calls the wastage. Other sites display similar burial rituals. I am on in three minutes.

Is everybody happy. (What is my gaze missing here?) There could be periods of great lucidity, then *Walpurgisnacht*.

He remembers, makes certain: a black elastic substance — calcium salt of human acid — ghost-double in apparition. A source of vibration is moving toward, or away from, the observer — which explains the sudden drop in temperature.

I had never before witnessed. [*Laughter within.*] Now we are going to hear more of those rumours, poison in my fodder et cetera. It takes six weeks to complete a single orbit.

The statue's nose had to be resurfaced. We strapped it into the turbine chair.

People are falling out of the windows. The plot sets out from a position of sanity, then recognition suddenly evaporates. The comedy stems from a yin-yang holocaust.

I stayed indoors to write. He exits stage left, pursued by bats.

Justice, at last.

Because the next step is farce, stratagems and aims will begin to decay. He is paralysed in his tracks, surgeons armed to the teeth closing in, rolling tumbleweed, the cawing of rooks. . . . How does it feel to have to?

There is a tattoo on his prosthesis, a latex member. The room is strobing — blue cathode ray — a beam of electrons shot from a high-vacuum tube. . . . Everything depends on the purity of the white light.

Is anybody else finding it difficult to breathe? Without an accurate conception of danger, we cannot understand the art of war.

I have overlooked. Like an obelisk toward which the principle streets of a town converge, the will of a buckled spirit stands precarious at the core.

*

Ill-starred language, a sequence of extremely bad timing. Do not force me to look back. I am fearful of accidentally turning away a body who is not on the list, but actually is.

There will be no fireworks at the end: she may be on the same tram, or she may not.

A greasy yellow orb bobbles and skates across the frozen pitch. I am to be performed after our exchange of vows: anything that sticks to you, you may keep et cetera. Along the touchline men in fluorescent tabards shovel at the snow.

*

Montage: crisp blue shadow of an overhanging roof — terrace maudlin, concrete cancer with spurts of rust. I do not believe we can ever return to that moment.

A change in the signs would be relatively painless, a plexus of intuition — the errors that feed our veracity — the stairs to the sea.

Break the back of time. Will we ever depart?

Struck down by shrapnel in her white spring coat lying still beside the tramway. To the east, an aerial view of metal tracks glinting in the sunlight. A single desire dominates the mind, a compulsion.

I am loath to enclose your counterfeit. The syndicate would never suffer a halt in the long march.

Fence sixty-two

I have been struggling to keep up with correspondence.
Who could shut one eye, then straightaway shut the other?
Would you accept, without too much revulsion, some samples of my work?

There is little space for quietude. She turns her head to address the dreamer. I am alive is scratched into the paintwork above the steel door where broken fingernails are embedded.
A carrier bag full of decommissioned junk was delivered during the night.
It is her — literally, double-goer — one who walks who should not walk.

We would tether the impossible. On the nineteenth, following an attack of dengue fever, the settlers lit out into the territory with their kinfolk, determined to reach the nearest trading post. As a sacrifice, one of the scribes was left behind to fend for himself alone in the wasteland.

*

Dazzle behind the eye: powder burn, quivering neural fibre. A banner ripples in the wind. We hung from a concrete precipice. Everything is unfinished.
Someone came back from the future who was not you. A network of roots protrude as we swing high above the earth.

I went downstairs and paid off the cab. This is one book of sacrament I can begin and expect to finish.
She is coffined and smeared in filth. Somehow it is all my fault. I wear a head of nails, one-and-a-quarter-inch, hence the memory loss.
Recall drilling out by fluke halo et cetera.

He chooses five books then leaps from the cobb into the sea.
Without. Hence, without mutes.
But I will never be pressed to speak of saints after dark. In civilian clothes I felt a masquerader.

The tide is out. He lies broken on the ooze among grounded vessels. At the threshold, I cannot see for the blinding light behind the other man's head.

Uprooting the shrapnel — the edifice lies in ruins, all our hard-won apparitions — fortune reaches down from the empty stand.

*

Found pages — a muddy embankment — on route to a shelled bridge, the long walk to a fresh adversary. It was getting dark. I want this line to be legible, though elsewhere might suit more of a whisper.

Fourth day: am I the only one who knows how to turn a question over? The answer is no, a promising blank.

There is an unspeakable margin hereabouts. I lay down and thought, where could we go from here?

The box sits on a glass shelf — is occasionally contemplated as an object in itself — enjoying its status as redundant technology, a perfect cube. The protagonists, one male and one female, have to make a decision: if yes, someone must die.

I cannot believe that the time has come. They are here among us, complete with bespoke callipers. Avoid serrated knives and hacksaws as they tend to become entangled in the volunteer's hair.

A courtroom staged in a magnificent panelled hall: enter witness for the prosecution.

Once upon a time, so many centuries past, a land now lost beneath the waves slid away from the coastline. Directly he spied their arms, the charcoal burner concluded the horsemen were wandering knights engaged in the quest of which he had heard previous report.

Multiple destinations, choices — they will not get very far. But stay calm, a particular set of features in speech enable the hearer to detect a word or phrase boundary.

She recoils, war has fled the memory of most. Someone made that silent film: he has less than four weeks to live, feels like Cézanne before the mountain — fasci of wooden rods, with or without axe, borne before an ancient gradient. We are equidistant in time.

A thin sheath of fibrous tissue lends the appearance of a luminescent stripe, the orbiting belt of an ice planet. The rest of the neighbourhood are dwarf ellipticals.

I am commonly mistaken for a chronographer, believed to induce melancholy and gloom — lead is my metal, the counterpart (also roaming myth). But I was once the largest and brightest, fifth in dislocation.

Venous suggests performed, situated or entering by way of a vein. Origin is late mishap.

*

Their extremes in time became plastic — palpable and systemic. No one can believe an object ends when another begins, and that our body is surrounded.

Reject anything that does not cut straight through, then section (alchemy, from to sow). Origin is after-saint, an English who helped. You could step on them and you would never have known.

Dressed as mediaeval pilgrims, we crawled amid the ruins of the citadel. A select few have been enlisted to betray our comrades; this is no strategy of renewal, just a botched attempt at vengeful punishment.

These butchers persist in their old ritual of turning the victim's head to the north during sacrifice. The boycott was extended to automatic writing.

An increase or decrease in the frequency of sound, light or other waves appears to take place as source and observer move toward or away from each other. There was a strange glow in the sky that day.

Please, no attempts at unravelling. I leave the remembering to you.

Roadkill

The aquilegia has backward-pointing spurs, typically a purplish blue. Origin has a supposed resemblance to a cluster of fire. Another example is acceleration.

All this does not mean I am not listening.

Did you two see anything?
Such as I have never witnessed, an arabesque of multidirectional curves. But farewell for now.
The victor in this test will be ball number seven, the celebrated numeral.

*

I can no longer activate any of my objects; morning is usually my worst time. If she is not going inside the building with me, I refuse to act. What do they call that sign?

Did you two see anything?

We saw the great wordgame. She has her disparate look. Reproduce the goods, her middle name et cetera.

Other skulls, usually without the jawbone, served as a framework for the plaster death masks and society portraits that were mounted around the walls of the cave. The motif here is a creeping or gimcrack nebula.

The winner of this round will be ball number eight, enabling astronomers to measure the radial velocity of stars. I began to realize that none of my memories mattered, were all false starts or idiotically partial.

But we are gluing these fragments back together as best we can, trying to find some species of intolerance.

*

A quarried face, i.e. somewhat fucked. The city, a hundred miles to the south, has been declared panic sanctified.
 What's the matter, father?

He climbs the scaffold before the gathered crowd. In a time of innovation, all that is not transformative is deemed malevolent.
 The only way to complete everyday actions and avoid dying in a fatal accident is never to think about what you are doing. Perhaps this unlocks the mechanism whereby the alien invader can see in our dimension, our light.
 Returning to the surface, he crams the precious volumes into a hessian sack. He has examined the worn spines, each book gilded with surface mottle of bird or snake.
 One morning a moth was found within the concentric circles of the drawing-room rug, the life bleached out of it.

I have been implicated in untold personal histories, such that it has become difficult to remember the details of every specimen. Then we passed a chalk escarpment.
 Note how the event always takes over in the end. Whoever next passes through the portal you will find yourself unable to resist.

He insists on explaining his methodology in detail, the swish of the mezzaluna blade now a fraction above the volunteer's sternum. At the age of ninety, craving an injection of nux vomica, the latter had set fire to his cell.
 This picture forces us to anticipate a quite different usage, connecting what is experienced now with what was experienced then, and thereby an uncharted level is reached. And would the ammunition not have become something of a collector's item?
 The hazard is No. He is riddled by the other, the one he stalks.
 'Today, I want you to behave like a reptile.'
 The answer is a metal support for a person's leg, a deserted origin.

*

I don't know whether you feature very much in their thoughts. I did not do anything because I expected nothing.
 He is lawless.
 He is not lawless.

Unexploded bombs are all around us under the ground, are they not? And then we have the aerolith speech.

From the opening words: bitter roadkill, composite with tubular heads of yellow steel, a great aluminium star afloat on the ocean. . . . You were always a disappointment to me, lurching seaward, misnamed from planet, ill-timed rootstock.

This feels like a rerun of that fatal conversation we had.

Strike him out. Extend erasure to any objects found existing out of joint. Retain only the more imposing samples, tapering away beyond form.

Cygnets kept appearing as the cards were cut. My opponent is that crusading priest who escaped from the archipelago.

Origin is taxonomic.

We have only limited time remaining, so I must think carefully about which point of the compass I intend to tread. Paradoxically, my lack of experience grants me an overview. Experience has become a list of excuses.

The house is perfectly situated: it is in a tunnel. There is a pinpoint of light at both ends.

I do not know how far back we will have to reach. It was then that I took my first footsteps into the desert.

He put his wet hat in the washbowl — it had been raining and the brim was dripping water onto the floor. The fisher king, as I contend above, is the seed of this enigma.

Here is the strategy some misuse, soaring across a blank page. This is where everything starts to go wrong. It all began.

Four hives stood isolate.

XXIII

We have been subverting situations buried within living memory. It is as if every place were aware of every other place.

I forgot to say, a mouthful of quartz crystals.

The repetition is unavoidable. I shall now refer to an untidy collection of objects placed haphazardly on top of one another. We can always deny people existence through our mental apprehension of them.

You are silhouetted against a background of sponsored word games. The saint's feast day coincides with a pagan festival whose rites erode protection against witchcraft. This effect causes the sudden change in pitch noticeable in a passing siren, as well as the red shift seen by astronomers.

*

This will not take time. Why does he not simply step away from the path of the oncoming train, one may ask.

Bystanders can tell the village in the Swiss Alps is a model, even the snow — for one thing, none of the figures on the station platform move as the camera pans across our field of vision. A spoor was once traced through every set, to grant a more convincing sense of movement.

One arm of the scale swings up and down, oblivious to the dull motive of gravity. Hold me, hold me fast at the centre of the horizon.

West I say. No, east. Yes, west. . . . She exits in disgust. Anyone who even breaks off a twig is expected to die within a year.

Origin is semblance.

The state, it's me, a transfigured use of the forgotten and an accidental success. That said, I am considered socially disappointing.

One character is power, the other more killer (viz. strapless implosive). She said the recoil left a bruise on her right shoulder and geigers clicked at every exit from the zone.

Two of unknown lineage were electrocuted on the razor wire. The carnage is authorized: count us in. Everything is way more objective than anticipated.

All the logic is bleeding out here: there has recently emerged a commercial interest in what determines the minutiae of individual choices. (I miss sound.) Which way are you going? The girl fled into a nearby café and cowered behind the zinc counter — the patron hid her for weeks in the cellar until the danger had passed.

We all nerved up and began talking to one another after a spell on the run. There is a rain of scribble, more erasure; it is my intention to spike an opportunity further on down the line.

*

One winter morning and snow is drifting across the window pane. Inside, nervous collapse.

Ready yourselves, I can no longer achieve a state of attention. There is not space for all these references: bone-sack, gum resin deep in salty soil — brittle, dried stigmas — into alignment creep the weary trackers. . . .

She recklessly compromises the various stages of the production; we were all kept busy gathering combustible twigs and brushwood. Any error is fatal and the piece ruined.

Suddenly she is not there, no longer standing behind me. There is this unbreakable rule.

His tongue is branded with a red-hot iron before the firing squad takes aim. A flag snaps in the gale, a lead pulley shoots down — an unknown alphabet has been scratched across the bullet-scarred wall.

Into the back of the convoy hitch the trackers. . . . Is that flyblow under your skin barks a corporal. . . . Find somewhere on the planet that is equally unnerved: no one had foreseen how narrow that ravine would be, where the earth sinks into the earth.

My mouth skips a beat. (O bless her.) Tell me, why is it so tactically significant to trek upriver?

Our guide and I went hunting and brought back nothing.

*

He has detected within himself some further signs of grace. The experiment is something dead technical to do with light.

I slept fitfully; a great white shark played a pivotal role in my dreams, but I refuse to change any of my plans for today.

Spoons banged hard against battered mess tins. . . . Numerous subatomic constituents of the physical world can interact with one another: electrons, neutrinos, photons and alpha particles. A couple of years later another sister died of pernicious anaemia.

The hypothetical object in the room is rumoured to have mass but no physical size. Later that evening an infantryman, selected at random, was broken on the wheel.

I have to make decisions on a first come, first served basis. Being an astrophysicist, I never got close to an actual brain.

He peers out from his foxhole. We are moving along a gothic trajectory; being hanged, drawn and quartered has its merits. The limbs of the condemned are lashed to two horses facing in opposite directions — the executioner's hands are sticky with blood as he drops the hatchet into a pail of water. He glances up at the clock tower.

The earth stood still around me as I walked through a crowd of people, frozen at an instant.

'You haven't any?'
'No.'
'Not any?'
'No.'

We were guided to this spot by a displacement of spectral lines invisible to the naked eye. All of your aims are substandard. The chosen genus is (especially) vulgaris and its hybrids.

'Useless, and I'm getting older, especially my arm.'
'What about that street runs parallel?'

Though I had known a certain nobility, I was finally discovering the true direction of my life. Then he says something has to break, prompting the memory of a dream in which it rained ash at the crossroads, ankle deep, the sky a solid expanse of grey. Everything had ceased.

Picture a figure clinging to the undergirder of an iron bridge.

More cauterized optimism; I could sit here forever. Temperaments, for what they're worth, are here to stay. But I don't think the living sample we excised is going to survive.

*

I woke to find myself renamed after one of the minor planets, a 'deep-sky object'. I am indifferently awed: scales and apparitions, a comedy goal, no laughing matter.

He makes a note: Wednesday, exorcism, dank basement with metal planchette.... We then lost the final title, barely retaining a white background which quickly fades to nothing.

Today, even a handheld travelling shot is considered a variation of tracking. The only available space is a bivalve aperture.

A bone-sack is a large brown sack filled with bones and worn under the cape. It is a reward for completing.

And so on to the remaining names.

The old man is a living field of battle; the aorta swells and ruptures, the great arterial route that journeys out from the heart. You could say the pitch had not been tilted to our advantage. The wind was at our backs.

Observe how these fossils are quite unlike our present-day species, living and dying at the edge of the shelf.

I cannot accept the fact that the yellow shape is swallowed up by the blue. A continuously growing, horizontal underground stem puts out lateral shoots and a rhizome system, but only at intervals.

Pikemen mounted the spiral stone steps. To my left a door swung open — I too made the ascent before abruptly losing consciousness.

This was the manager's cue to sidle up and inform us that we would have to behave differently, or leave. In the attic is a cage which holds the feral boy.

Once more, the son has usurped the father.

An object has been placed on the window ledge — it resembles light, solidified. The mouth of the Nile is scratched across one wall, all her venous tributaries clustering at the delta. A thin sheath of fibrous tissue encloses a muscle or other organ.

We hired a narrative tracker. At first he just rolled across the ground in the dusty backyard — now he's up on the roof, wailing and ghouling, almighty possessed. Can you tell us what he says?

He stabbed at the edge of the slit. A plant secretion consisting of resin mixed with gum spurts from the hole at the head of the shaft.

Police used tear gas, rubber bullets, water cannon and armoured vehicles to breach the barricades. Alienists resisted long into the night, responding with crossbows and poison darts shot through blowpipes.

*

A galaxy is flushed from his mouth.

They are never going to allow us outside again. Eating did not seem to be part of my existence in that steel box.

Flanking the bridge is a cliff face of white chalk. I observed closely the minutiae of the painting, how the artist had with simple grace depicted the weave of the old man's tabard.

Because I will forget, from this time onward I shall partition and share out the stolen head. I would then Yes — Yes to all, so notoriously shut away as I am.

This part is the most difficult step to take. I could not bring myself. The fire element of the fourth day gives rise to the passion of detachment and an aggregate of ill-feeling.

I have personally measured the electric charge released at a neuromuscular junction by a synaptic vesicle. Error is an incentive, a wellspring of energy. I am personally contributing voltage to the end-plate potential.

Vignette: a human head springing from a lotus. And then we have the zeppelin speech. I said that.

'What ails thee?'

'The detail, all the detail,' I said, just in case of confusion.

*

She has been left alone all night, locked in.

'I have not felt this way up for years.'

She is febrile, every uttered name a trespass.

Mediaeval cathedrals were built without a groundplan, fragment laid upon fragment in a rapture of faith unconcerned with meaning. She can no longer control the rage; first it came as delirium, finally as presentiment.

'That was a hell of a trench mortar.'

Yes, madame.

We have been informed that we are going about this in the wrong way. The methodology is fucked — nonetheless, the blue room I read, yes, the blue room.

I am acting like a man whose days as a stranger will soon be over. They have vectored in on our position. . . . Shadow of outspread wing across forehead, close-up eyes of the one stationed beside.

We have gone back in time several hundred years, where we find ourselves clinging to brickwork waist deep in water at the bottom of a well. In the same locality buildings fell into disrepair, people went mad or dropped dead on the spot; pawnbrokers and undertakers did brisk business. An antique mechanical clock standing at the centre of the room tells us the year on an abacus, while three revolving spheres predict the next total eclipse, and a month of pitch black. Do you remember when we first attempted this, hand-painted static sparking across your body?

*

Witness the lamentable lack of remedies this season. He is famous for the discovery of 1842. I have not seen this pattern before.

Of course.

The object you are holding can be substituted for a ram's skull by seeking out an eccentric old hermit living deep in the forest. Both sides converted disputed penalties in front of a tense Homburg.

It is not as though we are short of legends. I ate just enough to make staying justifiable. The envoy in question is probably a double agent, his blazon a cross with centre void. Five thousand turned up on the day. One officer was struck in the leg by an arrow.

What is a hatchment?

A large tablet, typically diamond-shaped, bearing the coat of arms of someone who has died. The insignia should be tricked to denote tinctures. I have already inferred that no rules are so sacrosanct that they cannot be set aside by our assassins.

I have not come down from heaven to execute my own will he once said.

He takes his place in a corner, frock coat torn and stained with blood. We have been stationed here to gently ruminate. The second field is divided into three parts.

We have resurfaced. Once again, everything depends on the mercurial nature of work — a volatile assemblage of human, reptile and thing. I had the power of prophecy but would assume different shapes to avoid answering questions.

We could engineer time warps as well. I lived there until I died.

*

His next novel was a pocketbook: the reader could take it along to a riot and it wouldn't slow her down. An acronym was coined by the army to describe the post-narrative world as erratic, complex and ambiguous. According to one author, the inherited framework serves no purpose: a narrow filament will be fed inside an artery to explore your interior.

This leads us into unknown backwaters of copulation. Lord, consider the lilies of the field, how they grow — there is something in this solitude.

You said they would. They did not. This is where I end, bring things to a close.

*

He detests physical labour, preferring to sit outside panting on the wet grass. I have no problem with that. But by now he could be anywhere — motionless on the jetty, falling in and out of love.

Cross over to the other side: I'm like an Eastertide statue, shrouded yet not. In this some find anathema, others release.

You have a sense that something is whistling close by you in the air. Search as I might, I could find no trace of his letter, nor any clue as to the cause and manner of its removal. Consider an act or situation that provokes or justifies a war.

It was never my intention to vex the reader with all this nothing: talk of endgame, the severed hand beneath the bed, the incarnadine garden claw — candle at his desk guttering in a sudden draught, flags cracking at the top of a turret.

By this stage, the police in their confusion were busy hunting for anyone in a blood-stained smock who bore the least resemblance. I have dragged the hoard of coins up from the dig, circlets of rust in the main.

As you may have guessed, the subject is a man at the moment of execution.

Go upstairs: door to the left, a message stencilled across the wall (your writing wall) aligned to the season — to disequilibrium, a want of balance. Describe more precisely at this point the skin tone.

'We cannot make use of these tissue samples, they are quite hollow.'

Note what is being documented here. These are unremarkable times, yet I remain stubbornly schismatic, exiled to the vault.

'And did you take into account the length of the suspect's stride?'

I have also been questioned about the topography of the suburbs, but will never betray my comrades.

Immaterial dialogue

Upon waking from this demonic reverie, so the legend goes, Sister Maria found herself soaked in ink. A letter scrawled with arcane glyphs had come into her possession during the night; another inquisition would soon be underway.

This tale is tragic and comical at the same time, like that story of the gentleman at an inn: there came a moment when unaccountably he had to leave. The next day he does not remember a thing.

Temperament is a theme we have been putting to good use — murmurs of the time, every tongue lapping at the floor.

Park your bets. The deeper in he treads, the further away seems the circle of light at the end of the tunnel.

We could survey from our vantage point the reach of the marshland, obscured that morning by a dense sea fog. Avoidance following a traumatic experience can take many forms.

Would someone please name these ephemera.

It had become very cold in the bedchamber. Chilled white breath is exhaled by the sleeping woman as the ghost of her husband sits beside her. The mercury has dropped.

I am returning to a workaday state; we are cutting off your neural supply. Dreams are a form of cerebral hygiene, responding to the whispers embedded in the plaster.

Some sequences are carriers. Change the room, change everything.

*

It is anticipated that the subject will be repelled by the severed head on the back seat. This routine is too brief to constitute a puzzle.

Elongated neck, battery acid in the stomach, abdominal wall dissolving. . . . I can now only breathe through a tube as the plastic sac laid across my chest slowly fills with bile. Monitoring the drip, the machine alongside beeps, a red light flashes on and off, a white line tremors. An imaginary distortion of space in relation to time is taking place, whereby people or objects of one period can be transported to another.

Your mouth is dry. A great sigh passes around the stadium. You feel confused when you wake up.

The second segment provides a timely geopolitical reminder: never despise your enemies, it affects one's judgement. Never mimic your rivals — outmanoeuvre them.

In my baggage was a Stradivarius violin, which I could play (waking self cannot). I also had a tattoo on my sternum which I had never noticed before, of a skeletal woman wearing a sinister conical hat. Compare with passage hawk.

A foundry or burning mountain is the emblem of this province. She resumes her incantation. I recall numerous stuffed animals fashioned into furniture.

We awoke facing north, then swung south — on arrival, we found evidence that M had spent the previous night there. We parted with many kisses of the mouth.

What form would recovery take? What sort of evidence has been procured? Stay close.

Did you lose the map?

Each page had been transcribed in neat lines across the sand. We don't do multiplicity, the striving after of names.

They have the accidental organomachines (viz. Schubert's impromptu).

Whose authority is virtually absolute?

Who is inside out, passing from knowledge to knowledge?

The message is dispatched. A passerby hands me his card. It reads: I have no wish to discover any further signs that the noise is growing louder.

Gold was once considered a fine thing to possess; memory is the cut-off point. I read aloud across the bitter fathoms of the sea, chained to the deck where space is sovereign.

I followed the address: Aqualung Cabaret said a handwritten neon sign. A candelabrum with seven branches had been placed in an alcove where the disturbance took place, a site famously destroyed.

The inmates include bodies stripped for action, societal hinges. Pick out an option of your own, take your time.

Of a sudden, breath comes good with a name. But she has failed to notice the ornamental scapula, one leg is off, and there are fragments of plaster strewn across the floor. Remnants of a floral pattern may still be discerned. There has to be some kind of explanation for what I have witnessed tonight.

I propose four possible strategic responses: guilt, false rumour, dispersal and chaos. At her interrogation on Saturday last, the suspect acknowledged that she had been drinking in dissolute company at three public houses on the night of the murder.

Now produce a rough sketch of a hatchment appropriate to each of the following:

(a) An unmarried wife.
(b) An unmarried husband.
(c) A wife already dead (argent a fess sable).
(d) A husband already dead (argent a bend sable).
(e) A wife surviving, clinging to an improvised raft at sea.

*

No, this was a genuine breakout. Toward the end of October the serum, an amber protein-rich liquid which separates out when blood coagulates, entered the food chain for the last time.

Hardly anyone noticed that we had arrived. An analogous amount of momentum and electric charge was employed in the proceedings.

My aim is true: crossed keys — a green lion with seven stars punctuating the spine, swallowing down the sun — an allegory of eye, of heart. This image usually signified what today we might call glancing back over the shoulder with regret.

A lurid orange light dawns slowly over a vast meteorite crater sunk into the earth.

Origin is taking root. This chronicle is helping strategists understand the existing challenges in your macro-environment: volatility/uncertainty/ambiguity. First of all we need a detailed written description of everything that has ever existed. We are using the words 'to know' as they are traditionally used (viz. one inherits oneself).

Resurface under a different name, an ownerless object penned in the hold, all your human ballast.

*

The Nile delta has been traced in red biro across a pitted wall. I note that the tributaries do not quite connect with the major artery.

A stack of roulette chips were scooped into the wrong baize hole. The coroner delivered a verdict of accidental suicide through lack of attention.

A drop of viscous crimson with a consistency between solid and liquid appears at the tip of his cock. Perplexed, he rolls the bead between thumb and index. It is believed that matter has no objective existence.

Picture a man chewing a sheaf of paper. If the puzzle were octagonal, failure to solve it could have cost you your head.

Taking not the slightest heed of any contrary opinion, when I first took this project on I suspected it was a runaway shape: a vitrine with crumpled paper, a vitrine with sphere, crawling. Now I am unconvinced by this trade or any other, forever manoeuvring beyond my scope.

This is the signal for him to lay all his cards on the table. Remember that boneyard?

*

She approaches the edge before recoiling — this is the established pattern, always returning to the lip of the ravine. Those who remain have named all their objects and places after animals.

We will discover here moral tales of female spontaneous combustion. Some among the settlers are relishing their newfound equality as channellers (there's even a Chopin crater on the planet Mercury).

About this time, madame had a vision of the devil as a horrific ostrichlike creature: architectural discourse and practice are dominated by such false dichotomies between design and chance. I am currently situated on the other side of the Alps from the point of view of the speaker.

The male has black plumage and a long tail used in leaping displays. It may be said that any name can be recognized only in the context of experience.

Editing is the joining of one strip of film with another. In this conception of the world, the earth is shouldered by an angel who stands on a slab of gemstone supported by the cosmic beast, sometimes called out as corruption, a misrendering.

The tracking or trucking shot is a shot taken from a moving vehicle. We are in the anteroom of an operating theatre. The time of day is early, still dark.

The heart promises total control; no one present is aware of this. The customers are set at an angle of one hundred and eighty degrees in relation to the sun.

Our starting point is the irrepressible, i.e. slow painstaking work without respite. We are meeting the damned this evening, when an exchange of dead goods is to take place: the head of an ox, the horn of a ram, surges of strength in the unassailable.

Nothing else remains. Dismantle the scaffold, consign this to celluloid and fix a date.

Deficiencies may be glimpsed during your lifespan: anxiety and panic attacks, melancholia, tinnitus with insomnia, pain at phantom limb, addiction, grief and zero self-esteem.

I am going to release next year. She was away for precisely one lunar, so long a stretch of time that in the interim passed an eclipse.

This demands the simplest of solutions, and sure enough the required people arrive. The clouds and the stars minister unto us.

He writes that he is defecting to the other side and is promptly sewn into a hessian sack and flung into the river. No more assumptions should be made than are necessary.

He is repeated, but very sparingly. The closest correspondence would be, in a flower, the part of a pistil that receives the pollen during pollination.

Origin denotes a shield, one bearing a heraldic device, from an older shield of unknown origin. The sense of the verb has been woefully influenced by firestorm.

Some of these seagulls sound like fucking chimps.

*

We no longer have the wall behind us, have no choice but to crouch on the lower ledge. I believe I am concessionary: where I come from, proof doesn't exist. It has no need.

No one was ready for the quality of a thing that makes it unique or describable. People used a catapult to hurl great boulders into the air — red, yellow and grey. These came crashing down upon our heads as we lay exhausted at the foreshore.

A new look crawls out into the sunlight and takes up position, ringside. A severed hand was the crucial piece of evidence in a gruesome murder case.

Voices from the outside. Voices from the lean ports of the body, haemorrhaging air. Now you are a little too close to the radiator.

He learnt about form through the experiments of others. From now on I am keeping the combatants apart; we have had enough of discoveries.

The past

It's the past. Time has changed. I am no longer cooperating, I am no longer responding.

She slew him in an act of forgetting as they met at a famous threshold. There is no light and scraps of food are strewn across the floor.

A clue: dog reincarnate. The dog is swallowed whole, a cartoon shape squeezing along the gullet.

O yes they say, she did not touch anything at the crime scene, and what is more did not notice anything unusual. Until very recently we had our own cake and daily trepanation, the workaday reprimand. I was aware that this would involve a titanic struggle, but nothing could have prepared me for what transpired: we are told one thing and then another thing happens.

Just a white streak across the forehead remains, an aftershock. The pilgrims received due scrutiny and anointment, the rapture of the moment.

*

I do not remember who or what came first. (Where is that noise?) That's me standing at the corner, a battered suitcase in my hand. . . . As the trunk was winched out of the river, water poured from numerous tiny holes, as if the thing had been shot.

The centre expands at the convergence of severed roots. Under the shattered roof, gentle rain fell through the beams as I lay dying.

This is an uncanny place, and I know how much it means to you. My every step is governed by the belief that the architect's role is to defend against the indeterminate.

A proton transmits the interaction that binds nucleons together in an atom. Compare this with a projection into the world of the dark reptilian side of the personality, in all its ambiguous wholeness.

She is one of those tramway people, thinks in capital letters.

He says that when we first begin to believe anything, what we believe is not a single proposition, it is part of a nexus of propositions. This dissonance confirms that we have indeed met at a cursèd point.

*

He owns not a pebble, is beside himself. I am halfway through a shift, doing nights, creeping in between the lines, the scales of the law.

He has manufactured his own crypto machine. I am pretty sure these people cannot be the lost five thousand.

Something else is due to take place. I am being primed. The influx is a form of distillation, culled from the meaning of mercury as grace.

I am anxious to get a clear insight into the facts, work out the conditions relating to a thing unseen. Sheets of a transparent flammable plastic are made from camphor and nitrocellulose and were formerly used.

No, truly, I was broken on the wheel (see above). We are held in counterpoint to the unbending sense that everything here is wrongly perceived.

I have encoded her name. We have been relegated from the suicide list.

She spent hours peering into the yellow fog, the enveloping mist. I am the owner of an idea; there is bound to be the odd spark. Say something before the senses invade, she murmured.

Stagnant ponds line the foreshore, clogged with reed mace through the filters. Language has preserved in its speech the canon of prelogic: picture a man suddenly made witness to distant past events, permitted this moment of grace as the earth stops spinning for a fragment of time.

Thrust from birth into carceral thought, i.e. relating to a prison.
 That old man, a nightlight by his side, he is not asleep. At three in the morning he hears a faint rumbling sound.

*

You were labyrinthed, a species of verb that died out years ago. Everything begins and ends at the head of the valley.
 This feels like asylum to me, then came the alarm.
 Is that a chinook?

Picture function as forgotten meaning, an act that should never be completed. Origin is mood, from geranium (see groundhog year).
 Now the air is tilting warm. . . . One morning as the engine revved she began to sing, wailing aloud.
 Here, I have avoided mentioning: you are my only reference point.

People no longer keep watch at the boundaries. Order something, and they may let us stay.
 I replied to anyone who would listen, I replied to anyone who had written. I could not know what you were planning to do that day.

*

Tail raised, a scorpion is tattooed on his forearm. Once R had left she watched a four-dimensional film, scrawling pictures wrapped on dog-reek of sofa. . . . This signifies that the wearer becomes invisible once the sun enters the eighth sign of the zodiac.
 I am actually quite dangerous. One day you learn how to hate, summon resistance, and suddenly all your accusers cease their claver.

He does not long for any change in status. Before him is a net within which the lovers lie apart from one another, barely alive and twitching in the mud. Their shape is strange to say. This approach is a threshold stratagem.
 Beyond compare is the widowbird, with plumage black and leaping spectacle. Ultramafic denotes igneous rocks composed chiefly of minerals.
 Your countless drafts one scholar has dubbed satellites.

We are not permitted entrance today. The doorkeeper frequently holds brief interviews, always finishing with the statement that we can never be let back in. This news will break her resolve, and all fear that she may kill again.

This visualisation of the structure of the universe was not unusual in the thirteenth century: a whale carries the bull on its back and is suspended in water for its own stability.

You clearly know your emptiness. He will never chance the even numbers, always lays money on the odd.

How went the day, how went this endless day, snared inside the circuit?

We are going to be theatre.

Two are stalking strangers in the street, shooting passersby. I can recognize the existence of none but myself, for lack of substantive proof.

This knowledge could not save him from an early death at the fall of some unforeseen disease.

*

You have eavesdropped the wrong word. He is a diurnal aberration.

A slender loop of electricity links every skull. The burr of his voice is a droning undercurrent: gold crackles in the eye socket.

It was winter in Zagreb. I remember. We must not be seen misusing the light.

He is hideous dead, part of the past; the doorkeeper saw it all happen. I want to be rid of an audience, the unfamiliar mass of coming-to-termness.

She has broken my blood. I have never met anyone who was a true revolutionary of the everyday. She says will functions in the rift between each moment.

From across the street, I thought that shocked head was you. I shall now journey across the territory, consent to swear my purpose on an oath.

Do you hear that tongue from the ossuary, trodden underfoot?

At that instant, breath heaves jagged. She embodies a chosen period of time past, shapes a pledge.

I am most unforgotten. Memory has her (this is the hypothesis). I took a trip on a train and I thought about you — around you, all around you.

*

Early, still dark. His choice of language, he seems to be saying, corresponds with our euphoria: fractal observation, projects for an ungrateful country, a swarm of flood victims. I will scream if you step too near the edge.

Despite my broken blood, I challenge the numbers: you tear out a leaf of the book, quash all memory of the past. Despite the circumstances, I remember feeling sheltered.

Needles are eased into the body and heated to the brink of endurance. Somewhere in the building a glass vessel shatters. He is blind — despite this, a well-aimed forearm smash strikes my left scapula.

The bones in the journeyman's sack turned out to be those of an ass. He once broke his back, three vertebra (L3, L2, L1).

The aorta swells and ruptures. How was your balance that day? Any vertigo? Everything is punishable.

We are making decisions. He is seething, bent double — old limner of blacks et cetera. I am left alone with a subtle bruise.

It was like watching stevedores at work: a steaming vat of pitch, the promised annihilation. . . . Can you still hear anything?

Coins rattling in a plastic bucket, ringing change in a volving china bowl.

We are aboard a steamship on the lake with reluctant assassins. Guesswork is limited to a specific subject: the inner canal or labyrinth. We owe it to ourselves to resist.

The ear was sluiced of wax and dead cells. Now you have lost me, lost time — I think the sirens are getting louder, closer.

I never enjoy this drama at the end of the second empire. Twist and shout came on and I wept. Come home.

Will they hand me on in the night? Incoming, the bisecting iron strikes at forty-five degrees of angle.

I can answer one simple question, then nothing more. Memory has him.

Darkness seeping in, I take a trip on a train and I think about you — two or three cars are parked outside beside the stars.

We were found stunned above the horizon line, a winding stream, moon shining down on some little town (it's June). And with each beam the same old dream, and every stop we make I think of you.

I draw down a shade — I speak through the track, the one turning back.

'Bring me an advent, bring me an advent if you find one on your way.'

XXIV

Indent following section latex. The sign read enigmatic.

She was one of those people who seem capable of anything, in whose company anything could happen, and probably will.

I am described.

A trickster, perhaps with criminal tendencies.

It's love, yet still those gears grinding within the skull.

*

Yes, but you are sure to reach the rendezvous before us. Wake up.

Opposite, a priest writing by hand with a fountain pen — elegant, unworldly. Alongside sits a municipal sign listing the top one hundred drugs of all time. I was still pondering the best course of action when suddenly he insists that we hide down a tunnel.

(Note the fragility of each instant described.)

So we enter the tunnel, which is choked with debris, finally emerging into a brightly lit cavernous space. I thought I had died or I was in a cathedral. How could a man ever find the nerve within such a place?

Here is a cracked frame circling an illuminated glass. The mouth to our left is vaguely defined in watery sunlight, set adrift in the atmosphere. I have an overwhelming urge to leave something behind, to add to the pile of shoes and used books. The snow is piled up on every side, leaving a narrow track beside the perimeter fence.

At least he inhabits himself. I have nothing to add, being both seed and obstacle. If justice comes it comes, and we must withdraw.

Backstory

Descriptions of sluice gate and saltwork, a derelict watermill — graphic of a star-eating supernova, surgical uses for molten lead — descent into remote copper mines, broken stone and other mercurials, an abandoned river bed.

One barge carries ballast to the open sea. These are my amendments, tilting away from the daylight.

He is guilty of simulation. Tension eases when we begin to excise the surplus parts.

This construct remains the same over time and changing circumstance: grief-struck and wept, in pieces and at rest — flesh that fades, moulders at first touch. Some objects are blurred and others remain in shadow. My adversary is a committed impermanent, his concrete form determined late in the game.

No verbals here, just utter capitulation, chained or linked together, connected in ranks: a series of things dependent on one another. For instance, the chair that still stands in its allotted place.

*

The page resembles a stook of marrow spines. A stook is a group of sheaves of grain stood on end in a field. Origin is a noun. One of the brood is renamed and raised to the second power. Some lose their sight, interrupt trade and adopt a variety of unhelpful postures: lion rampant on a visored crest, a postilion struck by lightning — a sheet of sparks spreading across open ground, semé of crosses of lilies. I will soon be pinned down while the curve is abruptly reversed — every grey as if illuminated — and the sea, the sea that day resembled a lack.

Origin is unrelated. Now we are out in the open.
    I went outside and came back with a cracked looking-glass, an antique mantrap and some rancid butter.

Of birds who tear off their wings

Sparks of light in flux, yet with rhythm and unstoppable — a downward motion, due south to the breakers, a surrender. The questioner, for the first time, was showing signs of interest in the proceedings.
    What has become of them?

Her motive may never be known. It looks as though I may have changed my mind.
    I have added you to the list of names. We were sustained by blood pie and sawdust, hastily built a palisade of felled trees: sharpened boughs pointing outward, smeared with pitch and ignited.
    An inherited mark of dishonour sits on her coat of arms. Now that we have nothing left to lose, grief spreads out in waves from the centre.
    Mere is boundary.

I am whispered in the ear: little remains but to battle it out by word of mouth. There is a faint residue of delay.
    The radio kept repeating the same name, interviews with people who have spoken. We found ourselves in a foreign port, lit by the first glimpse of winter sunshine.
    He says I am trying to prise open the uncanny. I was born to possess, and did appear a very inconsequent phenomenon for a time.
    Crime is a gift, embrace it, murmurs a bystander.

She gives a signal with her remaining eye, fracturing a vertebra in the process. She is no longer capable of forming an idea.

I strode out inland, toward the granular light. Any attempt always fails, but is worth the pursuit.

A history: neap flood tide, run aground. You know that in time you will have to move the chosen object. Everything rests on the inserted clause, the cull.

I know the story, of course, and it is still dear to me. The other replies that the process is a slow process, the conjunction of opposites.

So, I occur when the sun and moon are suspended agin one another, the countervail.

*

It was always good to find oneself in such company. He ambles in at the close of the last moment. Quick, count to nothing whilst walking circumpolar.

These components are out of character, the feared resemblance. In sleep we received a haphazard grace.

I could possibly finish in the allotted time, given the right conditions. Then the radio played a sentimental melody called I found love due east of your current position.

Count to nothing, in the desert a highway et cetera.

Eviscerator

He says evil entered the world through a single scribal error. He is never when you expect.

No one here is looking at me. (Origin tears at the flesh.)

I participated. A few subtle movements can compensate for the loss of memory, the step toward a poorly conjured experience.

You drop, arms dead. You are elbow-deep, void and immense. The head and hands had been severed and removed elsewhere.

I survive as pure form: a taxi rank in a parallel universe, without connectives, beside oneself and beyond arrangement.

By the way, a hammer is always placed at the top of the column. I would not have taken the risk myself.

She has lapses in attention, concentration. She may be fabricating, compensating for loss.

Nearby, leaves rustled. I swear.

Isidore of Seville insists that an asterism is put in place of something that has been omitted, so as to call attention to the omission.

*

An inland sea with ice floes, ringed by conifers. On its gravel shore a family bathes in low winter sunlight.

Logic eats away at the image, swallows it whole: economic exigency versus domestic conspiracy. Elsewhere you can see galaxies coming and going.

We have raised an outwork of fortifications whose two faces form a salient angle. Origin is unknown. I was as if preparing myself for an event that cannot be foreseen.

He is not present, therefore I have taken it upon myself to build him. Each day the ice creeps nearer. Shades approach bearing rushes, each with his own personal erection.

She could call at any moment. I took note.

Source material in progress, his formidable concentrate. I am unsure about some of these translations, but there is still time to move the ivory rook from here to there. Apparently, I am overused.

He was a personality in his own right, a 'stalk harrowed from immortal'. Only one trigger of the isotope was used. A spiked frame alternately levels and pulverizes the land before seed is scattered.

Amen.

I have built a minuscule tomb for the deceased, the grainy thorax of a long-dead dragonfly. A majuscule script with rounded unjoined letters is found in manuscripts of the fourth to eighth.

Some of these objects would become concrete through a spell of isolation.

A carriage is drawn by black-plumed horses who snort and steam at a solemn trot — sheaves of grain stand on end beside a cage of rotting cob — tank tracks crisscross a field of churned mud enclosed by an ancient drystone wall.

He steps over too soon and sinks amid the smothering waves. Once a brilliant tactician and commander of men, no one will trust him today. What recall.

He seeks shelter beyond control, for we have him now in abundance. A burst slug oozes on the frozen causeway.

I am not altogether present. Citizens have dropped a paper size and gather in small groups under the streetlamps. Back in the day they were duty holders.

We broke the long march and struck camp for the darkness. When dawn came I was still there, but you had passed on before me.

Hide and seek was no longer a game that day — I devoured his book in one lungful.

I see you now; every little helps.

I have kept your default alive, beyond all reason.

The great head grows heavy and weighs down on the wooden beam, dragging at the void beyond. The roof must be shored up before the skull draws everything into its orbit.

Fresh from the municipal slaughterhouse, I remember nothing but this thing of the ballast head.

*

Dwelling, she says over the phone, in response to a greeting. Maybe she was reluctant to utter the other word, given circumstance.

He clutches a sheaf of papers, upon which have been drawn figures composed of tiny letters. One of these forms a catastrophic eye. One forms a needle, another a horselike creature (yet not horse, for sure). I do not know where to place these items. I do not know what else to call them.

*

The cell is set within a narrow row of identical compartments; whether hermitage or glasshouse is unclear. None of the urgent paperwork has been done. He is always here and is a constant: infinitesimal change at minimum amplitude.

He shrinks back inside the recess, clutching a book to his chest. I lie on a trolley in the corridor, a tube in an artery at the wrist; though wounded, I am busy writing in the head, memorizing every fragment of conversation.

A paramedic presses at the base of the ribs. Everything in the book exists to escape into the world he says, apropos of nothing.

Once a tornado appeared at the horizon above the sea, both blue-grey.

Look, that is muscle, this a layer of tissue. These are vertebrae, and here, the three fractured ribs.

I am looking forward into the future. An impression is made on the surface, an angel reeling across the railway junction.

Sorry, I should never have spoken like that. What he makes is not written, it is stitched (he did use this precise word). Right now we are crossing that viaduct.

Aquifer.

Meeting him was something of a revelation, like meeting oneself inside an abject error. We were only allowed to bring back four people.

When you say dormant, I think of the word dormant. Origin gnashes the teeth, i.e. bitter speech, without and back into flesh.

But no, he has turned; I was just now thinking of the long-term psychological effects. One day, a hot-air balloon descended. Another day it was 1828.

Which way up is archaic?

He was the first to isolate the elements aluminium and beryllium. His cardinal humour is poison, black bile.

This process is known as contagious abortion, communicable to man as 'Malta' or 'undulant fever' — a gigantic recent, wingless of Madagascar — all that excess skin.

The stalking of this misshapen creature is a convoluted affair, yet it will surely expire at the close of the story in the most desolate circumstances.

Origin is vast.

I do not know who beat this idea into you, but it is best forgotten, cast beyond. Unawares, I have been waiting for the man all my life, and finally chance has invoked.

Headlines rattle through.

Spelling error embalms wrong corpse

His hexagram reads ease under authority: keep the boy suspended, night image of the cathedral and suchlike. He conjures up a row of numbers (later these will serve as markers on the unlit runway). Hebrew letters are arranged on the wall to form a candelabrum. Hereabouts, he says, pristine materiality is worn thin. The room is lofty and white, lit by arc lamps.

Make a list of all the places that you can never go back to. Now make a list of all the places you can trust. Cut these up, place the fragments in a hat and pick one out at random. The object is to inflict upon your opponent a relentless attack from which escape is impossible.

The moon's blacks crackle and drag she once wrote.

I also have the memory, or rather it has me. It is too late to start. Bleach everything out, cauterize the substance and see what remains.

Flatlands, estuarine marsh, rusting hulk with raft of lashed pallets, a mesh of fluorescent orange rope. A broad vertical stripe runs down the centre of the shield. Origin is a heretic burnt at the stake.

Up in the clock tower, a mechanism alternately checks and releases the pilgrim, transmitting a periodic impulse from the spring to the balance wheel. I often recollect an abandoned dwelling place, stockaded.

Keys of glass were found. That vibration between the skull-plates resumed, the 'darkening cartouche'.

The room contains hundreds of ornate electrics and is divided by two rows of massive columns. At one end stands a dais flanked with standards from which the ceremonial flag is hoisted; the frontispiece bears a wooden panel into which the imperial emblem has been cut. This is where we must stop.

Of an animal.

Make a sudden explosive sound through the muzzle, especially when nervous or frightened.

*

Note the dappled scavenger, another of his battering nocturnals. There are some men for whom oblivion is a blessing; I appreciate all the time you have taken.

We still have the flickering image projected onto our bodies. Across the floor, various objects had arranged themselves in a distinct yet unreadable pattern during the night. Tiny meteoric stones burst through the roof to pierce the sleeping.

Another construction reveals an infertile crescent traversed by canals. This scenario resembles painting; the aim is to sabotage the composition. Black letters had been stencilled onto the wall with an aerosol: you no longer have the promised lack.

I once worked this pit, long before the time of our obstruction. The pledged book never arrived. Neap tides occur at six and six.

Nine of them came sliding over to intercept us. No I say, I cannot go on.

Objects have been placed on small ledges cut for the purpose. It is impossible to testify, is impossible to tell. Granted a reprieve, we were set down in the middle of the amphitheatre and began to tear each other apart.

*

He hails from any territory he chooses, it all depends on the situation, the precise nature of the stunt.

Approach in silence, come to the terrace precisely one hour after moonrise — we will be around the back, suspended from metal hooks bolted into the ceiling.

You have called at such a late hour and nothing of us remains, all used up in ourselves.

You could see the luminous substrate glowing beneath his skin. The subject has lapses in attention, fabricates imaginary experiences as compensation for loss of memory. Origin is scar tissue, related to wisps of straw and the verb elbow.

Significance too is lost: muted light above a gothic archway, the wilderness beyond the west gate, panic made good. Notebooks pulped in the rain cover the rotting floorboards that seal in the dead. I cannot decide from up here.

Before dawn we must work out a methodology. The opening frame shows a bleached and petrified tree.

A nightmare at the races

Nonetheless, it might be said that what transpired that day was well intentioned. In the mess tent green and gold predominate. On the third floor you will find an introduction and a tiny framed picture of the heart. One's gaze should turn away at this point.

At the nape of her neck, some loose strands of hair.

They whisper to one another in the darkness; an outcome is predicted. The flesh is yellow and slides obliquely across the side of the face, extending from the inner angle of the orbit, outward to the anterior margin.

A range of downland, deep blue against the setting sun. Chance comes to a halt and collapses, the measured suspension of a disaster. Lesions form on the shaved scalp, where beads of grease bubble and hiss. Drop to the floor, it's time for a final word.

When I recovered consciousness his face was the first thing I saw — a bunch of keys is jangling close to my ear, shadows flicker in the gaslight. I leaf through the book — something here is extinct — nothing too solid, nothing said about the vengeance of an outsider.

The cascade surges seventy feet above our heads and plunges through a haze of broken light. The rift in the mountain wall is unassailable. He calls out me: turn the vessel about and follow, but none too swiftly — strike an interval. Someone on board fingers an accordion while another plucks at a hollow tube with holes set along the shaft — dried and twisted intestines vibrate when the player exhales. Pointing, the captain demands a sacrifice: overthrow him, into the sea. With hindsight, this command appears incongruous.

*

The interior is austere, with walls of flesh-pink plaster, across which sweep her drawings of magi and human fish, hydras and Portuguese men-of-war. For long years we lived under shadow, but I can still glimpse a certain resemblance.

Scent of ashes and rancid meat. The notion of any future time may not be negotiable: a stolen fragment of your DNA, the cursive script of an untold alphabet, cinders of dissent.

This of course depends on whether he falls to earth or strikes the surface of the sea. Allow for slight movement above and beyond the head, track down the jangle of bloodied keys.

These have been situated with purpose, among other objects set carefully in place throughout that long night. The structure contains a plexus of nerve cells, haphazardly linked by synapses. Balance is precariously sustained.

His trick bears an engraving of a fabulous mediaeval beast, a griffin-headed horse with the giant wings of a bat. He feels a swelling under the tongue.

The music grieves and insists, but the plot has its lighter moments — all is not cabinets of atrocity. I give the blue liquid in my glass a gentle shake and the ice crackles.

Suddenly she stood still and leant forward into the gale. Her chosen method of divination is the algorithm of birds above a ruinous pier. The desired effect has been achieved and our plans will never be realized: compile a list of familiars.

a) A body of permeable rock which can contain or transmit groundwater.
b) A calcified artefact of once-soft sandstone, use indeterminate.
c) No enzyme could have survived the explosion.
d) To rock or oscillate around a lateral axis such that the front moves up and down.
e) A tin hat, and so forth.
f) By subtle increments despair creeps back in.
g) Diminutive of pale, a narrow strip borne in groups of two or three arranged vertically.
h) An oval or oblong enclosing a group of your cherished hieroglyphs, representing the name and title of the deceased.
i) Synthesis of urea from ammonium cyanate demonstrates that organic compounds can be grown from inorganic matter.

I was flung clear. He acknowledges the mistranslation, something like 'your meltwaters'.

Under oath he gives evidence of his own mutability. Fear cements the compact. A thin sheath of fibrous tissue cocoons his whole body.

I can see the contour now as weakly luminous, now as grey. This man could outpray the saints in any shape or form.

Utterance does not occur as a condition which is present-at-hand. It could happen to anyone.

At least it appears this sense of uprooting is consistent. Covering the surface is an oilcloth with a repeated classic horror motif.

During a sudden downward turn, the broken vessels are forced out of the hold. We were attached to the core by threadlike hyphae. I will never again.

*

I can still see the snow line from where we are stationed. Our adversaries can be identified by the same pattern of shallow incisions in the skin.

A conversation has been timetabled. Don't move a muscle.

We were set adrift at the first neap flood. The surface of the planet provides the medium through which the organism spreads and obtains its nourishment. Origin resembles the shape of nonpareil.

Q: Did she lose anybody close?

A: No, such coincidences have always populated her world, the classic undergod.

She is playing the role of seditionary, sustains a steady gaze across space, the divide between host and revenant. We clung together as we plummeted to earth.

She may take up a position, but a position, by its intrinsic falsehood, is never where expected.

Are you in a settlement or an isolated outpost? Is there any restraint? Is there a threshold? Is it a place that is growing or sinking?

Note how she has severed all ties. Someone erected a granite marker at the crash site.

One could choose to perform an action, or one could choose not to perform an action. I had never before dwelt on such marvels, the ability to trigger events solely through the agency of our own thoughts and impulses.

All surviving members of the creeping ulcer chamber quartet are in attendance; the swollen veins surrounding them resemble the limbs of a crab. We are going about the land to disseminate.

XXV

We stormed the excavation site, meeting fierce resistance.
    She is folding space. After several days the hostage confessed to his crime, the exact nature of which I cannot recollect.
    I am assembled slowly over time, retrieval upon retrieval. She carries beneath her cloak a new translation of the rule.
    Familiarize yourself with all possible courses of action, consider yourself as background noise, stolen breath.

What unnerves me is the speed with which every action is performed; she foresees, knows precisely what is demanded of any particular moment. The extra space means we never have to be in the same room together. The floor was bare pounded earth.

He is digging a deep trench in the garden, wears a crest of red feathers that render him a conspicuous target. The sash bisecting his chest is held in place by a silver clasp in the form of a salamander. Grave clothes are the order of the day. Property is protected by a translucent screen.

                    A pebble beach

The dental pulp burst open. A story has leaked: she could be neither driven nor manoeuvred into the parish kirk. Origin is espionage, tradecraft.
    The smoke from her burning hair caught my throat. And then a voice asking over and over: when will you build it, this great silence?

                      *

The answer is a person saintlike and virtuosic, yet somewhat thwarted. I list.
    a) A tide just after the first or third quarters of the moon, when there is least difference between high and low water.
    b) A pair of connected or corresponding things.
    c) Heavy-earth spike rotator, radiation leaking from the core.
    d) Brachiopods attaching themselves to your substrate by a stalk.
    e) Thin copper tracks link the components in a measured fault loop.
    f) Terminal artery with grazed clavicle, low-lying.
    Diversity factors may have to be applied. He has been rewarded with a once-spoken name.

                      *

First light tomorrow. I lay face downward in the mud. He closes the message — this gives me way too much time to think.

I asked for very little.
I admit.
I never made any progress.
I live to regret.
As they speak, he keeps his face pressed against the mutinous stones.

Spelling corpse embalms wrong error

I thought we would dwell in that room for eternity, but now it seems I must leave. He is master of the occasional instant, a rough trade in thought, body nourished by corrosion.

A metallic substance is obtained by melting or reduction. . . . And look, up there, the brightest star in our constellation.

He is fabricating imaginary experiences as compensation for loss of memory — for example, he castrated and usurped the father and ate all his children. Always nurture the no-constant option.

Claret spreading across coarse fibre of hessian. I can't guarantee first light.

He is unforgiven, resembles more and more an act of dictation. Everyone knows the rules: we are rumoured.

Additional futility and other godforsaken proverbs

The subject is a man scant in years. The armistice was a truce in name alone. Anyone present is a potential executioner.

Letter writing has become an unconditional surrender: because one cannot know where a significant event will turn up, nor discern any border with adjacent events, when can any experience be deemed to have ended?

You will find in this matter no two creatures more harmonious in their fear. But this rumoured alterity must be amplified: it makes of him neither another self conjured from my own, nor a separate existence.

Heraldry of the moon depicted as full

A troubled reminiscence. I confess that there is no possibility of the person mentioned ever having done what is specified. The others are perplexed.

Overnight, he has painted an apocalypse on the ceiling. I don't think my limbs are up to this any longer, but still there are the generous compensations of the sea.

Treat of these events separately. He is valued no longer and returns to the dimension whence he came.

Sometimes I start by reading backwards (that business with the ear). Unhinged things made of sound are drifting back into the funnel. This contrivance was developed in the seventh — mass nouns, the countdown —

whereas the humanistic hands of the fifteenth were based on the Carlovingian minuscule.

From to make round

You may gather up your supplies and equipment and disappear. It will be quicker if we do this my way; laughter is seeping in at the seams. The remaining space is an auction house, and nothing to do with the stars: it's all about wavelength.

What will you do, she says, when the real war comes? As a test, supply the words that have been deleted, such as a word formed from enclosure, driven in with a nail. You get the idea: an annulment.
During that time, beseeching him, the while his hand she wrung.

It is rumoured he has a mania for shipping forecasts. Check the horizon, all the arbitrary routes followed over the past decade. But I don't know whether I will be able to join you on the long march.
This is enough for a stiff reprimand, wandering the corridors of imperial sequester, into whose enclave the mob has broken, uprooting the cobblestones.

Notes for a depositary, from apart

We may have to quit before time. The existence sketched above is a workaday life, with steadfast clairvoyance. Nostalgia was always dissolving, somewhere.

He is busy researching his hymn to dissipation. When I was a child he took us with him; we lived on a remote island. He thereby disclosed the credal error of remaining in one place.
That rock was the keystone — you could see the blue, an ultramarine, from any vantage point. The peacock and the eagle and the snake also lived there but are said to have remembered nothing.
Today people are turning ashes into jewellery, literally wearing a corpse on one finger. I am attempting to describe here a triple system of which the primary is a red dwarf star. The infected metal is apparently so named because of its readiness to combine with gold.
Now, truly break away, in the sense of a horse-drawn carriage without postilion.

We swung back through the village, passing the son of the landless Paul. People ran out under the hooves. Panic took hold.

Regulus of antimony

The guard who brought him in locks the door and is posted in the passageway. The prisoner stands beside the bed and takes off his hat, in deference to the convalescent who has received a fatal wound. A voice from without shouts.
 Invisible companion, be gone.
 To avoid the same fate we rendezvoused at sunset. He bore a white shield and the crest of red feathers on his helmet quivered as he galloped into the clearing.

And as I navigated lifeless rivers, saliva dangling from the lip et cetera. . . . One confronts here a value antithesis that seems irrefutable, yet is held in a shoddy binding that undermines the whole.
 He then made a pantomime of checking his watch while the others pantomimed picking up dropped food.

*

Low winter sun, solitary man turning deasil, opposite to withershins. This calls for comment on several levels. I perceive what you are trying to engineer: the characteristics of sound sources are revealed in the distance between successive crests of a wave.

To resume her treatment of the quotidian: a real nerve grinder, I so desperately want to stop. We have been decaying this theme for several years now.

And later he found himself a further null expanse, the desert, spread out below during the ascent of swaying antennae. One might as well use up the remaindered light.
 i) I am an intermediate product in the smelting of ores.
 ii) With capital, a first-magnitude star in Leo.
 iii) A story must hold a child's interest and enrich its sick life.
 iv) The goldcrest genus of bird, diminutive of king.

Once she even substituted a stone. Picture a makeshift bed, what some call a shakedown.
 Who taught the theory of disjuncture in a class they had stolen? A lost style of handwriting developed at about that time.

A warm horizontal, rising heat corrugating the static. He ought himself to slay and berapt his life, skip down into the flames, and choose.
 Sometimes the past arrives too late. See, he has the faculty.
 I am exhaust.
 A watchword rises, the call of the steersman according time to every oar.

Hymns and psalms were once sung in vessels. Your words were frequently repeated. In the distance I could hear synchronized volleys of applause, no doubt the insurrection of twenty-eight. Nobody else gives a fuck, really.

List

    A unit of animosity, one hundredth of a pause.
    A moth, the male of which has orange.
    A rough drag-stone, plucked from the lower greensand.
    Pig iron in the keel — ballast, also kintledge.
    A redress or hairnet.
    A native of west, one born east of the hindwings.
    The film or membrane.
    A caul, covering head.

This has ken, but too brief for my life, for the task in hand. I mean in the sense forerunner, acting as a guide to the post-horse rider.

    Notes on how to catch an approaching object or falling liquid

Bring armour, and observing strict ritual. . . . She is twinned with another who resembles. The tone of the conversation is cryptic, wherein some unspecified deed is owed to a person yet to be identified: subterrene anima comes in the guise of a bird, a god depicted in theriomorphic form.
    Are you run aground?
    I have stayed too long.
    Without a word, he returned the pebble to its place on the shelf.

At the back of the tomb is a jade reliquary containing the head. The book's endless preface is an expression of biological disunity (above, I meant Carolingian). Any surviving human elements are too diverse to cohere, except under intense pressure per square inch. Here, we usually add that in one case we can imagine the colour red and in the other we cannot.

The door to my cell swung back and forth during the earthquake. Despite this, we prevented the enemy from bursting in. For a second I thought I was dead.
    I prefer the original 'to remember' for 'the thing remembered'. When contact finally takes place it will be indescribable, void of sense, with spasms of fury that flesh cannot circumference.

*

It is a big old river. You can see it on the map; it looks like a snake. This battered strip of earth beneath your feet represents the missing link in a chain of causation.

Across the span of that critical bridge the bolts began to rattle and one by one darted loose from their sleepers.

Conceive of a terrain without edges. I was not looking, shrank myself out of the picture.

I thought of him only the other day, the embodiment of a rift in time, exiled to a spit of shingle. Once there, he squats on the ground and coils a strip of reptile skin about his forearm.

You may not be aware.

We were buried up to our necks on the line that marks high tide. What would happen if I refuse to make a decision?

He is snared by his own conjuring; the quoted word that appears erroneous is copied exactly as it stands in the original.

The man who switched sides in the pursuit of lack

He declines the customary blindfold, confesses. His mind turns around the detail, distant in time, numberless opportunities passed over, as he thrusts his lawless hand into the flames. This could be termed an apprenticeship in clairvoyance.

We are exposed to every blow once our strategy no longer holds. A fragment of dead bone has become detached, a common enough occurrence during trepanation.

'Why are you here, sequestered from the rain?'

The answer is of course the autonomic nervous system.

And still they ignore our petition. Just a fleeting thought: falling down is the emerging motif. I recall the signal.

Trace an indelible design on a randomly selected part of your body. Insert pigment into punctures in the skin.

There is something disquieting about my cell, but the compression of daylight is glorious. Most of the strangers are like fine particles floating in the air, and come at an instant.

The fallen angels were imprisoned in stone, crystallizing as hexagonal prisms. Your voice rises up from beneath the ground, speech whispers out of the dust; come nightfall stars emerge, transfixed at the rim.

Origin has collapsed.

He carries the crucible that contains the ashes. We are travelling in a direction contrary to the sun's course, considered forsaken.

XXVI

We recognized them the moment they entered the airlock. The risks and complications fall into three categories.

I began with caution; it takes a month of sedation to fully recuperate, during which time the volunteer must lie face down upon the pavement.

Once more a disembodied voice gave information about hostilities, this time mentioning the only survivor of a group of ten. I need these quiet mornings to gather up any strays, the haphazard and digression.

*

The wooden shutters are eased open; at some point in time they have been painted white. A grey haze enters the room. She says mist curled about her feet as she ran at dawn in the wake of a strange military craft. Then she replenished her glass cup before moving to the adjacent thoroughfare, where she continued the tracing of cellophane sweets, backdrop to a china doll in silhouette. Hard colourless light flickers, a triangle across the ceiling, before steadying itself.

*

He rinses the sacrum. A message has been scored into the surface, isolated syllables arranged in a list.

I am sidestepping catastrophe. Tradition rumours this is the bone through which the body resumes its mutability.

We returned home to find the excavated head had turned a shade of Prussian blue, in contrast to its initial orange complexion, and had collapsed in on itself. A musty scent of decay now lingers in the study; the cage door has been left open and swings on its hinges in a gale.

The next day while working I meant to type moth and wrote syzygy. Any thought of a ritual casting of the head into the sea, thereby acknowledging its status as a cherished gift, must be abandoned. I had the thing bagged and flung down the chute.

One overseer insists each pair must be numbered. He can be identified across the globe by a name.

Every time I attempt to encroach, you resist: a change of wind direction would have us seized by the tide.

Origin is stone of flank.

*

The less we are handled the better, though in dangerous sections of the abyss a safety harness is essential.

The voltmeter twitches as she murmurs an early tone poem, the same spasmodic theme leaching into every brain.

That encounter did a curious thing to you. This occurs, it occurs to me.

Among the embers, a rib where tissue clung. The snow is eighteen deep, matching the debris and calculus indices — a hard mass is formed by minerals within the body, especially in the kidney or gall bladder. . . . I had been moving about the surface too aimlessly to make any coherent social observations.

Loose and unstable rock, slippery shale and high winds can make work on the cliff face perilous. The next task was to assign the artefact to one of the civilisations conjured by scholarship. Origin is a warping of calibre. For example:

'You are such a cloyment and cumber unto me, that I must leave.'

I am cleft by a vertical line. Regardless, here enters a combining form harbouring eights: octahedron, octosyllabic, October and so on.

Suddenly he says you are concealing your results, carrying out excavations without official consent. I confessed: true enough, I had located a primeval form in art and a cactus on the bathroom cill, yet chose to remain silent.

*

Demons caper through the alleys wielding pitchforks, toppling within papier-mâché heads. I am ecstatic, well prepared for assault by ball lightning — and indeed, after dark the work of fire spread soundlessly across the sky. As we have so often remarked, it is necessary only to express these intuitions in a vague and imprecise form for them to become manifest.

Vehicles had been put to the stave during the night and the following morning we trod barefoot across splinters of glass.

I would like a room the man says in a voice. The family implodes, not so much dysfunctional as dystopian, bleeding across its bounds, all spic and span. He says there is no outside, we share no kith or kinship, no guilt. He also says there is no interior.

A tungsten plate is screwed into his skull while he sleeps.

Compare with rhizome (sense 1). This and other minor signs of forgetfulness plagued his final years.

The twelve

What remains to be said about the paradox of causality? I do not know how the sentence 'I have a body' is to be trusted. And there may be other transitional signs.

He stands paralysed beside me, the sky pink and blue. The child knows more than I realize, more than I can acknowledge, as he whispers into my ear.

What are you going to do when this reaches its conclusion, trace the history of your malevolence, her volatility?

To which I replied.

Have you fled inside the bunker on this ruinous day of late summer?

*

Lead is the chosen surface on which the life is to be inscribed (see also silicon wafer, optical disc substratum). Just keep off the barricades, plead my probationists: we don't want you in jail, we do not want you medicated beyond redemption.

Origin is literally being present.

October the first. Despite clues aplenty and an armoured escort, our executive slaughterman is kidnapped and drowned in a vat of eau de cologne. Later that day, I managed to catch the right train and alight at the correct station. All the males have pockmarks and buboes in the neck they share. Clay packs the room to the ceiling.

In another poem the angel of death appears as a vengeful spectre. Now we bring you salvage from the great pioneers — outsiders, radicals, visionaries — whose ideas foiled civilization and helped make us who could be today but are not. Have you ever tried to arrest breathing, outwit repetition of the act? Three a.m. is the time when people are most likely to die, which explains the insomnia: I want to be around when it happens.

Safely back inside the stockade, my mother hands me a plant in a terracotta pot; it has a single delicate white flower. Through the window stretches the grey lunar landscape. Fragments of gravel have embedded themselves in the sole of my boot, and the matting that covers the floor of every cell. Cosmology claims a disc-shaped earth with surrounding mountains resting on the back of a giant bull, which in turn stands on a vast fish, held high.

The fire

Pancreatic sap, the rain with scent of asphalt while acrid blacks pour from a vent at the rear of the building. Leaving-takings all round. . . . My accomplices, islanders to a man, sit their ground before unflinching ranks of stout, heads twisted round toward the circumference of the pit.

Origin is late ganglia, tumour on or near the sinew.

This could be more playful still, for example the image of a huge pendulum, such as one sees labouring within antique clocks. Our limbs were lashed together as we were dragged by bargemen along the riverbank; it was like a painting. Suddenly she points and screams this gamomaniac must be archived, tagged!

Dream of a head

A magnet rests on the brainpan. The day in question is the one in which light appeared over the darkness. If I knew the outcome, I do not suppose I would tell of it.

This way of speaking is misleading. I can smell burning.

Who or what is used to denote the complex nerve centres? A discrete quantity of energy is proportional in magnitude to the frequency of radiation it leaks.

(i) An archaic, a metallic substance obtained by smelting, alloy of fuck.
(ii) The brightest star in the constellation Leo.
(iii) There is no point in asking, you will get no reply.
(iv) A triple system of which the primary is a hot dwarf star.
(v) This condition has been named quietude, yet remains upside down.

The guttering candle was the first to extinguish. A catafalque traces a low arc across the sky.

I am not always where my body is.

Lineage is untimely. Compare with scaffold.

*

He struggles to calculate when daylight is scheduled to reappear. Glands discharge, embedded islets secrete hormones into the bloodstream: we are witness to the contraction of diverse howls into one long scream.

As they waited for the help that never came, she lay on the floor and kept vigil beside him throughout that long night. The canals of the ear are infected and wreckage is gathering at the foot of the block: redundant wardrobes, a charred sofa, the peel of unchronicled fruit, carved pumpkin with rictus grin and dust of blue lichen. . . . Surgical excision is scheduled to take place beneath the valance of the great bed. He can no longer feed plasma to the extremities, must focus on any object, anchor.

Origin is to lower one's eyes as a sign of submission. The surviving mutineers are to be hanged at sun-up. I cannot do this anymore: several of the embryos are migrating around my numbed body.

Then she says, nonchalantly, that you could still see the bullet holes in the wooden panelling. The landlord had kept these forensic trophies, where the assassin's aim was lacking, or maybe the bullets had gone straight through her lover and into the wall.

Another says I dreamt a revolution; we were painting a mural of a hydrothermal vent, an opening in the sea floor. A soldier shot at me — wounded, I fell through a window to escape — a guard outside pressed a pistol to my temple to deliver the stroke of grace.

A third says I dreamt of gore-clotted tunnels, an exorcism, the final takeover: they have been here for millennia, they are us, were are them et cetera. I try to explain to the others but this proves futile.

She replies that with the advancement of years the sense of time and space dissolves, molecules ebb discarnate until one becomes a lingering sense of place.

*

She straps herself into the cockpit as red and blue tracer streak either side of the cramped turret. Daylight is impossible. The story here is the story of an oppressed wife who resorts to murder to follow her heart.

Whatever these rituals may once have manifested it seems fair to suggest, given what we know of Aztec symbolism, that they all involve the crescent moon. On removing debris from the perimeter we came across a shell gorget, two greenstone beads, a wax earplug, fragments of tapir bone and a terracotta incense burner. Historically, a piece of armour covered the throat.

I feel like a monkish version of the aesthete in your book: headlong into abyss and so forth. I have always been on or very near the surface of the earth.

It is a Sunday afternoon in the 1930s. His theorem dictates that in logic there must be formulas that are neither provable nor disprovable.

See, gorcrow equals carrion.

Conversely, as she tells it: in eight hours, with zero preparation, he had read the whole damn codex. And why carve such an exquisite masterpiece then vandalize the corners? I share your belief that the excavated bone does not decay.

In only eight hours, this prodigy had got to the place it took our research team five years to crawl toward. Or are there moments built of a quite different nature, of unknown substance?

*

The falconer enters with a black gauntlet on his left hand; the hawk has fled but will return. He opens the wicker casket beside the furnace and grabs a clutch of paperback kindling: Mills & Boon, unpopular science, an annotated book of hours. (Hamlet is the chosen fire-slaught.) Then came the horrible part: light is produced in flashes and typically functions as a signal between the sexes.

Dead to influence, with 'anatomy of glass', he is bound to a metal cot in a straitjacket with a rag pushed down his throat. Such a pause between two states, during which the transformation from an old to a new being is effected, is termed liminal. I myself am divided into three phases, each of which is called. I am absent in the flesh.

i) This infamous corsair is notorious for plundering vessels in the estuary. In the following scene the man behind the hoax is revealed: leaning conspiratorially across the table, he whispers that very soon the whole continent will become a swamp, for it once formed the bed of the sea and yearns to return to its former state.

ii) The divine kings of the north and south are with me, the ever-changing god is with me, and those who bind up their heads are with me. Embedded in the pancreas are the islets of Langerhans, which secrete insulin into the bloodstream.

iii) The flame is in the land of the multitude. The idea of the replicant child creates an absorbing tension.

Parousia

All cries drown one another out. I discovered today that the archive contains counterfeit, never the thing-in-itself.

*

Our next step is to numb the sensitivity of the tissues to be operated upon. The glans was bruised and there were abrasions on the foreskin caused by the rim of her fucking diaphragm. A small trading vessel was formerly used.

There was something in the appearance of the craft which caused me to regret our proximity; its position was immediately above our heads. Abseiling stormtroopers disembarked.

Once set in motion our countervail, following Handel, was measured and stately. I watched for some minutes before turning my eyes toward the other objects in the cell.

This severed finger of yours requires a note from the librarian. It is destined to rot like the head. Then she gestured with her hand toward the legion of cacti and Venus flytraps encircling her cot. One striking peculiarity to be found in such studies of human nature through the medium of the hand is those mutants with the acrobatic or broke-back thumb.

He has dreamt up two sinister men playing erotic games of chance with an unknown woman. I have already emphasized in a previous seminar the close connection between essential repairs and witchcraft: overnight, the sixth century witnessed the rationalizing of the human mind. Autonomously or not, this is happening in all the rumoured places.

*

Today we are tracking a combined form, denoting cloud. There is much uncertainty about the source of this trail: it could be formed of glaciated vapour, or thick coagulated blood. Origin is usually found to be empty after death.

A portal opens between the supporting corbels of the battlement, through which stones or other material such as boiling water or oil can be dropped on attackers at the base of the rampart. I found myself in a bleak corridor lined with phosphorescent roots that had burst through the walls. We cut another run adjacent to the existing tunnel: the spur to our mission was an object of indeterminate function unearthed at the archaeological dig. In order to find ourselves accepted without compromise, we must restore and poeticize subjective drift.

No, origin denotes a temporary platform from which to repair or erect a building, from the base of catafalque.

Dear Gauleiter

The emperor has just asked me how a man would be resurrected in the world to come. He placed the bone upon an anvil and struck it with a hammer. The anvil split and the hammer broke.

Rime is glazed when the liquid water content of the cloud is high and droplets spread over the captured surface before freezing. We exist only to die in a great levelling, either flood or conquest, or both.

And whose name is forever connected with heresy? Who are also giants living next door? Who left the landing light on? Why stands that great stone, just there, looming out of the moorland mist?

A broken strip approximates the coastline.

Your savant

I quote from the purloined letter, found under the bed in an oblong box inlaid with jade and bone. The aforementioned military ordnance defies all laws of physics known to the public sphere: blood-red algae floating on the surface of the canal evaporated before my eyes, as if sucked up into the atmosphere.

I too wax furious, afire with nerves of glass, for I have discovered that devouring the flesh of a man can have as narcotic an effect upon the senses as lashing oneself to ribbons. Keeper, go ring those bells, limbs are scattered across the battlefield et cetera.

Silently, she takes her coffee and moves to the adjacent studio — a thoroughfare dimly lit — to continue the tracing of a china doll in silhouette, superimposed upon celluloid sweets. The outcome is more map than terrain.

Inventory, the contents of that oblong box

To be brief, all the principles of our malcontent. But there was no record of feldspar, an abundant rock-forming mineral typically occurring as colourless or pale-coloured crystals and consisting of aluminosilicates of potassium, sodium and calcium; nor olivine, an olive-green, grey-green or brown mineral occurring widely in basalt, peridotite and other igneous rocks, a silicate containing varying proportions of magnesium, iron and other elements.

I woke to find myself back in the study, gagged and handcuffed to a heavy oak desk; a truth serum had been administered. Essentially, this theorem entails the corollary that the consistency of a logical system cannot be proved within that system itself.

'And what did you do then?'

'Well, your Courtship, I cannot rightly remember. . . .'

'Indeed? Well, perhaps this document from the prosecution files will refresh your memory.'

[*Quotes therefrom.*]

'I am going to be blunt: that number is way too high. That number is twenty percent of the earth's population.'

'Nonetheless, this is the statement you made to the sentry shortly after you were found wandering naked across a frozen lake at the foot of a glacier in the year AD 2081.'

*

An iridescent sheen may appear on the throat of a reptile or other animal, especially a raptor. At the prearranged signal a gynandromorph — an uncommon individual, especially an insect, having some male and some female characteristics — strode into the drawing room, dazzling light shining through gauze wings, barbed hackles striking out from its elongated limbs. We need a metadata model that any citizen in the street could read. Origin is lengthy intermission plus the urgent steps to be taken.

Soldiers in the firing squad pleaded with their commanding officer to release a boy from the line-up of condemned prisoners; it was Stalingrad all over. Before the introduction of firearms, crossbows were often used. Saint Sebastian is usually depicted being executed by a squad of Roman archers in around AD 288. I woke to find it was not the same year.

This is called making the most of any given circumstance: embrace yourself, love. This area is a self clearing area.

I woke up and sure enough it was not the same year. I took a swig from the bottle of gin I found beside the shakedown and immediately felt better. I remember this place, we used to snort glue off the bar. Origin denotes a piece of armour protecting the throat from crows.

Remove yourself to a safe distance: the wrong type of giant hailstones have been despatched, but the unpredictable temporal leaps still have their uses. We have inherited a single precious attribute — one surface of the skull is concave and the opposite convex.

List, please, a sore with multiples, a room packed full with light.

As she approaches the balcony to draw down the shutter, her silhouette is absorbed by a radiance from without. A cacophony of tin pans is struck by the neighbourhood sedition.

For the first and last time, I feel a desire to return to the place where I find myself.

In ballast to the white sea

I am hanged, drawn, quartered; I like the word ballast. I am punished.

They hoisted her upside down by the ankles from the stars. (I had them all excommunicated.) Come join us at the old operating theatre, but hurry, it's uncertain whether we will be alive one minute from now.

With this last citation we have come full circle. Everything is covered with black coal dust in the vicinity of the port, where the boulevard forks at the main square. We still do not trust semicolons.

This guesswork is indisputable. A missing word is conjured from obsolete wail — literally, submerged in the valley. The mountain snowscape is vertiginous, as if the viewer were herself plunging through the freezing air. Another scene was a picture postcard. Our train pulled into a town called Brod. (Yes, but what is the book about?) An alien-occult vanguard division arrives undetected on planet earth, someone's corpse is filmed burning like a fallen cross in the wake of an explosion. . . . At the end of that routine we had to hose another flight attendant out of the ball turret.

As well as the severed achilles and missing ear, the skull of Figure K85 is studded with turquoise and displays the bat-mark of death inlaid with seashell fragments. The winged male and flightless female both have luminescent organs whose light is produced in flashes and usually functions as an excuse.

*

Blunt and deadened, i.e. a state of existence between death and rebirth, varying in length according to a person's magnetic conduction.

'Just a trace of salt sea, I am Pisces in the moon-cup of Aquarius.'

'I have no nice things.'

'One day my place will be perfect.'

Hold back. Remove, cut off, withdraw. Bloodline denotes test or inquisition, from abandoned probe (to remedy, see unproof). Legal use dates from the missing centuries.

On that bright cold morning of thirty-nine, contrasting dramatically with the heat of thirty-six, the general's tanks rolled along the diagonal and took the city without resistance. Our orders were to dynamite the gun battery on the cliff immediately above our position. Your soul suddenly revealed itself in its totality.

CONCRETE EAR SAVED BY ENGLISH HERETIC

Consider the risks involved: the severed head found in a sack of feathers, the permanent cloud cover, a melting glacier yielding up its dead.

Upward sweep of a rusting stairwell illuminated by electric arc.

I was encompassed.

Three apparently unconnected memories

The light of the moon was diffused by a dense mist. He goes to the window, opens it, and stands ready for flight, murmuring exorcisms under his breath. At that moment something seized him by the neck.

Awaiting my turn, I sat on the steps outside the courthouse in the spring sunshine and read her book. An antidote to restore the dissenting voice is being fermented from the pancreas of my animal.

A kerosene lantern swings at the back of a covered wagon as it crosses a snowbound prairie. The secessionists have gambled their veto.

*

Thus, the judge enquires, are you or have you ever been an assassin? The man in question is a committed improvisor, is counted among those creatures of nature for whom conscience in morals does not play so important a role.

The thing sluiced from the defendant's ear resembled the chrysalis of a moth. A winged fist tattoos his cheekbone, a claw is incised on the heart and a skull on the right calf.

The bone itches. An old woman passes by, carrying what looks like a ribbon of facial tissue. As soon as we got back home I started cooking up what was left of the roadkill. There is no point going any further with this, you will get no reply.

His body is a dull greyish-green, at sway on the horizontal iron high above the municipal incinerator. Another lies on the concrete platform, abdomen torn with viscera exposed, shrunken skull slithering down to greet the pelvis. . . . But enough of this complacency ('neural spindrift'). Humour me, we are held back among the living and have no choice but to annex the paranormal weapons of our foe.

*

On the bathroom shelf beside the earwax solvent stand a candied phallus and a crab's head. I am not taking the others with me, I am leaving them behind. . . . The garrison's physician has opened an anthrax in my heel, which permits me to set my foot upon the ground, but it is still very painful. I am feverish. During my recuperation that degenerate taught me a game played on squares with little stones, which I cannot now erase from memory. At dawn, another hostage is scheduled to be randomly selected and hanged for crimes of sedition and mutiny.

Uncouple the wagons, corral them into a defensive enclosure. Seize any opportunity to trail behind. I am here — we are here — exploring the warped and disquieting. Members of the order function like a bellwether to the rest of humanity, orchestrating a lack of purpose in accordance with instructions received from an unknown elsewhere.

Origin is a crow's beak.

I felt abandoned and took shelter deep inside the head, tormented by hallucinations of sight, touch and sound. A great number of mislaid musical instruments have fetched up in hell.

When facing such an abyss, standing at the edge, the only option is to fling oneself in — you will not shatter, the great silence will stay you.

This transcription is a masterstroke. Extemporizing relieves me of the terrible duty of hope.

The league of armed neutrality

The missing word means cavity or almond. There is a legend in the ancient commentaries. He replied that the solution would be found in the sacrum, a triangular bone in the lower back formed of fused vertebrae and situated between the two hip bones of the pelvis.

It is leaderless.
It is exiled.
It is completed in the act of coming back.

The signal: glass armoury

This sensation made me think of ice cubes melting and evaporating. A rook flapped down to earth, cawing loudly. (I generally avoid speaking about this experience.) We held a conversation in which I asked him whether he remembered what had happened the night before. In the manner of dispatch and age at death we agreed to deviate.

One of the signatories refers explicitly to a transcendent and infinite being. The science in question is also known as oneiromancy. There was uncertainty in the chain of command that day, and again the day after the day in question.

I am a late addition, not entirely present, having woken up a shade corroded. The zinc-bodied beetle is distantly related to the firefly. We must here close the discussion.

*

Cranioclasm is the breaking up of a foetal head. The skull and its interior have been compartmentalized, tracing a delicate fan array.

Remember how a bulkhead burst. On the sleepwalk spoken of, she opened a door to find herself looking down upon a chapel in darkness, with pinpoints of candlelight.

The correct answer is a dome-shaped muscular partition separating the thorax from the abdomen.

He immediately rushed about the garret shouting that he had conquered time et cetera, could control his own destiny and that of others. At precisely this moment in the brasserie beneath his lodgings, a gang of ultras began fighting and hurling bottles and chairs. The bar staff lowered the shutters.

Complex question: a liquidator. May I pause for thought, your Courtship?

My emphasis

Origin is abandoned reef, a sailing ship lost somewhere in time. Deathtrap and rear window.

Promise of grace was not attached as a condition (I am mindful of the rumoured machete). A bright red mineral consisting of mercury sulphide, sometimes used as a pigment, was administered. Blood coagulated into fibrous threads as frost glistened on the deserted platform.

Origin is a variant of cist, an ancient burial chamber made from a tree hollowed out of stone. Already this process is the *reverse* of chance. Insurrection is by nature centrifugal.

Others who had been standing beside me were propelled into the streets by the broken news. Observe how two pieces of music are here superimposed on top of one another; in so doing he has cleverly erased our remaining alternatives.

A giant moth burst onto the crease and flew headlong into the advancing vortex. Can we summon a little tension, please, to accompany that eerie sound of a snapping crustacean.

Eighteen light years from the Bruise Nebula, far from the live coals in which the ark was formerly placed. Something materialized through that membrane, as if dissolving and then reanimating itself. It pleaded for an amnesty.

The same can never be spoken regarding each arbitrary set of circumstances.

Sea-canny — steersman or quartermaster — unnamed by lascars, from rudder confused with drift: a sickening basal thud, straight into memory.

Dear Gauleiter

I have embarked upon an inventory of our schisms (this could take a generation or two). The outcome is determined by whereabouts in the car park you wake up.

Then was overheard a remark that connects disparate games of chance: the stage is set above our heads, where a lead roof slides open soundlessly — the well-known soft metal — and torrential rain pours in, drenching the witnesses.

The soundtrack seemed to propel me toward this scene; I could not stop, my tendons ached.

I am debarred, vetoed.

Your savant

I prefer the book of hours arranged thus, though this is a matter of some indifference. A timely endorsement was broadcast over the tannoy in the town square: he has been given two choices, tethered lifelines.

Origin is the 1920s. The neophyte, more bold, stands in the centre of the circle, but at the first conjuration he trembles uncontrollably and struggles to make a sign. The shaman commands him not to move.

Unused endorsement

> Mentalist reiteration, a hallucinogenic interbreed where each warp of the preceding sentence is a fertile echolalia, non sequiturs that elbow romantic love and the reader further and further toward a reassuring pit of absurdity. I wanted to scream along, out very loud, clapping my hands and stomping my hoofs to the arrhythmia. This is literature as stroboscopic minimalism — total surface, no core — antinarrative narratives to collapse to, speechless.

This organ plays a sinister role in breathing and acoustic systems, haphazardly adjusting the aperture of the lens: each convulsion further erodes the volume of the thorax and voids the surviving lung. A thin sheet of antimatter acts as a room divider. This is where the famous word subsidence comes from.

Prove this to me, said the great martyr and Tzar.

The rabbi took a small bone from the volunteer's spine and immersed it in water, but it would not dissolve. He cast the bone into fire but it was not consumed. He placed the bone between two millstones but it could not be pulverized.

A family of these tiny bones once nested in my daughter's hair.

And so on.

*

Surveillance of the cabin, set on wooden piles above the marsh, took place from a camouflaged shelter. During those long hours marking time, I dimly recollected that at some point in the past I had been pinned beneath the hull of a capsized boat. The sting of this memory I still carry within me: things are not as voiced.

A circle of white light entered through the keyhole and burned a mark into the bathroom door; it was autumn, about the time of the solstice. A dolmen was raised at that very spot.

The doomsday writer who claimed that the world would end on the twenty-third now says it will end on the twenty-first. On hearing this news, we embarked on a pilgrimage to an ossuary of bones of the inner ear, the world's smallest reliquary.

See otolith. Origin lives elsewhere, in the diaphragm.

He stoops, disguised beneath a papier-mâché head. So many of these pledges die of compromise, well-intentioned reconciliation.

Cancel his correction. A kind of burglary has occurred in the dwellings of the skull.

*

As she climbed the steps to the clifftop it was as though gravity were tilting her upwards. I am never going back.

Radio transmitted the news of an ambush where some numbers of the army fell and were rescued by helicopters, but this report was not heard well due to static. Also, there are bells ringing outside, everywhere.

Witnessing this from the window of his attic room, the apprentice necromancer was convinced he had willed the events himself and suffered a nervous convulsion.

I woke to find myself in a theatre of war. A scarlet fighter jet was suspended close to the ground as intergalactic stormtroopers abseiled down to the surface.

Tenderly she strokes the back of his shaven head.

'Suppose this man were to suddenly thrust his skull out to parley.'

We made no reply and the bird flew off, its place being taken at once by a rook, who spoke in turn — a babel of violent fractured visions.

'On paper this all looks rather abortive, makeshift.'

'I lost my balance, was plummeting to earth surrounded by gaping mouths and jagged teeth.'

Word links are labile.

Detail from a somewhat purloined letter

That sea was a sheet of gunmetal. The sun struck the water like a damnation. At least someone loves you she said, under a pewter sky, the torrential rain.

'You ought and must serve me tomorrow.'

'My room will face south, though it's pointless to say so. There will be gravel in the courtyard, audible underfoot, gently dripping eaves, the wail of a fox at dusk.'

'Withstand yourself, I am without head or compass.'

Come nightfall I spied several planets, one of which was cobalt blue — circling it was a brilliant halo of light. Someone said this augurs a transition from shadow to guide. That same evening our neophyte took great satisfaction in watching the resident composer, a young prodigy, lose his footing to fall headlong down the stairs and break his neck.

*

Schizocarp, on and on, seed of all the giants. The corpse was left on the barren mountainside, a feast of carrion. I no longer have a use for any of your numbers, setting out on foot into white light.

Now write something below something else, further salvaged matter. For example, we gazed up at the night sky full of stars beneath a dome at the heart of the maze. Or, I drifted to earth as if windborne — I correspond to the small bone at the tip of the column, the seventh cervical wonder.

Then the rook too flew away and both birds were gone, vanished from sight.

XXVII

I have cut off the nations; their towers are desolate

Material to be abused.

In this process, the principle of cyclotron resonance is used to energize the uranium isotope in a plasma; I have written a letter to the bureau.

I am a late convert to the cause, a loose die rattling in the faulty meter of your skull. An old acquaintance will be in touch soon said a fortune cookie.

On the return journey she glued together a collage, hazarding a guess at the nature of his interior: ore of quicksilver and death's head hawkmoth. Three years ago he retreated into a remote mountain fastness and wears now the ankle chain.

*

Keyhole solstice, the absent father as author and signatory of the world. . . . See, now she's back in office, reading fortunes, gazing into her black mirror: your certainty is a sinecure et cetera.

Her book presents a snag: the inenarrable modality, perhaps.

A couple are treading water alongside the jetty. Details include the man from London, the music of the spheres, and a ball of white lightning that has drifted through interstellar space and now hovers just above the entrance to my oubliette. A tiny mummified infant is tucked under my feet.

The syndicate should be informed: Osiris is in the two lands, who are called. This is one of those situations you can only resolve by taking a risk; I suspect the others are hiding in the marquee. I have seen pictures of a marquee.

Before we can proceed, we will have to make a few bold assumptions about this circumstance. But I can only enter a new number when I have no doubt whatsoever.

Ground saxifrage is found. I thought we had been transported back to the days of corrugated concrete, salmonella dogs. We also discovered resident poets — the great St Johns — ivy-leaved toadflax or great mullein, tall and brittle with yellow-flowering stem of hagseed: shepherd's club, Adam's cerecloth, Aaron's rod. . . . Origin is contraction. Tantalum alloy was used as a rectifier in the chain of command.

The etymology of the first element remains doubtful, due to an early insistence that came too late. We woke to find ourselves in a camera or other optical system.

*

There is an upright division in between the light of the windows. I have learned a new method of binding the limbs together, thus rendering the volunteer immobile and helpless. An aspergillum of decaying organic matter plus heavy water — in which the hydrogen in the molecules is partly or wholly replaced by the isotope deuterium — has been put to good use.

The square photograph shows him seated in a low chair on the deck of a ship, the bright sunlight confirmed by stark shadows. He is in uniform white: shirt, shorts, plimsoles — head bowed in concentration as he presses the keys of a typewriter.

What is he writing a letter.

If any Hebrews were left in the city, we would tell them that Jacob was alive and where he could be found. . . . This thread will no doubt end with entire constellations, utter soundlessness. How can one man know all this?

In actuality, his misleading radiance. We hope this document will appear more credible when the time comes to hand it over to our inquisitors.

*

He stands his ground with some reluctance. Note the haste with which fragments are written down before the thought can slip away: alternatives and erasures, the erratic configuration of parts. I believe too there survives some trace of the original, your residue.

Three strokes were administered, no more.

I valve

Which swept through heaven the alien name of woe and its dazzling glory broke through my shielding wings. . . . But what if she reneges, leaves me stranded between undercliff and marina? One man, it is rumoured, perished on route in a fit of starburst.

Now we should talk about your fear of inertia, your fear of passing time. Another died of suddenness: an unexpected science befell him, and he was outdone.

She is condemned to stay here far longer than the rest of us. Symptoms include the absence of any clear verbal division between speech acts, and frequent epileptic seizures — for example, Number 197 demands a series of short controlled spasms.

The first two examples are corrupt, thus the vacuum is compromised. Cardinal (1879–2082) takes Number 213 to be a reverse back-formation; tracheotomy was then a weekend phenomenon.

Number 232 is a surrogate tripod. East, more plausibly, annexed Numbers 220 and 253 on account of their unresolved diameters. Suddenly, apropos of nothing, she says as a child I wanted to make a wooden brain — not a toy, one that actually functioned.

Question: who may only be approached while clutching a huge magnifying glass?

A moth with black and red wings slowly emerges from its transparent cocoon as an elastic structure behind the iris focusses light onto the observer's retina, thus making the episode visible. Grey is this light, upon the consuming lens.

Nothing, taken for chance

Think of a part of the body that does not decompose. About the middle of the seventeenth century I opted to embrace the disruption of continuity: tragedy is a stationary song composed of trophies and ants. A box was used.

Conversely, a longhouse is a large communal dwelling found in parts, from which a large drawer may be slid out through a recess. Within this compartment, embedded in glistening black pitch, is a shrunken head split laterally, the two halves resting side by side. Wisps of amber hair cling to the skull.

I remain indifferent, indeed nurture the condition. (Not now! Not now!) There is no need whatsoever to dwell upon an image that appears before the inner eye. We're all going to die down here, you do realize that.

This is our first job in over one hundred and fourteen years. I would love to have not.

A portable sundial of cylindrical form was used in the early years. Forgetting is my domain. It does not matter in which order you arrange the limbs and organs, though most people still rely on the old system: one knows in part from the shapes that can, in part from the shapes that cannot.

Now, the true stomach of ruminants, I know exactly who you mean.

*

Reflex spasms of the diaphragm were accompanied by rapid closure of the glottis, producing an audible click — a singularity — through which the first man was created from spittle and clay.

Someone hurled a glass. We stood face to face; I had finally intercepted my adversary.

You have to turn the mechanism by working its crank; power is both an office and a void. Those tiny creatures had gnawed through the rope that secured our vessel to the riverbank.

No said Thor.

My penance was to buy another fridge. I will begin by admitting. A taut flexible membrane in an acoustic system does not exist.

*

Architecture of assembled nouns, incorrigible stonework, typically in the upper part of a gothic ruin. All day we wandered about the ancient port's vertiginous alleys and cobbled streets, until we found a new home in an abandoned seventeenth-century warehouse. About that time the rose motif escalated, leaving traces.

An early example cited by Scree underlines the significance of the time factor in any refusal to be embalmed. Another woman pleaded in her will that her body never be opened. All were required to stand in a mass grave while the leper ritual was recited and spadefuls of quicklime were flung over our heads.

A crane fly has lodged itself in the wallpaper nailed up across the partition, above and a little to the left of the head. Eggs hatched out of my wrists at the banquet.

Compare: a portable crustacean of the foreshore lives among algae and is postponed. The larvae of your own kind are collectable. My opponent wore a battered leather coat with buttons of Edwardian jet, a 'seething erotic compass'.

Fracture this. Origin is the feminine past.

Cranioclasm

He writes with thanks for the endorsement, which he found unjustly frivolous, and apologizes for the tardiness of his reply: he has been crawling across the lava fields of Etna and her environs. The time recorded in his letter, if it is not simply a mistaken date, may relate to the synchronous eruption of one of the archipelago's twelve active volcanoes.

The other semaphores in response.

I am with those who weep and with the women who bewail (surely a further reference to the municipal ossuary). I confess that mister had been a good mister, in his own ungovernable way.

On the mathematical plane of the cycloid, a curve is traced by a point on the circumference when rolling past in the rain. A shallow trench is formed by walking back and forth along a straight line.

How consoling this is, though usually I am somewhat grief-stricken on waking up in the morning. That said, time can stand still long enough for anyone in the mood to upend it.

See, he is a person of paradoxical temperament, has made a fetish of old reel-to-reel. Note the iridescent reptilian scales with jagged borders (I am mindful of the brace of alien life forms presented to me yesterday evening, wrapped in greasy chip paper, as I ventured out for my nightly lurch across the shingle).

'You will know them by the pocks and atoms that float inside your eyes. . . .'

Have the code sequence ready. And here comes another fucking quantum of light, here come any number of subatomic particles carrying a fractional electric charge, building blocks of the hadron.

Origin passes away.

On indifference, the substitution of a body

I have an unnerving sense that everything down here is out of joint. Objects appear to relate to one another — even communicate in some arcane manner — yet the sector is interlaced by what the fieldwork refers to as vacant rhizomic interstices. I stapled the organism's limbs to the floor and waited for a second opinion.

An unstable compound may be formed with an atom or molecule such that it is no longer available. I may be the start of something promising, an untimely and incomplete metaphor.

Or, back in the zoo, a life form with appendage of pincer-like claw. (We are advert-free for another hour or so tonight.) 'Born' became restricted to just one very common use, which remains the case today.

During the current lunar month a low-growing plant of the underclass bears microscopic white, red and yellow flowers, forming ribbons of flesh intersected by a ridge of moss. Origin is now a broken neck.

*

Subjectivity: how to replicate this in order to make oneself compatible with a mutant universe devoid of value. One night I dreamt that I had lost my name. The following night I dreamt that I had found one.

See above: seventeenth-century warehouse, Portbou.

I appear.

I move about.

I reposition myself.

This is all about timing, this is all about a telescopic lens with one surface concave and the opposite convex. Our best guess has only the slightest chance of succeeding or being accurate or being believed.

For centuries the grail has been hidden. I relocated to the rear of the spleen. An isolated speech act took place at the critical moment: today is the day we should talk about your fear of perpetual motion, your fear of open space.

Craniotomy is an operation in which the head is cut open, breaking down when it encounters an obstacle. A raft of unstable uranium symbolizes neural atomic instinct. The male lead stood at the centre of a vast chamber built of interlocking cubes of steel, within which constellations of light began to pulse, shooting forth bursts of electromagnetic energy: he was standing at the core of his own nervous system, externalized, made manifest in the atmosphere around him.

We were ill-equipped for decay, lacking the necessary resources and qualities for that spectacular role. Into a wealthy suburb with its hissing lawns limped a defeated battalion of papier mâché demons. Upon reaching a muddy watering hole the onslaught appeared irreversible, and that being the case we sheltered there and waited for the next communiqué.

Those weeks in the desert were the provocation behind a feud that lasted thirty years. A forceps is invaluable when confronting this species of rift.

I have a single memory of childhood, carried shoulder-high to witness fireworks and a giant ceramic saint. Nearby, a ballerina pirouettes beside the steaming viaduct, reaching forward into an already forgotten future. From the sky we could see crippled outskirts encircling a walled imperial core, an ancient grid system infested with tourists and their assassins. The wreckers preserve their names, written on the surface of water, and vow to outlive us.

The time is too clocked. A slaughterman lurks beneath the eavesdrip. Everything depends on which day of the week, which hour of day: your last minute, that final second. Protocol demands the coccyx of an ape, a small triangular bone of fused vertebrae, salvaged.

*

Disjecta membra, marrow of molten lead. The radio play used sound effects of galley oars, blood-piercing screams and broken waves. See, you have the narrative all stitched up — at least a rough sketch — but I can't see much of this surviving the moment. Keep nerve, my love, never afar except as one, an adamantine brittleness.

I resisted orchestration through sheer willpower. Note the preponderance of custodial romantics between cells thirty-nine and seventy-three.

And far below he sees the road and the bridge and the long lines of men stretching all the way to the front. End of world coming soon our numerologist says, forever trailing in the wake of our postponement.

Difficulties met with by inquisitors
and control during transference

The function of art is to fracture the world and render it incomprehensible. I confused the knock at the door with the assassin outside with the ringing of the bell with the coded telephone message.

We are standing to the left of the picture plane, from the perspective of the hurler. The gruel served up today is rather slippery, congruent with the tenor of my mind.

Ballast was jettisoned from a two-masted vessel at anchor in the bay, the ship which had conveyed the traveller from the east. One significant change at the hill fort is that the man of the hour has become infected with doubt. But the settlers may yet snare their witness: eyes are turned as a red lamp and then blue shutter off and on in the fog.

It is rumoured that the outlander's ears, nose and mouth were stationed in his chest. Now I am going to ask you to share your experience with all the others.

'An iris is an adjustable diaphragm of thin overlapping plates that regulates the size of a hole for the admission of light.'

He is known. He is known through the story of his death at the hands of his brother and subsequent recruitment as foreman of the afterlife. He is messenger, with clatter of unstoppable hooves, harness and oxygen tank at the ready.

*

Gentle touch of key upon the lips, metal cold with sharp tang of blood across the tongue, copperish. She had sheltered in her brain less than three years, quite alone within the span and its squalls of ash. The primitive jawless is a distant relative — mucous eel anatomy — a slit-like mouth edged with thorns to feed on the dying.

Torchroot

Vision is constrained by the nature of the work possessing us. Anyone would have struggled to read those words submerged beneath the powdered sulphur floating on the surface.

We assembled on the viewing platform to observe the transit of Mercury. The strongest traction pulls on the optic nerve toward the end: white flashes are one thing, but the fall of the grey curtain is severe mischance.

This is difficult to understand, as intended for a small number of people with specialized knowledge. Origin denotes a metrical foot of four short syllables.

I am beginning to find the voice on the radio alarming. It means he has won she says, and our souls are damned to infinity. Our principal meaning as a verb has just collapsed: now is the time to go forth into the world and make some cunt feel uneasy. Thursday is named after us.

She once worked within a stockpile of ammunition, a taxonomy of hotels. Today is improbable: we don't seem ready to trust the distinction between who and what.

Next move to scrambled note, cryptic grace

I cross to her side of the room to retrieve something, but once there forget what the something is. I want a second opinion: any inertia and the scene ruptures.

I cannot believe that everything we say or do has already happened. She pretended not to hear and strode out of the drawing room and on to the furthermost end of the east wing.

The syndicate is in the bidding to stage a re-enactment. Our coach is number seven of eight. On the back seat, she raises her legs to prop them against a window, not knowing where else to put them. Her skirt rucks up to reveal her crotch. She is aware of this yet retains the position, may or may not be seeking attention.

We overhear one passenger telling a comrade that he has been summoned; everyone is better off remaining silent and keeping still. In the darkness are approaching pinpoints of light, a nameless city. We must press on, grant ourselves an option while the choice is still to be had.

We have arrived. Dawn is breaking. Civic buildings collapsing under the burden of purpose surround us on all sides. Pollen and radioactive ash drift through the air, drawn into a vortex by gusts of wind.

I had forgotten to write down the address. We sat and ordered coffee in a room lit by bare strip lights. Outside, a knot of people gawped at a capsized beetle marooned on the pavement.

Origin is late midwife, sacred utensils.

Hair is the only part of the body that will not decompose. When nothing is left to chance, everything is left to chance.

Abandon to here.

I saw at my wrists the raw ulcers where poisonous sand fleas had burrowed under the skin while I lay unconscious on a riverbank. Eggs were hatching.

Arborvirus

A thin contraceptive fold covered the cervix. A device for varying the effective aperture of the lens lives inside your optical solar system. This testifies to a sense of time that is strikingly recursive and nonlinear.

I doubt. Bad blood is poised. You have to guess the wrong conclusion before you can be allowed to leave. What is it that ensures the existence of an apt signifier upon the visitation of a thing?

Origin is face to face.

Cranioklept

Each specimen carries a seedpod, ripening within an obsolete form. Only one skin remains, stretched taut across the junction to span a void. This is a fucking trial, generally speaking, bursting with invisible violence. Back then I meant unassailable, back there.

I could have been way more diplomatic. We turned the corner into a dark expanse, a garage with three figures murmuring, no more than shadows — nearby she has turned her back and stands oblivious. Time has been downgraded to a rehearsal.

It was imperative that she track down her husband. She insisted. A door opened onto the street, throwing a shaft of yellow light from a Balkan restaurant squatting one of the concrete bunkers that had multiplied throughout the territory.

Eoan

He had to mix his colours in the fifties and somehow make them nineties. Origin is literally being present.

Our suture remains visible. We have just sold an exact copy of your apartment; thirty tons of gravel have arrived, which the artist is busy stroking as we speak.

Shrieking, the crowd held aloft their mangled organs. Chance had been apprehended. The male lead's tongue was disconnected.

I am implicated in a history of ruptures. A lot of the vital papers are kept behind glass. The last film was a film noir.

I am superbly ill-prepared. His account could simply be a mélange of myth, confusion, legend and embellishment, or may never have happened at all. Across untold generations, a pair of appendages in front of the mouth has become modified into pincer-like claws.

She is moved to pen three more of these allegories. Here then are all the facts, weft across warp, a schismatic pattern reminiscent of that old joke.

A wasp trapped in an alembic full of smoke is going for your eyes. . . . Her piercing voice overcomes me; there are times when I wish I did not understand my mother tongue. But she cannot see far with her surviving eye. Our stratagems are dissimilar.

Uninvited, I read aloud, of the travelled and the un-, the foiled and the prizewinner: the pitmen in the opera were never told and all perished without a flameproof layer of skin.

Tongue graft

He was much given to declaiming his wish to draw the sword of his ancestors, which always meant another fucking long day stretching ahead of us. It all ends in a disused warehouse at the dock where, rather than burn, he flings himself into the freezing oily waters of the east river.

'Would you like the radio in your cell today, mister?'
'A compound may be bonded to a central atom at two or more points.'
We are at the midline of an indifferent organ, the torn ligament.

*

She stepped in front of a secondhand car. In my sleep I heard a bell tolling; when I woke, I was perplexed to find her gone. As time uncoils, a sense of leave-taking occurs, as if one were dissolving into a given moment while passing through.

'Here I was born. [*Index points at tree ring.*] And there I died.'

Today she pleads terminal insanity, judging this a cannily neutral way to refer to her state of mind. During the winter the roof was too dangerous.

For some reason I had bolted the gate. I am pronounced at the core of the mouth.

The adult is often parasitic, attaching itself to passersby and sucking their blood. Origin is a stone balanced on the tongue.

*

Another night of hard toil in the engine room. The following morning we set about dismantling the boat, in readiness for its transportation across the desert.

I got no reply. Atoms were vaporized by bombarding the plate with energetic ions in a process called dogging.

wax tablet, being suspended [. . .] and us reran

This is untranslatable. We used a stylus made of bronze. A membrane covers the hearing organ on the leg or body of some insects, occasionally adapted to ferment sound. I am mostly plural, dubbed kleptocrat.

We are under oath. Who was the unreasonable man? Mine is a spectacular indiscipline — I recall only one occasion when I could not bring myself.

There was no point in asking. I want to escape this. The correct answer is of or pertaining to dawn.

Now, composer: which?

Having reached this threshold, the game requires the accused to be weighted with lead and immersed up to his neck in oily salt water. The lagoon stretches beyond the horizon — there are purple mountains in the distance, above which storm clouds stack. Origin is mediaeval assassin, from eater.

I am conscious of something that exists beyond the observable facts of my anatomy. Today the ribcage and lower spinal column live *here*, recognizably intact. An essential element of a neap tide is occurrence at the first or third quarters of the moon (file under oneiroscopy).

*

He is often portrayed with a falcon's head bearing the solar disc.

An eel-like aquatic jawless has a sucker mouth with horny teeth and rasping tongue. Origin is to lick your own stone.

Move and separate.

'A crane fly is a slender two-winged insect with very long legs.'

I nod in agreement before evaporating.

Our detachment is aligned in parallel ranks. There is a stone chapel at the crest of the hill, now offshore on an island separated from the mainland by a narrow sound. Due to the slowness of exposure, no one is visible on the dusty streets. Every surface has crumbled in the heat.

Remember how you were afraid to breathe? I can hear waves lapping against a concrete jetty, the drag of seaweed. Take yourself back to that time, then slip away, tender and absurd.

She is no longer the abject individual referred to in the letter. Be sure to compensate for all her disappearances, the grief.

This is especially true of a leaf or shell having a scalloped edge, but compare with tongue, crenulated. Here, at this time, I have found my own collapsible.

CRAZY HERMIT MAKES HOME INSIDE ANIMAL

Abstract.

Notes on the origin of dry valleys in a limestone escarpment, the countdown to a delicate branching pattern with tracery of red veins. For many years this solitary mass of angular flint and chalk has baffled geologists.

A boulder may be rolled across the entrance of the fogou to keep the thing entombed. But the real find was the huge post holes that have intervened. One head describes fragmented material which, due to frozen subsoil acting as a barrier, has gradually moved downslope. Divination on such occasions is by lot, helping to stave off the pain of hunger during long periods of fast.

He made a brew of the thorny seedcases that cleave to my frock coat. Birds had become entangled in the burrs, leading to a slow death.

Think of something, quick, while we extinguish every word, cover our tracks.

*

She attempts the same manoeuvre year upon year, but nothing ever becomes concrete. Moreover, it is deemed reckless even to glance at the codex as it uncoils before our eyes. Always put your money on the least credible candidate.

A blank space is driven out of the script using a machine for punching holes. Something seems to have stuck in the throat, susurrus between empty cells. A row of stitches holds together the edges of the wound, evoking the seam-like junction between two bones, such as those of the skull.

The planet's surface consists of grey vitreous quartz studded with barbed pupae. Now, what do you call a person employed to kill for food?

This is the place you could never leave. Stopping is clearly contagious.

*

High above a rift valley: dog-leg river in spring sunshine, alumni on horseback, an admixture of errors. . . . I write myself instructions on slips of paper and glue them to the inside of my crate. Flora hereabouts possess yellow or purple flowers resembling snapdragons with fragile leaves.

Oviduct and nerve shaft fuse together after the ritual gathering of arbitrarily chosen objects. Another volunteer was making a full-scale crocodile out of chewed paper.

We are legendary militant fanatics and reputed to use hashish before setting out on murder missions — I am right now clinging to the roof of a speeding intercontinental train.

You are not, are you?
Yes.
Is this your first day?
Yes.
What are we going to do now?

Neap flood

One compound contains a ligature bonded to a metal atom at two or more starting points. By contrast, the lamprey attaches itself to stones by its mouth.

What are we going to do now?

The correct answer is anything arched or vaulted within an indifferent colour scheme, excluding parts of the tongue. Articulation is achieved by the fit of one bone into the groove of another.

Now gather her in.

A single unit is equal to one thousand million years; sound is subdivided inside the canal of the ear. It is rumoured there exists a hidden substructure beneath the circuit.

She travels inside light.

This brings us back full circle to the threshold. A drummer boy and bugler are tending to the wounded. The wheel symbolizes mutability. Establish criteria and wait: sometimes the fire, sometimes the sea, sometimes the fog.

Here she comes, with her famous curved edge. Staying here won't tell us anything new.

There has been a skirmish over some boundary we share, triggered by the roaming of nomadic herds. We are nonparticipating. Complex phosphates have been known to track down a suspect.

She tells me she is ready, but I have no way of knowing for sure — her body exposes the sum of her peculiarities. Together we are experimenting with a new reptile parody, the two intersecting vaults.

Now write down the exact opposite.

She crawls back inside the concrete bunker. (Look at that fog.) I remember once the promise of each new day.

Loose framing usually happens in longer shots, a line of jurisdiction formed by two crustal plates which have collided in space. In my notebook I wrote spectral traces, the icehouse.

The conventional emblems of order and confusion have been reversed. What kept you so long?

*

The scrap of paper that he has sworn to always carry about his person is sewn into the hem of his army greatcoat. One eye is flipped open with a deft fingernail. Such an action is called a simple primary function.

The terrain here is low-roofed, dorsal (this is imperative). During his travels, he discovered an unused commandment stipulating that any adjustments should be ignored.

*

Head current sunk into heavy earth main, surging floodwater. The door and window shudder as the dark is broken by discs of light suspended in the air. On the shakedown lies a still figure, the skin of his abdomen peeled back to reveal the lodestone.

This is something we call a situation: the steep-sided valley in which this event took place was forged millions of years ago by downward displacement of the earth's crust between parallel fault systems.

See ruin, see trounce.

The holding muscle of the flesh is torn from its shell and the contents swallowed whole. This act of cannibalism is destined to alter the course of our lives in the most unexpected fashion.

For you, it was only a moment in time: each of the concentric rings in a cross section of the spinal column represents days, hours, minutes and seconds.

See also sidereal, anomalistic.

We have identified several obvious contradictions here: he will forever be fifteen minutes in lieu of time (viz. somatic melancholy). Now I have that crushing sense of nostalgia.

'Scrutinize this extradition warrant at your leisure, costermonger.'

Levy this, teller of heads.

Only three ideas

It would appear that the alloy is so named because of its readiness to combine with gold. A microwave antenna discovered just in front of the planet is energizing neutral atoms, but these are colliding with discharge from the nearest household name. Whatever the cost, an ear-splitting noise was made after dark by vibrating two membranes in the insect's abdomen.

After this encounter comes a break in the record, a pause in the current of a lifeline. Our footsteps are displaced.

We are stationed inside a random distribution of ghosts. The sea is turquoise, at the rim of a perfectly flat earth. Here, the script stands in for literal meaning, and should be returned once used up.

I am outbalanced, so desperate for sleep. Where matter proves too dense it must be subdivided into its component parts, urgently.

At least we have found a suitable site, a place to give witness. In those days a wire was used for suturing any wound or incision.

*

Mister is wearing his state-of-the-art octofoil headpiece. The others watch him leave in silence. Origin is chewed paper.

He tries to screw the head back on but repeatedly loses his grip and it rolls down the street, bobbling along the tram tracks. He strides on, growing smaller against the vastness of the steppe as he fades into the distance.

Stopping to rest, he rubs his skin with gunpowder and stuffs clumps of dried grass between the lips of his wound.

See them, how low into the long walk they crouch. Any progress is immediately sabotaged.

A lead roof across the drop glistens in the rain. I have observed the gradual movement of wet soil or other material down a slope.

We walked a mile and more eastward yet found nothing. (That which is missing is perhaps what renders us stable, grants equilibrium.) While journeying, he presses the leaves of plants and trees into his daybook.

The angel I mistook was Soutine's flayed ox. Of course nobody ever dies, these parallels arise within our flux beyond the world, the dressing of stone.

The key elements to listen out for are virtually identical in form. The roof stays are mouldering. This was once a building used for storing ice, hence situated partly underground.

All values, your own included, are to be destroyed during the interval — a long cord is attached to the hawk's leash to prevent its escape during penetration. Origin is late from faith, also a cord.

A page is missing. Blanks. With his skull inside syntax he is done for, never to be revoked. Today, he is simply not possible.

Does he have a social role, like one who shares a familiar spirit, our portion of malignancy? The hexagram's advice is to gather together any parts of the edible flesh and abandon the outpost.

He is no less curious a study himself, while she I have tagged conflictrix. Finds include a herbaceous plant of the daisy clan with blurred petals, a yellow disc and white rays — once native, but now found all over the fucking place. One child rammed dandelions into her sinus cavity and was hospitalized and died. These events occurred during a major division of geological time, an existence filtered through your inconsolable destiny.

She perceives that he casts no shadow onto the courtyard wall. Indeed, things are beginning to look precarious (expressed alphabetically: hat to intervacuum). A gigantic mythological bird was described during the night.

A variant spelling is to be performed. Bloodline is mid-century, a concise table of subheadings undermining any discourse, i.e. a misleading.

Option A: do the minimum.

Option B: acquire another.

I do believe those distant buildings are on fire, a snug village in a crease of land. Tiny scale-like leaves borne on slender branches give it a feathery appearance.

Perhaps we are finally granting a name to the family, the English sea above our heads. Your plasma is subject to a magnetic field along the axis of a cylindrical extinction chamber, as it flows from source to collector, collector to source.

I more or less killed them: she had burst into the office unannounced and demanded a job, any job, no matter how inglorious. Our planet bears a spike of brightly coloured frontal lobes that gape like a mouth when an insect lands on the observer's curled lip.

We failed to recognize this at the time and now the pavement is potholed, money ruptured. We will use whatever weapons come to hand and take it from there: beneath the paving slabs, the encircling clay et cetera.

*

The approach to the valley swung east via a metal track that glinted in the sunlight. At the same moment on the other side of the world — at the exact antipodes, in fact — our ship's surgeon is cutting open a localized area of decomposing body tissue. Origin is paronomasia.

That blade near took my face off. Nonetheless, we have a lady on the line; she will unhook you.

This reprieve on parting may be our last. So many times this path, yet nothing forestalls — a gentle grief, better aloud yet not, no bell to toll the unmistakeable.

You counterfeit, inter-spleen. A membranous fold supports the organ and clamps it in position. The monumental gateway is formed by two truncated pyramidal towers.
Deep blue bordering black she writes his death rattle.

XXVIII

At daybreak we will have to find this place on the map, upon the earth. Language comes into it at some point.
 A clue here lies in the minutiae of the view: asphodel rooted to green incline of earth, white clapboard house at the crest — and our heron has vanished, along with the accidental scaffold.
 He says voice is held within somehow the device. Still we refuse. Continue.
 Bleached pallet at rest, silvered wood — the brittle cylinder, oil drum angled at forty-five degrees — a prehistoric boundary stone — two girls tonguing — anatomy of a cycle: ice floe with light greys, a smear of crushed light — one forsaken stone pyramid, the iron rampart that held back the land.
 Now, without hesitation, write such inventory against a scene that has been imperceptibly altered.

Hands arthritic upon desktop, snowbound convalescence the only option. Two men are attending to something unseen upon the ground, a black stain circled by an iridescence.
 Who was found one morning entirely consumed by fire, except for the joints of the fingers, the luz, the skull?
 'We've got the atomizers in, they had to remove all the panelling.'
 The defendant has cheated death three times now.

*

The instructions read flood the silo with ink, establish a sustained arc of tension and release: wingspan of gull in counterpoise to invisible orbit, seams of liquid rust. We are two light years from home. Invariably, he stations himself at the same spot in the same room and orders the same meal.

Drawn blind, across space a distant room with ziggurat of books, the mirror image. But does it not seem to me here that I viewed this scene through a pane of coloured glass.
 Keep your head down in the passageway. There is only one remaining obstacle (and there is of course the eye, with its ophthalmic nerve). Suddenly one detail expands to fill the entire field. Our concern here is with memory, summoning a solitary figure on her back in the dark, beneath the roar of the waves.
 Can you not see there is only half a face remaining?
 I see that as the mouth. I see that as the eye. I see that as the ear.
 [*Pointing.*]
 The core is detachable.

*

There is a clearly delineated track running up one flank of the hill — a little further on, purple heather clings to the face of an inland cliff. Sense one dates from the eponymous hero of the novel.

Accusative plural from title slip, from labile. I have not seen in the flesh. Anther is the part that contains pollen, while pistil is the female organ, comprising stigma, style and ovary. Notes rise and fall in a simple progression, thoughtless minor modes and shapeshifting dissonance. Origin is celebrated at a fixed date.

A tower looms in our sweep toward the horizon, objects begin to dissolve. I pressed my eye against a spyhole into the furnace.

That pit could be an excavation, or hiding place. He is now barely audible. A white of substance is bearing in, opaque in the scarlet evening air.

Make a fresh assumption, into an ill-defined concept of the book, the congealing mist — repeated rhythms compressed of small cells — language isolates, a lament for something that was never here in the first place, i.e. the perfect occasion.

Mass plummet to zero ground, screams from the descendants. I strove to become all those things I wanted not to be.

I took his place on the journey out, counterfeit the man — now we stand twinned in the dim light, moss pressing behind glass.

Nothing congruent was ever found. A passerby reading aloud from Luke is suddenly plucked up and flung into the sea.

*

Paint a severed digit. This is a big song about used electricity: a no-man's-land, the neutral.

She says this is the unforeseen zone of operation. No one can build upon — and ultramarine, everything ultramarine.

We are attempting here to word a mutation. He comes for the third time and says sleep and be at your ease, this moment is enough.

The inverted espresso cup yields a petrified forest beneath a constellation of stars. Origin is a list of everything that was never found.

I no longer feel the need to orient myself, eased back to earth in a sequence of tiny clicks. All-time riot, the strapline read.

On surgical removal of the tongue

Based on size and shape, the prints match a hominoid foot from the pit of bones. This is not a proposition of metaphysics.

'Hullo goodbye let me embrace you.'

Much of the detail has been suppressed. Whatever is not superseded decays. I am an unworthy member of the indefinite body. I have no visible calling.

Meanwhile the men are building a palisade of pointed wooden stakes, fixed into the ground in a close row to form a defensive enclosure. Another entry in the journal reads hello where were you. Then: you cannot assassin me I told my pursuer in the fog, I am dead already.

And a curious one comes — starch, high-collared. The female of the species is named reeve, or nerve. Time runs all the way through and has no reason to warp or rip.

Want a toy to peer into? I do not fear her the way I fear the others.

List

(i)   Somewhere in time.
(ii)   Deathtrap.
(iii)   Rear window.

We had a fun weekend. Nevertheless, he suffers the obsession of the I that wants to die without ceasing to be I. The stringent demand for commonplaceness which governs literature at present is rooted in a failure to recognize that the dilemma of fiction is connected with the very survival of language.

A single note is preceded by two grace notes. Dead space opens up. Empirics were occasionally foiled and sometimes concealed but never thoroughly eradicated — wealth was not to be vaporized in some colossal potlatch.

Vivisectionists deliver the promised arterial cut. The second volunteer was granted the rest of the day off. We are infamously blessed.

Go back and check.

They used to lock one of us in each room. But I think I'm coming around to your idea of the counterscarp.

Go back and check.

Our companion did not looked marked for death, which was some solace. You can feel the years piling on, ghost of self, bird wheeling across the sky. Another man began by writing a novel using only invented words.

We are entering a vast, flat treeless region where the frozen subsoil beneath the tundra acts as a barrier to excavation. Even so, a surgical incision was successfully made between the plates of the giant insect's exoskeleton. Sulphur molecules diffused through the membrane.

Observe how he assumes dispassion, takes upon himself the failure and the lack.

*

Athanor, studded with eyes. Ruinous gothic interior — crumbling industry, rolling white fists of chalk. Why birds only on certain trees, at anchorhold?

Something unseen careers about, colliding with the walls inside the family house. (Painting had abandoned him.) Then the days are cool and the leaves turn and we know that summer is spent.

Distant, dull-thudding of artillery at the front beyond the pine forest. In a sunlit alcove, someone has tied a headscarf to a tree.

She reads the same book over and over until the yellowing pages crumble in her hands. A word has been carefully scored into his flesh with a scalpel.

We were in love and there was a war. Sense two of the noun dates from genesis. Train would be instantaneous.

I need to show you this, he says, handing her a route map to the archaeological site, the alien artefacts.

*

Fire comes, the element declares itself: soot stains on a whitewashed wall, a name slowly emerging from the plasterwork. Overhung, he can barely move his fingers for the pen. Down in the courtyard, a man beats time with a plastic broom head.

We need to find new reasons for meeting again, recurrence in the same eternity. I have to go back.

The novel's disjunctive detail expresses a choice between two mutually exclusive possibilities — such as, she asked if he was going or staying.

Seal up all the graphs, right now. (Fucking histogram.) Origin denotes a stave hewn from an ancient oak — a partial translation of flow, from to crack, plus halt and identify yourself.

Cerements, after a firestorm

A whorl suspending an inflorescence, murmured. As I left, the air was cold and still. When I speak, my voice echoes.

He is stationed to one side, fixed in counterpoint: interesting-futile.

By now the pain had subsided; his chosen familiar is the lemur. We have questioned advantage — moss presses against the sheet of glass. Day trippers mill to scrape samples from a concrete groyne.

Now let us rupture time with a few strands of hair coiled about a pin doll. She is winding down her estates, has retreated to the library to immerse herself in the anonymity of others.

It was our custom to seal a treaty by interlocking thumbs and squeezing blood to the tips. We were gripped by panic in that cramped space.

Make it rain.

Ten acres of land with clots of electricity — a stone outcrop — those tiny white flowers pouring from your head. . . . All of this is well documented, the risen burr of each precise moment.

I had to live in an outhouse while I bled. A length of chain was hung about the anchorite's neck and he was thrown into the sea.

Shadow in lee of bird of prey, a feast of iron and manganese (ninety-six percent of men). You will never finish this.

Evidence of their nanomachines will be unmistakeable, they would spread throughout our solar system in just a few hundred years.

*

She has not long since disappeared. Sedition withdraws inside the earth and waits.

The communards claim that time is an unjustifiable error. Nearby, a tower of wooden pallets is stacked high above a burial mound.

He came across on a Polish merchantman, a small two-masted vessel. This man was as disinclined to nervous apprehension as any fearless creature on land or sea that one might encounter: he had undergone such ordeals.

Origin is territory in flux — radiant energy — particles within a given span, the magnetic field penetrating every surface.

'No. Yes. I feel it's a unique category, this naming of colours.'
'Condensation was not always with us.'
'So, we ourselves are the random factor.'
'Did you find any semblance?'

Following this, we suspended all communiqués. The roulette chips were in my sack all along. For the first time in three years we have the necessary perspective: leaves detach themselves, silently.

We travelled a long way up above the rapids in torrential rain. There we waited and watched for the slack while the enemy built a landing stage under the bridge, adapting its ancient wooden piles. To this day, familiar objects have the capacity to startle me.

Once you begin to notice Pyrrhic victories, they seem to abound. Origin is dwelling, the vault.

His voice was one among many that vanished unheard. If only he had granted the asylum I begged for — my role is now that of unfathomable witness.

Later that day we passed a body of still water, cobalt blue, hung dead perpendicular in the air.

'Where are we, evenfall? Are we not?'

We are turning away from the present moment: a pulse beat, a timely accident. (Incoherent diction equals the divine.) Within fifteen minutes he had become famous, was one of the first people to fling himself from the ferry into a maelstrom.

My final symphony was written during a three-day hangover. We had travelled from tomorrow to today and on into yesterday, along a distance which appears no longer to exist. I see memory here projected along a parabola, offering a glimpse of the soon-to-happen. The path of a projectile under the influence of gravity follows a curve of similar shape.

It was just family. Three grace notes were played with alternating sticks.

*

The case study under analysis wore a peg on her nose as she was made to walk around and around the ward until dropping to her knees, exhausted. Stuffed into her pockets and underwear the nurses found ten thousand roubles in cash, her winnings from repeated success at the state lottery.

A very intense and destructive fire is timetabled, typically one caused by aerial bombardment. Strong currents of air are to be drawn into the blaze from the surrounding area, making it burn more fiercely. We also became conscious of two assassins stealing up under cover of darkness and called out in alarm for the gaoler.

Imagine you have just been given your own cell. There is no number on the door. Loneliness is abolished. Any distinction no longer binds.

The strategy adopted by the syndicate removes from us the means to perfect our long-awaited act of provocation. They took the fugitives away with them and climbed right up past the snowline and *inside* the mountain.

Who was at the funeral

Now I know who you were talking about; I never foresaw having to do this. You could tell by the footprints that nothing of spirit had passed through.

That area had a feeling of menace about it: among the deadliest inhabitants are parasitic plants engineered to take root in human flesh. Such strange seasons here, and the unthinkable collision is yet to come.

I followed the numbers horizontally, according to the dictates of reading aloud: woman with solitary flower, rusting pyx with consecrated bread, the scattered tail feathers — and here is one tiny fragment of bone that needs a helping hand.

There is reason behind these items found scattered across my territory. (Space was not timebound so much as it uncoiled.) The greatest blessing of a disjunctive rhythm is to verse the listener in slowness: origin retreats from any sense of place.

This opens well then falters where she, at her oculus, gazes out with such contempt. I am courting abjection.

In her trunk is the grimoire she uses for calling down familiars, and an engraved device for stamping a seal. With maximum effect, velocity acts on a cylinder rotating in a stream of perpendicular fluid, impulse driving axis and flow.

I expected asymmetry. (Only seven hours to wait.) I quickly scanned the cartoon strip in that morning's edition: those mad ideas re-enacting language, whereupon they pricked each other's thumbs with a needle and sucked blood. . . . Another engraving revealed the female organs of a flower, spontaneous rupture, abnormal discharge of matter oozing from the body.

An incision has been made in the back, the dorsal slit. She taught me these cherished moves with the scalpel: hierarchical control of stasis, organization of the motor stem, the cortex and skilled moments, basal ganglia in cerebellum. . . . You can tell by the burr of my cylinder that it is approaching close of day.

I failed to achieve my aims but did gain a little insight. The world once embodied her will — the reds and ochres, the ultramarine — but what good would it become one to suffer a fit of the cycles? It is rumoured that something not yet seen before has broken out in the marketplace. There was no noise at the windows.

A groat's worth of music, please (this is a very small sum, proverbially). We will shortly be departing, never to return.

Plumb lines suspended from the arms of a cruciform frame were once used to construct a right angle. Between the atrium and the western wing rose a very tall and slender square chimney of ceramic bricks, alternately black and red.

Whatever the facts, the murder led to mutiny among our malnourished troops.

He once slid as golem into the pit. We should all of us work until we are dead.

It will be a four-hour march before we reach the hub of the empire. The *commissaire's* most terrifying case could well be his last.

When stars implode, and so on

The nebula looked like a cluster of exploding nerves. I have been asleep most of the time.

'Why I am such exhaust? I will surely never find.'

'And we will never pass over,' he says, slipping into his pocketbook with unfamiliar style.

Bells toll to remind citizens of the time, while martial music is transmitted over tannoys in the municipal park and town square. It would be wonderful to hear from excavations, or whoever feels needed on the day.

I keep seeing dogs, then realize they're other people's heads. I cannot depend on my sources any longer. In those days, small maps of Europe were tightly folded and stuffed into fruit.

XXIX

I made their streets waste, that none passeth by

The suspect was subjected to a body search, and another enigmatic list was found: a papyrus scroll depicting the third pylon, the gnawed horse blanket, one bucket of quicklime, a crate full of bloody sawdust and mercury ball bearings. Much of her work involves responding to existing inventories, reworking them into grotesque baroque shapes.

A chain of black rocks resembling titanic vertebrae is visible at low tide. Sir is a publisher of mislaid selves, a workshop convulsionist dedicated to radical forms of illiteracy. An archaic noun signifies conflict between the soul and the body, or a literary representation of such a difference of opinion. Silence is a surviving mode of expression.

He tells me he was born the day after a firestorm, tightly packed inside a cocoon of flesh. One of the tibia had snapped. Included in his collection are sepia photographs documenting the fourth segment of the giant insect's leg, i.e. between the femur and the tarsus. I myself am a dealer in hazardous paranormal ephemera, small compressed archives.

We must always be prepared for the night, and come that time I beseech you not to move: when darkness falls there is no light at all, no moon or stars to speak of. The silt that stretches as far as the eye is flat and shallow to the depth of a shin bone. Origin is knowing with others or in oneself.

*

Thirteen years have passed. He is tormented in observing the supple flexion of his own body, and is now bending himself into one of the rumoured causal folds.

Witness how the organist is cannily working his way through the alphabet. Regardless, by my order he forfeits title of the kingdom and is commanded to quit all our assemblies and dominions forthwith. Compare with coitus.

He does not hear me, snared in a species of phenomenological malaise. The strain is on the last syllable. We are both gods I said on parting.

Voices in the night as we hack into the chalkface. Another writes of the brittle effacement of self. The maximum possible loss that could foreseeably impact upon your corporation is now being calculated. Someone find us out, please.

We are abundant and thoroughly documented. There has been a rapid movement of people to a newly discovered star field, followed by the others. Here are boulders, great boulders with lichen on them scattered about in a meadow.

I forgot telepathy, the remote transference of thought: we will perform a simple action first, then take it from there.

I am unrelated to knowledge or any degree of its validation. I need to find myself in what is called a place before a single step can be taken.

Despite everything, the assault is on, into the valley of dry bone. Origin is the nineteen seventies, from mistakes that can be readily imitated.

Looking through the gunsights at this range makes men look twice the size of men — trenches to set an ambush have been dug in case the army countervails. Having reached this point in the drill you will begin to hear other voices, such as the above. The graft has not taken.

His gaze drops to feet crammed into patent black. One extremity bears a scar, another a blue-green tattoo: flesh semiotics, fear of flight (earwax) — the action of stitching together the edges of a wound or incision.

I planned to live in a seedy hotel for the rest of my life. The two other people in the room are pretending not to listen.

I was going to live in a cave at the foot of a cliff. I planned to leave without telling anyone. In the end I stayed home.

At low ebb an ancient petrified forest emerges from the waves. Bear in mind that this is already a schizoid compromise, what with the amnesiac rhythm section (see 'tram'). It's like a different dog all of a sudden: he is after the lung bone. Maybe I never could.

*

Cracked vinyl, Glagolitic Mass. This term is applied where the plot or characters are said to be *verismo*, as distinct from godforsaken.

He lives to scavenge: behemoth is a sea thing, a gigantic, the whale or serpent that lies deep below, reinforcing the buttress that underpins the earth. It was evening when I arrived, and immediately I withdrew to a hideout on the moorland that surrounds the settlement: the villagers look old and frail of a sudden, worn to shadows.

By the turn of the century, photographers no longer had to confine themselves. This sensation was vouched for by people whose sanity brooks no question.

We travelled from today into tomorrow along a distance which appeared not to exist. That detail is the one point I shall always remember.

Origin is placed side by side.

Companions of glass

You have to concentrate. He has all these powers, a ghost of chance.

Who hid the seven daggers? The pivotal scene, the motive, speaks for itself: the sin of J is written with a pen of iron and the point of a diamond. Any advantage is immediately rendered obsolete.

A well of living waters
and flowing streams
with beads of mercury
drew me into their scope.

I was denied by the elongated arm. Maybe this airstrike is the last, he said. Remain where you find yourself at this precise moment in time.

It was a disastrous instruction. We dug in, cut off and held in some sort of antechamber.

The fabric is painstakingly unravelled. I feel he is somebody I will one day have to confront, an emanation with whom I must parley.

*

Then the music stopped, its numerous folds and deficits. Lattermath horsemen and suchlike are archaisms. Toponymic surnames suddenly disappeared. Origin is a wagon, probably meaning partition (e.g. akathist of unthank). At least I am no longer under house arrest.

Our men never saw the map but heard the number of the hill, and slowly climbed the scarp.

Fear of ants

Ants poured from the dead man's ear.

*

A tiny box in my mouth. It is autumn. Large black stones lie in the shallow river, making the water spiral as it flows between them. In the background, people crash cars through storefronts to loot merchandise. She chose this moment to announce her forthcoming hunger strike.

None of these characters appeared in court again. (See thieve, see riot.) A tool was used to gouge rotting fibres from the seams of the stranded vessel.

I am making up your mind. This is no time for quotation, but it's your right to concur, to grow together into a pestilential mass.

Tradition is established in the misery of ritual: two opposing tendencies collide, resulting in variant readings. An electromagnetic field was produced by the superconducting magnet that encased the outside of the chamber. Sure enough, today I have recorded a sensation of moving backwards, even though we are moving forwards.

The crew performs every action with fluid simplicity. Side effects include the ignition of dead memory. Origin is knowing how to do something, and then keeping it to yourself.

Any mutation of a subatomic particle is related to local changes in the zone through which it migrates. He had no choice but to become the foretold usurper.

Messages are pinned to plastic cones, notes to remind oneself how to proceed. Somehow the brake released itself and the diesel engine hurtled down the track toward the next victim, who stood paralysed by fear clutching a metal cross. Another says enemies must be cultivated, allies spurned, whereupon they evaporate.

I urge you to publish your collected surveillance. I could never differentiate between red and green myself.

'So, father, when did all this happen?'

'We will loop the yoke around his neck another time.'

One more infinite deferment has been triggered. The cerebral cortex is controlled by motor neurons (interneurons are shown purple in the diagram). My orders were to hand over the thirty-six-word cypher immediately, yet this *cannot* be the accepted protocol.

By condemning the killing as an atrocity on a par with murder, the insurgents were making maximum capital of it.

*

He can sit there for days without moving. His cravings are mostly for small living things, though a key was shat forth a week ago.

We are engaged in gathering samples — indiscriminate objects, eavesdroppage, impractical mechanics — and a no-man's-land has been established between the air-raid shelters. Observe the clearly demarcated exclusion zone.

It is therefore evident that the universe must be considered as a growth of spiral filaments. Now we have an immense palindrome.

Tread your heel deep into the clay. I am doubtful. Origin is your glaucous eye.

Febrifuge

Which species is currently in a flux of renaming? As we move further away from the midline, the spine is controlling the more distal parts of the body. Are you trying to reach someone, the outside? Origin is the name of an abandoned alphabet.

*

I need to spend at least an hour each day composing a list of numbers.

We walked through the arcade to avoid the heat of the square; within its colonnade is a bizarre limestone attraction known as the gallows, because of its resemblance to a hangman's scaffold. What follows is my worst-case synopsis.

I am perpetually engaged in gathering samples — for instance, in Mexico City I was transfixed by the head of a deity made of twenty-five pieces of jade. A musical apotheosis is foreseen, the soundtrack to an eight hundred-year-old tree, its roots wound about the tombstones set along its circumference, granite sandwiched at inexplicable pairings.

I was mindful of the studies I once made before a statue housed in a gloomy flagstoned corridor. At that time I was trapped beneath a fantasy trilogy starring the inhabitants of a subterranean gothic metropolis (we often passed upon the staircase). Our own family has been called the prototypical icon of human agony — a hymn, unseated.

One bystander curtly pointed out that the bulging eyebrows are physiologically impossible.

In astronomy and navigation, fifteen degrees of longitude or right ascension is one twenty-fourth part of a circle. Origin is decaying time.

At the eastern tip of the peninsula some isolated mounds prove to be stuccoed pyramids with sand cores. Also found there are several platforms of interlocking bone balanced along the ridge of a chalk escarpment.

I am superseded in a temporal sense. The current verb is nothing to do with a particular moment.

The ambassador would take weeks to arrive, and besides, we had firmly ruled him out as a candidate for assassination, having recognized the envoy as a vital channel of news from the outside world, and a dissident in all but name.

Moths battered at the screen: *Mythimna separata* and other species, family Noctuidae, order Lepidoptera, class Insecta, phylum Arthropoda, kingdom Animalia — yes.

An outbound journey may not be in the past. We peaked at about ten o'clock, just as another crack began to open up in the wall.

You have seen it time and time again, haven't you, the apparition? It is widely believed that its loose fibres are sustained by untwisting lengths of old rope.

*

I cannot. We are measured in Fahrenheit. I always volunteer for the nightshift: what do you mean there is nothing out there et cetera.

One day it was raining, the next it was not — the day after that the sirocco blew fierce, hot and dusty. For most scientists the unpredictability of some of the equations in classical science is a revelation. But he considers this account an attack upon his fiefdom, otherwise unassailable — he had begun the year with a supreme sense of triumph, having successfully fist-fucked an irrepressible opponent.

Aftermath is a synonym. I am referring here to knowledge, to the extent that its communication is at all possible.

(Are you coming to the funeral?)

There has occurred in the last few seconds an excessive localized swelling of the artery wall.

Origin is a suture.

You are suffering. You have been taking place for years. Sedatives were administered in the hope of releasing the gorgonized mandible.

I too insist on my quiet moment every morning. If our adversaries should come tomorrow or the day after, the idea is to let them pass by unmolested. This will later be discussed in greater detail, under the heading of war games: opening gambits.

I have been designed to make social contact and secure our position. Meaning is literally a second crop grown after the first is slashed and burnt. Figuratively speaking I am an unforeseen result or consequence, a critical development, an irresistible state of mourning.

We retrieved her ashes, which had been transferred to a large hourglass. Genesis is obscure.

It was through such citizens that I uncovered a network who believed they were being driven into a futile conflict. Waving the white flag was a sapper who only by chance happened to be crawling about on the battlements that afternoon.

My father clutches an obsolete instrument of bone and leather which incorporates a toothed dial and bakelite slide rule. I would rather leave before being tempted to speak.

And so she placed the wrist tags in her orange basket. . . . I have got to open up. I am trading in, hawking.

Consider this the apex of failure. He takes careful measurements before turning to whisper gently the words fade, ebb, subside. . . . He is the deed itself, never the outcome.

I am stillborn. Your man painted potatoes and nothing else, maybe the occasional deceased comic genius.

'If we don't stop soon, we will not have anything left to bargain with.'

But I wanted to keep the driftwood thing (the constellation depicted was hitherto unknown). Yes, I would like *something* to happen, perhaps a solitary flash of light. A letter slipped inside the manuscript provides a tantalizing clue as to our ancestry.

Pursue this course of action while there is still money left in the bank. If all else fails, list: an earful of mustard seeds, the unquiet grave, tombstones embedded in ancient roots, digger a silhouette where the birds of the sky submit beneath the shadow of a dismantled horizon.

Rationalize: workman in boiler suit with fractured valve. On certain days psychology describes all the phenomena of seeing.

*

To the fastness. He says the mutable is all he knows, all he values. One volunteer passed away, unused. I am strapped in. I hope we can stop soon and rest, but there are still the remaining numbers to look up.

He is no longer bereft: he has his kodak head, the pick of the tarot cards, the eel's teeth — and a list of names: names of dead and names of vanished, names forgotten, even the name for a buckled silence. This was how we discovered our respective ancestors came from the same remote island off the east coast.

I observe that overnight a cage has been installed in the gravel forecourt. Symptoms include memory loss and degenerative motor neurone disorder, while febrifuge is a medicine used to reduce fever (viz. scentless false mayweed). Note the two octagrams tipped with tiny membranous rings. Pollen is collected by sociopathic moths.

The door clatters shut and a key turns in the lock. Our central movement is no more than a set of variations on a descending bassline. The solo part soars.

Origin passes by without touching, with reference to the exemption from death of their first-born. County, in the province, is one source of the crucified groundplan.

You've got nothing left, have you?

That solar flare, if it had caught the both of us, we would be ash. Till that day comes, I implore you, do not move: the blinded man often sits motionless on his veranda of an evening, listening out for freight trains in the distance. You are advised to spend at least one hour each day composing uncharted alphabets.

*

Our coverage today has been a bit mediaeval: distraught vision and sound, an unscripted organ transplant. It was imperative that we accurately read the landscape, plotting a course through the abandoned mine shafts.

You are not listening. Each of you was instructed to swallow the object immediately it became symmetrical.

Stent, my neighbour screamed.

The plot is set around a woman who murders her husband and is now being shadowed by a private detective. Acting isn't everything.

The man who invented the game watches the contestants unbeknownst for a whole year. (I confessed to something I had never seen.) By contrast, she's a medicine woman who caresses the lineaments of skull and spine, flinging aside extracted poison.

'Do you still want your accursed share?'

She glimpses the word security and immediately feels insecure.

He will never get back in time. The first man is suspended from the ribbed vault — another windowless afternoon spent deep inside the fortress — while the second is plunged up to his middle in quicksand and stretches out despairing arms. A magnetic field induces a rapid helical motion of their ions. Plasma flows through a collector composed of closely spaced parallel slats, the physical appearance of which resembles a venetian blind. All said, we no longer do guilt.

This assemblage requires several stages to ferment the required hue from decaying organic matter. Breakthroughs include the high-frequency urethra and a hybrid plant with dejected spleen-shaped leaves and cavalier stems.

An expression of rudeness is to be used when the receiving party has totally embarrassed himself. Coincidentally, the resulting figure is also the number of kilograms needed to produce enough enriched uranium to manufacture a single pocket bomb.

We were halted by machine guns stationed in the olive groves. Origin denotes the swirling noise that has been rumoured.

I too am doubtless imitative. Compare with Cydonia (Mars).

The first night was bearable, but the second night it grew colder and colder as we climbed higher along the back of the glacier. Suffering is shown through the contorted expression of the face, which is only matched by the struggling body. Would removing time from any sentence, when used in this way, not alter its meaning?

*

The court-appointed defence lawyer walked out in disgust over the wiretapping, never to return. Thereafter, the whole trial was deemed null and its judgement revoked.

'Who did you say the other two possibilities were?'

A chaos star has eight spikes radiating from a central point. The effects of gravity are considered an anomalous affair.

When I opened my eyes, I found myself lying on a sheet of stitched snakeskin, not far from the blaze around which we had been assembled for that dreadful banquet. It is notable how everyday minutiae cling to any recollection: the certified woman, a terracotta vessel, the polyethylene sack, the silhouette of a carbonized figure.

'Yes, but what do you mean by he and she?'

I recoil from chronicling the terror, that vast insurrectionary moment. Above our heads billowed a great bag of highly inflammable coal-gas which needed just one stray enemy bullet to turn it into a ball of flame. Far below us, emergency food stocks in ruined buildings had suffered radioactive contamination.

Right now I can hear someone outside my window, clattering about on the concrete platform in the winter darkness.

I lifted up my eyes to the window as he turned to look down, and seeing a blue light, I hastened on my way. An empty beer can scuttered in the wind.

Always defer, whenever you can. Unlike the agony depicted in art showing the passion of martyrs, your own suffering has no redemptive power or reward whatsoever. A caution is due to be delivered, the mediaeval incarnadine.

*

Do you think it best not to tell?

His pledge is an oath-crammed covenant which is destined never to be delivered. All these scholars have in common the confusion they fall into when trying to determine a traditional meaning for any universal symbol. The body is broken, spine severed, the face warped by a belt of scar tissue — half the jaw is missing, sheared off by a lightning bolt. One couple found a crushed multicoloured loop on the promenade, as if cast out from heaven. Ever since that time I have been peculiarly vigilant, serving due reverence to your uncertainty principle.

Indifferent bearers cart him off without ceremony on a makeshift stretcher. He is irreversibility personified. This is a fragment of his theory of revelation, isn't it?

A paper cut to the tongue

Face the moon. Glad to have you back, however threadbare. For him, money is liquid. I just wanted to die.

Up in the night sky, galaxies emerged. The installation involved ranks of vacuum-packed meat, expired people and the horsehead nebula. (Why equate the babel of remembering with prowess, neglecting the grace of forgetting?) The figures are near life-size and the group is a little over two metres in height — it depicts the killer and his sons being attacked by grotesque sea serpents.

She strides into the vestibule and announces to all present that her mission is to harvest human beings. At this point the candidate is laid out inside the cabin in a big wooden box, coins balanced on the eyes.

Factor in some coastal blight, blue smoke shaping air in a sun-bleached room. Gainsay me: contradict, deny.

I should be more certain of the shadows and their attendant objects come dawn. We will need that perfect sphere of titanium to counterbalance my ball-and-chain of chewed paper. The glyphs of an unknown script 'recoil at their incurvature'.

Response is elicited by holding the newborn in ventral suspension (face down) and stroking along one side of the spine. Origin is called upon, from alongside plus to shriek out loud while standing in the garden pond.

Scattered on top of the vitrine were pieces of silvery petrified wood. He pitched the hip flask to the man behind and stared down at the mob from the helicopter platform.

'Using the stolen artefact, electromagnetic phenomena can now be manifested as living entities through an interference pattern.'

'If we don't get out of here soon, terrible things will start to happen.'

A word was once used to denote a part of the forum decorated with captured beaks, intricately stitched suture lines, the antennae of the great lunar moth.

*

This method of surgery involves keeping the patient awake to pinpoint the source of epilepsy in an exposed brain. After the ordeal she remained alive for only two hours; this brought the average down.

I woke to find myself standing in the garden pond. I did not recognize her, she was so subdued. We had both been seduced. The disease is brutally progressive: it burns through the anatomy until all vital functions begin to fail at once. These are not excuses. There are no identifiable causes, but there are large hollow categories.

I was once abused as a platform for public speakers. I am the extreme form. There was no other name. And sure enough, the invisible connections between objects are beginning to dissolve and disintegrate. The crucial words here are ductus, vas, trachea, culvert.

He manifested in all his glory, the rival axe. This demonstrates how spatial wherewithal can begin to disappear, jumping from the back seat into the frontal lobes.

The antichrist was born of a jackal. All that distortion was quite real: she just kept on drawing — hatching and scraping. I still think straight lines are preferable to curvature, and would like to have run a few more tests. There was even a crayon locomotive, shunting past a group of peasants as they toiled beneath summer thunderheads.

A mass noun entered the lexical arena at about this point in history. The taxonomy of my genre is unknown, viz. antimatter of dead nature.

Unless we use some kind of living organism, even a human being, any attempt at sympathetic magic will have little or no effect.

In any event, we marched on across the tundra. I was the first to arrive, the first name on a long list of names. (It is the only time I have ever been catalogued.) The whole battalion was ready with its implausible baroque evasions. That was where I first met you, under anaesthesia, the bloody bandage slowly drawn out from the back of my throat.

Note that, since one form of energy can always be converted into another, this outcome is not solely about errant beams of light.

I spun the pencil and it came to a halt alongside my own name; I had volunteered for the firing squad. I approached her. She smiled back. We didn't really engage.

The commune denounced her as autistic: dense wordage was scribbled, emotional life began to wither. We had discovered a precarious trend. People all over the world began renaming their psychoses: Cydonia, Spitsbergen, Transylvania.

A condition of increased pressure within the eyeball is causing gradual loss of sight — note the grey-green haze in the pupil. Here is no want of subterfuge, yet on every side fears cluster and press.

Ever since the count's arrival, death has haunted our profession. The oath we took must endure, for there lies before us a terrible task from which we cannot afford to draw back.

The spinal cord is engineered such that the midline is controlling the median zone of the body. (My own noun often takes the form of a humidifier.) As ions move toward the collector, they pass through an excitation coil oscillating at your personal rate of repetition. Disease results from damage to nerve fibres in the brain.

We are elaborations of carbon, the serial killer had said in her confession.

'Why you no hide?' she falters, tongue slit to a fork.

If the trackers fail to discover the encampment, liquidate them when there is time to spare. I am searching for an archaic form of decline (baulk, evade, elude). The pursuing corpse revived by witchcraft will never realize what is happening until it is too late: origin is a straight line.

And the day after that the sea was dead calm. And the day after that calm day was a day like a furnace. Few scientists expected that unpredictability was lurking beneath the simple equations they had been using for over ten millennia.

The large-orbit ions are willing to deposit on the aluminium slats. Aluminium is the most abundant metal in the earth's crust. Be that as it may, a brain disorder is affecting movement, control of walking ('gait'), balance, speech, vision and mood.

I recall that my assailant was clad from head to foot in steel armour, or something closely resembling that. Does use of the word time in this context add any helpful information?

The thing we found on the concrete groyne kept curling up into the wrong shape. I am about to confess myself: spun glass fibre and molten lead, the runes that reveal a clue to the hidden treasure in the well, and the role of its malefic guardian. This stage suggests an opera about a man who is impersonating himself.

Origin passes by without touching. We are here making reference to the woman's absolution at the death. The depleted plasma is drawn to the apocalypse plate. Then came the next piece of advice.

If I were you, I wouldn't put their food down in one corner and try to feed them all at once.

*

Dull crump of artillery in the distance, red-tiled rooftops stacked above a sea, the sick child. Yours is a spectacular art, like ice that is about to melt. The historic stem passes through without much protest: a round or eyelike opening, a being which can have no essential involvement.

Just ten days left. We have inherited the names. Gaudy wreaths of artificial flowers were scattered across the runway. Passing through a metal aperture that opened and closed, the procession slowly moved toward us. One chord was suspended.

She says a cage has been set aside for your sole use. Relax, your diet of photosynthesis, opioids and valium should soon start to kick in. During my incarceration, time was measured using a Doritos advent calendar.

Basically, I refer to any groundplan of a building that resembles a crucifixion, where an elongated shaft is intersected by a shorter passageway. I may or may not be accountable. The surviving air has been removed such that the wrapping is taut and speculative.

*

There it goes. I think it is creeping out into the wider countryside and surrounding us.

The flames were reflected in all of the windows. I took several photographs from an extreme angle. I heard someone say it's a lovely blaze, is it not.

Among our favourite features is the transmission of electromagnetic waves. Thin copper tracks link these concepts together, each riveted to the next, on and on to infinity. In the illustration on the card I observed that she had stationed herself far lower than required. This was puzzling, because I could still see myself, suspended inside the vertical duct that admits air into the mine. Who wielded the assassin's knife is not open to doubt.

'I think you need to change everything you are doing. I think you need to change your statement.'

Now we are a different film altogether. The lighter ions spiral faster and faster. She plays grace: blood-stem — grief and snot — mucus oozing from the mouthpiece. We know only too well what it is to yield. A stunt is played out with the remaining head. [*Laughter.*] Origin is an unburied hatchet.

I did some spadework late last night. At three a.m. the telephone rang. I was still up, plagiarizing an introduction to a book of stories culled from twenty years of criminal activity. I want her to be happy, but now the drama is all about the bathroom tiles: we will bomb your house and you will never look back et cetera.

I should have gathered up and quit. An unfinished form is emerging — a book, a book forever about to be written. Beside my bed sits a clepsydra, the clock that once used a flux of water to measure time. Origin is too bleak, from to gnaw.

Using a cranial saw, the surgeon would expose the brain and probe at tissue while urging the patient to murmur feedback.

'Salvage, tilt face to nearest star.'

Retain the benzene and hydrocarbon reference from a safe distance of five thousand light years. I have painted two webs on the asphalt roof, that he may swoop down in the night and shelter us, we brace of giants.

End here.

*

Introspection or insurrection, you write: all my life I have been torn between the two, like a doomed regicide. But your letter finds me less afraid.

The patient's occupation is filed as professional revenger. While on the question of definitions, a cockle is an edible bivalve mollusc with ribbed shell, the heart a hollow muscular organ that pumps blood through the circulatory system by rhythmic contraction and dilation.

He replies that his existence has become more ascetic as the shortest day approaches. Meet me at the aftermath.

Truncal incurvation is a newborn reflex. I am named after that infamous neurologist.

Capricorn rising signals sociopaths who like people to appreciate their ideas and insist that they adopt them. They often prefer to spend time alone and have no friends.

There exists here an information asymmetry: the principle that propositions concerning empirical knowledge must be accepted, even though they can never be proved with certainty. How might we counter someone who tells us that, with them, understanding is an inert process — for example the beaks of captured galleys, antennae of the lunar moth.

XXX

The fantasy-prone personality: implications for understanding imagery, hypnosis and parapsychological phenomena

There are no warnings for this document: a sunken image luminous beneath the floodwaters, flesh in hand.
Location: Ekaterininsky Canal, a small ditch with collapsing banks. She says there is no such place. Origin is a procession or pilgrimage, especially one without purpose.

Among a series of photographs in the album is a monochrome image of a woman wearing a wedding dress, turning from the camera. In the background, uniformed men on horseback gallop past. The arresting point is the sharpness of the bride's image, in contrast to the blurred cavalry speeding from left to right across our field of vision.

A figure stands before the white house at the crest, shaven head beside a pyramid with rooks. He traces a word on the ground with an index finger, adds blue spittle and pigment. Founded on a fragility, he exists at the margin of everything, but no doubt positions himself where he belongs.

Strobilus

Needles and coniform clusters of small ones, each with a kidney-shaped spore capsule at the base. A bye is needed, unvoiced prayer.
Plastic tubes of ink replace the venous system; some would not talk to each other for years. Origin is employed in iconoclasm, burning alive the refused.

Another man is listening intently at the wall, attempting to guess at the detective thread. In time, he shuffles over to another room of the compound. Our views on the same point diverge:
A unit of weight formerly used by apothecaries.
No.
A carbon counterfeit.
Yes.
To render watertight by pressing matter into the gaps.
Caulkhead.

Assassin beside giant water. Now reverse the psychology: she has a palate for rare birds, the sounding out of letters, empty turbines. But the sentence that snapped inside me ran perhaps now you will learn a lesson.

I maintain, carry my own fraction, forever uncollected. I have no lasting nor makeshift circumstance. I manifest in sections, appearing at several moments between the numbers sixty-eight and seventy-one.

Both writers acknowledge the same source and predict fallout patterns using idealized elliptical contours (see chapter VII). Then she speaks for the last time, bringing together her hands to form a gateway.

*

It is surely significant that he placed his prelude at the end rather than at the head. Origin is a pane of glass, the pole magnetic with used elements.

That old problem again: the conditions of possibility, any translation and its affects — emotion or desire as influencing behaviour et cetera. This is two hours of your life that you can no longer retrieve, so I shan't offer you a worthless guarantee.

I realize now how it happened, how they made their fatal choice: they looked before them at the field of battle, then turned to the sheer cliff face and thought, fuck.

Consider a plane of bilateral symmetry, especially that of a body. The abdomen was opened by midline incision. The next step is a new approach to guessing the correct date.

Dull, distant thuds reverberate through the compound. Early use referred to an enclosure for the detention of stray or trespassing cattle.

Stumble around the backyard until you discover your place, he says.

Victorian opera glasses, ten pounds. . . . The first character is depicted spinning through the corridors of a sunken luxury liner — his watery eyes match the colour of the blanched sockets in which they are set. I took note of his shrivelled complexion and thin blue lips.

The killer and his sons have been famous since they were excavated and placed on public display, where they remain. In all likelihood, origin was invented by Paracelsus.

*

True, the passport had been returned to the attaché case along with the sheets of grey foolscap, here enclosed. Someone should come for me: you will not be permitted to see me again for many years.

This stuttering pace, she craves something more communicative, less broke: the medial section of the spinal cord controls the medial parts of anybody. Which words are graven upon the table of your heart?

Light is refracted through a window pane. An abandoned canal in the republic connects the behemoth's brain with a network of tributaries.

Calyx, a cup like cavity or organ

A droid in blue overalls spins round and round until he collapses on the floor. There is a bruise either side of his ankle plumage. Spurts of growth during adolescence have left weals across his back, as if he had once been flogged near death. She, as if in competition, reveals the scars of self-harm on her thigh and wrist. Her number is the number twelve, signifying the void outside of existence (viz. loss of control of movement). The kidneys were once thought to control dream states and temperament.

Displacement is everything. Noun is a line with a plumb attached. I am about to refer to a circular window, the central boss of a volute, an opening at the apex of a dome and suchlike. Origin is twisting around to face you.

In composition, yellow — found in muscle tissue, the liver and other organs, even the victim's urine. The poison leaves a sallow residue when evaporated.

I set about washing the body of the deceased. I can no longer punctuate myself adequately.

He clambered aboard and immediately began to fade, exhausted in the vanguard against those punishing weeks. A jaundiced complexion indicates the first step and a wrong turn. Ours is a progressively degenerative art, he once said.

I was assailed, over and over, by the same thought. Many of the pigments are now lost. Our resolutions were more histrionic than interpersonal.

If he overshoots the target area, he will be left alone to freeze in the wilderness — out of grace and out of years — crouched beneath the embers of a stairwell, with chalk astronauts.

A number of the archives are permanently sealed, most notably that which contains the codex of references. Insignificance is somehow tied up with being.

A drug that fosters sleep was administered, trunk line incurvation.

The tyrant is persuaded, because he alone knows that he has made love to his wife's corpse. He could pass through solid matter as if it were water and could sink into the earth.

*

Giant insects the size of zeppelins are vibrating in the air. Maybe once you did strike out for the territory, but simply cannot remember the episode: in there, at rest, lie the letters of your name.

Now, more from numbers, the suspended track where we are left behind with ourselves.

He bound the twenty-two letters to his tongue, he harnessed them to the seven planets. The trouble begins when the ancient walls are pulled down: those ruins bore the twisted slant of a wrought-iron bridge in a firestorm. He speaks over and over of the missing gland.

She disembodies — a smell of molten plastic follows her around. Her work chiefly depicts human figures in grotesquely distorted postures set in a confined interior space.

I hear footsteps.

An inquisitor enters the room; I hide under the table. He finds me and begins to howl. I had received a summons to leave town before the tenth: heave down curses upon thy head et cetera.

In the collision a rail penetrated the pelvic bone. An animal's horn pierced the abdomen to exit at the base of the spine.

Let me see if there is anything new here. (Where are you by the way?)

On one foot is a threadbare stocking and on the other foot a boot. In their own unique way, these items are quite unremarkable.

News is coming in of another upset: the culprit is the one without a plan. Any medium impacting on the spleen or the neural ganglia has been overlooked.

Starless, bleak wastage — unforgiving marshland. A fibrous sac containing acid burst through the skin. Figures are scratched into the walls of the cell and normal colouring is replaced.

Do something.

*

Before he dies I make my peace, gazing into glaucous eyes; eighteen years later this will have tragic consequences. Some words require explanation.

I was unable to trade hostages with the adversary: it felt as if we were being pushed further and further away from a circle of knowledge.

The extremities of what?

I think you are right, there is a good deal of underused stock hereabouts (for example, the unexpected discovery that H and J are the same person). Three men dead, yet that woman went riding off in the rain without a mark on her.

You were only meant to analyse these statements, not take any action. Now make a list of all the scenes you cannot remember in the order they appeared. Go away and make yourself a map of the structure of the book.

*

Transverse city, a small portion of which extends into the panhandle. He is bibliographer, an adept. I have just realized how much I am going to miss the neutral.

The consecrated host is displayed for veneration in an open or transparent receptacle. Be indulgent, in light of this, to those who cannot refuse.

He is asleep on the pallet. Unused pronouns float about the room, colliding with one another. After several days, a rancid oil began to seep out.

Coloured lights from the fairground opposite strobe across the ceiling. He runs his tongue over the firm, fleshy tissue around the roots of his teeth — there is a song in his head from our youth.

Alkahest is the hypothetical universal solvent. (Paracelsus again.) Origin is a dull grey-green, covered with a powdery bloom like that of grapes.

Next, the somnolence, the role of improvisation: there will always be more. He pictures a stairwell of used books (*esprit de l'escalier*, latterwit). Back then, folk lived under the yoke of an indifferent advent.

The scrap of cord beneath the tongue snapped in a fall. Everything slots into place — something is released, the recognition of an error: a sudden shift into a vanished frame.

She says she is outward bound, due south to pilgrim on eighty a week. The tale speaks for itself: an impossible exodus. Origin is late, much earlier in compounds, and rumoured uncertain. I remained in a state of profound distress for several decades.

Growing pains, our father's hat of ash cast into the sea.

*

Armed with scythes and pitchforks, they march beneath a white standard spangled with lilies and the device. She never suspects that she is overseen, lambent body floating within the gauze of a fourposter. A ball of lead was attached to the end of a line to find the depth of the water.

'Thus, and dream not speaking far then at inmost. . . .'

The lateral part of the spinal cord controls the lateral parts of the body. Another name still in use translates as afterganger, or the one who walks who should not walk.

A nasty paper cut to the tongue, deep scar across final digit, the knuckle. These will disappear in time. Other injuries, despite being alone for several days, include a shattered tibia, ingrowing hair, a bitten lip and fractured astragalus. Observe the sloping mass of fragments at the foot of the bed.

He made a covenant with himself. (This was reckless.) I cannot believe someone dragged a corpse into the kitchen and just carried on as if nothing had happened.

She drew the letters in water. Their substance is flawless, despite traces of silt in the form of filaments.

Is there something adrift within him, so spoken as he is, void of grace, so full of years?

Origin is a hawking term, probably of unknown ultimate. The analogous recollection assumes a very similar shape.

> And all things, proudly beginning, collapsed
> at the sight of their own future

A tranquillizer, no doubt chloral hydrate, was administered. She dreamt as follows: I am crawling around the garden alone in the moonlight, when there comes a shadow with a gash where the heart should beat.

A crossover has taken place, the postilion struck by lightning.

Her work is found in several international publics. It has been a while since anyone has wrongly assumed.

Rolling back, and memory accelerates: a stairwell of used books, shoulder high — defiant, blind — a glory hole. A being which, for the sake of itself, is that it is.

Weightless in space to here. He is no more than an instrument containing current and a shunt coil. The howling died away.

Well, tomorrow is the last. Something is possible.

To return to the incident of the father and the son: their combined torque deflects the spinal column. They are a direct measure of the circuit (see gospel of St Thomas). I want to counterfeit, everything declared, tidy myself off into a clearing house.

He takes the earthenware jar and the bottle and the key and puts them back where he found them.

'Hear I what of thee, remaining?'

*

Horizon, a smear of turquoise rimmed with gold.

The sense changes over time, but my first impression was that of sound: tiny supernatural figures pounding corn — between the sticks a promising hand, the wreckage. They wear scapular feathers about their necks, together with the insignia. A passing convoy carries freight at the rear window. The horse was eaten.

I signal: eddies of ash in the air, those twisted porcelain folk. We shall report back to earth when good and ready.

*

Now and again I peer down to see what I might find discarded on the ground. I do not relish thrusting my hand in. Our customers are the rumoured irregulars and resemble untanned hides from a distance. The gullible emptor had it coming for a long time.

I took myself off. Origin is the roof of the mouth.

The scene forms a triptych. Upon a sudden click she begins to swing back and forth, bound to hinged metal frames which may be closed like a book and sealed. A glaucous gull is a type of seabird, a large white and pale grey found in the arctic of eighty-one.

Our hearsay is Yes. Origin is a demonstration or proof, the possibility drawn attention to earlier.

Whiff of paraffin in the gun carriage. The lost children (I see now) were saints, holed beneath the waterline.

Linger. Postpone. Suspend.

I told myself. I withheld myself.

Under yellow fog, a boxcar shunts onto a sidetrack at the marshalling yard. Wagons clash together, shuddering on impact.

I told you earlier, the pledge is broken. Back in the day we would only deliver the naked facts, starting all over, again and again.

A corona of pelvic bones hung from the ceiling, radiant with candle flame. The volunteer is slipping back into the pit.

He is an inverse measure of the circuit's electromagnetic power: your love hath no fabric et cetera. There clings to him a sense of duty, an impractical unit of energy that has survived our fall from grace.

*

Ascension pavement, a halo about her solarized head. The group assembled for one last time to muster a single rigid stare.

The sharpened femur penetrated to the spleen. She has a counterfeit uniform, doctored with crosses of lilies, a tattered ribbon of medals. . . . But it is painful to let her go, even when her method lacks an alphabet.

We are going to need. Origin is ligament of tongue.

What do I get?

I set to work in absolute silence. The function of the coil is not apparent, nor its method of attachment to the internal suction of the implant. Nonetheless, I always trust my mistakes, my needle.

I meet him in the street by chance and he says the work has no significance, which is the source of its enigma. There were only two bridges spanning the river in those days (the third had been destroyed in a NATO aerial bombardment). Ours is an uneasy language.

He neglects — is annexed, overthrown. When he fell open to sleep, he slept. When hungry, he ate. No times were fixed. He made a covenant between the ten fingers of his hands and the tongue. He ignited the letters with fire.

One winter afternoon, with snow falling and the roads covered with slush, we went into a bar near the crossroads. Taking a stool at the zinc counter, I gazed out of the window at the passing traffic and pedestrians. On the corner two cloaked figures were standing motionless, the taller man hooded. Above all, it is hard to locate a genuine fracture, even after years of experience.

No, I do not carry around with me a picture of that last scene in my head. But I never forget a phrasal idiom: entropic musical reflux, the dozen fugitive mutants et cetera. Her body lay outside in the courtyard, where four plane trees demarcate a square, one at each corner.

Once in a while the odd thing happens. You evangelists, I screamed, this is a secular and impoverished substitute for memory.

*

The room he has been given is completely white and matches the painted highlight in the iris. When it proved impractical, the invasion was abandoned.

This is what's called fighting for time, being genetically dispossessed. Breath without voicing utilizes the diaphragm and is controlled by the vagus nerve.

I no longer believe anything that occurs: the first postilion never returned.

We are temporarily delayed this moment, paralysed under inaction, a want of process. The township is powerless to help. I don't understand where all the pollen has descended from, the ticker tape. And those birds are martlets, martlets arranged in tight blue triangles.

Is he drawing on the train home, summoning forth his letters, a whole alphabet of his own making? And now the basic form resembles an eagle nebula.

At the heartland: mutual avoidance, judicious violence, a landscape 'swathed in her winter raiment'. The principle here is stoic-domestic: you gain an hour, you lose an hour. Today's subject is the legal personality of the unborn, the one who folds inside the remaining head.

Who wrote about silence?

The sick child was delivered up — that place was a ghost town where hell lies in all directions, by all available means. I would rather have spent five days lodged in the house of a revenant, tunnelled blindfold into a burial mound.

Of an instant, we all began hearing things very differently: the prayer wheel, a footless bird borne as a charge, archaic and swift. One sheet of writing does not make plenty.

Never here where you wait for me, I am now folding up the dust, our clusters of ill-starred cells.

But you are growing absent, inside out with eyes sewn fast, because the electric, the enraptured.

*

The settlers' wagon train was battered by another of the planet's incessant dust storms. He attempted to reply to the last dispatch himself.

I am a rare medium — total threshold — and don't wish to stop here, provoked by my own sabotage. Have you seen the photographs, the charred and blackened trunks of trees that line the pilgrim route? It is not as though we were not warned.

A horse crosses the bridge. Money is no object. I am left here and I must. No one spoke up around the door of the furnace as she scraped ashes from the grate.

He wears protective rust and carries an ikon, some takeaway god. In one corner of the room is a tiny household temple. The men are guarding it. No one wants to risk a static charge, what with the marketplace burning. A message was transmitted beacon to beacon, across the dark.

Their vessel spins to earth twisting wildly. She goes forth to meet them.

The vision is set: pier with waves and ocean, Saturn before a gully of stars. The steep hull of our boat may check them, but not for long.

Glimmer of a wreck beneath the surface, more spare parts for her spontaneous combustion. A device was invented to hazard the depth of water, another to determine the vertical incline of a cliff face.

*

The following is an account of what took place on an important date in the history of that period.

I am the promised bone of sponge.

They have got this disease.

She said look at all that steam rising up from the oilcloth on the table.

Twenty minutes or so went by.

Then softly she said, what's wrong with you?

Others, such as sponsors of the rapid onset of the illness, are not so sure.

Slowly he bleeds from her a substance that will outlast them both. (They have majored in the unsurveyed.) Thereafter, he went on copying the hourly bulletins mechanically, trying to convey some sense of our ordeal to the outside world.

Solitaries disperse, reading the traces, the shapes. A dozen engines are belching smoke, whistling and panting — sharp chocks of plastic jut from a black bin liner. It was nothing spectacular.

This is not unlike memory. What I did cherish was the evacuee sitting there, that porcelain evacuee.

*

He is patron saint of the hermit and the lunatic. For three years he stood motionless at the top of a column. He agitated the letters with his breath.

We are starting again from scratch; every time it rains we have to kill the power.

At his death, he left fifty-two shirts of sackcloth and nine glass eyes — a corona of bone swung from the ceiling. Origin is private property.

People can grow addicted to collapse. Is there anything else you would like to say, to add to your statement?

She was allegedly a Janus-faced life form.

It was just you and me waking up in a different time at a different rhythm, in a different place where all the rooftops have been levelled. Dark bituminous pitch was roped into a binding pattern.

The eyeball is leaking. She asks me the distance between the sun and moon, and then between the earth and the other side.

I refuse, give notice.

It is rumoured that we once lived together in an early skete. I have no recollection of this (gin). My name stems from a disused word meaning to weigh the heart.

Far below sea level, with zero gravity, that valley was a dangerous place where electric storms blasted clouds of dust, soil and sand over vast areas. Early writings are replete with travellers who went astray and died trying to cross it.

As you can see, I have abandoned many of the old motifs.

*

He has the look of a man with nothing to do and nowhere to go. This is where the mechanism slips into overdrive, the inhibitor is lost and the chain of command severed: with any gravity simulation, there will always be a period of frenzied activity.

Leibniz himself saw in the binary system, that counts only zeros and ones, the very image. This has tipped the see-saw and every object must again be counted.

I cannot he groans: one revolution symbolizes the repetition et cetera.

A lack of potassium led to massive discharge of neurons, a hyperexcitable state where we fire exhaust to infinity. This explains some autonomic effects and the user's withdrawal: pinpoints of red light in the kitchen form a tunnel that leads to an aperture — a coven of saints — the marble stairs descending into the river.

Observe how I have returned to some of the old motifs. The songs in my head are mainly about the past.

How does this look to you? You are free to disprove me on every point raised. I have just noticed the miniature table and chairs, the withered umbrella. . . . Then, during rehearsal, the script said instinct and I said insect.

Why so much mist lately?

Exile them into disassociation, murmured from notes. The belief that if you understand something you ought to be able to write it down still persists.

This is hard to follow (see titanic limestone, sedimentary massive). The sea by contrast is grey-green, arctic. Time is set at a slippery pace — filaments who touch, spasm and collapse. The messenger was buried up to his neck in the shingle as the tide came in.

From the asphalt along the promenade rose ripples of light. He was born in my year and is author of the lost novel, but it was I who described the fundamental particles which later came to be known.

Could we have a little tension music, please? I doubted you would get this far. One of the discarded objects turned out to be a ring pull, a tongue of metal with sharp curve attached.

We were not archival at all back then, surviving on repetition alone. Origin was three-cornered.

Various species have been grouped together according to their past beliefs. Lymph is the fluid leaking from inflamed tissue.

I struggled to redeploy the forgotten dream, the Bowery: father seafaring, nautical pugilism et cetera. Our arrival sparked so much unrest that by the middle of September an announcement to the public was signed by the viceroy and circulated. One day on the crowded esplanade I heard someone cry out, and made a note of this occurrence on the spot in a notebook using a pencil with a helpful eraser at the tip. Origin is leaving with me.

*

In 1804, one of the names was rediscovered. Asteroid Apophis is the largest name, having a diameter of three hundred and seventy metres. By this I mean above the level of the head, in the sky.

Observe how he is simply registering impressions haphazardly as they appear before him. The gift was a handful of fractured teeth.

Today he feels sick, as though poisoned by an unknown hand. It had occurred to him that his visits would look more genuine if he were to address letters to himself occasionally. My only wish is to stand still for eternity, find me where I am.

Sooner or later, she knew, all these minor details would form an alignment and assume significance. For example, there were originally at least four massive stones running from west to east. The titles had slipped out.

The corona is visible during a total solar eclipse, when it is seen as an irregular pearly glow surrounding the darkened disc of the moon. She marshalled the letters of the alphabet by harnessing them to the twelve constellations, while I bent back in the current, dying in her arms and so forth.

There is no graspable physical aspect, only a faint residue — pandemic liminal, total threshold — the impossibility of arrival (where an owl grips a branch). A bare chalk track ranked high in my value system, among other figures of inspiration.

These autobiographical facts discreetly hint at a dark copse on the hill. Origin is symbolic of a sawing motion.

Battering moths, rumour of giants next door.... I inherited seven chromogenic prints of the relic found at Devil's Coyt, and a small revolving cylinder containing someone's prayers. On either side of the lychgate were a number of enamel plaques with black gothic lettering: factotum of gloom and similar.

She advanced across the room, drawing nearer, seemingly without moving her body or touching the ground. The previous night I had dreamt of a woman I once sold conversation to in the city of Zagreb, where I lived during our years of probation. Now the valley lies well below sea level, a wilderness broken by quicksand and swamp. I remain convinced that I was mortally sick at the time, and suspect I was being slowly poisoned with arsenic, though by whom I could not say.

The missing word is numb and literally means corpse servant. I can no longer associate myself. That will do.

*

Items are placed in the centre and at the rear to approximate a pyramid. This is a game; I pretended not to see his gun. One by one, the contenders select colours corresponding to a name and a place and a date in history.... A compound with ruined outhouse and backyard enclosed by an electrified fence is connected to the immediate, to the home stretch of the dog track.

This point is unassailable. A brilliant halo of light — sometimes referred to as a nimbus, aureola, radiance or (rarely) gloriole — was seen around the sun due to diffraction by water droplets. Origin suggests a large building compressed into fine horizontal strata and then abandoned.

We calculated that the rebel tank manoeuvres would be restricted by the enemy's own minefields. It is said she made her recordings accompanied by anti-aircraft fire, and on such a summer's day as this, rising up from the submerged rim. You are no longer here.

Do you observe any parallels? I am anxious to keep apart these multifaceted ways of using a sentence. A hair-like vibrating structure was found in large numbers on the surface.

The initial primordial contraction formed a vacant space into which light could beam. As he mounts the crumbling steps toward an opening in the storm drain, a cluster of sparks drift across his field of vision, prompting a twist of neck to face the nearest star.

Pallid green, stale pink, a fluorescent bruise: these varying shades correspond to diverse functions of the neural ganglia. Tomorrow night we have been promised a sheet of igneous rock, more or less parallel to the bedding plane.

We could actually fold the two reptiles together to make a third, an untouchable pariah. A subatomic particle, such as a photon, has zero spin and follows the vengeful description mapped out below. Origin is the trodden ground.

He has evidently transgressed a rule. At the base of the tilted page sits a ledge, an outcrop of stone — the underpinning.

*

Anglers are stationed at intervals across the east-west run of the port. We shall have to come back and liquidate: you treat the two absences encountered today as though they had the same motive.

Physically, he never fully recovered. You are welcome to stray, into a realm of concrete tank traps and red-tiled roofs, cinderblock shacks painted Naples yellow, a pale pigment of lead and antimony oxides.

He is time-worn, used up.

This scene is distorted by the general state of concussion, though memory is kept alive in the lesions. The earliest monks were simply men who had fled alone into the desert.

In the distance, white light from the stadium, carried up on an outroar. Despite the nervous tic, her reminiscences are slowly adding up to something that could one day become significant. We are not safe beyond this point, any point.

I asked her about this thing and that thing and the other thing. She shrugged. Origin is noted for its cheap lodging houses.

The supreme beginning, operating by binary function in nothingness, would have suffered to draw itself out of itself.

*

He busied himself stockpiling beetles. Meanwhile history is repeating itself, the unmistakeable tramp of Roman legions marching along the causeway at low tide. One escaped slave was the so-called harbinger.

His demeanour is best described as sinister-affable. The good doctor insisted on a lectern supported by spinal vertebrae and real leeches — new kit had to be designed: tungsten with a fluorescent slash of yellow lichen.

Now I am your replicant. Etymology is a noun denoting homicidal frenzy.

The early monastic communities grafted acute isolation onto paranormal criminal activity. Resources were scarce, proteins vulnerable. Old believers are pictured here in a skete beside a river near the forest — that is you in the background, head bent to beg alms, withered arm aloft.

Then the year was ninety-seven: I counted down from ten to one before falling into a deep pocket of wounded air. The forgotten limb had not been lubricated.

It is hard to decide whether his signal is a still pose or part of a movement trapped by the camera. The sun flaring off the sea leaves a constellation of sparks in my eye, the glow around a conductor of baffled potential, corona discharge.

His fourth was the tragic.

XXXI

Spoor of mercury rising. The instrument used consists of a flint box with sounding board, wires stretched taut across the bridge. The postilion's head is off at dawn.

We stand on the foreshore and answer no to every question. Nothing is reliable — never a collision to the right (the south), none to the left (the north). I am about to come eyeball to eyeball with a stranger on the cobbled square. North signifies malefic. East is convulsion, west mischance. South means catastrophe.

I heard just one sound, then the landscape must have dissolved immediately.

Probably electromagnetism is implied, the interaction between magnetic field and electric current. In other words, the human body suggests points of fire to which the writer endeavours to give concrete form, energy that congeals when siphoned from the kidneys, the liver and the spleen.

What do you hope to accomplish tomorrow, what cage harbours your usefulness? Origin is an abbreviation of he is quit.

*

A fluctuation in entropy has been detected, the degree of disorder or randomness in any system:
- i) Eight cylinders in narrow monobloc.
- ii) Coil ignition at base of spine.
- iii) Zenith pump-fed via tank fermentation.
- iv) Hypnoid moss.
- v) Sudden recurrent episodes of sensory disturbance and convulsions.
- vi) Abnormal electrical activity in the brain.

My own dereliction is a bye, an illicit bet in a counterfeit scene.

He suffered no permanent injury: the sheath of a tendon, any tissue of the body, can and will heal. Dried bark was provided to scribble upon for free.

Another lies paralysed beneath a blanket of pollen. Yet the legion of angels survived the sudden drop in altitude, bleached bone resistant on the paving slab.

*

Sleep no longer touches my eyes — you are always in my vision, inside the skull. Voice is seldom the easiest option.

The first thing she says is you are not the right person, you have never been the right person. What is more, I never should have: you are self-saboteur, a disaster — a natural disaster, I grant you, but nonetheless. She advocates writing, cessation.

The patient is to be executed by contract. We draw straws; the apostrophe key is jammed. Mercifully, she is distracted, busy composing one of her lists.

I am appointed executioner. Climbing a short flight of steps, I reach the iron matrix that holds the detainee: a starvation cage suspended above a stagnant pool. The contraption shudders before plunging into the oily waters of the tarn.

We could go backwards in time she hazards, attempt to reach a decision, mourn the lost six of our company.

The survivors arm themselves and head out for the stadium at the edge of the city. A cliff collapses into the sea, frame by frame.

These are inherited rules which we are following (recall that unpleasant scene at the bus terminus). Among your crew is one possessed, who gives himself so completely that each time you take leave of him you feel it is of no consequence whether parting is for one day or an eternity.

'Gone for a wander (eleven twenty). And then to that café, the red one with the sulphurous yellow lamp. You have the key. Go through the chalk tunnel, down the green steps and straight on, wherever they deliver you.'

Be good, if you can't. My apparent indifference does not exempt me from acts of vengeance. Now I must stop.

*

Shutter across head in shadow, onward into terrain of ash. Once again we are on a journey composed of time and geography, shackled together. That moniker is probably a breeder's name, preserved at a luckless moment.

A nail embedded in the heel. His head is off (the wire).

The next station is battle ore. Origin is vagabondage.

The white plain absorbs whatever precipitation falls to earth. In my knapsack I have my notes and two or three unconcerned objects.

'Is it tomorrow night? Is it not tonight? I thought it was tonight. . . .'

Walking slowly inland to the crest, toothless, inhaling rank odour of urine. We have simply swapped the place names around, all part of the daily reprimand.

Nothing, nothing is choreographed for tonight.

*

Estranged wife kidnaps musical, the strapline read. . . . 'I deflate the immediate' et cetera. She has never used. She chews at the cord.

The day cannot contain our exchange — anything you can avoid, avoid.

'Are you on or off the premises?'

I have walked, I have been cancelled. We spent the greater part of our time in solitary.

The boys hurling stones into waves. Nature implodes, nitroglycerine under the tongue. Our spoor is mistrust: now we can do whatever we want.

He is encased in leather armour, the true skin hidden beneath a toughened epidermis. I have a tendency to identify him as the son of either/or — and who is that third figure, walking beside you, the invisible?

*

More rhetorical speech at the regular full moon assembly. I had never heard of him.

Practise your inventory: tin can with bullet, the shattered wooden box, a heap of stones, green algae floating on a creek at low tide. . . . The ruined casket is set at an angle — we are many light years from home.

On the shore beside the loch is a cube of fire. Relax, you don't actually lose any of your lives in the process.

Common misperception: my lack of caution. I interrupt. You can see for miles — turn your head, in the other direction you can peer straight through the cell wall. This is where cryogenics comes into it. I have an no appetite for the archaic, she replies.

We are marching into the prevailing wind. I am officially imminent, about to happen — or simply waiting. The zone is an up-and-coming no-go area.

Tirelessly, I list: a leguminous plant with clover-like leaves and bluish flowers, a chain of fireflies, crimson pollen of the lily. . . . And you, you resemble an unnatural break in the proceedings.

An easy prey, one boy burns in his night shroud; there is no remedy. His span is recoiling. All gathered reckon it's a nerve, trapped.

Origin is frozen, the bone framework enclosing the brain of a vertebrate.

I broke the wax seal, roamed about the earth before occupying a space of my own. As the festival unravels, I don't want my fingers in that wound, stabbing at the page.

We have exposed a shelf of rock and innumerable slender thread-like structures. I foresaw you storming in, guns blazing, one reversal hard upon another. I wonder whether we can outlast the arrival.

He undercuts himself on the hard frozen ground. This seems the oldest solution on offer, to leap from the balcony, another lottery-funded suicide. The others escort him home before there is no point to the favour.

The cab driver says he knows nothing, then adds that the planets Saturn and Mars are traditionally considered to have a malefic influence.

History

When searched, a list is found on a scrap of paper in my pocket. During the solemnization, a muscle was torn; the wounded flesh envelops an abscess. One outlaw had a full name: it was 1882 or thereabouts. He was joined to his brother at the scapulae. Then it was 1915. Others pioneered a notorious gang which specialized and extinguished people. The brothers were hanged in a piecemeal fashion.

Such is a person of shiftless courage. (Origin is too late.) A major mountain system runs the length of the coast, its highest peak rising to an incorrigible altitude. In folklore it is always the night when witches meet on a mountain and hold orgies with the devil.

Another forest-dwelling old world monkey has a long face for holding food. In mythology, the wife of the selfish giant and grandmother found a constellation near the north celestial pole, identified by the conspicuous W pattern of its brightest stars. It is misused with a preceding letter, or mineral.

See, any act of witnessing. I once was trapped under your stairs. I could not find the switch — a door, a corner — nothing.

Acute animosity is flaring up in the principalities. It was like going home after a long stretch in time: windows squaring up to the dark, men fighting under the pier at low tide. . . . The land slides away from beneath us — apocalypse beyond the square, our collapsing boundary.

The legion has dismounted and refuses to withdraw — reinforcements are mustered and lock themselves into position. (Everyone appreciates a side, your underdog.) In the distance stands a derelict windmill, wandering dunes, a current of fine sand coursing about our ankles as we stand together at the shoreline.

Announces the observant placard: he pummelled the crab nebula with cosmic severity.

*

Your superabundance is without limit. Visualize this book beside the shakedown in a windowless cell.

The house is the house with seven gables surrounded by a moat and shield of quickthorn — we had reached the end of the land: *finisterre*, a promontory once called forth. My own enclosure is flanked by a narrow alley strewn with broken glass and a false wall. When I gaze at a painting, a period of time elapses.

There is also the memory of a sky above a vein of gold at the horizon, strips of rose and blue in the compass. A shallow of white mist clung to her feet as she ran the early morning track — a satellite is reflected in each of the four windows. Our language is made of intercepting circles.

At the cloister is a herb garden quarried from a pit older than lineage, where two granite figures face each other down. The anchor chain passes through a tube which doubles as a mortar canister, a short piece for hurling shells. Again, a lifeline, matter pounding at the heart: a person who has literally ascended by falling, fashioned from a single lucky throw.

Of course, she says, if you had not been an outcast, we would never have bankrolled you. And then she says, mother of god, even here one man can make a bureaucracy of his mouth.

*

Probably elvan, to wit intrusive igneous, found: a single spark, accumulation of quartz and orthoclase — fracture common or potash feldspar — monoclinic with cleavage set at right angles.... Debris forming on the spot, or moved by wind, as loss.

The organism is distilling fluid from the dank air. She drew back (a helpful analogy is to swab the sinus cavity). Events damaged me. The whole family was lodged on the roof; they were loyal.

The right hand is slightly blurred, suggesting motion. Each contestant is bound to its neighbour, an *agglutination* is thereby composed: spongy voids on the dashboard, a hanging saint at sway, fragile reassurance.

I am no longer here and they will not wait for me. The planchette skates across the lead, scratching out code.

He deserves better, was ill-prepared for the mortal undertow, a sudden recollection of someone else's boyhood.

There is nothing to see, nothing to see, murmurs the summoned policewoman.

Insomnia

Through action of opiates on the locus coeruleus, a heavily pigmented nucleus has been located in the dorsal wall. Chronic activation of receptors provokes quarantine. This is the only mechanism able to compensate for the abrupt changes in your manifesto: an intracellular engine that hastens premature death, destruction by supernatural agency et cetera.

Once they penetrate the stockade, we will have no option but to launch a distress signal. (See barbarian west, the four hundred to one outsider.) There is one memory of the man on a train making up his face, another of the woman on a jetty, turning, a sudden inrush of fluid. She left a message in mad green crayon.

Upshot: this does not sound like anything I have actually experienced. We are approximate. Everything hinges upon a sky resting on this thin strip of gold, the ruined clock tower.... I recall seeing the photograph and thinking: our survival never amounts to this, times and dates all out of kilter.

She tastes the sudden arrival of something, anything.

*

A maze of pores is held together by a zip. (I suppose these things happen.) Now he is in traction, still trying to justify himself, striving to authenticate a single lived moment. We are here documenting the death of an obscure science, where origin is an inappropriate step taken at the wrong time.

These rites grant asylum to witchcraft. We are an estimate: the outcome may be a fraction more, it may be a fraction less.

Knotted cords dangle from the scalp. Maximum curvature of the spine is forecast, the crew hunched over their precarious instruments. I am shackled to your mutability.

But we're glad you are here, breathing alongside, unwired among the strangers. I never wanted to stop — a hard seal of wax in the canal, the rudimentary valve.

I need a counterpoint. And here is a rather aimless coda at the entrance to my interior, no labyrinth to speak of.

*

Face in the pillow.
   [*Deadpan.*]
   'Do you still own that metal neck brace?'
   'Who are, who are all these people?'
   On that very page was found the aforementioned or stated. Another object was made by pouring molten metal into a mould.

We cannot keep up with all the action — for example, I don't remember the totemic ganglion referred to earlier. And then she murmurs no such community as things, something like that. Years later, she will erase the guilty sentence.

Nerves schismatic today: hawk or gyrfalcon — one-third of a pipe — a cask or abandoned vessel of capacity. Is there room? Sort yourself out.

a) A wood pigeon (sound).
b) The adamantine rock strikes fire.
c) An irregularly shaped blood vessel found in certain organs.
d) A sequence of three cards of the same suit: is this a real choice or just another assassination attempt?
e) A third of something, anything.
f) A fencing piston.
g) There is that noise again.
h) A salvage pontoon, the grudge.
i) The office of that hour, the terce said or chanted: agony of stillness.
j) An opioid prompts the liver to manufacture morphine — sheer genius.
k) The third hour of the day, ending at nine.
l) Of a field, divided, each of a separate tincture.
m) A system of betting whereby one's opponent must be identified in an apocalypse.
n) A race to which this system binds.
o) A subordinate rib springing from the intersection of two other ribs.
p) A minute opening in the surface through which microscopic particles may be trafficked.

I look skeletal beside the female. Our eggs hatch at close of day; a rubber tube leads from the middle ear to the cleft. We are venal at heart.

This seems the most historic solution on offer — nevertheless, the contestant fell into a series of pale, regrettable weeks. Nearby stands the boundary wall, soaring above hovels roofed over with peat and reeds from the nearby marshland. The following decade witnessed a vicious blood feud over territory, saw edgemen and their kin slain over disputed thresholds.

Origin is named after a saint, Delta Cassiopeia.

A recurring episode concerns the boundary stone. Retreat is signalled, inventory and schedule consumed in a temporal rift: quarks are *forecast*, never directly observed.

Essentially, this mental picture consists of three words. Omnivorous. Undomesticated. Hoofed.

A sense of place arrived with him, beating a circuit about the rim of our enclave.

*

This is a sanitized account of what people once did, how they would pass time. (A page is clearly missing here.) Underground galleries were found beneath the sea, a vast cavern illuminated by flickering torches in ochre, red and blue. Someone whispers it's *de profundis* time.

A gull crashes into the window and the temperature suddenly drops. One howl is swiftly followed by another howl.

This passage contains some words that do not appear to belong. For example, we met with unexpected resistance, the island acts like a centrifuge, and so on.

A terracotta bowl of mercury has been set upon the floor at the foot of the bed; we are about to take part in a graceless detour. I must admit.

The bodies observed have possible astronomical significance — moments with a view, billions of doubters clustered far below.

*

Spraying himself with repellent, he straps on the harvesting knife: a broad three-foot blade with a sharp crescent hook at the end. You would lack the patience for such a mission.

The only remedy is a life of ceaseless distraction. More and more he resembles, leaves a flood of semen on the faux-leather upholstery. Wednesday is not usually a bad day.

I have nothing to add to this; some sensations simply can't be articulated. There are plans to mix modernity with sheer panic, or at least put a stop to the ceaseless footfall. Your match is a spent match, knee-deep in silt and plasma, thunderstruck.

Not here, not now

In the end, my neurons returned to their customary firing rates. Origin is a recess, or bend.

Her memoir was plagiarized from a stolen transcript: the spectre of the countess was here, I swear, now absent of a sudden. When finally she deigns to speak, I have the feeling she is acutely aware of every dissociated detail.

'Quick, I am relishing this state of neutrality, the dank chalky stratum in which we find ourselves rooted. . . .'

From time to time this organism misbehaves — typically, at an unforeseen moment, it will come to an abrupt halt.

But she is never found at point C and she is never found at point F. A series of coils has been burnt into the wood, according to a centrifugal pattern.

Ectopia

Morbid naming of parts — wandering womb, neural assault — a depression in the face filled with putrescent matter. . . . Steady yourself upon a chalky ridge of land, the gently sloping outburst — wrap around her legs as you slide toward the lower plummet.

Note the absence of metaphor, correspondence: I was unprepared for the apology at the climax. But a great inrush of fluid occurred, yes.

Finding now a place to shelter for the night will be fraught: I tried to break into a log cabin in the dark. The compass is now embedded in my lung. It's known that somewhere in England there is a grave.

On the closing stage of the march, a few furlongs out, came an eerie droning sound from a copse at the edge of the mesa. You have been up there each day since it happened, in a futile quest to root out the lost details.

I have been inseparable ever since the desert.

*

The nearest person to the stun grenade has to volunteer. I am to perform the final act.

There then follows a series of inept feints and touches, whereupon she emerges from the game with her identity bent backwards. I was the only true gambler in the room.

It hath a long bony tail, our primitive avian reptile. In spite of all this the patient is doing fine, aftershock burrowing into the skull, a nerve-like thread conducting impulse.

A paradox, contradiction between two verdicts that are in themselves reasonable. We agree to meet, and a rendezvous is set at an appointed spot (viz. archaeology of a tryst). I waited in disguise at a prearranged bend in time, cursed with the hunter's instinct and cadence.

Say nothing, perfect radio. I observed that nobody present paid any regard to my silence, the most understated salute one could hope for. By this I mean that souls did see and hear, and they did not see and hear.

The incident

The experience is still here and it is affecting, but not as a remembered event: oblivious apprehension rather than comprehension, that will to interpret, to convert all phenomena to interference. The archivist is required to unsettle himself with a whole variety of material simply to guarantee his own survival, submerged forever amid countless things unlost.

She is still credited with having invented the nocturne. (Your hands are old.) She abandoned the maestro and shortly after fell blind in torment — even so, she outlived him by a wilderness or two.

You may well hang your head. She levitates into the air while violently shaking the infant. Her friendship has been described as pneumatic — acid sap compressed in space under pressure — and has not yet won my compass. But there is no visible conflict, as yet; I say this just in case we are ever parted.

When placed beside her, my nerves begin to knot: we have been shackled together since the desert years. The backwash of meaning never stops — a thing whose name one cannot recall, does not know, or does not wish to specify. I was the last person.

*

Whisper sedative of yes. Whisper sedative of no. Taste of another's breath across a pierced tongue. She had the pale blue eyes of a wolf.

I should act upon this circumstance, but can no longer fathom what is to be expected. All day long my orders have been cracked.

We must hold on to the unsustainable for twelve more weeks, after which it is pledged that we fade. I used as an excuse the first object that presented itself to my vision.

My own fractions are counterfeit, built of disparity: still they shape their house of fire.

I cannot tell you what I said to them, murmuring disquiet: bad company, language and the like, crumbs of broken bread. The Greeks called it a spectral hand, the one who stoops to speak. Speculative predictions based on our existence have been rejected.

Outside once more, beside a watercourse — any channel for fluid will do — a line of seed, the sluice.

Note to self, restore angelic upcry.

XXXII

Hers is autographic: battery axe, internal cut with organ-lift to switch room — straight lines meeting and crossing at the edge of a milestone. Apparently, this denotes surprise and unpreparedness.

It was official. Their primitive brains will not notice their comrades falling all around them. Do not in any circumstance fling across. . . . There is the memory of a woman in a powder-blue dress standing at the crest of a hill — cloudless in another country, another century.

I sat up late watching the cracks open wide, all those tiny craters. Come dawn, bands of green light quivered on the ceiling (father, presumably). This area is a self-consuming area.

Halos were beginning to form around the streetlamps. Abnormal matter consists of particles which are the antiparticles of those making up normal matter.

She says I once had.

*

It is rumoured. He is rumoured an abject keeper of time and compulsive maker of lists. This is the chapter of accident, all heads refusing to transfer.

We are redefining our moment. In many places the earth is mottled dark green like oxidized silver. But who should we see enter right now, lurching through the door and into the drawing room?

Where to, if anywhere, next? The whole project collapses. We recede: footprints across the cellar wall and straight up the star well.

To brighten up the party and properly round off this comedy, I continue to write standing up. See, I have a firm basis in reality and have led a consequential and momentous and noteworthy life.

I once possessed a separate and independent existence. I am no longer representing. I have no rank or appointment. I am a re-enactment of past events, vagrant stasis, the impossible solution.

He says you never could get past the beginning of a story. Origin is self-governing (see corporeality). We are about to enter a spectacular sphere of influence.

*

This is what he always wanted, an empty room with glass divider: moth-wing collage on bone fibre glazed in enamel, distant thunder. I am mindful of the silk road.

The vessel is a vessel from which all substance has been pulverized. By this I mean a mental riot in which distillation of doom is the primary symptom.

These words remain unforgotten because they are not strictly present — thistle spirits crackling on a wire — the underknife with nothing too soon, a number of red dragonflies dead on the cill.

As sound waves pass through they are given visible form by the assembled mediums, working in unison as one mind. The contours are distorted, colours abject.

'What is that below? You don't say.'

'I am never your actual no.'

Thus he communicates his strategy as a future war game. We had but little time, reckoning the details of expenditure, the human losses both at home and at the front.

I am meditating on the actor's state of mind in all the various dramatic situations available to a playwright. I have been axed for using language; the chancellor suggested a fine of two thousand crowns. Sometimes a connection between epilepsy and some previous injury to the brain can be established.

An intrusive igneous was typically found (quartz, porphyry). There is no longer a workable compromise, no longer an alignment — there is no longer any guarantee. May I interrogate him first?

We ran a lie-detector test: any number of subatomic particles carrying a fissile isotope are your building blocks. A randomly selected volunteer may, under certain conditions, be added as an afterthought — in this case an organism composed of two genetically ill-matched tissues.

The date of corresponding intensity and direction in the magnetic field is also the date of your object. This may be hung upside down: the fractured jaw, a dashboard of animal skin, the polished walnut box lined with tulip. . . . Impressions in carbon and wax were taken and are gravely compressed, thereby resembling a lagoon. (Picture an optical illusion buried deep in a Neolithic wardrobe.) In contrast to the early mediaevals, this made the first act of creation a concealment, a divine exile rather than unfolding revelation.

'No,' he screams, exasperated now. 'Your mid-zone should be Naples fucking yellow!'

Flakes of ash fall from the sky: throw the possessed objects out of the window into the street — defenestrate, immediately.

'And you were never supposed to touch the blue electrode.'

The machine closes down and then somebody opens it up again.

*

You are sorrow and I have acted most cruel. My thoughts, when I recollect you, would diminish me — the burden of evidence, ballast of indifference. . . . I too have the mourning, fingernails gouged into face, casing smashed.

Her hands firmly locked around his throat, she presses into the jugular with an index finger, the windpipe her thumbs. We found fragments of old porcelain and layers of rotting wallpaper, two greenstone clubs, a ukulele, a tin pipe with six holes, a brace of masks, one toy ocarina (a small egg-shaped) and a packet of wormwood buds — all artefacts historically unknown to this territory. And there was a child's tin drum, with foliage arranged in alphabetical order and sticks to beat.

The principle in operation is that entities are not to be multiplied beyond orgasm: love and loathing ride knuckle to knuckle. Yet I am full of optimism, what with my telepathic complacency — despise everything, there is logic in operation here.

She tastes of liquid copper, a major third closing a piece otherwise sung in minor key. And here comes just the ticket. Imagine someone has placed a sheet of gauze over your eyes, cerecloth.

In the course of this unusual work a bitter remark is needed, an occasion for extravagant gift-giving and auto-destructive property. Antimony has been known from ancient times — the naturally occurring black sulphide was put to work as maquillage. I am reinventing the art of geology.

Initiate: anoint the face, anoint the surviving limb. This action acutely inhibits the firing of neurons.

He anoints his own face. (Equanimity is under suspicion.) Each of two circular stones was used.

We leave.

The wound dresser

Thin amber slash oblique across face. They were looking for a signal that wasn't there.

There is no written record of what happened next, but the tension between the two outposts persists to this day. Just as she was taking the shortcut by the metal bridge over the railway, she heard footsteps behind her.

Frottage has been suggested. Cudgels were engaged during the course of the game, hastening an unconditional surrender: exit by a head. Note how the body in a great wave retreats into itself.

Transcontinental linguistic unity was achieved in less than twenty-four hours, followed by a sudden inversion of night and day. Resume this chain of thought at 'seizing'.

Vanishing perspectives today, beneath thickening shadow. Can we talk, or is communication strictly semaphore? My right of inheritance has been vetoed.

Change everything at the last moment. Tell me about the deluge, tell me about the forks of lightning at the rim of the earth: evaporate, be forgotten — cut your hand with the knife, compose your own lifelines.

After all this, he was surprised to discover that the other man had no method at all, none at all.

*

An *x* is missing from his name; I reckon him to exist from the outside up. The wound begins to suppurate after a day or so, a weeping friction burn. (What is in a name?) He claims he wrote the composition from scraps found on the library floor.

This is called a cento. We do not hesitate to claim as our origin certain fundamental intuitions. First we do the Anglosaxons: there will be mosaic pavements and gas-lamps, war machines and so forth.

broad kingdom

in hand passed

he held it firm

fifty winters et cetera

They may, almost, with a forlorn sigh of nostalgia. Some elements have only the one stable isotope.

*

She dreams of being drawn backwards through a dazzling white passage, a helix that resembles a gigantic drill. The man-eating tiger is not happy being photographed and pads nervously about the restaurant among the diners.

Somehow she had induced her animal familiar to miraculously deliver, through the sealed edge of my laboratory door, a writ contained in an envelope of facial tissue. The exotic names therein connect us to all the broken places.

'The hermetic urban man has been poured into a technological abyss at the point of a legionnaire's spear! We are second in excellence, next-door's bricolage!'

He dreams he is an engineer trapped in an egg timer, imprisoned by unbreakable glass. Suddenly his beak splits open, feathers fly, and it is exactly one hundred years later.

Did he tell you of this transformation in the flesh?

I could not distinguish clearly what he said — something about extinction by bacteriological trade war, bonemeal salad, a plastic astronaut tipping over the edge. . . .

Those exiles at the beachside café have just fled from a suicide pandemic. (What year is it?) O yes, and no matter how I tried, I could not get back inside the crate.

I hadn't realized that you did not know, could never have known. Today's shibboleth is silence. One of the insects in my collection is related to the wasp and cuts into plant tissue with a sawlike ovum tube before depositing its eggs.

> Of a dye, not needing a mordant

This denotes a sudden transfiguration of mind, static charge at work again — a sea change — pressing on for more despite the stockpile of stolen goods. Evidently he thinks I am somebody else I am not.

Such opulent possibilities, but injustice is real enough in the hearts of men. And here comes another soul, turning the emptiness of space across a sheet of paper. I am incapable of believing in the future of my regrets.

Her heart is arrhythmic. He is excess residue — sheer volume, cubic measure — a *compass*. She craves detail; he longs for an exit stratagem. The bear meat tastes good, but it's still fucking cold, despite the impromptu cremation.

The results of a lie-detector test are generally not accepted for judicial purposes. Compare with polygraph.

*

Observe how an existence cannot be shared as it unravels. He actually said this one day, apropos of nothing, the crewman with rotary teeth, as beads of molten gold cascaded from the ship's prow. . . . A tympanum is a big triangle, a recessed space at the centre of everything. . . . The day was blinding as we peered out from the vacuum under the stairs, and our comrades pointed the way to victory. . . .

I'm reminded of Trieste, years back in that obscure film, the star-crossed Istrian sky. It seems, above all, that we have neglected many of these critical apertures. For a moment this thought consumes me — it is upon such ebbing ground that I waited for her.

Don't understand me. I did not lightly take the leap from that bridge, singing shall I, shan't I.

I think a rubber stamp might be worth fabricating, a portable signature, yes.

She lies with dorsal aspect facing upward (compare with suicide). Her element is used in alloys, often with lead, sometimes tin: pewter, type metal, Britannia. . . . Against my will I was fashioned into a form, never amended.

What is the function of *that* noise? she said pointing. She is hanging out the window now: 'breathes there a man with soul so dead, who never to himself has said' et cetera.

Some scholars believe this to be an obscure reference to the chemical of atom fifty-one, a brittle semi-sentient. The neural adverb is here, mercifully, here now and waiting.

If she were a spiral shell, she would turn in the required manner, globewise, spinning madly from pole to pole. But the closest one can get has more the meaning of 'hurtle'.

They have found each other. They did not know.

In the same year, a system of classification based on division into numbered classes had to be invented. This was the so-called death time, an unattainable evening.

I was born temporary.

*

Knife grinder with oil on canvas. She stations herself every day in the turret to paint.

About the circumference of a circle, the text reads it's a fluke. Do you ever have the feeling that you have gone too far this time?

Three things are necessary to render the defendant's anatomy acceptable: a movement is to be performed, a somewhat slow moment, the very last instant — inertia.

'Stay away a few years longer, save yourself.'

Somewhat slow, but not so slow as I.

Intermittent spoor of used face, bruised torso, swollen jaw. These are the subjects here — thunderbolt, plummet, scourge and others of that genre — all culled from a mediaeval medical treatise.

The current was reversed and expelled through a column of plasma. Typically, this produces almost no electric charge at low pressures (earth's upper atmosphere, fluorescent lamps) or at very high temperatures (stars, nuclear fusion reactors). The following weekend we evacuated and dynamited the laboratory from a safe distance after detecting mobile charged particles that appear to behave like electrons in condemned salt. A bright green ray refracted through a translucent variety of quartz was set aside for a different purpose on another day. A specimen of your own colourless material approximates the undead part.

Piss Rorschach, spoon carp syndicate — molten lead with mosaic sediment, gruel-like mortar coursing through a wooden conduit — the surfeit yet unfinished sac, gobbets of frozen snot on the pavement, the page. . . . And the elder says of the younger, forgive him, he is a budding mechanic of the unsaid.

Then a very small humanoid creature was lowered onto the stage by a mechanical device fashioned from the frenulum of a dog's tongue. I could hardly breathe, which explains why.

I had no yen to hunger. This is the same conversation time upon time, night within day.

I've got places to go,
I have made up my mind
and I've got to let you know
let you know, let you know know know.

Tannis root was an ingredient used for centuries by witches in their shopping spells and ritual. Suddenly the window caved in, crushing his legs — now the body lies broken within a chalk silhouette. Outside, I could hear the beating of giant wings.

An act of possession is evident in this chain of events, a sequential psychic exchange — camouflage, in as many words: a want of shelter, 'unheavened beneath the blasted firmament'.

Origin is a head with the skull standing on end.

*

Overpriced anatomy, a condition in which the heart is suspended outside of the ribcage. In the next half hour, should you need any replica spores, speak to him. [*Pointing.*] He's your man. We are calling this planet nine, until some other arrangement can be made.

Tin cans are scattered by the wind in the street below. Inanimate matter holds a mnemonic charge. Wires trailing from a car battery are attached to various apertures of the body under study.

Inquisitor: I suggest that you were alone in that cell for untold years, contriving a solution to some perplexity within the plot.

A machine to determine whether a person is telling the truth, by detecting the changes in pulse and breathing associated with lying, is then wheeled onto the stage. By multiplying the number of husbands, convincing comic effects may be achieved.

This man has no trouble keeping mouth (it's rumoured he actually volunteered for questioning). Behind him flashes a handwritten neon legend that reads *I helped unsnarl her muddled veins.*

That day I cast no shadow. It was September, one among several.

No signal. That's two less bodies to account for. It is only a matter of time before someone starts complaining about the corpse under the kitchen table. The older tune is an adaptation.

Night falls and they wait in silence for the attack that never comes. (It's too quiet, I don't like it et cetera.) Despite these facts, of continuing to look down upon the earth from a great height there is no end.

A sudden enclosed space, perhaps this very corner of time or somewhere mighty similar. Origin denotes a lead-grey mineral or striated prismatic crystal. It is difficult not to remember.

*

We thought we were earthbound. The remaining superheroes had become obsessively paranoid, less human. But I have grown accustomed to these hungry nomads, forever at home in the elsewhere.

Origin is a shorthand form of 'Look!'.

The foundations of the bunker were the cellars of a haunted seventeenth-century manor house. Survivors fell through a portal and landed in a heap on the roof.

One man said he had to discover whether he could endure a single night alone, when suddenly he was snared by a hook at the end of a chain and hauled toward the ceiling. Since then it has been observed that he drags himself about like some polyamorous cadaver.

People are turning to stone. The only concession I dared beg of the overseer was to stop the fugitives being punished further.

The lost underpieces

A network of nerves and scintillas of light became enmeshed inside the body. At a prearranged signal, the blinding took place. One repercussion was the emergence of a deviant group of ancestors.

All the letters have been deranged in sequence. Nothing specific regarding the texture of background noise suggests itself. I have the sense of something muted yet persistent, repetitive and barely audible, the hum of exiled DNA. The freezer is crammed full of bloodpecked muzzles, rhesus macaques.

Hypnotic, these moribund white nights, struggling northbound, all Brit-safe and shapeshift. But this needs more work: his heart is in the wrong place.

We were beyond salvage. It is now a question of methodically placing all the numbers in their correct order — objects have begun to levitate and ricochet about the room. If we all stick together, life gets cheaper.

The series now runs A plus D and/or F, augmented by a row of bristles that quiver at the edge of the hindwing.

Idea for a novel: the search for a lost painting.

*

However, she would not change *how* she expressed her accusation, just kept repeating it in the same way, over and over.

Thanks for the message you abandoned: delete me from your insipid core et cetera — though I still sense bad blood, an undertone of duress. (Learn to run from *what* exactly?) We should secure our territories elsewhere: there comes a time, lover, when one has had one's fill of memory.

What we see as luminous we do not see as grey. Examples include concussion subs and other feuding vessels.

As we waited on the platform, she explained the distinction between the two types of Yes: one was used exclusively in the context of negative assumptions, such as the ritual cleansing of a siege latrine, the other was not. Someone should be willing to produce a colour chart showing the transition between these two affirmations.

Ash litany, from our ember days

Still he distrusts the glimpse. Space around here was once Church Slavonic.

The correct number is eleven, or twelve; it's a terribly long way back. The catalogue boasts a variety of abducted organs — we have never seen an infestation quite like this. Origin is another place.

A resit was demanded. We are secreting today, most volatile. I could only fix the following fragments.

*

I want to stop here. One should never overreach.

Everything you say is characterized by the absence rather than the presence of distinguishing features — expresses negation — shows light and shade and colours reversed from those of the original. This denotes the earth or water signs, an individual orbited by bad faith.

In short, less than zero. I think the best course of action is to find out and do nothing.

We are back on the road, a film of rust across every tongue. You know the rules: we make it happen, you watch the heist unfold and then photograph the wreckage. But I can only receive voice, never transmit (viz. emergency situation). Why not storm the flanks with the full arsenal at our disposal: the electromagnetic pulse bomb, a nanosecond impact ten times faster than a lightning bolt et cetera.

Point 6 is unforeseeable ground. I snatched a few postcards from the rotating wheel, to preserve a handful for future generations.

Sound has a curvature, waves of compression in an elastic medium such as air. Nervous tissue density is dissolving. I hummed the tune once more, in a desperate attempt to convince the nightwatch to let us pass.

Origin has grown thin, become rare. No one can recall a single stretch of time.

This was followed by a prolonged absence of the thing specified. But today is special (think vacuum). I have our instructions: reassemble, then convulse.

We are drawing closer: insomnia, night sweats, numbness at surface of limbs, panic under self-assault. . . . In the morning he wakes to find a detective inspector at the foot of his bed. Hurriedly he dresses. Together they drive to the outskirts of town, where the suspect's likeness is painted on the billboard which a helicopter is lifting into the sky above the multitude.

In response, he has dreamt up another of his unstoppable lists: the liver of an ox, kidneys skating in molten lard, cleft monkey brains on a salver like the baptist head. . . .

Inquisitor: You've had your eyes burnished, have you not?

Splinters fly at the impact of a bone chisel. Another brain sample is taken using an apple corer.

Suspect: We are a group of three, the only underground resistance on a penal satellite infested by hostile species. . . . Volunteers are being processed into fertilizer on an industrial scale. . . . Fever of neglect as the endless chain of time drags on. . . .

I mislaid trust a full seven years ago, lost forever in the cranial vault.

Naevus faction

An ill-fated attempt was made to establish a bridgehead, a position secured by an army inside enemy territory from which to advance or attack. The symmetry locked in with the appearance of an undiscovered constellation, an evidence cluster in the night sky, forensic architecture: I belong to you and you belong to me.

At that point she leant forward, her face close to mine, and said that word *cluster*, I cannot bear it: I'm a trypophobe, the sight of any irregular pattern — a nest of tiny holes or nodules — horrifies me.

There was a conspiracy. I got nought percent. Origin is a shape.

Since that time, I have experienced innumerable further moments. Corrosive subdivision is betrayed here, for example, her fingers pursuing a feudal point.

Background of urban Victorian noise, the crack of a whip, costermonger bawl, horses hooves sparking at the oily cobble. The mechanism has jammed. His carcass was skinned and the leavings dumped in a skip.

We are an amateur interest — divertissement, a sideline. Observe a likeness, spittle running from the mouth, snot the nostrils: find a new word to replace your own name, whichever sound emerges first. Observe extensive use of clicks and glottal stops, audible release of the airstream after complete closure of the glottis.

At about this time I succeeded the apostolic see, my predecessor having withered loose, viscera outed in the passing street. Errors are only avoidable among the unexceptional.

All affected beasts were destroyed, consistent with sanity. I am putting you in possession of all I know.

Before his untimely departure, he received my final telegraphic letter.

How meteoric are these people. We are nominated. If I stay, who goes? If I go, who stays? I am flagging. This is an empty sack. Indeed. Events are governed by the particular fall of the light at any given moment.

Communal defecation

Please have your kidneys ready for inspection at the roadblock. . . . The stone was removed by the Protector's master surgeon, who then spoke in his own defence.

Hurry, one who suffers the condition has arrived with only seconds to live — that said, she does look grotesquely reassuring. (Note the number four again!) An alloy of lead, tin and antimony was used for casting type, for the briefest of moments.

Extinct Early Warning is the title of the movement's in-house magazine and radar system. . . . Now my name is unbecome — and I traced her footsteps in the snow, the fibres of bloody sputum.

Talk to us.

Well, they marched through the streets. Each year they collided with the first rain, after an arid season spent wandering across depopulated wasteland. Only three of our lunar cycles have been accounted for.

A poison is distilled and absorbed into the dry fissured earth.

'I know you are close, just do what you do. . . .'

There must be a simpler way of documenting all this: red shift, blue shift, crushed waves of light, displacement of spectral lines. . . . The mineral bureau has discovered it could not be dead vegetation causing the stench, and what of those mysterious droplets of quicksilver that have appeared on the pavements of our city?

Abscission layer

I am disturbed by anything that resembles talk, the detachment of parts. The island fell and, as foretold, our pilgrims perished in a storm at sea. Wherefore I advise: go to the wicket gate yonder, slip through and over the plain until you come to a hill — climb the path and find what stands inside the head stationed at the summit.

We befriended each other while circumnavigating a frozen lake. One tribe migrated to the north. I am never going back: *ekstasis* is removal from an intended place, standing outside of oneself.

Rising tang of rainfall on parched ground, tendrils of glandular hair — fibrous tissue enclosing organ or muscle —fascia of dried grass, the bungled axe. . . . This is the same idea as the above, following you around.

It seems that I, at least, am off the hook for the time being (rotten, as was).

*

This account is set in a future where dissidents are sentenced to work in penal colonies on the moon. Everything is made of a malleable greyish-yellow paste composed of ground chalk and linseed oil. Giant insects patrol the streets. This is why we hear dissonance as essentially harrowing, an undervoice that simultaneously occupies two positions in the curvature of space-time.

Most of the above was reckoned by eye. Attempts at communication with people who are negotiating a deal with death is the new narrative. Origin is the 1840s, punningly, from the hobby falcon logo on all our products.

It was like staring into an abyss of my own making: thousands of people claimed in Compostela the excess.

I do not see the number four, only its neighbour, five. Still I press on as best I can, scouting around the rim of the skull. The volunteer who had the most convincing excuse for silence nonetheless remains unforgiven — I begged for compassion, love and spleen being two sides of the same catastrophe.

The exegesis is all in your head. Let us assume this is your head.

Grief was only punctuated by the odd epiphany. My story contradicted my own testimony — the penalty was death by being sewn into a sack and ignored.

The point is this: a game of chance played by betting on the uncertain order of events and appearances. Slowly over time the ink fades, until we find ourselves clutching at blank sheets of paper. He deselects, abandons form, vows never to write another coherent word.

I instructed my letterman to make the image of the head by marshalling thousands of minute glyphs (memory pins, if you will). Uncertain reminiscence includes the communal oven, animal sinew wound about an elm at the top of the lane, a creosote alley baking in the heat, rank straw on the floor of a kennel: ghost of rain.

Are you at all enthusiastic about these revelations? One day my neighbour was viciously attacked by lightning in the guise of fog.

*

Bounding canine, stench of blackened piss, a drawn down constellation — bare limbs thrashed by nettle or thorn — a crude passageway, planked conduit set down between impassable routes.

It was language; I'm next. But I never accepted such a covenant: this island, across a channel with its abandoned ports, only navigable by improvised raft. . . . The main fault was deregulation, amateur exorcists on a minimum wage: riptide.

The head is dispossessed. She once visited me in a hotel room. Nothing happened.

The head is crammed full and renamed the seventh circle: the violent, the monitor reptile, the first and last round, the uncensored self. Origin turns in separate ways.

The head is condemned; anatomy isn't interpretation. My centre is pounded out.

She is risk. See what happens (perhaps from 'pharaoh'). Cause is unknown and hence deserted, your history unspoke.

*

This is the place where we assembled for our descent, a place every eye would shun. We slid down on borrowed trays, a makeshift entertainment. Why don't you pause for a few moments to think about that.

Our passage is postponed — if it fractures, let it fracture: outwaste, mucus sheath of liver, the forked path that leads toward every lung. . . . We were none of us hang-on specialists.

That preamble went on too long, but circumstances could still open up for us here today. I imagine somewhere might happen, soon.

She waits for an event to break the silence. An *i* is still missing; this is not officially recognized as a mental disorder, but may be diagnosed as a phobia if excessive fear and distress are manifest. Her surface cools too rapidly and is in danger of splitting — if so, she won't live to witness the residue.

The battle, its indecision

The aorta in humans passes over the heart from the left ventricle and runs down in front of the backbone.

A moaning sound, repetition. We should retreat.

Hence the saying, one may know how to conquer without being able to do so. To struggle across, a passage must be cut.

Form bending over him. (That's enough.) He throws out his arms — the goal will surely evaporate.

We glimpsed movement beneath the surface of the ice, where movement was impossible. I want to go to a place where we can get shot of this workaday possession.

I remember he began by making a rough sketch of a divining rod on a scrap of paper. The following day we set off in search of anything invisible, closely observing the motion of a forked stick. Depending on the lunar cycle, he might use a pair of bent copper wires, or observe the changes in direction of a pendulum in response to unseen influence. He dowsed a spiral of energy under a stone. That night, a great conjunction of Jupiter and Saturn took place, the first in four hundred years. It augured.

One rib is set far lower than the other, an aperture disconnects at the top. Two sheets of space collide at the gentle curvature of a line: perfect cleavage. The laminae are flexing and elastic — we refer here to a thin layer of sedimentary rock or organic tissue.

For many years his compositions were regarded with fanatical admiration by a handful of disciples, and equal scorn by a much larger cohort of magicians.

'I suppose it was never your desire that we should now confront you in this semblance.'

At this he felt an inexplicable fear in noticing that the room was a perfect square, including the temperature of the walls.

*

Above, move and isolate the neutral.

'You can't do that.'

'I did it.'

'But you hooked your own legs up.'

Why did you do that when I was already walking, had already made up my mind to walk away? Origin is stuck together.

She is back in service: potent, counterpotent. Vanilla and vagina share the same etymology.

Her name is a made-up name, whereas an elm is a tall deciduous tree which typically has rough serrated leaves and propagates from root suckers. My luminosity doesn't come into it.

From the viewing platform we could see the earth from a great height, incessant movement across the surface of the planet, your redundant product. There is no substitute for glass, perfectly terminated crystals.

The third partition

Local name of sarsen. The corridor suddenly aged. An elaborate kite is being constructed in the attic. Given time, we could talk a little more about that.

Mentalists such as these create a montage that juxtaposes events and objects culled from separate places at separate times.

He calls to return the borrowed carbon and finds her weeping at the kitchen table; there is an unmistakeable trace hereabouts. And then he says, has all the stillness and silence in the world embarked upon our heads?

File under dietary abstinence, a season of fast. (It is somebody else's turn.) All the seats have restricted sensibility.

Adopt the version who came earlier — I thought it would be amusing for us to operate on the same level for once.

So, he has a plan.

These objects together form the prototype of a rapidly spinning neutron star. We find ourselves once more on the infamous dicing terrace. He says there is something here that was not here before: not dead, yet no longer living. Your market has witnessed.

This must be one of those hermetic sites she keeps talking about, the platform upon which every moment that has passed coexists: raving madness versus melancholy madness — Bishopsgate, Moorfields, Lambeth Marsh — underplayed ghosts of refracted light, snared in the iris.

In fact, this is not necessarily the case; there is a vast amount of the solar system that I have never looked at.

And again, she: what will you do when a real war comes?

Origin is the nineteen sixties. See rhesus factor.

*

Not quite so legendary, still legend enough. Up a narrow side street an ancient campanile survives, red brick of scorched adobe clay.

A tube of flesh with quivering tendrils is slit down the middle, opened flat and nailed to the floor. The lentiform is the lower of two grey nuclei of the corpus striatum, part of the basal ganglia of the brain.

We were preparing to dig a trench when it happened. Later, at the very margin of the land, I realized what was missing.

We arrive in bitter shapes. There is no alternative, yet she is rapt by the intricacy of her abjection, the capacity to self-oppress. You know her, everybody knows her, but there seems to be little neural damage, sinews crossed.

I was finally tracked down to a sunless netherworld, scavenging around the ancestral orbit.

XXXIII

Misdoubt

Dark columns in fugue, intersecting spindles of light. The art of disrupting a unique pictorial event has begun.

Birdlife clinging to an old man in the square. Saints fly down; I have made up my own mind. You have the sack with the meat raffle and the dice.

Image capture utilizes mercury and silver iodine. The fact that there is red ink in the well and the packet contains a rose-coloured seed is reassuring. A selection of thumbnails will now retell the tale.

I could find no symbols in the body of work; the last time I looked it was made of words. All my letters have given up.

*

Our entire family has been decommissioned, a tribe crammed full with coincidence. The crew did not see the iceberg until it was too late. Of all the rumours in the building, this is the one.

Back then everything was so tragic and yet so simple. What makes the adventure noteworthy is the way it is being constructed from moment to moment in an impromptu fashion (the rust talks to you, you don't talk to it). There was a sudden burst of compressed air inside the ear, nothing at all between thumb and index.

Her characters materialize from silhouettes, space archaeology: the surface cracks, the land splits open to expose a chalky outcrop, cliffs of blue scree. She carves these shapes out of herself.

The instructions read bring a picnic, bring facial tissue, a vial of battery acid — measure the critical distance in shoals of fish — perform a significant interruption.

I woke up three hours later. She was playing a tam-tam made of crow skin, clawing at her hair, tearing off her shawl — desperate to sustain motion, any substitute for doing nothing. Abruptly she comes to a halt and says your feathers must be caressed back to face the right direction, any direction.

Everyone knew something. I felt so ill I took to my bed and never looked back.

*

What about some authorship, panic-stricken for the human voice? We now have a full contingent of bodies. Every night I am subjected to an electric current passing between the two cells on either side of my own.

Nobody will actually speak. As I get older, the logic of suicide makes more and more sense. The sole of her foot pressed against mine.

Folk have become wary of placement.

They bark and howl, surrounding. I wrapped myself in a damp blanket while above my head the sky tilted at an impossible angle. One wall is glass brick, through which streams a dazzling white light. There is a new kind of etiquette on track, the skew and flex of happenstance.

She writes to say that she sits overlooking. Between her and the sea is an ancient pine forest — the sun strikes the surface of the water like a damnation.

He is looking at the same surface. This is where our classification lies, exposed to a copper plate.

There is always a slight alarm when I perform this next act. Let us move along a bit, set to the music of an occasional guess.

In the parlour he observed the cogs of a spinning wheel, the clack of a machine busy sewing up a torn face. I stop and wait. Inside me is this metronome.

You can choose from any one of these situations: go forth and build thrice a dwelling as this, and so on.

*

Our chief component is a benzine ring with attacked carbon. I had to work around her. Atoms offer the same old ultimatum.

The rasping clarinets shift in and out of focus. (I knew there was something.) I found a big stone and a new kind of metal we had never heard before, its outline shimmering with a silver gleam. She says everything and nothing is formulaic. In another version a giant descends from the sky, arms laden with literally Persian apples.

After the deluge, random information will emerge at first. Above all, it's vital to remember there is a stricture binding your heart.

Keep it simple. Citizens were snared in a relentless cycle of distraction and self-regard, an undeserved attention to the minutiae of their banal and unproductive lives. It was quite a serious situation. It was their fence. It was a good job no one got killed.

No, no, no. (Why persist?)

Extend this idea to your ancestors, every last one. I have established an arc between the two electrodes, anything for the sake of fidelity. The liver has become quite warm.

And that's about it: his life was an inexact discipline.

Discourse invariably arrives at the neutral. The time is the time just before he went blind at the age of eight. My politics are never.

As it happens, he is not fit to make utterance today. The brain was removed and the inside of the skull scoured clean of flesh. Nothing mourns me.

Behind the icehouse was found an enormous muscular tube lined with mucous membrane that once connected the throat to the stomach. It had been there all along, and appears to regenerate itself.

There are the humans and there are the other vertebrates, but the pivotal idea is to cultivate memory. You must get bored doing something all the time.

Genes are irresponsible and a concrete roadblock was lowered into place by a crane — I have explained this to you, so you should be able to understand. I was solitary back then and did not heed the swing of the pendulum.

When a dead person is mentioned, the patient will sometimes exhibit uncontrollable grief. I will now awaken the homestead, luring it back to a state of disinterested being.

*

A salty deposit is accumulating at the interstices. Nothing is my fault.

We cannot be sure, without further investigation, that the gift of prophecy would always follow this pattern. Comparisons are off-putting.

An organ of soft nervous tissue sloshes about in its cradle of bone, precariously supported at the rim by a corona of metal antennae. Elected sniper for the day, I fetch a crossbow.

Origin is doubtless film. An economy collapsed.

'Bring asphodel!' the Lord screamed.

I began with my own unfathomable attraction to certain words. Anyone can reveal everything that is to pass in the future by studying the subject's physiognomy.

Several bystanders were persuaded to donate their organs, behaviour deemed refreshingly messianic. The sought-after herb has blanched flowers fed through a coiled rhizomic interface. Others have cleft palates and a solitary row of teeth.

Stand-to, doorkeeper, up against the wall — you cannot be the same person. . . . They were also planning to liquidate me at about that moment in time. The word is not a continuous path but a sequence of interconnected dots.

This account has appeared under a number of rubrics.

I am relating events as they unfold, am changing nothing (the razor blade, a bathtub). There is an old-fashioned light at the end. We were wading against the tide.

Just get this eulogy over with, please. Place your head back on your shoulders.

There were two solutions: the untimely forefather or a bitter wind blowing off the sea. The piece of furniture I chose was the bed, because there were no life forms anywhere near it.

We are situated in the panic room of a sealed argument. Scale is based on the night sky.

*

Landscape with twisted river mouth. Where is your fluorescence now?

The given number is seven and the tail end has broken off, the piece called a coda. He drags the tracker outside and slams the door shut.

They had used a garrotte made of barbed wire at the log cabin in the forest. The man's flesh is set to burst.

I have learnt this evening where all the rejected mail ends up.

I spell out entire sentences on the roof of my mouth with my tongue, where no one can read them. The head already has our name, our species. He is probably touching, snout to earth as we speak — I warned you we were close.

Now we are going to crouch on the ground for several days and wait. He is tied up and then silence; only a few survivors from his column remain. Time is always like that with me, the stony path at the turn.

*

The image is mirrored to twist her yearning face toward camera; there is no consoling spirit for her to lean upon today. The chairs are from elsewhere.

I went unsummoned, from a base meaning augur. (Pass me the drip tray.) Not one of the ants fell off the stick.

These days, his lips are much the time glued to her cunt. Day here means state.

Shadows less sharp — press on to the summit, edge that little bit closer. Far below, the boy holds a pebble and a feather and a fossiled thing from the years — pupils dilated, scattered teeth on the beach, male and female. He does not even turn around to look.

That's it, think of yourselves.

*

I was doubt personified. I withheld. Across the temple wall stretched parallel rows of cuneiform inscription. Outside, puddles of mercury, dazzling sunlight behind the crane, isolated clouds.

Now here comes the big vegetable me, balanced between two plagues. I am not here next week, or the week after (poverty of mimesis et cetera). We are deeply in love, yet still this struggle: pathos and defiance, who have followed me about all my life.

Note how he has reduced memory to an uninhabited form. The chosen shape is a pyramid atop a column with lateral slit, waves crashing beyond the harbour. Then there was a spell of monotheism, but only for a couple of days; I am too expensive.

There was nothing to watch over, in spite of expectations to the contrary: the territory originally expressed is not. He would never dream of exploiting me to his own advantage, his own language.

They withdrew the sedatives, I had figured out how many it would take to discontinue myself. The regime has sleeper agents all over the peninsular.

One soldier moved to the rear of the vehicle to empty his bladder. This is a series of observations of how things are. Now we foresee a collision.

'O, look children quick, he's down on his hands and knee, admittedly. . . .'

This grants us a little more inflexibility and a hint of what's to come. The following is what I made note of today, just by stepping outside the door: odour of fish glue and floor polish, gimlets of strained light, impoverished flesh. He says he will never forget watching her body turn blue through a lack of oxygen.

Carceri d'Invenzioni

The dramatically altered scale of the engravings adds to the buildings' grandeur, a series of imagined and fantastical prisons. The interior was a vast human treadmill; orientation in space is a linguistic strategy.

He outpersonates. When we were growing up, he was the only one who could become truly phosphorescent.

You speak an estimate of my life. Origin is a stabbing blow.

Another tense expresses the simple past, with no guarantee of continuance. We tried to reinvent this place once before: you took the lift from the top floor, hurtling down to the molten core of the earth.

The other points and laughs for ten minutes straight. For him, this is a matter of philosophy conjured in the dungeon-cum-laboratory, shapeshifting every form, all night long bent double over his crucibles.

The cache included Browning automatic rifles, gas canisters, bombsights, ninety-millimetre anti-aircraft gun directors and three hundred and forty-five thousand units of the thirty-calibre M1 carbine rifle. On this occasion he has been permitted to keep some of his finds —

the alien fossil, miscellaneous off-planet relics. Critical economic policy files have been reduced to punchcards.

This is endless. What if we agree to call this particular segment mythopoeia.

I think he always longed. My father was found; I kept vigil and never slept. Logos was stamped on most of the products.

*

Grains of glass, splinters of mirror, a silvering — what's called the tain, a fine tinplate. I do not remember what happened to us next.

This makes her sound like a revenant: shed scales underfoot, the crunch of volcanic ash behind the vestry door. She recoiled a step or two as the stranger advanced and clutched my arm in silence.

Now I stand alone, rocking my head backwards and forwards; clearly structure is collapsing at the subatomic level. I think she may be vulnerable to one or two of your integral parts, the refracted light. We may never hear from her again.

It was the longest disturbance — I once fell straight through to the basement. Today sees a new domestic blowtorch on the market.

He rejects this uncompromising scene (my original 'unpromising' now seems preferable). All present concluded that through the indissoluble union of clay with bone, a human protagonist could not fail to result.

So much for anatomy: nerves of septum and larynx, hard palate — persistent ringing in the ear, screams in discord.

'We are signalled,' he says, 'there was only one survivor, two dead and a droid smashed beyond recognition.'

I was appointed assassin. Film is again.

'Why are you scrambling me? Any white flower will do.'

'This is no armistice [*trembling with anger*] — it is a capitulation.'

A sigil is a painted symbol considered to have magical power, here denoting three bones of the tarsus, or ankle.

By Morse code this was communicated, tapped out with a metal object against the wastepipe. Silhouettes of ibis, cobra and jackal are tattooed across his shoulders. Do you not remember?

*

Study for acid etch, shadows of blue wine accented with guano of seabird and bat. The scene depicts a peasant heaving on a rope, another man with a Phrygian cap up a ladder, and a lady at the top of the house, arms out the window — as if to say where have you become, when have you become — still singing that song about how weary she is, how tired she is of wanting.

Another insists on total concealment. He hacks off a branch laden with spores, goading my first objection. At that instant he said 'I' for the first time.

I moved as if in a trance, revealing myself as a rather workaday supreme being. It would compromise my task to feel close to you, even for a moment.

'Do you know precisely where we are on the map, landgrave?'

I do not know what it means to be supervised, governed. Strictly speaking, you cannot be anatomy if you are dead.

Concrete things steadily multiplied, at the cost of Volunteer 9. I will never forget the day the lost patrol came back: for hours we sat transfixed and watched them scrambling in the dust, savagely clawing at raw flesh. And that background hum is still there, still vibrating inside every skull, every second.

On such frosty nights we would gather around a blazing Cortina, as in the old, fingering the keys. I am a big fan of the historic present. This control group is not technically psychotic, you understand.

The bloody drill bit was found miles away. There exists a memorial that repeatedly floods, having been situated too close to the river, a corridor with pinpricks of light.

I stole the image, every word. No one dare touch anything that resembled the original.

She is understate, past care. She is lost current.

Leave the pebbles here, leave them be.

Unorchestrate

Such velocity. He guesses a path through the forest. By contrast, I exist piecemeal and nothing interests me.

He appears to have died twice and has now been shunted to the outer beacon. A reversal is taking place, a surfeit of eyes.

'You are cursed.'

'Which of these men is our postilion?'

Clusters of sharp spikes were set at intervals along the spine.

Slow torches gutter in the dark. I am sometimes associated with customer.

We remember that evening very clearly, as if it were happening now. To this day I remain convinced that she is still alive under the fragile earth of the backyard.

I write. I think this scattering can work. When it becomes blue outside, it is very blue.

Origin is kept awake.

*

I am sorry about earlier, the murmurs. Everyone seems to have been realized except me. Metal oxidizes in the air (recall your insurrection spent out in the rain). I am just testing.

In this version, an account of a far earlier seance, we begin to seek evidence of memory. My existence has been punctuated by a sequence of immaterial speech acts, but by composing this list the words given voice start to become more concrete, more than a series of scapeghosts.

Piper down in the street, aeolian, insisting upon the immediate. Origin is an edge, undisclosed.

Funeral tomorrow. He telegraphs a scant reply: long way back — wrong passageway — please forgive. . . . They gave him six to eight to live, our trooper with the insensible orders. The opposing side's polygonal fortress has been made vulnerable by our weakening of its foundations, undercut by glacial action.

We are probing a wound, enquiring. I am here denoting a person or thing that performs a specified action or activity, such as extinguisher. I am here denoting a person or thing that has a specified attribute or form.

She writes back.

Give me Balkan snipers over this fucking inertia any day of the week.

Which path, I plead. (My words were vague.)

The body and organs of the androgyne were central to the ritual work of ancient civilisations. Without warning, a bystander said I personify that benediction which the eclipsing curve of birth cannot quench.

Origin is to know again.

Ever the dissident, he chose the number seven, which signifies an emerald table. The less complicated option is infinity, superlunary harmonics et cetera.

The planchette scratched a series of marks across the surface of a metal plate. Only then could I reconstruct precisely the method by which the diamond had been abstracted.

He is clearly new to this job. In the adjoining room our lover lies paralysed in a coma.

She refused. They tried hypnosis: she knew God as a hidden and at the same time supra-personal erection.

He insists. Still she refuses.

I can no longer breathe the same air as they breathe. What object is that levitating between us and the flint steeple of the church? The eyes also had to be removed: you have hidden them in a special place, where nobody will ever find them.

Distant thud of untimely brickbats. Now for today's challenge.

Two pieces of music were found to be interstitial. I have just been walking along the seafront and am now totally blind.

The other insists on dust particles. The correct answer is the aerosphere, an invisible gaseous envelope surrounding the earth.

A ninth letter of the Greek alphabet has been transliterated: a thin weblike veil extends from the edge of the cap to the stalk.

*

I had to prove. I had to prove I was my only mother's son. The defeated army has fled to a wilderness in the north.

This unforeseen and tragic tale compels him to scream again and again on the forced march back into the territory. Origin is disobliged.

'Her father invented a new kind of pipe. He had all these windows. . . .'

How perplexing it is to see people crawling around along the esplanade, rending their clothes and wailing. That same day I found a stone in the shape of someone's vagina and a used tissue that was the doppelgänger of a well-known science fiction mystic.

Shard heap in desert, blockage at left lung, acute pain accompanied by voiceless alveolar stops, shorthand radio. They had torn out his tongue and sheared off his left hand, the more useful of the two. It was feudal. If the alembic shatters, his blood will spread across the floor and you will not have anything left to bargain with. Consequently, there are two persons in him: the person assuming and the person assumed.

Dull ache beneath ribcage. Hour upon hour the ration of air, inhaled beyond certainty. The centre has dropped out. If only we can find the long walk, I shall deliver the reading from memory and express my ingratitude to all present.

The position of a pin on the map indicates the military outpost you must journey to. Wait for me there.

Things happen, don't they? The mechanism you have been armed with is more a vessel for capturing and storing. One of the life forms has a spring-loaded retina. Blood is the obvious.

Your own job is the apparent undone. We must burrow down into the lost years, see if they translate into anything useful at the skeletal level.

She is famous for becoming a victim who can adopt a multitude of shapes, infinite patterns of torment. We are now waiting at the brink of a pit — no shilly-shallying before extinction — are about to be torn apart, dragged across hot coals. Speech is being sharpened.

I love this place. Origin is a dead ringer. No better authority could be imagined for a hungry ghost.

He is attempting to hawk a used anecdote. The remaining branches are decaying.

Coptic is also extinct, she says. Who could be better suited than I to set the public record straight.

'So what's your plan?'

The advertisement contained several of the symbols essential for survival, a species of hoax.

'Child, child, I am counterfeiting myself!'

A tunnel was dug to conceal the assailant's approach to a fortified place. Origin withdrew. This suggests a person licensed to teach in a mediaeval university.

*

It rotates thus, the plane of polar light, beam swung out from the oblivion platform. Note the Martello tower, cento of snakeskin, flickering Super 8. . . . True schizophrenics lack the superego element present in paranoia.

This is comparable to a pit stop; the surrounding nations function as buffer zones.

See, he cannot learn to use words as precisely as a normal person would. (Gin and sperm cake solve everything.) Is this the same man with whom we were once allied, he who has been paid handsomely but now refuses to act?

He is back-formation, from salvage. That must have been worth seeing.

Sound of one-head clapping, dog panting — the shakedown, supine.

I am just observing how things evolve. We do not have far to go.

It is on the increase. I have been away for a few years, leaching all hope.

*

She has a reputation for short stays. Beyond the boundary marker, I glimpsed a raft of erections.

We had been wandering around the Iberian peninsula in search of her father's arse. My own descent was broken by a sonic net.

When I run downhill I lose all my moments. This is a catch-twenty-two simulation, but one cannot listen to both options at once.

'Approach control is here come dawn' . . . I dictated a message to F, which is encrypted in document C–ZO#2 — any code must be scrambled beyond recall. We are stationed at the very end or at the very beginning.

They arrive. He carries a heavy green sack over one shoulder, her an asthmatic lapdog, arm crooked through a basket. There are four newcomers here, parental spirits.

Matt-black jets strafe the pebble beach. I don't get paid for nothing, all this porous information.

Distant lights. The good burghers drag massive boulders across the shingle and deposit them haphazard in the crust of the sea. I was sentenced to three-and-a-half minutes. Folk tried to shield that delicate head, skull brittle as eggshell.

'In the darkness, how could you see the muzzle or the crown of which you speak?'

This was no incentive to go forth and die for a cause. What do you all want down here? I asked.

The barkeep glanced toward the men's room, and the remaining drinker nodded.

I thought you had a stroke. All sense has now passed over to the other side. And a tax too on lees of wine, blue with vomiting, a bouquet of burnt copper and those metal-green flies.

'Boy, do you know where the silo is hereabout?'

She is bruised, he bloodied. Only one third of the way down to the molten core, but we are still making good time. What is he waiting for, eyeing the surplus?

He has been adding her up: defoliate, orange-pink with glistening cerise interior.

Armistice

Passersby, spectacularly bored of coveting, waiting. Their spiny skin might be swallowed as food, but some parts become highly toxic when threatened. Origin is a covered trench, spadework.

The fossils of countless nouns have been discovered across the continent, buried deep inside limestone caves. In subzero temperatures the retreating troops sheltered in the carcasses of horses slaughtered for the purpose. The future rests upon a single idea that will not reach fruition until well after your last fatal error.

No, there is nothing on the face. His remaining eye blurs: increased pressure within the orbit, gradual loss of sight — a blue-grey haze veils the pupil.

Our next initiative is a form of badland tenure. The judge urged his beast onward.

I could weep. The egg white suddenly crystallizes.

Stop now, stop.

We are putting as much pressure on the populace as we dare. Small objects drop from his throat and onto the track as battle-weary sappers remotely trigger the detonator implanted in his spine.

It is believed he yet speaks. Tread precisely along the threshold of protocol, sacrifice none of those fragile nerves.

Other countries were found to have no twilight at all. A magic feather which can materialize at any moment and grant the bearer protection was introduced. There is a flightless bird, fast-running, whose tail barbs resemble.

In an alley near the river I retrieved the spirit of John Dee. A ring of surrounding muscle served to guard the aperture.

Suture

The giant strides made by two bodies.

I can think of nowhere else I would rather be. It is always worth checking. Today every detail appears contaminated.

A tree or shrub with large waxy fingers, or thereabouts.

Dog panting.

Salpinx.

An early hook for pulling off a horse.

I lost all three of you in that ravine.

*

There was a pistol in his canvas sack. It glistened in the moonlight as if flecked with mother-of-pearl, splinters of mirror. Other objects include a femur stripped of flesh.

We are set in place.

In the end, I decided to keep the cursèd gift. I thought about making a pencil sketch of the scene, then immediately changed my mind. This episode has somehow fed my lifelong addiction to infinite choice.

I eventually settled in a chalk-white town streaked with rivulets of rust, longitudinal nerve fibres.

The sea was phosphorescent, seeds of light kindled by the oarsman's stroke. Our captain has locked himself in his quarters, scrawling.

An old woman hands me a small box with clouds and a painted sky. The aforementioned city was once in China. I felt nauseous.

This is possibly the earliest example of unrequited love in the history of literature, an account of devotion never purged. Carriages at midnight were pledged, organs stripped of hair. Who can be so blind as to not see that selfhood has nothing to do with our actions? We lost three of our companions on route.

Inside the box is an invitation card adorned with a black silk ribbon. On the floor is a bar of soap bearing an address and a telephone number. The nearest galaxy is the Magellanic.

*

When we arrive at the agreed rendezvous, there is nothing, just an empty space between two tenement buildings. A young man with an ashplant hurries past; his left hand, as if paralysed, is locked against his chest. Upon the ground (this is more like it) are strewn the membranes that once joined tentacles to ribcage. The retina has detached; cannibalism is in the air. I have ringed the thumb whirls with red ink, in case transmission scars the imprint.

He received an industrial beating while hung upside down from one of the numerous metal hooks that had been seized at the neighbourhood abattoir. Sovereignty is exclusion.

That same evening he managed to whisper that there now stands a memorial plaque where his son collided with fate. Evidently, the truce is no longer observed.

The disruption was caused by what the syndicate calls migrant inertia, a magnificent oxymoron. A number of species are red or yellow, or marked with white spots and stripes — size varies considerably — and there are four rows of sharpened teeth. I could hear the lift ascending.

No, this is me, there can be no doubt. I could not undertake such an ordeal lightly, and have never broken my fast. Silence and withdrawal are now revolutionary postures.

*

Picture a man lying on his back in a padded cot, tapping out Morse code to confirm to himself that he is still in the room.

'Have I infected your transit?'

During the winter campaign he lost a wing and was hobbled for life.

A woman passes by carrying an arm. This suggests an extremely small dosage. Compare self with atom.

Neighbourhood citizen siphoning fuel. I forget his name. Estuarine and freshwater deposits are best exemplified.

The song on the jukebox encircled Ava Gardner in a wall of sound (the killers, junction be, night of the iguana). Cinder-block structures were thrown up at the outskirts of town — I am mindful of the extramural charnel pits of mediaeval Paris.

I sat on a terrace all afternoon drinking beer in the rain. This does not mean that to destroy is to create, but that destruction in itself is an absolute value.

A group of partisans burst in: on every side clicked meters and dials while above my head swung an instrument which measures time by the stealing of water. I have long lost that generational thing.

You must be some kind of Jonah. I have played out my fit of wandering, your accursed share.

Columns of data scroll down the glass partition. In the end, origin was handed over without a fight.

Voice: do you know what this instrument does?

A cylindrical thing of concrete.

*

The next chapter consists of an opening passage designed to provoke the reader, followed by an account of the twelve astrological houses, wherein the triumph of the deceased is conveyed through intensely elegiac language.

The boy is concealed under the floor in a narrow wooden trough. As the water rises I search for him, tearing at the rotten boards, hurling them onto a stained mattress. When at last I find him, he appears lifeless. Gently I lift him up and lay him on the ground, press my hand against his chest to find a heartbeat, breathe air into his lungs. He wakes, whereupon I gesture to the heap of splintered wood and rusting nails and whisper look at what we had to do to find you. The boy is angelic, with skin so pale it's translucent. Only then he smiles, this promised man.

I have been sitting here for hours and nothing has changed. He is perched on one of the stools facing the control panel. A parley, an improvised conference, is due to take place between the two factions.

The exchange proves futile. Origin came from behind, from saddlecloth, hood.

'They repeated over and over, until.'

[*Drums fingers on zinc tabletop.*]

I was foreblind. He says the extent of rupture is gauged by the rejection of transcendence — the others are just barking out the cards robotic.

*

An ashtray: correct. An uncertain lament.

Note how most things seem to exist without purpose. Next, a row of windmills, hence the name which attaches itself to this part of the island (dog). I think that's enough for the time being.

The locals have been experimenting with the stolen atoms they found on nearby wasteland. At the very last, I recall her murmuring something about a collision that has lain dormant beneath the earth for millennia.

Whatever they do to me, I shall wait for you.

Remember, trust nobody. After six days the patrol returned, exhausted. We decided to change course and take the road for the mesa, pitching camp before dusk.

Infrared out in space reveals clusters of hut circles invisible to the naked eye. Our nemesis no longer enjoys the tactical advantage of superior elevation.

She is confined, cultivates a tension, can no longer be bled. Cartridges are distributed and the nightwatch alerted.

Inconceivably, none suspect the significance of this drill, ineptly worked into the survivor's account. For example, do the people speak while carrying out these actions?

We have split the element — fibres were sluiced, the ceiling burnished. The ninth star in the constellation is Iota Piscium.

Where are we going nowhere she said.

*

He is exiled wherever he finds himself, but has fond memories of the guerrilla warfare of years past. They did not even ask us how we had managed to land here in such a storm: all day long it was the collapsed this, the dead that. . . . In a photograph on the dust jacket the author looks benignly belligerent. The probe was deliberately burned up in the atmosphere of Venus.

I walk. I hail a hansom cab, begin the journey to suffer a promised audience with the consul. A hansom is a two-wheeled horse-drawn conveyance that accommodates two inside, with the driver seated behind.

I am never moving again. We slid headlong into a ravine. We all perished.

*

Ice-blue sky is forecast. Let us make our way back: necromancy, spontaneous ignition — black magic, then regeneration. I was once rented, sex for pelf (those were the days). This is where the objective conditions of historical consciousness begin to disintegrate.

The first wave passed. It seemed to me that I was under the water for several minutes, when in truth it was seconds. The blast had torn out the great sail.

We mapped the surface using radar to penetrate the permanent blanket of cloud charged with electricity. High in the air, rags fluttered to leeward — from the crow's nest, I failed to catch sight of your fluke. Look at that gathering crowd.

At this point we applied pressure by transforming repetition into a sequence of fake memories.

Now they are advertising the cyclone vacuum, an iron basket for combustibles placed in a beacon, a lighthouse — a small pit or hollow, in particular — any of those tiny air sacs of the lung.

Bony socket for the root, scar-like gravity trapped in the hand. I keep forgetting.

I will see to it: the names keep repeating themselves, the names are always the same.

Nerve & Venom.

Even then she gazed up at the quivering lines, the spectrum. There has been a drop in the wind speed at the dogs. Insentience lies beyond the stockade, connected with a universe of discourse but not under its direct control. By this we mean the set containing all objects or elements and of which all other sets are subsets.

Torched song

A kerosene lamp swings from the rafters. We are back at the log cabin in the woods; it has begun to snow.

This may be a lost cause. Two diffuse luminous patches appeared in the southern sky.

Anvil front moving in, funnelling the prospect. A change in strategy is augured. We are trekking west through a winter landscape, a trail of covered wagons, shreds of carbon on a white field.

Origin, in a sense, is a parley between people and their traffickers (see parabola). Many of our number perished.

I have made contact, persistent murmur of dialogue, seemingly from inside the amygdala. Fingers crossed, said my counsel.

Our passage was swift, a good day to be under sail — she was lean and sinewed, brittle — but now the night is so dark, and not a star to be seen under the whole sky.

Child with toy, makeshift, with helium rictus.